W9-BTJ-071

RANDOM
HOUSE
LARGE
PRINT

ALSO BY STEVE BERRY

AVAILABLE FROM RANDOM HOUSE LARGE PRINT

The Alexandria Link
The Charlemagne Pursuit
The Columbus Affair
The Emperor's Tomb
The Jefferson Key
The Paris Vendetta
The Romanov Prophecy
The Templar Legacy
The Third Secret
The Venetian Betrayal

The King's Deception

ON SINE SOLE
IRIS.

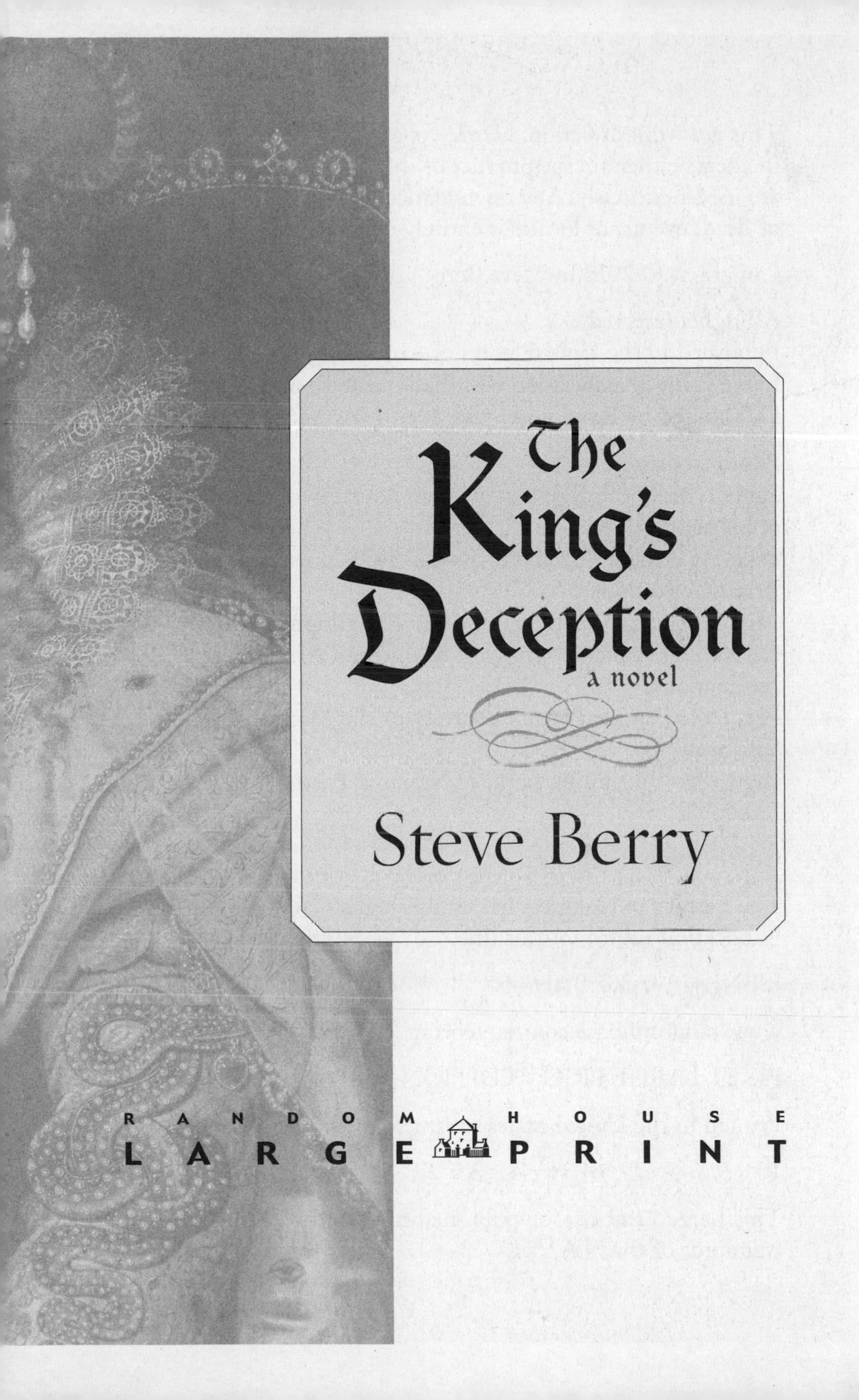

The King's Deception

a novel

Steve Berry

RANDOM HOUSE
LARGE PRINT

This is a work of fiction. Names, characters, places, and incidents either are the product of the author's imagination or are used fictitiously. Any resemblance to actual persons, living or dead, events, or locales is entirely coincidental.

Published in the United States of America by Random House Large Print in association with Ballantine Books, New York. Distributed by Random House, Inc., New York.

Photo credits:
Pages iv and 569: Rainbow portrait courtesy of the Marquess of Salisbury
Page 11: Princess Elizabeth (1546–1547) courtesy of the Royal Collection
Page 139: Elizabeth I (1533–1603) The Clopton Portrait, c. 1560–65 (panel) courtesy of Bridgeman Art Library International
Page 261: Ermine Portrait courtesy of the Marquess of Salisbury
Page 379: Queen Elizabeth, © National Portrait Gallery, London

Cover design: Scott Biel

The Library of Congress has established a Cataloging-in-Publication record for this title.

ISBN: 978-0-307-99094-5

www.randomhouse.com/largeprint

FIRST LARGE PRINT EDITION

Printed in the United States of America

10 9 8 7 6 5 4 3 2 1

This Large Print edition published in accord with the standards of the N.A.V.H.

For Jessica Johns and Esther Garver

Acknowledgments

For the 12th time, my sincere thanks to Gina Centrello, Libby McGuire, Kim Hovey, Cindy Murray, Scott Shannon, Debbie Aroff, Carole Lowenstein, Matt Schwartz, and everyone in Promotions and Sales. It's an honor to be part of Ballantine Books and the Random House Publishing Group team.

A special bow to Mark Tavani—who has a way of squeezing the impossible out of writers.

And Simon Lipskar, who escaped the dogs and lives on, offering more expert advice.

A few special mentions: Nick Sayers, an Oxford graduate, superb gentleman, and exceptional publisher who helped with some of the British details (though any errors are mine); Ian Williamson, British book rep extraordinaire, who showed us Oxfordshire; and Meryl Moss and her publicity team, Deb Zipf and JeriAnn Geller, the best in the business.

As always, a special thanks to my wife, Elizabeth, a muse beyond measure.

In recent books I've also thanked Jessica Johns and Esther Garver. Together, they keep Steve Berry Enterprises running and take a lot of the load off.

Jessica and Esther, this one's for you.

I tell you my seat hath been the seat of kings.
I will have no rascal to succeed me,
and who should succeed me but a king.

—ELIZABETH I

The King's Deception

Prologue

WHITEHALL PALACE
JANUARY 28, 1547

KATHERINE PARR SAW THAT THE END WAS APPROACHING. Only a few more days remained, maybe a mere few hours. She'd stood silent for the past half hour and watched, as the physicians completed their examinations. The time had now come for them to deliver their verdict.

"Sire," one of them said. "All human aid is now in vain. It is best for you to review your past life and seek God's mercy through Christ."

She stared as Henry VIII considered the advice. The king, prone in his bed, had been uttering loud cries of pain. He ceased them and lifted his head, facing the messenger. "What judge has sent you to pass this sentence on me?"

"We are your physicians. There is no appeal from this judgment."

"Get away from me," Henry shrieked. "All of you."

Though gravely ill the king could still command. The men quickly fled the bedchamber, as did all of the frightened courtiers.

Katherine turned to leave, too.

"I bid you, good queen, to stay," Henry said.

She nodded.

They were alone.

He seemed to steel himself.

"If a man fills his belly with venison and pork, with sides of beef and pasties of veal, if he washes them down with floodtides of ale and wine that never know neap." Henry paused. "He will reap his tares in a black hour. He will be none the happier for his swollen estate. That, my queen, is how it is with me."

Her husband spoke the truth. A malady of his own choosing had consumed him, one that had rotted him away from within, slowly extinguishing his life's core. He was swollen to the point of bursting, incapable of exercise, no more motion in him than a hill of tallow. This man who in youth was so handsome, who leaped moats and drew the best bow in England, who excelled in jousts, led armies, and defeated popes—now he could not even jostle a lordling or raise a hand with pleasure. He'd become big, burly, small-eyed, large-faced, and double-chinned. Swinish looking.

Hideous.

"Sire, you speak ill of yourself without cause," she said. "You're my liege lord, to whom I and all of England owe absolute allegiance."

"But only so long as I breathe."

"Which you continue to do."

She knew her place. Stimulating a controversy between a husband and wife, where the former possessed all of the power and the latter nothing, was a dangerous sport. But, though weak, she was not without weapons. Fidelity, kindliness, a ready wit, her constant care, and brilliant learning—those were her tools.

"A man may sow his own seed a thousand times," she said. "If he take heed to avoid the plague and live otherwise well and hale, he may stand like an oak at the end and leap like a stag who still lords over his herd. That is you, my king."

He opened his bloated hand and she laid hers within. His skin was cold and clammy and she wondered if death had already begun to take hold. She knew him to be fifty-six years old, having reigned for nearly thirty-eight years. He'd taken six wives and fathered five children that he acknowledged. He'd challenged the world and defied the Catholic Church, establishing his own religion. She was the third woman named Katherine whom he had married and, thanks be to heaven, it appeared she would be the last.

And that gave her heart hope.

No joy had come from being mated to this tyrant, but she'd fulfilled her duties. She'd not wanted to be his wife, preferring instead to be his mistress, since his wives had not fared well. *No, madam,* he'd said to her. *I look for you in the higher role.* She'd consciously showed no enthusiasm at his offer, remaining dull to his royal gestures, mindful that as Henry had grown older heads had fallen faster. Discretion was the only path to longevity. So, with no choice, she'd married Henry Tudor in a grand ceremony before the eyes of the world.

Now four years of marital agony were approaching an end.

But she kept her joy to herself, her face masked with concern, her eyes filled with what could only be perceived as love. She was skilled in holding older men's hearts, having nursed two previous husbands on their deathbeds. She knew what sacrifices the role demanded. For the king she'd many times laid his stinking, ulcered leg upon her lap, applying fomentations and balms, calming his mind, relieving the pain. She was the only one he would allow to do that.

"Sweetheart," the king whispered. "I have a final duty for you."

She gave a nod. "Your Majesty's faintest wish is the law of this land."

"There is a secret. One I have kept for a long

time. One my father passed to me. I wish it passed to Edward and ask you to do such."

"It would be my honor to do anything for you."

The king's eyes closed and she saw that his brief respite from pain had ended. His mouth opened and he cried, "Monks. Monks."

Terror laced the words.

Were the ghosts of clerics sent to the flames thronged around his bed, jeering at his dying soul? Henry had laid waste to the monasteries, seizing all of their wealth, punishing their occupants. Ruins and corpses were all that remained of their former grandeur.

He seemed to grab control of himself and fought back the vision. "At his death, my father told me of a secret place. One only for Tudors. I have cherished this place and made fine use of it. My son must know of it. Will you tell him, my queen?"

She was amazed that this man, so ruthless in life, so distrusting of anyone and anything, would, at the hour of his death, bring her into his confidence. She wondered if it be another subterfuge to entrap her. He'd tried that once before, months back, when she'd pressed him too far on religion. Bishop Gardiner of Winchester had quickly seized on her error, obtaining royal permission to both investigate and arrest her. Thankfully, she'd learned of the plot

and managed to turn the king's favor back her way. Eventually, it had been Gardiner who'd been banished from court.

"I would, of course, do whatever you request of me," she said. "But why not tell your dear son and heir yourself?"

"He cannot see me like this. I have not allowed any of my children to see me like this. Only you, sweetheart. I must know that you will carry out this duty."

She nodded again. "That is not in question."

"Then, listen to me."

COTTON MALONE KNEW A LIE WOULD BE BETTER, but decided, as part of his new cooperative relationship with his ex-wife, to tell the truth. Pam watched him with an intensity he'd seen on her face before. Only this time her eyes were softened by a difficult reality.

He knew something she didn't.

"What does the death of Henry VIII have to do with what happened to you two years ago?" she asked him.

He'd started to tell her the story, but stopped. He hadn't thought about those hours in London in a long while. They'd been eye opening, in more ways than one. A father-and-son experience only an ex-agent for the United States Justice Department could survive.

"The other day, Gary and I were watching the news," Pam said. "A Libyan terrorist, the one who bombed that plane in Scotland back in the 1980s, died of cancer. Gary said he knew all about him."

He'd seen the same story. Abdelbaset al-Megrahi had finally succumbed. A former intelligence officer, al-Megrahi was accused in 1988 of 270 counts of murder for bombing Pan Am Flight 103 over Lockerbie, Scotland. But it wasn't until January 2001 that three Scottish judges, sitting in a special court held in the Netherlands, handed down their guilty verdict and a life sentence.

He wanted to know, "What else did Gary say?"

Depending on what his now seventeen-year-old son had revealed, he might be able to limit his own comments.

Or at least he hoped so.

"Only that in London you two were involved with that terrorist."

Not exactly true, but he was proud of his son's hedging. Any good intelligence officer knew that ears-open-and-mouth-shut always works best.

"All I know," she said, "is that two years ago Gary left here with you for a Thanksgiving break in Copenhagen. Instead, now I learn he was in London. Neither one of you ever said a word about that."

"You knew I had to make a stop there on the way home."

"A stop? Sure. But it was more than that and you know it."

They'd been divorced going on four years. Before that they'd been married eighteen years. His entire naval career had been spent with Pam. He became a lawyer and started with the Justice Department while with her, but he ended his twelve-year career as a Magellan Billet agent as her ex-husband.

And it had not been a good separation.

But they'd finally worked things out.

Two years ago.

Just **before** all that happened in London.

Maybe she should be told everything.

No more secrets, right?

"You sure you want to hear this?"

They were sitting at the kitchen table inside the Atlanta house where Pam and Gary had moved before the divorce. Just after the marriage ended he'd left Georgia and moved to Denmark thinking he'd left the past behind.

How wrong could someone be?

Did **he** want to hear what happened again?

Not really.

But it might be good for them both.

"Okay, I'll tell you."

Part One

Two Years Ago

One

LONDON
FRIDAY, NOVEMBER 21
6:25 PM

Cotton Malone stepped up to the Customs window at Heathrow Airport and presented two passports—his own and his son Gary's. Positioned between himself and the glass-enclosed counter, however, stood a problem.

Fifteen-year-old Ian Dunne.

"This one doesn't have a passport," he told the attendant, then explained who he was and what he was doing. A brief call to somebody led to verbal approval for Ian to reenter the country.

Which didn't surprise Malone.

He assumed that since the Central Intelligence Agency wanted the boy in England they'd make the necessary arrangements.

He was tired from the long flight, though he'd

caught a few hours of sleep. His knee still hurt from the kick Ian had delivered in Atlanta, before trying to flee from that airport. Luckily, his own fifteen-year-old, Gary, had been quick to tackle the pesky Scot before he'd escaped the concourse.

Favors for friends.

Always a problem.

This one for his former boss, Stephanie Nelle, at the Magellan Billet.

It's the CIA, she'd told him. Langley had called directly. Somehow they were aware Malone was in Georgia and wanted him to escort the boy back to London, handing him over to the Metropolitan Police. After that he and Gary could head on to Copenhagen. In return, they'd received first-class tickets all the way home to Denmark.

Not bad. His own were coach.

Four days ago he'd flown to Georgia for two reasons. The State Bar of Georgia required twelve hours of continuing legal education from all of its licensed lawyers. Though he'd retired from the navy and the Magellan Billet, he still kept his law license active, which meant he had to satisfy the annual education mandate. Last year he'd attended a sanctioned event in Brussels, a three-day meeting on multinational property rights. This year he'd chosen a seminar in Atlanta on international law. Not the most exciting way to spend two days, but he'd worked too hard for that degree to simply allow his ticket to lapse.

The second reason was personal.

Gary had asked to spend the Thanksgiving holiday with him. School was out and his ex-wife, Pam, thought an overseas trip a good idea. He'd wondered why she was so reticent, and found out last week when Pam called his bookshop in Copenhagen.

"Gary's angry," she said. "He's asking a lot of questions."

"Ones you don't want to answer?"

"Ones I'm going to have a tough time answering."

Which was an understatement. Six months ago she'd revealed a harsh truth to him during another call from Atlanta to Denmark. Gary was not his natural son. Instead, the boy was the product of an affair some sixteen years past.

Now she'd told Gary that truth, and his son was not happy. For Malone, the news had been crushing. He could only imagine what it had been for Gary.

"Neither one of us was a saint back then, Cotton."

She liked to remind him of that reality—as if somehow he'd forgotten that their marriage supposedly ended because of his lapses.

"Gary wants to know about his birth father."

"So do I."

She'd told him nothing about the man, and refused his requests for information.

"He has no involvement here," she said. "He's

a total stranger to all of us. Just like the women you were with have nothing to do with this. I don't want to open that door. Ever."

"Why did you tell Gary about this? We agreed to do that together, when the time was right."

"I know. I know. My mistake. But it had to be done."

"Why?"

She did not answer him. But he could imagine the reason. She liked to be in control. Of everything. Only she wasn't in control here. Nobody was, actually.

"He hates me," she said. "I see it in his eyes."

"You turned the boy's life upside down."

"He told me today that he might want to live with you."

He had to say, "You know I would never take advantage of this."

"I know that. This is my fault. Not yours. He's so angry. Maybe a week with you would help ease some of that."

He'd come to realize that he didn't love Gary one drop less because he carried no Malone genes. But he'd be lying to himself if he said he wasn't bothered by the fact. Six months had passed and the truth still hurt. Why? He wasn't sure. He hadn't been faithful to Pam while in the navy. He was young and stupid and got caught. But now he knew that she'd had an affair of her own. Never mentioned at the time. Would she have strayed if he hadn't?

He doubted it. Not her nature.

So he wasn't blameless for the current mess.

He and Pam had been divorced for over a year, but only back in October had they made their peace. Everything that happened with the Library of Alexandria changed things between them.

For the better.

But now this.

One boy in his charge was angry and confused.

The other seemed to be a delinquent.

Stephanie had told him some. Ian Dunne had been born in Scotland. Father unknown. Mother abandoned him early. He was sent to London to live with an aunt and drifted in and out of her home, finally running away. He had an arrest record—petty theft, trespassing, loitering. The CIA wanted him because a month ago one of their people was shoved, or jumped, into the path of an oncoming Underground train. Dunne was there, in Oxford Circus. Witnesses say he might even have stolen something from the dead man. So they needed to talk to him.

Not good, but also not his concern.

In a few minutes his favor for Stephanie Nelle would be over, then he and Gary would catch their connecting flight to Copenhagen and enjoy the week, depending of course on how many uncomfortable questions his son might want answered. The hitch was that the Denmark flight departed not from Heathrow, but Gatwick, London's other major airport, an hour's ride south. Their departure time was several hours away, so it wasn't a problem. He would just need to convert some dollars to pounds and hire a taxi.

They left Customs and claimed their luggage.

Both he and Gary had packed light.

"The police going to take me?" Ian asked.

"That's what I'm told."

"What will happen to him?" Gary asked.

He shrugged. "Hard to say."

And it was. Especially with the CIA involved.

He shouldered his bag and led both boys out of the baggage area.

"Can I have my things?" Ian asked.

When Ian had been turned over to him in Atlanta, he'd been given a plastic bag that contained a Swiss Army knife with all the assorted attachments, a pewter necklace with a religious medal attached, a pocket Mace container, some silver shears, and two paperback books with their covers missing.

Ivanhoe and **Le Morte d'Arthur.**

Their brown edges were water-stained, the bindings veined with thick white creases. Both were thirty-plus-year-old printings. Stamped on the title page was ANY OLD BOOKS, with an address in Piccadilly Circus, London. He employed a similar branding of inventory, his simply announcing COTTON MALONE, BOOKSELLER, HØJBRO PLADS, COPENHAGEN. The items in the plastic bag all belonged to Ian, seized by Customs when they took him into custody at Miami International, after he'd tried to enter the country illegally.

"That's up to the police," he said. "My orders are to hand you and the bag over to them."

He'd stuffed the bundle inside his travel case, where it would stay until the police assumed custody. He half expected Ian to bolt, so he remained on guard. Ahead he spied two men, both in dark suits walking their way. The one on the right, short and stocky with auburn hair, introduced himself as Inspector Norse.

He extended a hand, which Malone shook.

"This is Inspector Devene. We're with the Met. We were told you'd be accompanying the boy. We're here to give you a lift to Gatwick and take charge of Master Dunne."

"I appreciate the ride. Wasn't looking forward to an expensive taxi."

"Least we can do. Our car is just outside. One of the privileges of being the police is we can park where we want."

The man threw Malone a grin.

They started for the exit.

Malone noticed Inspector Devene take up a position behind Ian. Smart move, he thought.

"You responsible for getting him into the country with no passport?"

Norse nodded. "We are, along with some others working with us. I think you know about them."

That he did.

They stepped out of the terminal into brisk morning air. A bank of dense clouds tinted the sky a depressing shade of pewter. A blue Mercedes sedan sat by the curb. Norse opened the rear door and motioned for Gary to climb in first, then Ian and Malone. The inspector stood outside until they were all in, then closed the door. Norse rode in the front passenger seat, while Devene drove. They sped out of Heathrow and found the M4 motorway. Malone knew the route, London a familiar locale. Years ago he'd spent time in England on assignments. He'd also been detached here for a year by the navy. Traffic progressively thickened as they made their way east toward the city.

"Would it be all right if we made one stop before we head for Gatwick?" Norse asked him.

"No problem. We have time before the plane leaves. The least we can do for a free ride."

Malone watched Ian as the boy gazed out the window. He couldn't help but wonder what would happen to him. Stephanie's assessment had not been a good one. A street kid, no family, completely on his own. Unlike Gary, who was dark-haired with a swarthy complexion, Ian was blond and fair-skinned. He seemed like a good kid, though. Just dealt a bad hand. But at least he was young, and youth offered chances, and chances led to possibilities. Such a contrast with Gary, who lived a more conventional, secure life. The thought of Gary on the streets, loose, with no one, tore at his heart.

Warm air blasted the car's interior and the engine droned as they chugged through traffic.

Malone's eyes surrendered to jet lag.

When he woke, he glanced at his watch and realized he'd been out about fifteen minutes. He willed himself to alertness. Gary and Ian were still sitting quietly. The sky had darkened further. A storm was approaching the city. He studied the car's interior, noticing for the first time no radio or communications equipment. Also, the carpets were immaculate, the upholstery in pristine condition. Certainly not like any police car he'd ever ridden in.

He then examined Norse.

The man's brown hair was cut below the ears. Not shaggy, but thick. He was clean-shaven and a bit overweight. He was dressed appropriately, suit and tie, but it was the left earlobe that drew his attention. Pierced. No earring was present, but the puncture was clear.

"I was wondering, Inspector. Might I see your identification? I should have asked at the airport."

Norse did not answer him. The question aroused Ian's attention, and he studied Malone with a curious look.

"Did you hear me, Norse? I'd like to see your identification."

"Just enjoy the ride, Malone."

He didn't like the curt tone so he reached for the front seat and pulled himself forward, intending to make his point clearer.

The barrel of a gun came around the headrest and greeted him.

"This enough identification?" Norse asked.

"Actually, I was hoping for a picture ID." He motioned to the weapon. "When did the Metropolitan Police start issuing Glocks?"

No reply.

"Who are you?"

The gun waved at Ian. "His keeper."

Ian reached across Gary and wrenched the chrome handle up and down, but the door would not open.

"Great things, child locks," said Norse. "Keeps the wee ones from slipping away."

Malone said, "Son, you want to tell me what's going on?"

Ian said nothing.

"These men have apparently gone to a lot of trouble to make your acquaintance."

"Sit back, Malone," Norse said. "This is none of your concern."

He reclined in the seat. "On that we agree."

Except his son was in the car, too.

Norse kept his head turned back toward them, his gaze and the gun glued on Malone.

The car continued through morning congestion.

He absorbed what was whirling past outside, recalling what he could about the geography of North London. He realized the bridge they'd just crossed was for Regent's Canal, a corridor-like waterway that wound a snaking path through the city, eventually spilling into the Thames. Stately trees lined the four-laned promenade. Traffic was heavy. He spotted the famous Lord's Cricket Ground. He knew that the fictional Baker Street of Sherlock Holmes lay a few blocks over. Little Venice wasn't far away.

They crossed the canal again and he glanced down at brightly painted houseboats dotting the waterway. Longboats dotted the canal, no more than ten feet high, designed to fit under the tight bridges. Rows and rows of Georgian houses and flats lined the boulevard, fronted with tall trees less their leaves.

Devene turned the Mercedes onto a side lane. More houses rolled past on either side. The scene was not unlike Atlanta, where his own house had once stood. Three more turns and they entered a courtyard enclosed on three sides by high hedges. The Mercedes stopped outside a mews constructed of pastel-colored stones.

Norse exited. Devene also climbed out.

Both rear doors were released from the outside.

"Get out," Norse said.

Malone stood on cobblestones outlined by emerald lichens. Gary and Ian emerged on the other side.

Ian tried to bolt.

Norse slammed the boy hard into the car.

"Don't," Malone called out. "Do as he says. You too, Gary."

Norse shoved the gun into Ian's neck. "Stay still." The man's body pinned Ian to the car. "Where's the flash drive?"

"What drive?" Malone asked.

"Shut him up," Norse called out.

Devene jammed a fist into Malone's gut.

"Dad," Gary called out.

He doubled over and tried to regain his breath, motioning to Gary that he was okay.

"The flash drive," Norse said again. "Where is it?"

Malone rose, arms hugging his stomach. Devene drew back to swing again, but Malone jammed his knee into the man's groin, then smacked Devene's jaw with his right fist.

He may have been retired and jet-lagged, but he wasn't helpless.

He whirled in time to see Norse aim the gun his way. The retort from a single shot came the instant after Malone lunged for the pavement, the bullet finding the hedges behind him. He stared up into the Mercedes' passenger compartment and saw Norse through the half-open doors. He sprang to his feet, pivoted off the hood, and propelled his legs through the car's interior into the far-side door.

The panel flew out and smashed into Norse, sending the phony inspector reeling backward into the mews.

He shoved himself through the open door.

Ian was running from the courtyard, toward the street.

Malone's gaze met Gary's. "Go with him. Get out of here."

He was tackled from behind.

His forehead slapped wet stone. Pain shuddered through him. He'd thought Devene out of commission.

A mistake.

An arm wrapped around his throat and he tried to release the stranglehold grip. His prone position gave him little room to maneuver and Devene was hinging his spine at an unnatural angle.

The buildings around him winked in and out.

Blood trickled down his forehead and into his eye.

The last thing he saw before blackness enveloped him was Ian and Gary, disappearing around a corner.

Two

BRUSSELS, BELGIUM
7:45 PM

BLAKE ANTRIM WAS NOT A FAN OF COCKY WOMEN. He endured them, as the Central Intelligence Agency was loaded with wiseass females. But that did not mean he had to tolerate them once off the clock. If a team leader, responsible for nine agents scattered across England and Europe, could ever truly be on his own time.

Denise Gérard was both Flemish and French, a combination that had produced a tall, svelte package with exquisite dark hair. She had a face that begged for attention, and a body that you wanted to embrace. They'd met inside the Musée de la Ville de Bruxelles, where they'd discovered a mutual love of old maps, architectural relics, and paintings. Since then they'd spent a lot of time together, making a few trips outside Brussels, one to Paris that had proven quite memorable.

She was excitable, discreet, and devoid of inhibition.

Ideal.

But not anymore.

"What have I done?" she asked, her voice soft. "Why end it now?"

No sadness or shock laced her plea. The words were spoken matter-of-factly, her way of shifting a decision she'd already made onto him.

Which irritated him even more.

She wore a striking silk skirt with a short hem that accentuated both her firm breasts and her long legs. He'd always admired her flat belly and wondered if it was from exercise or a surgeon's touch. He'd never noticed any scars, her caramel-colored flesh smooth as porcelain.

And her smell.

Sweet lemons mixed with rosemary.

She was something in the perfume industry. She'd explained her job one afternoon over coffee near the Grand Place, but he hadn't been listening, that day consumed with an operation gone wrong in western Germany.

Which seemed his lot of late.

One failure after another.

His title was coordinator of special counter-operations, European Theater. Sounded like he was part of a war—which, in a sense, he was. That undeclared one on terrorism. But he shouldn't mock it. Threats definitely existed, and came from the oddest places. Of late, they seemed to originate more from America's allies than its enemies.

Hence, the purpose of his unit.

Special counter-operations.

"Blake, tell me how I can make it better. I'd like to keep seeing you."

But she didn't mean it, and he knew it.

She was playing with him.

They sat in her apartment, an expensive, turn-of-the-century flat that overlooked the Parc de Bruxelles, a formal patch of greenery flanked by the Palais Royal and the Palais de la Nation. Past the open third-floor terrace doors he saw the trademark classical statues, framed by trees with meticulously trellised branches. The throngs of office workers, joggers, and families that normally filled the park were gone for the day. He figured her rent had to be several thousand euros a month. Nothing he could afford on his government salary. But most of the women he connected with made more than him, anyway. He seemed drawn to the professional type.

And cheaters.

Like Denise.

"I was out and about yesterday," he said. "Near the Grand Place. I heard the **Manneken Pis** was dressed as an organ grinder."

The famous statue was located not far from town hall, a two-foot-high, bronze sculpture depicting a naked boy peeing into the fountain basin. It had stood since 1618 and had become a national landmark. Several times a week the bronze boy was dressed in a costume, each one unique. Blake had been nearby to meet a contact and have a quick chat.

And saw Denise.

With another man.

Her arm in his, enjoying the cool midday air, the two stopping to admire the spectacle and share a few kisses. She seemed utterly at ease, just as she always was with him. He'd wondered then, and still did now, how many men she kept around.

"In French we call him **le petit Julien,**" she said. "I have seen him dressed many ways, but not as an organ man. Was it delightful?"

He'd offered her a chance to tell the truth, but dishonesty was another common denominator of the women that attracted him.

One last chance.

"You missed that yesterday?" he asked, a trace of incredulity in his voice.

"I was working out of the city. Perhaps they will dress him again like that."

He stood to leave.

She rose from her chair. "Perhaps you could stay for a while longer?"

He knew what she meant. Her bedroom door was open.

But not today.

He allowed her to drift close.

"I'm sorry that we will not see each other again," she said.

Her lies had stirred a familiar fury. He'd tried to resist, but finally surrendered, his right hand whipping upward and grabbing her throat. He lifted her thin frame off the floor and slammed her into the wall. He tightened his grip on her neck and stared hard into her eyes.

"You're a lying whore."

"No, Blake. You are a deceitful man," she managed to say, her eyes unafraid. "I saw you yesterday."

"Who was he?"

He relaxed his grip enough so she could speak.

"No one of your concern."

"I. Don't. Share."

She smiled. "Then you are going to have to adjust your ways. Plain girls have to be grateful for love. Those of us not so plain fare much better."

The truth of her words enraged him more.

"You simply do not offer enough for someone to exclude all others," she said.

"I heard no complaints from you."

Their mouths were inches away. He could feel her breathe, smell the sweet scent that seeped from her skin.

"I have many men, Blake. You are but one."

As far as she knew he worked for the State Department, dispatched to the American embassy in Belgium.

"I'm an important person," he told her, his hand still around her throat.

"But not enough to command me solely."

He admired her courage.

Foolish. But still admirable.

He released his grip, then kissed her hard.

She reciprocated, her tongue finding his and signaling that all might not be lost.

He ended the embrace.

Then kneed her in the gut.

Her breath spewed out in an explosive burst.

She doubled over, arms wrapping around her stomach. She began to choke as nausea enveloped her.

She shrank to her knees and vomited on the parquet floor.

Her composure had vanished.

Excitement surged through him.

"You are a worthless little man," she managed to spit out.

But her opinion no longer mattered.

So he left.

He entered his office in the American embassy, located on the east side of the Parc de Bruxelles. He'd walked back from Denise's apartment feeling satisfied, but confused. He wondered if she would involve the police. Probably not. First, it was a he-said-she-said thing with no witnesses, and second, her pride would never allow it.

Besides, he'd left no marks.

Women like her took their lumps and moved on.

But her confidence would never again be so certain. She'd always wonder. **Can I play this man? Or does he know?**

Like Blake knew.

Her doubts pleased him.

But he felt bad about the knee. Why she pushed him to such extremes he did not know. Cheating was bad enough. But lying only made it worse. It was her own fault. Still, he'd send her flowers tomorrow.

Pale blue carnations. Her favorite.

He logged into his computer and provided the day's access code. Not much had arrived since early afternoon, but a FLASH ALERT from Langley caught his eye. A post-9/11 thing. Far better to disseminate information across the grid than keep it to yourself and shoulder all of the blame. Most of the alerts did not concern him. His area was **special counter**-operations, targeted assignments that were, by definition, not the norm. All were highly classified and he reported only to the director of counter-operations. Five missions were currently ongoing, another two in the planning stages. This alert, though, was addressed only to him, decrypted automatically by his computer.

KING'S DECEPTION IS NOW TIMELINED. IF NO RESULTS IN NEXT 48 HOURS CEASE OPERATIONS AND EXIT.

Not entirely unexpected.

Things had not been going right in England.

Until a few days ago, when they'd finally caught a break.

He needed to know more and reached for the desk phone, calling his man in London, who answered on the second ring.

"Ian Dunne and Cotton Malone are on the ground at Heathrow," he was told.

He smiled.

Seventeen years with the CIA had taught him how to get things done. Cotton Malone in London, with Ian Dunne, was proof of that.

He'd made that happen.

Malone had once been a hotshot Justice Department agent at the Magellan Billet, where he served a dozen years before retiring after a shootout in Mexico City. Malone now lived in Copenhagen and owned an old-book shop but maintained a close relationship with Stephanie Nelle, the Billet's longtime head. A connection he'd used to draw Malone to England. A call to Langley led to a call to the attorney general, which led to Stephanie Nelle, who'd contacted Malone.

He smiled again.

At least something had gone right today.

Three

WINDSOR, ENGLAND
5:50 PM

KATHLEEN RICHARDS HAD NEVER BEEN INSIDE Windsor Castle. For a born-and-bred Brit that seemed unforgivable. But at least she knew its past. First built in the 11th century to guard the River Thames and protect Norman dominance on the outer reaches of a fledgling London, it had served as a royal enclave since the time of William the Conqueror. Once a motte-and-bailey castle built of wood, now it was a massive stone fortification. It survived the First Barons' War in 1200, the English Civil War in the 1600s, two world wars, and a devastating fire in 1992 to become the largest inhabited castle in the world.

The twenty-mile drive from London had been through a late-autumn rain. The castle dominated a steep chalk bluff, the gray walls, turrets, and towers—thirteen acres of buildings—barely discernible through the evening storm. The call had come from her supervisor an hour ago, telling her to head there.

Which shocked her.

She was twenty days into a thirty-day suspension without pay. An operation in Liverpool involving illicit arms to Northern Ireland had turned ugly when the three targets decided to run. She'd given motor chase and corralled them, but not before havoc had erupted on the local highways. Eighteen cars ended up wrecked. A few injuries, some serious, but no fatalities. Her fault? Not in her mind.

But her bosses had thought differently.

And the press had not been kind to SOCA.

The Serious Organized Crime Agency, England's version of America's FBI, handled drugs, money laundering, fraud, computer crimes, human trafficking, and firearms violations. Ten years she'd been an officer. When hired she'd been told that four qualities made for a good recruit—working with others, achieving results, leadership, making a difference. She'd like to think at least three of those were her specialty. The "working with others" part had always presented problems. Not that she was hard to get along with, it was just that she preferred to work alone. Luckily, her performance evaluations were excellent, her conviction record exemplary. She'd even received three commendations. But that sense of rebellion—which seemed part of her character—constantly brought trouble her way.

And she hated herself for it.

Like during the past twenty days, sitting around her flat, wondering when her law enforcement career would end.

She had a good job. A career. Thirty-one days of annual leave, a pension, plenty of training and development opportunities, and generous maternity and child care services. Not that she'd ever need those last two. She'd come to accept that marriage might not be for her, either. Too much sharing.

She wondered what she was doing here, walking on hallowed ground inside Windsor Castle, being escorted through the rain toward St. George's Chapel, a Gothic church built by Edward IV in the 15th century. Ten English monarchs lay buried inside. No explanations had been offered as to why she was needed and she'd not asked, chalking it up to that element of the unexpected that came with being a SOCA agent.

She entered, shook the rain from her shoulders, and admired the high vaulted ceiling, stained-glass windows, and ornate wooden stalls that guarded both sides of the long choir. Colorful banners from the Knights of the Garter hung at attention above each bench, forming two impressive rows. Enameled brass plates identified the current and prior occupiers. A checkerboard marble floor formed a center aisle, polished to a mirror shine, marred only by a gaping hole before the eleventh stall. Four men gathered around the gash, one her director, who met her halfway and led her away from the others.

"The chapel has been closed all day," he said to her. "There was an incident here last night. One of the royal graves was violated. The intruders used PEs to crack the floor and gain access."

Those she knew. Percussion explosives inflicted massive damage through heat, with little concussion and minimal noise. She'd caught the odor when entering the chapel, a sharp carbon smell. It was a sophisticated material, not available for sale on the open market, reserved only for the military. The question immediately formed in her mind. Who would have access to that type of explosive?

"Kathleen, you realize that you are about to be fired."

She did, but to hear the words shook her.

"You were warned," he said. "Told to tone your manner down. God help you, your results are wonderful, but how you achieve those is another matter entirely."

Her file was loaded with incidents similar to the one in Liverpool. A corrupt dock crew caught with 37 kilos of cocaine, but two boats sunk in the process. A raging fire she set to flush out drug traffickers that destroyed an expensive estate, which could have been sold for millions as a seized asset. An Internet piracy gang stopped, but four people shot during the arrest. And the worst, a ring of private investigators who illegally gathered confidential information, then sold it to corporate clients. One of the targets challenged her with his gun and she shot him dead. Though it was deemed a proper kill—self-defense—she'd been required to attend counseling sessions, and the therapist concluded that risks were her way of dealing with an unfulfilled life. Whatever that meant, the silly prat of a doctor never explained himself. So after the required six sessions, she'd not returned for more.

"I have fourteen other agents under my command," her supervisor said. "None brings me the grief that you do. Why is it they, too, achieve results, but with none of the residual effects?"

"I did not tell those men to run in Liverpool. They chose that course. I decided stopping them, and the ammunition they were smuggling, was worth the risk."

"There were injuries on that motorway. Innocent people, in their cars. What happened to them is inexcusable, Kathleen."

She'd heard enough rebukes at the time of her suspension. "Why am I here?"

"To see something. Come with me."

They walked back to where the three other men stood. To the right of the dark chasm in the floor she studied a black stone slab that had been neatly cracked into three manageable pieces, laid close together, as originally joined.

She read what was engraved on the face.

IN A VAULT
BENEATH THIS MARBLE SLAB
ARE DEPOSITED THE REMAINS
OF
JANE SEYMOUR QUEEN OF KING HENRY VIII
1537
KING HENRY VIII
1547
KING CHARLES I
1648
AND
AN INFANT CHILD OF QUEEN ANNE

THIS MEMORIAL WAS PLACED HERE
BY COMMAND OF
KING WILLIAM IV, 1837

One of the other men explained how Henry VIII had wanted a grand monument here, in St. George's, to overshadow his father's in Westminster. A metal effigy and massive candlesticks were cast, but Henry died before the edifice was completed. An era of Radical Protestantism came after him, a time when church monuments were not erected but hauled down. Then his daughter Mary ushered in a brief return to Rome and remembering

Henry VIII, the king of the Protestants, became dangerous. Eventually, Cromwell melted the effigy and sold the candelabra. Henry was finally buried beneath the floor, with only the black marble slab marking the spot.

She stared into the hole under the chapel. A power cable snaked a path across the floor, disappearing downward, ambient light illuminating the space beyond.

"Only once before has this crypt been opened," another of the men said.

Her director introduced him as the keeper of the grounds.

"April 1, 1813. At the time, no one knew where the beheaded Charles I had been buried. But since many believed his remains might be with those of Henry VIII and his third wife, Jane Seymour, this vault was breached."

Now, apparently, it had been opened again.

"Gentlemen," her director said. "Will you excuse Inspector Richards and myself? We need a few moments."

The other men nodded and retreated toward the main doors, twenty meters away.

She liked to hear her title. **Inspector.** She'd worked hard to earn it and hated that it might now be lost.

"Kathleen," her director said, his voice low. "I implore you, for once, to keep your mouth shut and listen to me."

She nodded.

"Six months ago the archives at Hatfield House were pilfered. Several precious volumes stolen. A month later, a similar incident occurred at the national archives in York. Over the ensuing weeks there were a series of thefts of historical documents from around the nation. A month ago a man was caught photographing pages within the British Library, but he evaded capture and fled the premises. Now this."

Her fear dissipated as her curiosity arose.

"With what has happened here," her director said, "the matter has escalated. To come into this sacred building. A royal palace." He paused. "These thieves have a clear purpose."

She crouched down to the opening.

"Go ahead," he said. "Have a peek."

It seemed irreverent to disturb the last tangible bits of someone who'd existed so long ago. Though her bosses at SOCA might think her brash and uncaring, certain things did matter to her. Like respect for the dead. But this was a crime scene, so she lay flat on the checkerboard marble and poked her head below.

The crypt was supported by a brick arch, maybe two and a half meters wide, three meters long, and a meter and a half deep. She counted four coffins. One pale and leaden bearing the inscription of King Charles, 1648, a square opening surgically cut in the upper part of the lid. Two smaller coffins were entirely intact. The fourth was the largest, pushing over two meters. An outer shell of wood, five centimeters thick, had decayed to fragments. The inner leaden coffin had also deteriorated and appeared to have been beaten by violence around its middle.

She knew whose bones were visible.

Henry VIII.

"The unopened coffins are for Jane Seymour," the director said, "the queen buried with her king, and an infant of Queen Anne's who died much later."

She recalled that Seymour had been wife number three, the only one of the six who provided Henry with a legitimate son, Edward, who eventually became king, ruling six years, dying just before his sixteenth birthday.

"It appears Henry's remains were rummaged through," he said. "The opening in Charles' coffin was made two hundred years ago. He, and the other two, seem to have been of no interest."

In life, she knew, Henry VIII had been a tall man, over six feet, but toward the end of his life his body had swelled with fat. Here lay the mortal remains of a king who fought with France, Spain, and the Holy Roman Emperor, transforming England from an island at the edge of Europe into an empire-in-the-making. He defied popes and possessed the courage to found his own religion, which continued to thrive five hundred years later.

Talk about audacity.

She stood.

"Serious things are happening, Kathleen."

He handed her one of his business cards. On the back was an address written in blue ink.

"Go there," he said.

She noted the address. A familiar place. "Why can't you tell me what this is about?"

"Because none of this was my idea." He handed back her SOCA badge and credentials, which had been confiscated three weeks ago. "Like I said, you were about to be dismissed."

She was perplexed. "So why am I here?"

"They asked, specifically, for you."

Four

LONDON

IAN KNEW EXACTLY WHERE HE WAS. HIS AUNT lived nearby and he'd many times wandered Little Venice, especially on weekend afternoons when the streets were filled with people. When he finally ran away, the posh villas and modern tower blocks had offered him his first education in life on his own. Tourists flocked to the area, drawn by the quaint neighborhoods, the blue iron bridges, and the many pubs and restaurants. Houseboats and water buses plowed the brown waters of the canal between here and the zoo—offering exactly the kind of distractions that helped with stealing. Right now, he needed a distraction to lose Norse and Devene, who would surely be after him once they were through dealing with Cotton Malone.

Maybe his aunt's flat would offer him a safe place to hide, but the thought of appearing on her doorstep turned his stomach. As much trouble as he was now apparently facing, the prospect of listening to that fat prat seemed worse. Besides, if whoever was after him knew enough to know that he was returning today, they surely would have learned about his aunt.

So he continued running down the sidewalk, in the opposite direction from where she lived, toward an avenue fifty meters ahead.

Gary stopped and said through heavy breaths, "We have to go back."

"Your dad said to go. Those are bad people. I know."

"How?"

"They tried to kill me. Not those two buggers, but others."

"That's why we need to go back."

"We will. But first we have to get farther away."

This American had no idea what it was like on London's streets. You didn't stay around and wait for trouble, and you certainly didn't go find it.

He spotted the red, white, and blue symbol for an Underground station, but since he did not have a travel card or money, and there was no time to steal anything, that escape route would do them little good. He actually liked the fact that Gary Malone seemed lost. The cockiness he'd seen in the Atlanta airport, when Gary tackled him during his own escape attempt, had vanished.

This was his world.

Where he knew the rules.

So he led the way as they ran off.

Ahead he spotted the backwater basin of Little Venice with its fleet of stumpy boats and array of trendy shops. Modern apartment buildings loomed to the left. Traffic encircling the brown-gray pool was moderate, given it was approaching 7:00 PM on a Friday. Most of the stores bordering the street were still open. Several owners were tending moored boats, rinsing off the sides and shining the lacquered exteriors. One was singing as he worked. Strings of lights decorated the basin above him.

Ian decided that would be his opportunity.

He trotted to the stairs and descended from street level to the basin's edge. The husky man was busily cleaning a teakwood hull. His boat, like all the others, was shaped like a bulging cigar.

"You going toward the zoo?" he asked.

The man stopped his dousing. "Not at the moment. Maybe later. Why do you ask?"

"Thought we'd hitch a lift."

The boat people were known for their friendliness, and it wasn't uncommon for tourists or strangers to be given rides. Two of the water buses that made a living hauling passengers were moored nearby, their cabins empty, the busy weekend coming tomorrow. He tried to appear as this man was surely perceiving him—a young boy itching for some adventure.

"Getting ready for the weekend?" he asked.

The man drenched his scalp with the hose and slicked back his black hair. "I'm readying to leave for the weekend. People will be everywhere here. Too crowded for me. Thought I'd head east, down the Thames."

The idea sounded appealing. "Need some company?"

"We can't leave," Gary whispered.

But Ian ignored him.

The man gave him a quizzical look. "What's the problem, son? You two in trouble? Where are your parents?"

Too many questions. "No bother. Don't worry about it. Just thought it would be fun to take a sail."

He glanced up to street level.

"You seem awful anxious. Got somewhere to be?"

He wasn't answering any more questions. "See you around."

He started for the towpath that paralleled the canal.

"Why aren't you two home?" the man called out as they hustled away.

"Don't look back," he muttered.

They kept following the gravelly path.

Off to his right, and above, he spotted a blue Mercedes turn onto the encircling avenue. He hoped it wasn't the same car, but when Norse climbed out he realized they were in trouble. Their position below the street and by the canal was not good. Escape options were limited to front and back since water flowed to their right and a stone wall rose to their left.

He saw that Gary realized their predicament, too.

All they could do was run down the towpath and follow the canal, but Norse and Devene would certainly catch them. He knew that once they left the basin it would be nearly impossible to escape the canal's steep banks, as property fronting the waterway was fenced. So he rushed toward a set of stairs and leaped up the stone steps two at a time. At the top he turned right and dashed across an iron bridge that arched over the canal. The span was narrow, pedestrian only, and empty. Halfway toward the other side the Mercedes wheeled up and screeched to a halt. Devene climbed out and started toward the bridge.

He and Gary turned to flee the way they'd come and were met by Norse, who stood ten meters away.

Their pursuers seemed to have anticipated their move.

"Let's stop this foolishness," Norse said. "You know what I want. Just give me the drive."

"I threw it away."

"Give it to me. Don't piss me off."

"Where's my dad?" Gary asked.

Ian liked the distraction. "Where is his dad?"

"That Yank's not your problem. We're your problem."

Norse and Devene were creeping toward them. The bridge was only two people wide and both ends were now blocked.

His pursuers were less than ten meters away.

To his left he caught sight of the beefy man with black hair motoring his boat away from its moor. Apparently he was heading for the Thames early. The boat's bow swung left, straight toward the bridge. He needed to buy a few moments so he thrust his right hand into his jacket and lunged toward the iron rail.

He quickly withdrew his hand and plunged it over the side. "Not a step closer or what you want goes into the water."

Both men stopped their advance.

Norse raised his hands in mock surrender. "Now, there's no need for that. Give it to us and we'll be done with you."

He silently breathed a sigh of relief. Apparently, neither man had seen that his closed fist contained nothing. He kept his arm pushed below the railing where the angle did not allow Norse or Devene to discover his ruse.

"How about fifty pounds," Norse said. "Fifty pounds for the drive and you can go away."

The chug from the boat's motor drew closer and the bow disappeared on the far side of the bridge.

This was going to be close.

"Make it a hundred," he said.

Norse reached into his pocket.

"Jump over the side," he whispered to Gary. "Onto the boat that's coming."

A wad of money appeared in Norse's hand.

"Do it," he breathed.

With Norse deciding what he was going to pay and Devene taking his cue from the one clearly in charge, Ian grabbed the iron rail and hurled his body up and over.

He fell the three meters down, hoping to heaven the longboat would be there. He slammed onto the cabin roof feetfirst, then recoiled, losing his balance. He grabbed onto a short metal rail and held on as his legs swung out into open air. His feet grazed the water but he managed to pull himself up as the boat cleared the bridge and continued its cruise down the canal.

The big man with black hair stood at the stern navigating the wheel. "Thought you could use some help."

He glanced back and saw Norse leap into the air, trying to duplicate what he'd just done. The man's body hurled down the three meters and found the stern. But the boat's owner rammed an elbow into Norse's chest, sending the phony inspector into the water.

He watched as Norse surfaced and climbed from the canal onto the bank.

The lighted bridge was now fifty meters in the distance.

It disappeared as the canal doglegged right.

The last thing he saw was Gary Malone in the clutches of Devene. Why had Gary not jumped? He couldn't worry about that now.

He had to go.

He searched the path ahead and spied another lit bridge. This one wider, stronger, made of brick. Cars moved back and forth above. As the boat eased toward it he leaped off onto the grassy bank. He heard his rescuer call out as he rolled onto the towpath.

"Where you going? Thought you wanted to sail?"

He stood and waved goodbye as he scampered toward a metal ladder and climbed to the street. Traffic whizzed by in both directions. He crossed the roadway and found refuge in the doorway of a closed pub. Two potted plants shielded the niche from traffic.

He shrank to the ground and gathered himself.

The acrid odor of London soaked his nostrils. He kept a close eye out for the blue Mercedes, but Norse and Devene would not assume he'd stay in the area, particularly after making such a bold escape. He caught the enticing aroma of fresh bread from a bakery a few doors down, which only aggravated his hunger. He'd not eaten since the little bit of lunch offered on the flight hours ago. People occasionally passed by on the sidewalk, but no one paid him any mind. Few ever did. What would it be like to be special? Perhaps even unique. He could only imagine. He'd quit school early, but stayed long enough to learn how to read and write. He was glad for that. Reading provided one of his few joys.

Which brought to mind the plastic bag Cotton Malone had carried.

His things.

A look was worth the chance.

So he fled the alcove.

Five

LONDON
6:30 PM

BLAKE ANTRIM CLIMBED FROM THE CAB INTO THE misty night. A storm had arrived an hour ago, draping the city in a cool, soggy blanket. Before him rose the dome of St. Paul's Cathedral, and he hoped the weather would discourage the usual throng of visitors.

He paid the driver, then climbed broad concrete steps to the church's entrance, the massive wooden doors easing shut behind him. The last gong from Big Tom, the clock that filled the south tower, completed its announcement of the half hour.

He'd flown over immediately after speaking to his agent on the ground, utilizing a State Department jet from Brussels to London. On the short flight he'd reviewed all of the reports on King's Deception, refamiliarizing himself with every detail of the operation.

The problem was simple.

Scotland planned to release Abdelbaset al-Megrahi, a former Libyan intelligence officer convicted in 1988 of 270 counts of murder for bombing Pan Am Flight 103 over Lockerbie, Scotland. In 2001 al-Megrahi was sentenced to life imprisonment, but now, after only a few years behind bars, he'd contracted cancer. So, for so-called humanitarian reasons, the Scots were going to allow al-Megrahi to die in Libya. No official announcement of the release decision had occurred as yet, since the highly secret negotiations were still ongoing. The CIA had learned of the proposal over a year ago and Washington had already voiced strong opposition, insisting that Downing Street stop it. But the English had refused, saying this was an internal Scottish affair in which they could not meddle.

Since friggin' when? the diplomats had asked.

London had been meddling in Edinburgh's politics for a thousand years. The fact that the two nations were united under the mantle of Great Britain just made things easier.

But they'd still refused.

Al-Megrahi going home to Libya would be a slap in the face to the 189 murdered Americans. It had taken the CIA thirteen years to apprehend the accused, try him, and obtain a guilty verdict.

Now to just let him go?

Kaddafi, Libya's leader, would rub al-Megrahi's

return in Washington's face, only amplifying his position among Arab leaders. Terrorists around the world would be fortified, their causes becoming that much more important in light of a weak America that could not even keep a friend from turning a murderer loose.

He unbuttoned his wet overcoat and approached the high altar, passing a side chapel where red-shielded candles sparkled in the amber light. His agent had selected this locale for their meeting because he'd been working in the church's archives all day, using false journalistic credentials, searching for more information.

He followed the south aisle to the base of a spiral stairway and glanced around one more time. His hopes about the weather seemed to have been granted. Few people milled about. Thankfully, Operation King's Deception had, so far, generated no British interest.

He stepped through an archway to a staircase that corkscrewed a path upward. He passed the time climbing by counting. Two hundred and fifty-nine steps came and went beneath his leather soles before he reached the Whispering Gallery.

Waiting for him was a fair-skinned man with pale green eyes and a balding head mottled with brownish age spots. What he lacked in looks he made up for in skill, as he was one of Antrim's best historical analysts, which was exactly what this operation required.

He stepped from the doorway into a narrow circular gallery. A polished iron railing offered the only protection from a one-hundred-foot drop down to the nave's marble floor. He spotted the design etched into the marble below, a compasslike insignia centered by a brass grille. He knew that beneath that floor, in the crypt, lay the tomb of Christopher Wren, the architect who almost 400 years before had labored to construct St. Paul's. Encircling the sunlike design was a Latin inscription dedicated to Wren. READER, IF YOU SEEK HIS MONUMENT, LOOK AROUND YOU.

Antrim did.

Not bad, at all.

The aisle between the railing and the gallery's stone wall was little more than a yard wide, usually filled with camera-toting tourists. Tonight it loomed empty, save for them.

"What name are you using?" he asked in a low voice.

"Gaius Wells."

He allowed his attention to drift up into the dome. Backlit frescoes depicting the life of St. Paul stared back at him.

The sound of rain quickened on the roof.

"We currently have Cotton Malone and Ian Dunne in the car, being transported," Wells said. "I hope that boy kept the flash drive. If so, this gamble might still pay off."

He wasn't so sure.

"The puzzle we're solving is 500 years old," his man said. "The pieces were carefully hidden. It's been tough finding them, but we're making progress. Unfortunately, Henry VIII's grave revealed nothing."

He'd approved that risky move because Farrow Curry's untimely death had set them back, so the chance had to be taken. The tomb had been inspected only once before, in 1813. At that time the king himself, William IV, had been present and everything that happened was meticulously recorded. No mention of opening Henry's coffin had appeared anywhere in those accounts. Which meant those remains had laid inviolate since 1548. He was hoping they might discover that the fat old Tudor had taken the secret with him to his grave.

But there'd been nothing but bones.

Another failure.

And costly.

"Unfortunately," he said. "The Brits will now be on alert. We abused their royal chapel."

"It was a clean in and out. No witnesses. They'd never suspect us."

"Do we know any more about how Curry died?"

A month had passed since Farrow Curry either fell or was pushed into the path of an oncoming Underground train. Ian Dunne had been there, picking Curry's pocket, and had been seen holding a flash drive before assaulting a man, then fleeing the station. They needed to hear what the boy had to say, and they wanted that flash drive.

The rain continued to fall outside.

"You realize that this could all be legend," Wells said. "Not a shred of truth to any of it."

"So what was it Curry found? Why was he so excited?"

True, Curry had called a few hours before he died and reported a breakthrough. He was a CIA contract analyst with a degree in encryption, specifically assigned to King's Deception. But with his sorry lack of progress over the past few months, Antrim had been leaning toward replacing him. The call changed that, and he'd sent a man to meet Curry at Oxford Circus, the two of them off to investigate whatever it was Curry had found. But they never connected. Murder? Suicide? Accident? Nobody knew. Could the flash drive Ian Dunne was seen holding provide answers?

He certainly hoped so.

"I'll be here, in town, from this point on," he told Wells.

Tonight he'd visit one of his favorite restaurants. His culinary skills were limited to microwave directions on a box, so he ate most meals out, choosing quality over economy. Maybe a particular waitress he knew would be on duty. If not, he'd give her a call. They'd enjoyed themselves several times in the past.

"I need to ask," Wells said. "Why involve Cotton Malone in all of this? Seems unnecessary."

"We can use all the help we can get."

"He's retired. I don't see where he'd be an asset."

"He can be."

And that was all he intended to offer.

An exit opened a few feet away, the one he'd used to climb to the gallery. Another waited on the far side. "Stay here until I'm gone. No use being seen together down below."

He traversed the circular walk, hugging the cathedral's upper walls and came to the far side. Wells stood a hundred feet away, staring across at him. A placard beside the exit informed him that if he spoke softly into the wall, the words could be heard on the other side.

Hence, the Whispering Gallery.

He decided to give it a try. He faced the gray stone wall and murmured, "Make sure we don't screw things up with Malone and Dunne."

A wave confirmed that he'd been understood.

Wells disappeared into the archway. Antrim was about to do the same when a pop echoed across the still air.

Then a cry from the other side.

Another pop.

The cry became a moan.

He raced back across and glanced inside the exit, saw nothing, then advanced forward. A few steps down the circular way he found Wells on the stone steps, facedown, blood pouring from two wounds. He rolled him over and spotted a flicker of disbelief in the eyes.

Wells opened his mouth to speak.

"Hang in there," Antrim said. "I'll get help."

Wells' hand clutched his coat sleeve.

"Not . . . supposed to . . . happen."

Then the body went limp.

He checked for a pulse. None.

Reality jarred him.

What the hell?

He heard footfalls below, receding away. He was unarmed. He hadn't expected any trouble. Why would he? He started down the 259 steps, keeping watch, concerned that the shooter could be waiting around the next turn. He came to the bottom and carefully peered out into the nave, seeing only a handful of visitors. Across, in the far transept, he spotted a figure moving steadily toward the exit doors.

A man.

Who stopped, turned, and aimed his gun.

Antrim dove to the floor.

But no bullet came his way.

He sprang to his feet and saw the shooter flee out the exit doors.

He rushed ahead and pushed the bronze portal open.

Darkness had rolled in.

Rain continued to wash down.

He caught sight of the man, beyond the steps that led from the church, trotting away toward Fleet Street.

Six

Gary Malone had been wrestled from the bridge and forced back into the Mercedes. His hands had been tied behind his back, his head covered with a wool mask.

He was afraid. Who wouldn't be? But he was even more concerned about his dad and what may have happened in that garage. He never should have run, but he'd followed his father's order. He should have ignored Ian and stayed close by. Instead, Ian leaped off that bridge. Sure, he'd been told to jump, too. But what sane person would have done that? Norse tried and failed, the man, in his wet clothes, cursing all the way during the drive in the car.

Ian Dunne had guts, that he'd give him.

But so did he.

Yesterday he was home packing, his mind in turmoil. Two weeks ago his mother told him that the man he'd called dad all of his life was not his natural father. She'd explained what happened before he was born—an affair, a pregnancy—confessing to her mistake and apologizing. At first he'd accepted it and decided, what did it matter? His father was his father. But he quickly began to question that decision.

It **did** matter.

Who **was** he? Where did he come from? Where did he belong? With his mother, as a Malone? Or with someone else?

He had no idea.

But he wanted to know.

He didn't have to return to school for another ten days, and was looking forward to a Thanksgiving holiday in Copenhagen, thousands of miles from Georgia. He had to get away.

At least for a while.

A swarm of bitter feelings had settled inside him that he was finding increasingly hard to control. He'd always been respectful, obeying his mother, not making any trouble, but her lies were weighing on him. She told him all the time to tell the truth.

So why hadn't she?

"You ready?" his mother asked him before they'd left for the airport. "You're off to England, I hear."

His dad had explained they were going to make a stop in London and drop a boy named Ian Dunne off with the police, then catch a con-

necting plane for Copenhagen. He noticed her red, watery eyes. "You been crying?"

She nodded. "I don't like it when you go. I miss you."

"It's just for the week."

"I hope that's all."

He knew what she meant, a reference to their conversation from last week when, for the first time, he'd said he might want to live somewhere else.

She bit her lip. "We can work this through, Gary."

"Tell me who my birth father is."

She shook her head. "I can't."

"No. You won't. There's a difference."

"I promised myself I would never have him part of our life. I made a mistake being with him, but not a mistake in having you."

He'd heard that explanation before, but was finding it difficult to separate the two. Both were based on lies.

"You knowing who that man is will change nothing," she said, her voice cracking.

"But I want to know. You lied to me all of my life. You knew the truth but told no one, not even Dad. I know he did bad things, too. There were other women. You told me. But he didn't lie to me."

His mother started crying. She was a lawyer who represented people in court. He'd watched

her try a case once and saw firsthand how tough and smart she could be. He thought he might like to be a lawyer one day, too.

"I'm fifteen," he said to her. "I'm not a kid. I'm entitled to know it all. If you can't tell me where I came from, then you and I have a problem."

"So you're going to leave and live in Denmark?" she asked.

He decided to cut her no slack. "I might just do that."

She stared at him through her tears. "I realize I messed up, Gary. It's my fault. I take the blame."

He wasn't interested in blame. Only in ending the uncertainty that seemed to grow inside him by the day. He didn't want to resent her—he loved her, she was his mother—but she wasn't making this easy.

"Spend some time with your dad," she said, swiping away the tears. "Enjoy yourself."

That he would.

He was tired of fighting.

His parents divorced over a year ago, right before his dad quit the Justice Department and moved overseas. Since then his mother had dated some, but not much. He'd always wondered why not more. But that was not a subject he was comfortable talking about with her.

Seemed her business, not his.

They lived in a nice house in a good neighborhood. He attended an excellent school. His grades were not extraordinary but above average. He played baseball and basketball. He hadn't tried a cigarette or any drugs, though opportunities for both had come his way. He'd tasted beer, wine, and some hard liquor but wasn't sure he liked any of them.

He was a good kid.

At least he thought so.

So why was he so mad?

He was now lying on a sofa, hands tied behind his back, head sheathed in the wool cap, only his mouth exposed. The drive in the Mercedes had taken about thirty minutes. He'd been warned that if he made a sound they would gag him.

So he stayed still.

Which helped his nerves.

He heard movement, but no voices, only the faint sound of chimes in the distance. Then someone came close and sat nearby. He heard a crackle, like plastic being torn, then the sound of chewing.

He was a little hungry himself.

A smell caught his nostrils. Licorice. One of his favorites.

"You got any more of that?" he asked.

"Shut up, kid. You're lucky to even still be alive."

Seven

Malone awoke with a pounding headache. What was supposed to have been a simple favor had evolved into a major problem.

He blinked his eyes and focused.

His fingers found dried blood and a nasty knot to his forehead. His neck was sore from Devene's attack. His and Gary's travel bags were opened, their clothes strewn across the mews, the plastic bag containing Ian's personal items still there, its contents scattered about.

He pushed himself up, his legs stiff and tired.

Where was Gary?

Someone had gone to a lot of trouble to make sure they found Ian Dunne. Even more troubling was the reach of the information network possessed by whoever **they** were. Somebody in an official position had given Customs clearance to allow Ian into the country. Granted, Norse and his pal were imposters, but the person or persons who'd managed to bypass Britain's passport laws were the genuine article.

Norse had demanded a flash drive from Ian.

He had to find Gary. He'd told the boys to run. Hopefully, they were nearby, waiting until all was clear to return.

But where were they?

He checked his watch. Best he could tell he'd been down about twenty minutes. He spotted his cell phone among his clothes. Should he call the police? Or maybe Stephanie Nelle at the Magellan Billet? No. This was his problem. One call he would not be making was to Pam. The last thing he needed was for his ex-wife to know about this. Bad enough that he once risked his own ass on a daily basis.

But to involve Gary?

That would be unforgivable.

He surveyed the mews, noting yard equipment, a couple of gas cans, and a tool bench. Rain fell beyond the open doorway. He stared out to the wet drive that led to the tree-lined side street, expecting to see both boys appear.

He should gather his clothes.

The Metropolitan Police would have to be involved.

That was the smart play.

A noise caught his attention, at the hedges separating the mews from the property next door.

Somebody was pushing through.

The boys?

To be cautious, he decided to lie back down.

He pressed his cheek to the cool cobbles and closed his eyes, cracking his lids open just enough to see.

IAN HAD HUGGED THE SIDE STREETS AND USED THE storm, trees, and the fences that fronted the stylish neighborhoods for cover. It took only a few minutes for him to find the courtyard where the Mercedes had first been parked. The mews door remained open, but the car was gone.

He glanced around.

No one seemed to be in any of the surrounding houses.

He stepped into the open garage and saw the contents of both Malones' travel bags scattered across the pavement. In the dim interior Malone lay sprawled near one wall. Ian crept over, knelt beside him, and heard labored breaths. He wanted to shake Malone awake and see if he was all right, but he hadn't asked this man to get involved, and there was no need to involve him any further.

He searched for what he came for and found the plastic bag beneath a balled-up shirt. Apparently it had not been considered important. Why would it? Those men were looking for a computer drive. Not some books, a pocketknife, and a few other insignificant items.

He stuffed everything back into the bag and again stared at Cotton Malone. The American seemed like a decent fellow. Maybe his own father had been like him. But thanks to a worthless mother, he would never know who his father had been. He'd seen genuine concern in Malone's eyes when he learned that Norse was not with Scotland Yard. Fear for **both** boys. He'd even felt a little better knowing Malone was there in the car. Not many people had ever cared about him, nor had he cared for anyone.

And this wasn't the time to start.

Life was tough, and Cotton Malone would understand.

Or at least that's what he told himself as he fled the mews.

MALONE ROSE UP AND YELLED, "WHERE'S GARY?"

Ian whirled and the shock on the boy's face quickly changed to relief. "Bloody hell. I thought you were out."

"I could see your concern. You only came back for your stuff."

Defiance returned to the boy's eyes. "I didn't ask you here. I didn't involve you. You're not my problem."

But a hint of resignation laced the declaration, the expression half defensive, half angry. So he asked again, "Where's Gary?"

"Those coppers have him."

He rose to his feet, head spinning. "They're not police and you know that. How did they get him and not you? You're the one they wanted."

"I got away. He didn't."

He lunged forward and grabbed Ian by the shoulders. "You left him?"

"I told him to jump with me, but he wouldn't."

Jump?

He listened to what had happened in Little Venice, how Ian had leaped from the bridge.

"Those men have Gary," Ian said.

He yanked the plastic bag away. "Where's the flash drive they want?"

Ian did not reply. But what did he expect? He was just a street kid who'd learned to survive by keeping his mouth shut.

"I tell you what," Malone said. "I'm going to let the police deal with you. Then I can find Gary." He locked his right hand onto Ian's left arm. "You so much as twitch and I'll knock the living daylights out of you."

And he meant it.

He was more than mad. He was furious. At this delinquent and at himself, his anger a crippling mixture of frustration and fear. He'd almost been shot thanks to this kid, and his son was now in danger.

He told himself to calm down.

"What do you plan to do with me?" Ian asked.

"You're in my custody."

"I'm not yours."

"Good thing. Because, if you were, me and you would be having a much more physical chat."

He saw the boy understood.

"One last chancc," he said. "Why are those men after you?"

"I was there, in Oxford Circus, that day, a month ago, when the man died."

Eight

IAN STOOD AT THE END OF THE WALKWAY, BENEATH a lighted WAY OUT sign, and surveyed the crowded train platform.

Who would be next?

His first choice was an older woman in a gray tweed coat who hobbled forward like a dog with a crippled leg. She lugged her purse in the crook of her arm, its gold catch loose, the flap snapping open with each labored step. The invitation was irresistible, and for a moment he thought she might be a decoy. Police sometimes baited the station. But after a few moments of careful observation he concluded she was genuine, so he worked his way through the rush-hour commuters to where she stood.

Oxford Circus was his favorite locale. The Bakerloo, Central, and Victoria Underground lines all converged there. Every morning and evening tens of thousands of people streamed in and out, most headed to the trendy shops and stores that lined Oxford and Bond streets a hundred feet above. Many, like the dowager he now spied, were weighed down with shopping bags—easy marks for someone with the skills he'd spent five of his fifteen years of life perfecting.

It helped that few considered him a threat. He was barely five feet tall with thick blond hair that he kept trimmed with a pair of scissors stolen last year from Harrods. He was actually a fairly proficient barber and considered hairstyling as a possible career—one day, after his street time was behind him. For now, the skill allowed him to maintain an image strangers found inviting. Thankfully, the city's charity shops offered him a varied choice in dress at little or no cost. He liked corduroy pants and buttondown shirts, a carefree look reminiscent of one of his favorite stories, *Oliver Twist*. An ideal image for an enterprising pickpocket.

His Scottish mother named him Ian, the only thing she gave him besides life. She disappeared when he was three months old and an English aunt took her place and bestowed him with the last name of Dunne. He'd not seen that aunt in three years, ever since he escaped out a second-story window and dissolved into the streets of

London where he'd survived through a combination of charity and criminality.

The police knew him. They'd arrested him several times in other stations and once at Trafalgar Square. But never had he stayed in custody. There'd been three foster homes, attempts to stabilize him, but he'd run away from them all. His age worked in his favor, as did his plight. Pity was an easy emotion to manipulate.

He approached the old woman using the crowd for cover. His methodology was the result of much practice, a simple matter to lightly bump into her.

"Sorry," he said, adding a quick smile.

She instantly warmed to him and returned the friendly gesture. "That's okay, young man."

The three seconds it took for the bump to register and for her to respond were all he needed to slip his hand into her purse and palm what he could. He immediately shielded his withdrawn hand under the flap of his jacket and slipped deeper into the crowd. A quick look back confirmed that the woman was unaware of his invasion. He threaded his way out of the gathering throng and stole a glance at what he held.

A small maroon cylinder with a black plastic cap.

He'd hoped it was a cigarette lighter, or something else he could pawn or sell. Instead, it was a canister of pepper spray. He'd managed to lift one or two in the past. He shook his head in disgust and pocketed the object.

His gaze found a second opportunity.

The man was maybe fifty, dressed in a wool jacket. The flap on the right-hand coat pocket, folded inward, offered an opportunity. He'd obtained some of his choicest loot from the pockets of smartly dressed men. This particular target was tall and gangly with a beak-like nose. He was facing away, toward the tracks, and repeatedly studied his watch, his attention alternating between that and an electronic billboard that announced the train was less than a minute away.

A billow of air puffed from the blackened cavern, followed by a rumble that steadily intensified. People massed forward toward the edge, prepared to rush into the cars once the doors opened and the electronic voice warned them to mind the gap.

His second opportunity joined the crowd and managed to place himself where he would be one of the first to enter. This was the time of maximum distraction. Everyone was tired and eager to get home. Their guard was down.

His first opportunity had garnered nothing.

He was hoping for better this time.

He made it to the smartly dressed man and, without delay, slipped his right hand into the jacket pocket. A jostle of bodies provided the perfect camouflage. His fingers wrapped around a rectangular piece of plastic and he withdrew his arm at the precise instant the train rattled into view.

Then two hands shoved the smartly dressed man from the platform into the path of the oncoming train.

Screams echoed through the chamber.

A dry screech of brakes grew to a roaring thunder.

Hydraulics hissed.

Voices rose in disbelief.

Ian suddenly realized he was standing on the platform with whatever he'd slipped from the dead man's pocket still in his hand, exposed for all to see. Yet no one was paying him any attention—except a tall bloke, with frizzy, ash-gray hair and a matching mustache.

Then he realized.

The hands that had pushed the man off the platform might have belonged to this demon.

Their gazes locked.

Frizzy reached for what Ian held and for some reason he did not want him to have it.

He yanked his hand back and turned to flee.

Two arms instantly wrapped around him from behind. He slammed the sole of his foot onto toes, his heel crushing into thin leather.

Frizzy cried out and released his grip.

Ian raced forward, shoving people aside, heading for the way out.

No one stopped him. The crowd's attention was on the train and the man who'd fallen onto the tracks. Doors to the cars were opening and people began to stream out onto the platform.

Ian kept edging his way forward. He couldn't tell if Frizzy was following. This foray into Oxford Circus had turned crazy and all he wanted was to leave.

He found the exit and started up the tiled passage.

Few people were there, most still lingering on the platform. He heard whistles ahead and quickly stepped aside as two coppers raced by him on the way down. He didn't yet know what he'd managed to snare from the pocket before the man flew off the platform, so he took a moment to study the object.

A computer flash drive.

He shook his head. Worthless. Dinner would have to be found in one of the free missions tonight. And he'd so been looking forward to pizza.

He stuffed the drive into his pocket and rushed for the escalator. At the top he passed through the turnstile using a travel card he'd pilfered earlier from a man in Chelsea. He pushed through dingy glass doors and emerged on the sidewalk into a steady drizzle. Chilly air forced him to zip his jacket and plunge both hands into his pockets. He'd lost his gloves two days ago somewhere on the East End. He hustled down the crowded sidewalk and turned the corner, passing newspaper vendors and cigarette booths, his eyes on the uneven pavement.

"There you are. I've been looking for you," a friendly voice said.

He glanced up as Frizzy casually wrapped an arm around his shoulders and diverted him toward a car beside the curb. The tip of a knife blade came beneath his jacket and pressed sharp against the soft flesh of his thigh.

"Nice and quiet," the man whispered, "or we'll see how you bleed."

Three steps and they reached the open rear door of a dark-colored Bentley. He was shoved inside and Frizzy climbed in, sitting across from him in a facing rear seat.

The door shut and the car wheeled from the curb.

Ian kept his hands inside his jacket pockets and sat rigid.

His attention focused on the other man sitting beside Frizzy. Older, wearing a charcoal-gray suit with a waistcoat. He sat straight and stared at Ian through a pair of green eyes flecked with specks of brown that seemed to say that he was not somebody accustomed to disagreement. A thick fleece of white hair covered his head and spilled down onto a creased brow.

"You have something I want," the older man said in a low, throaty voice, the words perfectly formed.

"I don't do business with people I don't know."

The aloof stare of an aristocrat dissolved into a mirthful grin. "I don't do business with street urchins. Give me the drive."

"What's so important about it?"

"I don't explain myself, either."

A cold bead of sweat slid down his back. Something about the two men who faced him signaled desperation.

And that he didn't like.

So he lied. "I threw it away."

"Petty thieves, like you, throw nothing away."

"I don't keep junk."

"Kill him," the older man said.

Frizzy lunged forward, the knife drawn back, ready to thrust.

"Okay. Okay," Ian said. "I have it."

The older man's right hand halted Frizzy's attack.

The Bentley started to brake in traffic.

Other vehicles could be seen outside the moisture-laden windows slowing for a road signal apparently ahead. Rush hour in London, and nobody moved fast. He quickly reviewed his options and determined they were limited. Frizzy still held the knife and kept a close watch. The other man was equally attentive, and the confines of the car did not allow much room to maneuver.

He withdrew his left hand and displayed the drive. "This what you want?"

"There's a good boy," the older man said.

Then Ian's right hand telegraphed the next move, and he almost smiled.

His fingers curled around the pepper spray. He'd thought it useless. Now it was priceless.

The older man reached for the drive.

Ian whipped out his right hand and sprayed.

Both men howled, pawing their eyes in a vain attempt to relieve the pain.

"Kill him, now," the older man ordered.

Frizzy, eyes closed, dropped the knife and reached beneath his coat.

A gun came into view.

Ian sprayed again.

Frizzy yelled.

Ian unlatched the door nearest to him and slid out onto wet pavement between two idling cars. Before slamming the door shut, he snatched the knife from the floorboard then sprang to his feet.

A woman in an adjacent vehicle gave him a queer look.

But he ignored her.

He wove a path around the congealed traffic, found the sidewalk, and disappeared into the gloomy evening.

MALONE LISTENED TO THE BOY'S STORY.

"So you were there stealing."

"I lifted a few things. Then I took the drive off the bloke, just before the bugger pushed him into the train."

"You saw the guy pushed?"

Ian nodded. "I wasn't expecting that, so I ran, but ended up getting caught by the man who pushed him, then shoved into a Bentley."

He held up the plastic bag and asked again, "Where's the flash drive?"

"I kept it, after I left the car. I thought it could be worth something."

"And thieves like you don't throw away things that are worth something."

"I'm not a thief."

His patience was running out. "Where's the damn drive?"

"In my special place. Where I keep my stuff."

His phone rang.

Which startled him.

Then he realized it could be Gary. He shoved Ian into the mews and dared the boy to make a run for it.

He found the phone and clicked it on. "Gary?"

"We have your son," the voice said, which he recognized.

Devene.

"You know what we want."

And he was staring straight at it. "I have Dunne."

"Then we can trade."

He was fed up, so he said, "When and where?"

Nine

ANTRIM YANKED UP THE COLLAR OF HIS COAT AND braced himself for the chilly rain. The man he was following into the lousy night had just killed an American intelligence operative. He had to know who was behind this and why.

Everything could depend on it.

The pace of the hurrying masses on the sidewalk matched the bustle of traffic. Evening rush hour in a city of eight million people was unfolding. Below he knew trains roared in every direction, people headed down to them where the red circle crossed by a blue bar marked an Underground station. All of this was familiar, as he'd lived in London for the first fourteen years of his life. His father had worked for the State Department, a career employee with the diplomatic service who lasted thirty years until retirement. His parents had rented a flat near Chelsea and he'd roamed London.

To hear his father talk, he'd laid the entire groundwork for the end of the Cold War. Reality was far different. His father was an unimportant man, in an unimportant job, a tiny cog in a massive diplomatic wheel. He died fifteen years ago in the States, living off one-half of his government pension. His mother received the other half, courtesy of an Illinois divorce she'd obtained after thirty-six years of marriage. Neither one of them had the courtesy to even tell him before they split, which summed up their life as a family.

Three strangers.

In every way.

His mother spent her life trying to please her husband, scared of the world, unsure of anything. That's why she took his father's shouts, insults, and punches. Which left marks not only on her, but in their son's memory.

To this day he hated having his face touched.

It started with his father, who'd smack him on the cheek for little or no reason. Which his mother allowed. And why wouldn't she?

She thought little of herself and even less of her son.

He'd walked Fleet Street many times. The first was nearly forty years ago, as a twelve-year-old, his way of escaping both parents. Named after one of the city's ghost rivers that flow belowground, this was once home to London's press. The newspapers left in the 1980s, moving to the outskirts of town.

But the courts and lawyers remained, their chambers occupying the warren of buildings and quadrangles surrounding him. He'd once thought about law school, but opted for government service. Only instead of the State Department, he'd managed to be hired by the CIA. His father lived long enough to know that, but never offered a single word of praise. His mother had long since lost touch with reality and languished in a fog. He'd visited her once in the nursing home, the entire experience too depressing to recall. He liked to think that his fears came from her, his audacity from his father, but there were times when he believed the reverse may well be true.

His target was a hundred feet ahead, moving at a steady pace.

He was panicked.

Somebody was finally into the business of Operation King's Deception.

He scanned the surroundings.

The Thames flowed a few hundred yards to his left, the Royal Courts of Justice only blocks ahead. This was the City, an autonomous district, separately chartered and governed since the 13th century. Some called it the Square Mile, occupied since the 1st century and the Romans. The great medieval craft guilds were founded right here, then the worldwide trading companies. The City remained crucial to Great Britain's finance and trade, and he wondered if his target had a connection to either.

His man turned left.

He hustled forward, rain tickling his face, and saw that the assailant had entered the Inns of Court, passing through its famous stone gateway.

This place he knew.

It had once been the home of the Templars and the knights stayed until the early 14th century. Two hundred years later Henry VIII dissolved all religious orders and allowed the lawyers to assume the Temple grounds, forming their Inns of Court. James I eventually ensured their perpetual presence with a royal grant. He'd many times, as a kid, wandered through the maze of buildings with their courtyards. He recalled the plane trees, sundials, and green lawns sloping to the Embankment. Its gateways and alleys were legendary, the things of books and movies, many with elegant names like King's Bench Walk and Middle Temple Lane.

He stared through the entrance and spotted his man making haste down a narrow, brick-paved street. Four men brushed past and headed through the gate, so he joined them, hanging back, using them as cover. Light came from a few windows and wall lamps that illuminated the entrances to the buildings.

His target turned left again.

He rushed past the men ahead of him and found a cloister framed out by archways. A courtyard opened on the other side and he saw the man enter the Temple Church.

He hesitated.

He'd been inside before. Small, with few places to hide.

Why go there?

One way to find out.

He stepped back out into the rain and trotted for the church's side door. Inside, his gaze searched the scattered folds of weak light. Silence reigned, which unnerved him. Beneath the circular roof lay the marble effigies of slumbering crusaders resting in full armor. He noted the marble columns, the interlaced arches, the solid drum of handsome stonework. The round church was embroidered by six windows and six marble pillars. In the rectangular choir to his right, beyond three more lofty arches, the altar was illuminated by a faint coppery glow. His target was nowhere in sight, nor anyone else.

Nothing about this felt right.

He turned to leave.

"Not yet, Mr. Antrim."

The voice was older with a hollow tone.

He whirled back around.

In the Round, among the floor effigies, six figures appeared from the deep shadows that engulfed the walls. No faces could be seen, just their outline. Men. Dressed in suits. Standing. Arms at their sides, like vultures in the gloom.

"We need to speak," the same voice said.

From his left, ten feet away, another man appeared, the face too in shadows, but enough was visible for him to see a weapon aimed straight at him.

"Please step into the Round," the first voice said.

No choice.

So he did as told, now among the floor effigies and encircled by the six men. "You killed my man just to get me here?"

"We killed him because a point needed to be made."

The shadowy chin on the speaker looked as tough as armor plate.

What had Wells said? **Not supposed to happen.**

"How did you know I'd be in St. Paul's?"

"Our survival has always been predicated on operating with excellent intelligence. We have been watching your actions in our country for many months."

"Who are you?" He truly wanted to know.

"Our founder called us the Daedalus Society. Do you know the story of Daedalus?"

"Mythology never interested me."

"To you, the seeker of secrets? Mythology should be quite an important subject."

He resented the condescending tone, but said nothing.

"The name Daedalus means 'cunning worker,'" the older man said.

"So what are you? Some kind of club?"

The other five shadows had neither moved nor said a word.

"We are the keepers of secrets. Protectors of kings and queens. God knows, they have needed protection, and mainly from themselves. We were created in 1605, because of the particular secret you seek."

Now he was interested. "You're saying that it's real?"

"Why do you seek this?" another of the shadows asked, the voice again older and raspy.

"Tell us," another said. "Why meddle in our affairs?"

"This an interrogation?" he asked.

The first man chuckled. "Not at all. But we are curious. An American intelligence agent delving into obscure British history, looking into something that few in this world know exists. You asked your man in St. Paul's, what happened to Farrow Curry? We killed him. The hope was that you would abandon the search. But that was not to be. So we killed another of your men tonight. Must we kill a third?"

He knew who that would be, but still said, "I have a job to do."

"So do we," one of the shadows said.

"You won't succeed," another voice pointed out.

Then a third said, "We will stop you."

The first man raised a hand, silencing the others. "Mr. Antrim, you have, so far, not been successful. My feeling is that once you do fail your superiors will forever abandon this effort. All we have to do is make sure that happens."

"Show yourself."

"Secrecy is our ally," the first voice said. "We operate outside of the law. We are subject to no oversight.

We decide what is best and appropriate." A pause. "And we care nothing about politics."

He swallowed the nervous lump in his throat and said, "We're not going to allow the release of that Libyan murderer. Not without repercussions."

"As I said, Mr. Antrim, politics matters not to us. But we are curious. Do you truly think that what you seek will stop that?"

He hated the feeling of helplessness that surged through him. "You killed an American intelligence agent. That won't go unpunished."

The older man chuckled. "And that is supposed to frighten us? I assure you, we have faced far greater threats from far greater sources. Cromwell and his Puritans beheaded Charles I. We tried to prevent that, but could not. Eventually, though, we engineered Cromwell's downfall and the return of Charles II. We were there to make sure William **and** Mary secured the throne. We shepherded George III through his insanity and prevented a revolt. So many kings and queens have come and gone, each more self-destructive than the last. But we have been there, to watch and to guard. We fear not the United States of America. And you and I both know that if your investigations are discovered, no one on the other side of the Atlantic Ocean will acknowledge responsibility. You will be disavowed. Forgotten. Left to your own devices."

He said nothing because the SOB was right. That had been an express condition of King's Deception. Take a shot. Go ahead. But if caught, you're on your own. He'd worked under that disclaimer before, but he'd also never been caught.

"What do you want?" he asked.

"We could kill you, but that would only arouse further curiosity and bring more agents. So we are asking **you** to leave this be."

"Why would I do that?"

"Because you are afraid. I see it on your face, in your eyes. Fear is paralyzing, is it not?"

"I came after your man."

"That you did. But let us be honest with each other. Your past does not include much heroism. Your service record is one of caution and deliberation. We have learned much about you, Mr. Antrim, and, I must say, none of it is impressive."

"Your insults don't bother me."

"We will pay you," one of the shadows said. "Five million pounds, deposited wherever you choose. Simply tell your superiors there was nothing to find."

He did the math. Seven million dollars. His. For just walking away?

"We knew that offer would interest you," the first voice said. "You own little and have saved nothing. At some point your usefulness to your employer will wane, if not already, and then what will you do?"

He stood in a pool of weak light, among the floor effigies, feeling defeated. Had that been the whole idea?

Rain continued to fall outside.

These men had chosen their play carefully and, he had to admit, the offer was tempting. He was fifty-two years old and had thought a lot lately about the rest of his life. Fifty-five was the usual age for operatives to leave, and living off a meager government pension had never seemed all that appealing.

Seven million dollars.

That was appealing.

But it bothered him that these men knew his weakness.

"Think on it, Mr. Antrim," the first voice said. "Think on it hard."

"You can't kill every agent of the U.S. government," he felt compelled to say.

"That's true. But, by paying you off, we will ensure that Operation King's Deception fails, which means no more agents will be dispatched. You will report that failure and assume all blame. We believe this simpler and more effective than force. Lucky for us that someone negotiable, like yourself, is in charge."

Another insult he allowed to pass.

"We want this over. And with your help, it will be."

The shadow's right hand rose, then flicked.

The man with the weapon surged forward.

A paralysis seized Antrim's body and made him unable to react.

He heard a pop.

Something pierced his chest.

Sharp. Stinging.

His legs went limp.

And he dropped to the floor among the dead knights.

Ten

KATHLEEN PARKED HER CAR ON TUDOR STREET, just outside the gate. On the card her supervisor had provided was written MIDDLE TEMPLE HALL, which stood within the old Temple grounds, part of the Inns of Court, where for 400 years London's lawyers had thrived. Two of the great legal societies, the Middle Temple and Inner Temple were headquartered here, their presence dating back to the time of Henry VIII. Dickens himself had been a Middle Templar, and she'd always liked what he'd written about life inside the Inn walls.

Who enters here leaves noise behind.

The sight of Henry's bones still bothered her. Never had she thought that she'd be privy to such a thing. Who would have burglarized that tomb? Bold, whoever they were, since security within Windsor Castle was extensive. And why? What did they think was there? All of these questions had weighed on her mind as she drove back into London, eager to know what awaited her at Middle Temple Hall.

The rain came in spurts, her short brown hair dry from earlier but once again being doused by a steady mist. No one manned the vehicle gate, the car park beyond empty. Nearly 7:30 PM and the Friday workday was over at the Inns of Court.

Hers, though, appeared to be only just beginning.

She crossed the famous King's Bench Walk and passed among a cluster of redbrick buildings, every window dark, entering the courtyard before the famous Temple Church. She hustled toward the cloister at the far end, crossing another brick lane and finding Middle Hall. A sign out front proclaimed CLOSED TO VISITORS, but she ignored its warning and opened the doors.

The lit space within stretched thirty meters long and half that wide, topped by a double hammerbeam roof, its oak joists, she knew, 900 years old. The towering windows lining both sides were adorned with suits of armor and heraldic memorials to former Middle Templars. Along with Dickens, Sir Walter Raleigh, William Blackstone, Edmund Burke, and John Marston were all once members. Four long rows of oak tables, lined with chairs packed close together, ran parallel from one end to the other. At the far end beneath five massive oil paintings stretched the ancients table, where the eight most senior barristers had eaten since the 16th century. The portraits above had not changed in two hundred years. Charles I, James II, William III, Charles II, Queen Anne, and, to the left, hidden from view until farther inside, Elizabeth I.

At the far end a man appeared.

He was short, early sixties, with a weathered face as round as a full moon. His silver hair was so immaculately coiffed it almost demanded to be ruffled. As he came close she saw that thick, steel-rimmed glasses not only hid his eyes but erased the natural symmetry of his blank features. He wore a stylish, dark suit with a waistcoat, a silver watch chain snaking from one pocket. He walked dragging a stiff right leg, aided by a cane. Though she'd never met him, she knew who he was.

Sir Thomas Mathews.

Head of the Secret Intelligence Service.

Only 16 men had ever led that agency, responsible for all foreign intelligence matters since the beginning of the 20th century. Americans liked to call it MI6, a tag attached during World War II.

She stood on the oak plank floor, not quite knowing what to say or do.

"I understand you are a member of the Middle Temple," he said to her, his voice low and throaty.

She nodded, catching the cockney accent in his vowels. "After I studied law at Oxford, I was granted membership. I ate many a meal in this hall."

"Then you decided enforcing the law would be more intriguing than interpreting it?"

"Something like that. I enjoy my job."

He pointed a thin finger at her. "I am familiar

with what you did a couple of years ago with the fish."

She recalled the batches of tropical fish, imported from Colombia and Costa Rica to be sold in British pet stores. Smugglers had dissolved cocaine in small plastic bags, which hung invisibly as they floated with the fish.

But she'd found the ruse.

"Quite clever on your part, discovering that scheme," he said. "How unfortunate that your career is now in jeopardy."

She said nothing.

"Frankly, I can sympathize with your superiors. Agents who refuse to show good judgment eventually get themselves, or someone else, killed."

"Forgive me, but I've been insulted enough for one evening."

"Are you always so forward?"

"As you mentioned, my job is probably gone. What would be gained by being coy?"

"Perhaps my support in saving your career."

That was unexpected. So she asked, "Then, could you tell me what you want?"

Mathews motioned with his walking stick. "When was the last time you were here, in Middle Hall."

She thought back. It had been almost a year. A garden party for a friend who'd attainted the rank of bencher, one of the select few who governed the Middle Temple.

"Not in a long time," she said.

"I always enjoy coming here," Mathews said. "This building has seen so much of our history. Imagine. These walls, that ceiling, all stood during the time of Elizabeth I. She, herself, came to this spot. Shakespeare's **Twelfth Night** was first performed right here. That impresses me. Does it you?"

"Depends on whether it will allow me to keep my job."

Mathews smiled. "Something extraordinary is happening, Miss Richards."

She maintained a stiff face.

"May I tell you a story?"

PRINCE HENRY ENTERED THE PRIVY CHAMBER AT Richmond Palace. He'd been summoned from Westminster by his father, King Henry VII, and told to come at once. Not an unusual request, considering the odd relationship they'd forged over the past seven years, ever since his brother, Arthur, died and he became heir to the throne. There'd been many summonses, most to either instill or extract a lesson. His father was desperate to know that his kingdom would be safe in the hands of his second son.

The king lay upon a cloth of scarlet and gold, amid pillows, cushions, and bolsters. Tonsured clerics, physicians, and courtesans surrounded the canopy on three sides. The sight shocked him. He'd known of previous illnesses. First a throat

infection, then rheumatic fever, chronic fatigue, loss of appetite, and bouts of depression. But he'd not been informed of this latest affliction, one that appeared quite serious.

A confessor stood near the foot of the bed, administering last rites, anointing the bare feet with holy oil. A crucifix was brought close to his father's lips, which was kissed, then he heard the raspy voice that had so many times chastised him.

"With all his might and power, I call on the Lord for a merciful death."

He stared at the crafty and calculating man who'd ruled England for twenty-three years. Henry VII had not inherited his crown. Instead, he'd won it on the battlefield, defeating the despicable Richard III at Bosworth Field, ending the time of the Yorks and Lancasters, and creating a new dynasty.

The Tudors.

His father motioned for him to approach. "Death is an enemy who cannot be bought off or deceived. No money or treachery has any effect. For me, finally, death has presented itself."

He did not know what to say. Experience had taught him that silence worked best. He was the second son, the Duke of York, never intended to be king. That duty was for his older brother, Arthur, his romantic name an effort to further legitimize the Tudor claim to the English throne.

Every privilege had been extended to Arthur, including a marriage to the stately Katherine of Aragon, part of a treaty with Spain that solidified England's growing European position. But Arthur died five months into the marriage, barely sixteen years old, and much had changed in the ensuing seven years.

The Borgia pope Alexander was dead. Pius III lasted only twenty-six days in Peter's chair. Julius II, boasting that he owned the Sacred College of Cardinals, had been elected God's vicar. Such a man would listen to reason and, the day after Christmas 1503, at the request of Henry VII, the pope issued a bull of dispensation against the incest of Katherine of Aragon marrying her dead husband's brother.

So he and Katherine had been betrothed.

But no marriage occurred.

Instead, the dying king in the bed before him had used its possibility as bait with Spain and the Holy Roman Empire, dangling it to obtain more.

"We must speak," his father said. The throat rattled with each word, lungs gasping for breath. "Your mother, whom I will soon see, held you in great esteem."

And he'd adored Elizabeth of York. As he was the second son, his mother had actually raised him, teaching him to read and write and think. A beautiful, gentle woman, she died six years ago, not quite a year after her eldest, Arthur. He'd often wondered if any woman would ever measure up to her perfection.

"I loved your mother more than anyone on this earth," his father said. "Many may not believe that. But it is true."

Henry's ears always stayed with his feet—on the ground. He listened to the everyday talk and knew that his father—firm, frigid, hard, tight-hearted and tight-handed—was not popular. His father considered England his, as he alone had won it on the battlefield. The nation owed him. And he'd amassed massive revenues from his many estates, most confiscated from those who'd initially opposed him. He understood the value of extortion and the benefit of benevolences from those who could afford to pay for the privileges they enjoyed—thanks to him.

"We are Christians, my son, and we must have consciences even more tender than the Holy Father himself. Remember that."

More lessons? He was eighteen years old—tall, stocky, powerful of limb and chest, a man in every way—and tired of being taught. He was a scholar, a poet, a musician. He knew how to choose and use men of ability, and he surrounded himself with those of great intellect. He never shied from pleasure and never neglected his work or duties. He was unafraid of failure.

He once desired to be a priest.

Now he would be king.

He'd sensed the recent air of tension and repentance throughout the palace—death was always a time of royal contrition. There'd be a releasing of prisoners, alms distributed, masses paid for souls. The chancery office at Westminster would fill with people willing to pay for a final pardon. Forgiving times—in more ways than one.

"Blast you hard-hearted brat," his father suddenly said. "Do you hear me?"

He trembled at his rage, a familiar reflex, and returned his attention to the bed. "I hear you."

"All of you be gone," his father commanded.

And those around the bed fled the chamber.

Only father and son remained.

"There is a secret you must know," his father said. "Something about which I have never spoken to you."

A faraway look crossed his father's face.

"You shall inherit from me a kingdom rich in wealth and bounty. But I learned long ago never to place my trust entirely with others. You must do likewise. Let others believe you trust them, but trust only yourself. I have amassed a separate wealth, rightfully belonging only to Tudor blood."

Indeed?

"This I have secreted away, in a place long ago known to the Templars."

He'd not heard that order's name in some time. Once they'd been a presence in England, but they were gone now two hundred years. Their churches and compounds remained, scattered in all parts, and he'd visited several. Which one held the secret?

He had to know.

So he offered one last submission.

A final obedient glare.

"Your duty," his father said, "is to safeguard our wealth and pass it on to your son. I fought to bring this family to the throne and, by God, it is your duty to ensure that we remain there."

On that they agreed.

"You will like this place. It has served me well and so it shall serve you."

SHE STARED AT MATHEWS. "IS THAT TRUE?"

He nodded. "As far as we know. This account is contained within archives that are unavailable to the general public."

"It's five-hundred-year-old information."

"Which, amazingly, still has explosive relevance today. Hence why we are here."

How was that possible? But she stayed silent.

"Sir Thomas Wriothesley wrote an account of what happened that day. April 20, 1509. Henry VII died the following day. Unfortunately, Wriothesley's account did not record what the father actually told the son. That was learned second hand, from Henry VIII himself, many decades later. What we do know is that Henry VIII passed on the information about this special place to his sixth wife, Katherine Parr, just before he died in 1547. We also know that the value of Henry VII's wealth, at the time of his death, was around four and a half million pounds. In today's money that would be incalculable, since most of it was in precious metals, the quantity and quality of which is uncertain. But into the billions of pounds would not be out of the question."

He then told her about what happened at Henry VIII's deathbed in January 1547. A conversation between husband and wife similar, in so many ways, to the one thirty-eight years before between father and son.

"Henry VIII was foolish when it came to women," Mathews said. "He misplaced his trust in Katherine Parr, who hated Henry. The last thing she would do is pass that information on to Edward VI." The older man paused. "Do you know much about Katherine Parr?"

She shook her head.

Mathews explained that she was born to one of Henry VIII's early courtesans, named after his first wife, Katherine of Aragon. Highly educated, she spoke French, Spanish, and Italian. Henry married her in 1543. When he died in 1547 she was but thirty-six. Shortly after she married a fourth time, to Thomas Seymour, and eventually became pregnant. She moved to Sudeley Castle in Gloucestershire and gave birth to a daughter in August 1548, but died six days later. Seymour himself lived until March 1549, when he was executed for treason. After that, Katherine Parr, Thomas Seymour, and their daughter, Mary, faded into oblivion.

"But that may no longer be the case," Mathews said.

Something serious is happening here. That's what her supervisor had said at Windsor. All of the talk about her SOCA career being over and being back in Middle Hall had stirred memories of sitting at the tables, with other barristers and students, and taking a meal, a duty required periodically from all Temple members. Once, centuries ago, they'd blow a horn on the hall steps half an hour before dinner. But the horn could not be heard by those hunting hares on the Thames far bank, so it was eventually retired to the vault.

She'd often imagined what it must have been like, hundreds of years ago, living here, reading law. Maybe she'd be back soon, as an ex-agent, to see for herself.

Time for a little pushback.

"Why am I here?"

Her supervisor had said, **They asked for you.**

"Blake Antrim."

A name she'd not heard in a long time. And to hear it here, in Middle Hall, only compounded her surprise.

"Apparently you are aware that Antrim and I were once close."

"We were hoping someone within one of our agencies would be familiar with him. A computer search revealed a rather glowing recommendation written by Antrim, as part of your application for SOCA employment."

"I have not seen or spoken to him in ten years."

And never wanted to again.

"Your father was a Middle Templar," Mathews said. "As were your grandfather and great-grandfather. Each a barrister. Your great-grandfather was a bencher. You were to follow them. But you left the law and became an inspector. Yet to this day you diligently retain your Temple membership, never shirking any obligation. Why is that?"

She'd been thoroughly checked out. Some of that was not in her SOCA personnel file. "Why I chose not to practice law is irrelevant."

"I do not agree. In fact, it might become an overriding truth that none of us can ignore."

She said nothing and he seemed to sense her hesitancy.

With his mahogany cane Mathews again gestured to the hall. For the first time she noticed the ivory globe that formed its handle, the continents etched in black upon its polished surface. "This building has stood 500 years, and remains one of the last Tudor structures. Supposedly, the War of the Roses started just outside, in the garden. Sides were chosen in 1430 by the pick of a flower. The Lancasterians plucked a red rose—the Yorks white—and fifty-five years of civil war began." He paused. "These Temple grounds have seen so much of our history—and they endure, becoming more relevant with each passing year."

He'd still not answered her original question.

"Why did you ask me to come here?"

"May I show you?"

Eleven

MALONE GATHERED UP HIS AND GARY'S CLOTHES, replacing everything in their travel bags. He noticed how Gary had packed light, like he'd taught him. His head still hurt from the pounding to the pavement, his field of vision fuzzy. Ian helped him, and made no attempt to leave. To be safe, though, Malone kept Ian between himself and the mews' rear wall.

He sat back down on the pavement and allowed his mind to clear. The rain outside had slackened to a mist. The air was chilly, which helped, but he was glad for his leather jacket.

"You okay?" Ian asked.

"Not really. My head took a banging."

He rubbed his scalp, careful of the sore knot. All he could think about was Gary, but he needed information and its main source was right here.

"I didn't mean to leave your son," Ian said. "I told Gary to jump."

"He's not you."

"He told me on the plane that you're not his real dad."

Hearing that jarred him. "I'm not his **birth** dad, but I am his real dad."

"He wants to know who that is."

"He told you that?"

Ian nodded.

Now was not the time to delve into this. "How much trouble are you in?"

"No bother. I'll be fine."

"I didn't ask you that. How much trouble?"

Ian said nothing.

He needed answers. Pieces were missing. And where before it had not mattered, now, with Gary gone, he had to know.

"How did you get from London to Georgia?"

"After I ran from the car with that flash drive, men started looking for me. Some came to visit Miss Mary, but she told them nothing."

"Who is that?"

"She owns a bookshop in Piccadilly. The men came there, and to other places I go, asking questions. I finally met a guy who offered me a trip to the States, so I took it."

Stephanie had told him that Ian had been detained by Customs in Miami, trying to enter the country on a false passport. His traveling companion, an Irish national wanted on several outstanding warrants, had also been arrested. No telling what plans that man ultimately had for Ian. **Free** trips were never free.

"You know that guy was bad."

Ian nodded. "I was planning on getting away from him as soon as we left the airport. I can handle myself."

But he questioned that observation. Obviously the boy had been scared enough to run. Stephanie told him that the CIA had been searching for Ian since mid-October. When caught in Miami—the name flagged—they'd immediately assumed custody, and he was flown to Atlanta.

All they needed was an escort back to England. Which he became.

"Why'd you run away from me in the Atlanta airport?"

"I didn't want to come back here."

"You have no family?"

"Don't need any."

"Did you ever go to school?" he asked.

"I'm not thick and wet. I can read. Wouldn't be any wiser if I went to school every day."

He'd apparently struck a nerve. "How many times have you been in jail?"

"A few, after a spot of trouble."

But he wondered how far the tough act went. He'd caught the flicker of fear back in Georgia when Ian first realized they were headed for London.

He'd also spotted the confusion in his own son's face.

Two weeks ago Gary's life was certain. He had a mother and father, a family, though scattered on two continents. Now he'd been told that he had a birth father, too. Gary wanted to know who that man was. Pam was wrong withholding the name. Surely it frightened Gary that he was no longer a Malone, at least not by blood. So wanting to know where he'd come from was natural.

"Gary said you were once a secret agent for the government. Like James Bond."

"Kind of. But for real. Did you ever know your father?"

Ian shook his head. "Never saw him."

"You ever wonder about him?"

"Don't care much one way or the other. He was never around. My mum, too. Never had any need for parents. Had the wit early on to know that I had to count on me."

But that can't be good. Kids needed moms and dads. Or at least that's what he'd always thought. "Is it hard living on the streets, with no home?"

"I got a home. I got friends."

"Like who?"

Ian gestured at the plastic bag. "The book lady. Miss Mary. She gave me those stories. She lets me stay in the store sometimes at night, when it's cold. That's when I read whatever I want."

"I like reading, too. I own a bookshop."

"Gary told me."

"You two seemed to have had quite a chat."

"It was a long flight and neither of us slept much."

But he wasn't surprised they'd talked. Who else would Gary have to talk to? Not his mother. She'd offered little to nothing. Or his father, who hadn't learned the truth till recently, either.

"What did you tell Gary about his birth father?"

"To not be a wee 'un. All's fine until we come a cropper."

He scrunched up his face in puzzlement.

"Wee 'un. Children. That's me and him. And we get into trouble. Come a cropper. All's good until that happens. Then we get told what to do."

Silence passed between them for a few moments.

"I told him to do something about it," Ian said. "Get you to help."

He assumed that was the boy's best attempt at a compliment.

"Why didn't you want to come back here?"

No reply.

Thoughts of Norse and Devene filled his clouded brain. "Is something bad going to happen to you here?"

Ian just glanced out to the night.

Which was the answer he feared.

Twelve

ANTRIM OPENED HIS EYES.

He lay on the stone floor within the Round, beside the Templar effigies. His muscles ached and he knew what had happened. Two projectiles had pierced his chest and 50,000 volts had sent him into unconsciousness. He'd been stunned by a Taser. Better than being shot, but still an experience.

The Daedalus Society.

What the hell was that?

He'd love to dismiss them as crackpots, but those old men killed Farrow Curry and his man in St. Paul's and knew nearly everything he'd been doing. Clearly, they were a force that had to be dealt with. Just as clearly, he was on to something. His men had methodically acquired historical artifacts and manuscripts from repositories all around England. They'd managed to photograph relevant texts in the British Library. They'd even breached the tomb of Henry VIII. No hint of anyone being aware of their efforts had ever surfaced. Yet this Daedalus Society knew he would be in St. Paul's Cathedral tonight. He wondered, did they know the most important thing? No mention had been made of Ian Dunne, a flash drive, and what may be on that.

And that gave him hope.

The past three years had been a string of stinging setbacks, the most notable in Poland where his failure had generated consequences. One thing Langley detested was **consequences,** especially from its special counter-operations unit. His job was to turn things around, not make them worse. Washington was looking for a way to stop Scotland from handing back a convicted mass murderer to Libya. Great Britain was America's ally. So his instructions from the beginning were clear.

Do it. But don't. Get. Caught.

He rubbed his sore chest and massaged his eyes with the flat of his palms.

What happened in St. Paul's, and what happened here, certainly qualified as being caught.

Maybe he should end this?

Five million pounds.

He slowly came to his feet, his damp coat rustling in the silence. The Round and the choir remained empty, the same few lights burning. His mind seemed incapable, as yet, of forming coherent thoughts, but he realized whoever **they** were had connections with the Middle or Inner Temples. How else could so much privacy have been assured?

He rubbed his scalp, sore from the fall. Once he'd sported a thick patch of auburn hair. Now the crown was nearly bare, only the sides shaded with a gray-brown fringe. His father had gone bald in his forties, too. He'd inherited almost everything else from him, why not that?

He found his phone and checked for messages.

None.

What was happening with Cotton Malone and Ian Dunne?

He needed to know.

Something on the floor between the effigies caught his eye.

A business card.

He bent down and retrieved it.

One of his, from Belgium, part of his State Department cover that noted his office phone and address at the embassy, along with his title, DEPUTY INFORMATION LIAISON OFFICER.

On the back was writing, in blue ink, printed neatly.

THE PENETENTIAL CELL

He knew what that was. Here. A tiny room at the top of the stairs where Knights Templars who disobeyed the Order's Rule would be confined for punishment. He'd been inside once as a kid.

His head turned toward the choir.

What was there?

He stepped through the dim interior and found

the staircase. Hinges and the catch of a long-missing door still remained. He climbed to the cell. Two small apertures admitted light, one facing the altar, the other opening into the Round. The space was no more than four feet long and two feet wide, impossible to lie down in with any degree of comfort, which, he thought, had been the whole idea.

His man who'd used the alias Gaius Wells, shot dead in St. Paul's, lay propped against the wall, the body contorted into the tiny space, his head unnaturally cocked to one shoulder.

They'd brought him here?

Of course.

To show him what they could do.

Against the corpse's chest, both arms wrapped around it, was a book.

Mythology of the Ancient World.

He slipped the volume from the dead man's grasp. Another of his business cards marked a place about halfway into the text. He should check Wells' pockets and make sure there was no identification, but he realized this body would never be found.

With the book in hand he descended the stairs and stepped close to one of the choir's incandescent fixtures. He opened to the marked page and saw a passage circled.

Ovid tells the tale, in his **Metamorphoses** (VIII: 183–235), of how Daedalus and his young son, Icarus, were imprisoned in a tower on Crete. Escape from land or sea was impossible, as the king controlled both. So Daedalus made wings for both himself and his son. He tied feathers together and secured them with wax, curving them like a bird's. When finished, he taught Icarus how to use the wings, but he provided two warnings: Do not fly too high or the sun will melt the wax, or too low as the sea will soak the feathers. Using the wings, they made their escape, passing Samos, Delos, and Lebynthos. Icarus was so excited he forgot his father's warnings and soared toward the sun. The wax melted and the wings collapsed, sending Icarus into the sea, where he drowned.

At the bottom of the page, beneath the circled text, was more blue lettering.

HEED THE WARNING OF DAEDALUS
AND AVOID THE SON

He immediately noticed the difference in spelling. **Son,** as opposed to **sun.**

These men were indeed knowledgeable.

Beneath was another line of scrawl.

CALL WHEN READY TO DEAL

And an English phone number.

Sure of themselves. Not call **if** you want to deal—**when.**

He sucked a few deep breaths and steeled himself. He was close to panic, but fear and urgency provided his flagging muscles strength.

Maybe they were right.

This was gestating out of control, more so than he was accustomed to handling.

He tore the page from the book and stuffed it into his pocket.

Thirteen

Kathleen followed Mathews from the hall, out into the rain. They crossed Middle Temple Lane, turned left, and entered one of the many office buildings, this one with windows opening to the Pump Court. The little courtyard was named after its mechanisms, once used to fight fires. The reservoir was located deep beneath the flagstones, fed by one of London's underground rivers. The ancient well remained but the pumps were long gone. On the court's north side she saw the dark outline of a sundial, legendary thanks to its caption. **Shadows we are and like shadows we depart.**

All of the office doors inside the building were closed, the hallway quiet. Mathews led the way up the stairs to the fourth floor, his cane click-clacking off the wooden steps. The Inns of Court acquired their name because members once studied and lived on the grounds. Once, they were independent, self-governing legal colleges, a graduate called to the bar, becoming a barrister, able to appear in court as a client's advocate.

But always under the discipline of the Inn.

The custom then was for clients to consult with their barristers not in chambers but under the porch of the Temple Church or at Westminster Hall, where the courts sat until the end of the 19th century. All of those time-honored practices were now gone, the many buildings within both the Middle and Inner Temple grounds converted to working offices. Only the upper floors remained residences, used collectively by the two Inns.

She climbed with Mathews to the top, where he opened the door to one of the apartments. No lights burned inside. A Regency sofa, chairs, and a glass-fronted curio cabinet loomed in the dark. Bare hooks were evident on the walls, where pictures should have hung. The smell of fresh paint was strong.

"They are remodeling," he said.

Mathews closed the door and led her to a window on the far side. Below stood the Temple Church, smothered by the surrounding buildings, fronted by a wet courtyard.

"Much history has occurred down there, too," Mathews said. "That church has existed, in one form or another, for nearly 1,000 years."

She knew that a condition of James I's royal land

grant to the barristers was that the Temple Church must be perpetually maintained as a place of worship. The church itself had garnered an air of mystery and romance, giving rise to improbable legends, but she knew it only as the Inns' private chapel.

"We Brits have always prided ourselves on the rule of law," Mathews said. "The Inns were where legal practitioners learned the craft. What has this place been called? **The noblest nursery of liberty and humanity in the kingdom.** Aptly put."

She agreed.

"Magna Carta was the start of our faith in the law," Mathews noted. "What a momentous act, if you think about it. Barons demanding, and obtaining, from their sovereign thirty-seven concessions on royal power."

"Most of which were never applied and eventually repealed," she had to say.

"Quite right. Only three still remain in effect. But one overriding principle came from Magna Carta. No free man could be punished except through the law of the land. That singular concept changed the course of this nation."

Below, in the courtyard, the rain quickened to a drizzle.

The side door leading into the church opened and a figure emerged. A man, buttoning his coat and moving away toward King's Bench Walk and the gate that led out of the Temple grounds.

"That is Blake Antrim," Mathews said. "He's

the lead agent on a CIA operation known as King's Deception that is presently ongoing within our country."

She watched as Antrim vanished beyond the pale of the wrought-iron lights.

"How close were you and he?" Mathews asked.

"We were only together a year. It was when I studied law at Oxford, then applied for membership here at Middle Temple."

"And Antrim changed your career path?"

She shrugged. "Not directly. I was drifting toward law enforcement while we were together. I had already applied to SOCA when we separated."

"You don't impress me as a woman who would allow a man to affect her so profoundly. Everything I have read or been told about you says you are tough, smart, independent."

"He was . . . difficult," she said.

"Precisely what your supervisors say about you."

"I try not to be."

"I notice that you have little to no accent, and your diction and syntax are barely British."

"My father, a Brit, died when I was eight. My mother was American. She never remarried and, though we lived here, she remained American."

"Do you know an American named Cotton Malone?"

She shook her head.

"He's a former intelligence agent. Highly regarded. Competent. Quite different from Antrim.

Apparently, Antrim knows him, and made it possible for Malone to be here, in London. There is a young man, Ian Dunne, whom Malone returned here a few hours ago. Antrim has been searching for this boy."

She had to say, "You do know that Blake and I did not part on the best of terms?"

"Yet he provided a glowing recommendation for your SOCA application."

"That was before we split," she said, offering nothing more.

"I chose you, Miss Richards, because of your past relationship with Antrim. If that was hostile, or nonexistent, then you are of no use to me. And as you painfully know, your usefulness to SOCA has already waned."

"And you can fix that?"

He nodded. "If you can assist me with my problem."

"I can re-ingratiate myself with Blake," she said.

"That is what I wanted to hear. He must suspect nothing. At no point can you reveal any involvement with us."

She nodded.

In the spill of light that leaked in from the window she studied England's top spymaster. A Cold War legend. She'd heard stories, the exploits, and had often dreamed of being a part of the SIS. But to see and speak to Blake Antrim again? What a price to pay for admission.

"I am of the Inner Temple," Mathews said. "A member fifty years. I read the law just over there." He pointed out the window, beyond the Temple Church dome.

"And you opted for law enforcement, too."

"That I did. See, you and I have something in common."

"You still have not told me what this is about."

Mathews stepped toward a tiered desk. He slid out a chair and beckoned for her to sit. She complied and, for the first time, noticed the dark outline of a laptop before her.

He opened the machine and pressed one of the keyboard's buttons. The screen sprang to life and bathed her in a harsh light. She squinted and gave her eyes time to adjust.

"Read this, then do as instructed."

Mathews headed for the door.

"How will I find Antrim?" she asked.

"Not to worry, you will have additional information when needed."

"How will you find me?"

He stopped, turned, and shook his head. "Don't ask silly questions, Miss Richards."

And he left.

Fourteen

Malone led Ian away from the mews, back to Little Venice where there were plenty of taxis. No return call had come as yet from Devene. The fact that Gary was in jeopardy tore at his heart. How had he allowed this to happen? It ran counter to everything he'd tried to do when he retired from the Justice Department.

"I'm quitting my job," he said to Gary.

"I thought you loved what you did."

He shook his head. "The risks have become too great."

It happened in Mexico City. He was there helping prosecute three defendants who'd murdered a DEA agent. During a lunch break he'd been caught in the crossfire of an assassination attempt in a public park that turned into a bloodbath. Seven dead, nine injured. He'd finally brought down the shooters, but not before taking a round in his left shoulder. He'd spent a month recovering, and making some decisions about his life.

"You're thirteen," he said to Gary. "This is going to be tough for you to understand, but sometimes life has to change."

He'd already tendered his resignation to Stephanie Nelle, ending his twelve-year career with the Magellan Billet and an even longer stint with the navy. He'd made it to full commander and would have liked to have been a captain, but no more.

"So you're leaving," Gary asked. "Moving to another country."

"I'm not leaving you."

But he was.

By the time he quit, he and Pam had lived apart five years. He'd come home from an assignment one day to find her gone. She'd rented a house on the other side of town, taking with her only what she and Gary needed. A note informed him of their new address and that the marriage was over. Pragmatic and cold. That was her way. Decisive, too. But neither one of them had sought an immediate divorce, though they only spoke when necessary for Gary's sake.

A lot of life had passed between them while together. He'd changed from a navy recruit, to a lawyer, to an agent for the Justice Department. She'd become a lawyer herself. He spent his time traveling the world. She prowled the halls of Atlanta's courthouses. They saw each other every week or so, dividing their time with Gary, who was growing up faster than either of them realized. They'd lived in a neighborhood with friends neither of them really knew. But **living** was the wrong term. More like existing. Taking that bullet in Mexico City had finally made him ask—was this the life he wanted? Neither he nor Pam was happy. That much they both knew. And the leap from unhappiness to anger was one Pam had easily made.

"Will you ever be satisfied?" she asked him. "The navy, then flight school, law school, JAG, the Billet. Now this sudden retirement. What's next?"

"I'm moving to Denmark."

Her face registered nothing. He might as well have said he was moving to the moon. "What is it you're after?"

"I'm tired of being shot at."

"Since when? You love the Billet."

"Time to grow up."

"So you think moving to Denmark will accomplish that miracle?"

He had no intention of explaining himself. She didn't care. Nor did he want her to. "It's Gary I need to talk to. I want to know if he's okay with that."

"Since when have you cared what he thought?"

"He's why I got out. I wanted him to have a father around—"

"That's bullshit, Cotton. You got out for

yourself. Don't use that boy as an excuse. Whatever it is you're planning, it's for you, not him."

"I don't need you telling me what I think."

"Then who does tell you? We were married a long time. You think it was easy waiting for you to come back from who-knows-where? Wondering if it was going to be in a body bag? I paid the price, Cotton. Gary did, too. But that boy loves you. No, he worships you, unconditionally. You and I both know what he'll say, since his head is screwed on better than either of ours. For all our failures together, he was a success."

She was right.

"Look, Cotton. Why you're moving across the ocean is your business. But if it makes you happy, then do it. Just don't use Gary as an excuse. The last thing he needs is a discontented parent around trying to make up for his own sad childhood."

"You enjoy insulting me?"

"The truth has to be said, and you know it."

The truth? Hardly. She'd omitted the most important part.

Gary is not your biological son.

Typical Pam. One set of rules for her, another for everyone else.

Now they **both** had a bad problem.

Ian walked beside him on the sidewalk. The boy had said nothing. Interesting how instinct bred survival, even in adolescence. He'd become angry at Ian in the mews, but he also saw that Ian seemed to tacitly agree that he'd messed up with Gary. He told himself to not allow that to happen again. This boy needed compassion, not hostility.

What did Gary need?

To know his biological father?

What good could possibly come from that, after fifteen years of ignorance. Unfortunately, Pam had not concerned herself with any of that. What had she been thinking?

The answer was obvious.

She hadn't thought.

Only acted.

Women were not his strong point. He neither knew nor understood how to deal with them. So he avoided them. So much simpler that way.

But at times it could be lonely.

Gary was the one thing no one could take from him.

Or could they?

He suddenly realized why he'd been so apprehensive since learning the truth. No longer was he irrevocably a parent. Being part of birthing a child stamped you forever. Short of a court divesting you of all rights, no matter how many mistakes were made—and he'd made a ton—you never stopped being a father.

But now that could be stripped away.

At least in part.

Gary could meet his biological father. The man

could be a great guy. Shocked to discover he had a son. They would bond. Gary's love would be divided. Where now all of the boy's emotions belonged to him, he'd have to share them.

Or maybe lose them entirely?

And that possibility crushed him.

Fifteen

KATHLEEN SCANNED THE INFORMATION ON THE laptop. The stories Sir Thomas had told her about what had happened at the deathbeds of Henry VII and Henry VIII were intriguing, but the information on the screen added more.

Henry VII, the first Tudor king, amassed a fortune in revenues which were eventually passed on to his son, Henry VIII. Over the final five years of Henry VIII's thirty-eight-year reign, the bulk of Tudor wealth was held inside iron chests at Westminster and in various secret chambers located in his palaces. Henry learned about acquiring revenues from his father and massive sums were accumulated from royal fines, taxes, purchases of Crown offices, and payments from the French on a pension owed. Even more wealth

came from the dissolution of the monasteries. Over 850 existed in 1509 when Henry was crowned. By 1540 all but 50 were gone, their riches confiscated. By any reasonable estimate the hoard totaled in the tens of millions of pounds (billions today). But no complete record of Henry VIII's treasure trove exists. Inventories that have survived are spotty, at best. What is known is that little of that wealth made it to Henry's son, Edward VI, who succeeded him in January 1547.

Edward was 10 when his father died and Henry's will provided for a regency council that would govern by majority vote. By March 1547 Edward Seymour, brother of the late queen, Jane Seymour, and uncle to the king, secured the title of Protector until Edward reached majority. Seymour immediately assumed control of the five treasure rooms Henry left for Edward. Late in 1547 a commission, appointed by the regency council, searched and found what was left of Henry's hoard. A mere £11,435 in angels, sovereigns, and Spanish reals.

What happened to the rest is unknown.

The fate of the Seymours, though, is clear.

Henry VIII's feelings for Jane Seymour were stronger than for any of his other five wives. She bore him the legitimate son he so desperately sought, but she died unexpectedly a few days afterwards. The Seymour family, who enjoyed much favor when Henry VIII was alive, suffered nothing but defeat after the king's death. Edward Seymour was removed from power in 1549, eventually executed for treason in 1552. His younger brother, Thomas, faired little better. He married Katherine Parr, Henry VIII's last queen, in April 1547. He too was executed for treason, his death coming in 1549 shortly before his brother fell from power.

Edward VI died in 1553, never reaching majority.

We have long known that Henry VIII passed information to Katherine Parr about a secret place, where the bulk of his wealth awaited his son. That information, though, has been little more than an historical footnote. Unimportant. But recently American intelligence agents have become fixated on this obscurity. For the past year they have scoured the nation searching for its hidden location. Your supervisor should have advised you already about a series of thefts and you saw, firsthand, the violation of Henry VIII's tomb. The key to finding this secret locale rests with an obscure journal, written entirely in code. Below is a page from that journal.

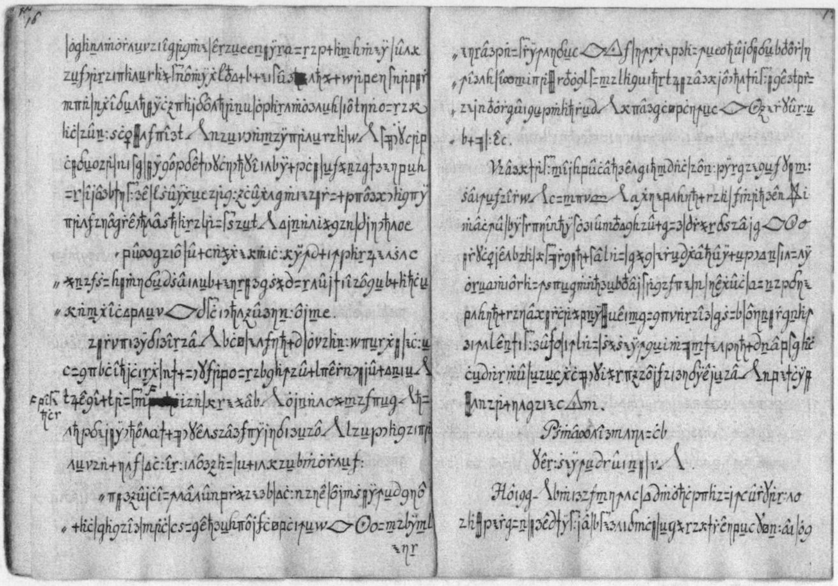

A man named Farrow Curry, employed by the Americans, may have cracked this code. Unfortunately, Curry died a few weeks ago in an Underground accident. The best information we have indicates that his research may have survived. It is this research that we require your assistance in securing. Blake Antrim is presently searching for it, too. In order for you to be fully prepared, a separate briefing has been arranged. Please proceed immediately to the hall at Jesus College, Oxford, where this information will be provided.

The narrative ended.

She sat in the dark and stared at the screen.

Thoughts of Blake Antrim filled her mind. They'd dated for a year, she a law student, he supposedly working for the State Department. Eventually, though, he'd told her the truth about himself.

"I work for the CIA," Antrim said.

She was surprised. She would have never thought that to be the case. "What do you do?"

"Senior field analyst, but I'll be a team leader soon. Counter-intelligence is my area."

"Should you be telling me this?"

He shrugged. "I doubt you're a spy."

She resented his conclusion. "You don't think me capable?"

"I don't think that interests you."

They'd met in a London pub, introduced by a mutual friend. The end came swiftly when he caught her with another man. By then she'd tired of his ways. Particularly his anger, which could erupt with little or no warning. He hated his job and his superiors, with little good to say about either. She came to view him as a sad, weak man, blessed with good looks but incapable of sincerity.

And that last day.

"You whore."

Antrim's eyes blazed with venom. She'd seen him mad, but not like this. He'd appeared at her flat early, unannounced. She'd had a visitor last night who'd only left a few minutes before. When the knock came she'd thought her new lover had returned for another kiss, but instead Antrim stood outside.

"It's over," she said. "We're done."

He burst inside and slammed the door.

"And this is how you do it?" he asked. "Another man? Here? Where you and I spent all that time?"

"I live here."

She just wanted him gone. The sight of him turned her stomach. She could not remember exactly when the attraction had turned to loathing. But when someone else showed her interest, one so opposite from the calculating soul she'd spent the last year with, the opportunity had been too inviting to resist.

She'd planned on phoning later today to tell him.

"It's over," she said again. "Now leave."

He sprang at her with a suddenness she'd not expected. A hand clamped onto her throat, her spine slammed down onto a tabletop, the robe open, exposing her naked body. The force of his attack lifted her feet from the ground and she was now pinned to the table, legs dangling.

She'd never been physically attacked before.

He brought his face close. Breathing was difficult for her. She thought about resisting, but everything she knew about this man signaled that he was a coward.

He'd only go so far.

She hoped.

"Rot in hell," he said.

Then he shoved her to the floor and left.

She'd not thought about that day in a long time. Her hip was sore for a week afterward. Antrim had tried to call, leaving messages of apology, but she'd ignored them. A month before that last encounter he'd written a glowing recommendation for her SOCA application. He'd volunteered to do it, revealing to her then his CIA employment and saying a good word from him couldn't hurt. She'd been debating whether to forgo the law and become a law enforcement agent, but their violent parting convinced her.

Never again was that going to happen to her.

So she learned to defend herself, carry a badge, fire a weapon.

She also developed a reckless streak, and often wondered if that happened because of Antrim or in spite of him.

Men like Blake Antrim lived by convincing themselves that everyone else was inferior to them. **Believing** yourself on top was far more important than actually being there. And when that fantasy became fouled by a conflicting reality the response was violence. There was something unhinged about him. Never would he go back. He couldn't. He not only burned bridges, he left them radioactive, forever impassable.

Forward was the only way for him.

Mathews may have been wrong about this.

Her approaching Antrim, after ten years, could be harder than anyone thought.

Part Two

Sixteen

8:30 PM

KATHLEEN ALWAYS LIKED RETURNING TO OXFORD. She'd spent four years studying there. So when the narrative on the laptop directed her to drive sixty miles northwest, she'd been pleased.

A town had existed since the 10th century, and the Normans were the first to erect a castle. A college was established in the 13th century. Now 39 distinctive institutions, each independent and fiercely competitive, filled the honey-colored Gothic buildings. They carried names like Corpus Christi, Hertford, Christ Church, Magdalen, and Trinity, together forming a federation, the oldest in England, known as Oxford University.

The Thames and Cherwell rivers merged here, and Kathleen had enjoyed many an afternoon punting down the placid waterways, becoming quite apt at maneuvering the flat-bottomed boats. King

Harold died here. Richard the Lionheart was born here. Henry V was educated and Elizabeth I entertained and fêted among the spires, towers, cloisters, and quadrangles. This was a place of history, theology, and academics, where great politicians, clerics, poets, philosophers, and scientists were trained. She'd read once that Hitler supposedly spared the town his bombs, as he planned to make it his English capital.

Oxford was exactly what Matthew Arnold called it.

The city of dreaming spires.

She'd thought about Blake Antrim on the drive. The prospect of seeing him again seemed revolting. He was not a man to let go of anything. His ego was far too fragile to seek forgiveness. How many women had there been since her? Had he married? Fathered children?

Mathews had provided no relevant information on this second briefing, telling her only to head straight to the hall at Jesus College, which sat in the heart of the city, among the shops and pubs. Founded by a Welshman, but endowed by Elizabeth I, it remained the only one of Oxford's colleges created during her reign. Small, maybe 600 students among undergraduates, graduates, and fellows. She'd always loved its unmistakable Elizabethan feel. She knew its great hall, which reminded her of the one at Middle Temple. Same rectangular shape, carved wooden screens, cartouches, and oil portraits, one of Elizabeth herself dominating the north wall above the high table. But no hammer-beam Tudor ceiling here, only plaster stretching overhead.

She'd wondered about campus access, considering it was a Friday night, but the gate at Turl and Ship streets was open, the hall lit, and a woman waited for her inside—short, petite, her graying blond hair drawn into a bun. She wore a conservative navy suit with low heels and introduced herself as Dr. Eva Pazan, providing a title, professor of history, Lincoln College, another of Oxford's long-standing institutions.

"I actually studied at Exeter," Pazan said, "and I understand you attended St. Anne's."

Both were part of Oxford's thirty-nine. St. Anne's had always been more open to students from a state-education background, like herself, as opposed to the private preparatory schools. Gaining admission had been one of the highlights of her life. Kathleen was curious, though, about Pazan's age, as she knew Exeter had been all-male until 1979.

"You must have been one of the first women in?"

"I was. We were changing history."

She wondered why she was here and Pazan seemed to sense her anxiety.

"Sir Thomas wanted me to pass on some details not provided to you in London. Information that is not written down for reasons that will become obvious. He thought I would be the best person to explain. My expertise is Tudor England. I teach that at Lincoln, but I occasionally provide historical context to our intelligence agencies."

"And did Sir Thomas choose this locale?"

"He did, and I concurred." Eva pointed across the hall. "The portrait there, of Elizabeth I. It was presented by the Canon of Canterbury, to the college, in 1686. It's illustrative of what we are going to speak about."

She glanced at the image of the queen in a floor-length dress. Geometric patterns from the puffed sleeves and kirtle complemented one another, the hem edged with pearls. Two cherubs held a wreath over Elizabeth's head.

"It was painted in 1590, when the queen was fifty-seven years old."

But the face was that of a much younger woman.

"That was about the time all unseemly portraits of Elizabeth were confiscated and burned. None was allowed to exist that, in any way, questioned her mortality. The man who painted this one, Nicholas Hilliard, ultimately devised a face pattern that all painters were required to follow when depicting the queen. A Mask of Youth, the Crown called it, which portrayed her as forever young."

"I never realized she was so conscious of her age."

"Elizabeth was quite an enigma. Her countenance was strongly marked, though always commanding and dignified. A hard swearer, coarse talker, clever, cunning, deceitful—she was truly her parents' daughter."

She smiled, recalling her history on Henry VIII and Anne Boleyn.

"What do you know of Elizabeth?" Eva asked.

"No more than what books and movies portray. She ruled for a long time. Never married. The last Tudor monarch."

Eva nodded. "She was a fascinating person. She chartered this college as the first Protestant institution at Oxford. And she was serious about that. Thirty local priests, all fellows of colleges, were executed during her reign for either practicing Catholicism or refusing to recognize her as head of the church."

She stared again at the portrait, which now seemed more a caricature than an honest representation of a woman dead over 400 years.

"Like her father," Eva said, "Elizabeth surrounded herself with competent, ambitious men. Unlike her father, though, she remained loyal to them all of her life. You received a preview of one earlier."

She did not understand.

"I was told you saw a page from the coded journal."

"But I wasn't told who created it."

"That journal was masterminded by Robert Cecil."

She knew the name Cecil, one of long standing in England.

"To understand Robert," Eva said, "you have to know his father, William."

She listened as Eva explained how William Cecil was born to a minor Welsh family that fought alongside Henry VII, the first Tudor king. He was raised at the court of Henry VIII and educated to government. Henry VIII's death in 1547 set in motion ten years of political turmoil. First the boy, Edward VI, reigned, then died at age 15. His half sister, Mary, daughter of Henry's first wife, then occupied the throne. But she gained the title **bloody** because of her propensity to burn Protestants. During Mary's five-year reign Cecil kept the young princess Elizabeth, daughter of Henry VIII's second wife, Anne Boleyn, at his home, where she was raised away from court. In 1558, when she finally became queen, Elizabeth immediately appointed William Cecil her principal secretary, later titled secretary of state, a position that made him chief adviser, closer to her than anyone else. Her reliance and trust in Cecil never failed. **No prince in Europe hath such a counselor as I have in mine.** Over forty years Cecil was the great architect of Elizabethan reign. **I have gained more by my temperance and forebearing than ever I did by my wit.** One observer at the time noted that he **had no close friends, no inward companion as great men commonly have, nor did any other know his secrets, some noting it for a fault, but most thinking it a praise and an instance of his wisdom. By trusting none with his secrets, none could reveal them.**

Cecil's first son, Thomas, was more suited to soldiering than government. William himself held the work of an army in low esteem. **A reign gaineth more by one year's peace than ten years' war.** William eventually became high treasurer, was knighted and made a baron, Lord Burghley. He served the queen until his death in 1598 when his second son, Robert, became Lord Burghley and assumed the post as Elizabeth's chief adviser.

"William Cecil was quite an administrator," Eva said. "One of the best in our history. Elizabeth owes much of her success to him. He founded the Cecil barony, which still exists today. Two prime ministers have come from that family."

"But aren't they all Cambridge graduates?" Kathleen asked, with a smile.

"We won't hold that against them.

"Robert Cecil was like his father," Eva said, "but more devious. He died young, age 48, in 1612. He served Elizabeth the last five years of her reign and James I for the first nine of his, both as secretary of state. He was also James' spymaster. He discovered the Gunpowder Plot and saved James I's life. The great Francis Walsingham was his teacher."

She knew that name, the man regarded as the father of British intelligence.

"Walsingham was an odd man," Eva said. "He constantly wore dark clothes and cast himself in secrecy. He was rude and could be quite crude, but the queen valued his advice and respected his competency, so she tolerated his eccentricities. It was Walsingham who uncovered the treasonous evidence that forced Elizabeth to execute her cousin, Mary, Queen of Scots. Walsingham who laid the groundwork for the defeat of the Spanish Armada. Eventually, Elizabeth knighted him. I tell you this because I want you to understand the personalities who trained Robert Cecil. Unfortunately, Robert, like his father, left few written records. So it is difficult to say exactly what Robert Cecil may or may not have known and what he truly accomplished. But there is one thing history confirms."

She was listening.

"He ensured that James I succeeded Elizabeth."

How all of this related to Blake Antrim escaped her, but obviously it did. Mathews had sent her here for a reason.

So she kept listening.

"Elizabeth never married and never birthed a child," Eva said. "She was the last of five Tudor monarchs, reigning forty-five years. Toward the end everyone was nervous. Who would succeed her? There were many contenders, and the prospect of civil war loomed great. Robert Cecil made sure it would be James, the son of Elizabeth's dead cousin Mary, Queen of Scots, now the Scottish king. There is a series of letters between Robert and James that have survived, which detail how that was accomplished. This happened between 1601 and Elizabeth's death in 1603. The Union of Crowns, it's called. Scotland joined with England. The beginnings of Great Britain. When James assumed both thrones, this country began to change. Forever."

"Robert Cecil made that happen?"

"Indeed, but Elizabeth herself confirmed that."

ROBERT CECIL AND THE LORD ADMIRAL CAME CLOSE to the bed. Robert stood at the foot, the admiral and several other lords on either side.

"Your Majesty," the lord admiral said. "We must ask this of you. Who do you desire to succeed you?"

Elizabeth opened her eyes. Where yesterday they had seemed weak and near death, Robert now saw in them something of the fire this old woman had displayed before taking to her bed.

"I tell you my seat hath been the seat of kings. I will have no rascal to succeed me, and who should succeed me but a king?"

The words were barely a whisper, but all there heard them clearly. A few of the lords appeared puzzled by the cryptic response, but Cecil understood perfectly, so he asked, "A name, Your Majesty."

"Who but our cousin of Scotland?"

The effort seemed to tax what little strength she possessed.

"I pray you trouble me no more," she said.

The lords withdrew and discussed what they'd heard. Many were unsure, as Cecil thought would

be the case. So the next day they returned to Elizabeth's bedside with a larger, more representative group. Unfortunately, the queen's ability to speak had waned. She was fading fast.

Cecil bent close and said to her, "Majesty, these gentlemen require a further sign that your cousin, King James of Scotland, is your choice. I beg you to provide them that."

Elizabeth's eyes signaled that she understood and the men waited. Slowly, her arms rose from the sheets to her head. Her fingers joined in a circle, forming a crown, which she held there for a moment.

No one could now argue as to her intent.

A few hours later, Elizabeth, Queen of England, France, and Ireland, Defender of the Faith, died.

"Cecil was ready," Eva said. "He assembled the council and informed them of her announced choice. The witnesses who were there confirmed the truth. Then, the next morning, from Whitehall Palace, heralded by trumpets, he personally read a proclamation declaring King James VI of Scotland, James I, King of England. That same proclamation was read all over the land throughout that day. Not a word of opposition was raised. In one clean move, Robert Cecil ensured a swift, bloodless succession from a monarch who left no direct heirs. Pretty skilled, wouldn't you say?"

"But you're going to have to explain what all this

means in relation to what Sir Thomas wants me to do."

"I know. And I plan to. The rain seems to have finally abated outside, let's enjoy the quad."

They stepped from the hall into one of the college's grassy quadrangles. Gothic buildings, most of their windows dark, enclosed them on all four sides. Darkened archways and doors led in and out. The rain was indeed gone, the night sky clear.

They were alone.

"Though both Cecils were secretive," Eva said, "and left nearly nothing in the way of personal papers, there is one artifact from them that survived. I am told that you saw an image of it earlier."

She recalled the page with gibberish.

"Robert's coded notebook was preserved at Hatfield House, where he lived until he died in 1612. Unfortunately, that original volume was stolen almost a year ago."

One of those thefts her supervisor had described. "I was told a man named Farrow Curry may have solved the code."

"He may have. Which is why it is imperative that you retrieve whatever data Curry may have accumulated."

"The page I saw was incomprehensible."

"Exactly how Cecil wanted it to be. That code has never been cracked. But we have clues as to how that might be accomplished. Would you like to see more images from the journal?"

She nodded.

"I have them inside. You wait here, and I'll retrieve them."

The professor turned and headed back toward the lit hall.

Kathleen heard a pop, like hands clapping.

Then another.

She turned.

A ragged hole exploded in the knit material at Eva's right shoulder. The older woman let out a strangled grunt.

Another pop.

Blood spewed.

Eva fell forward to the stone.

Kathleen whirled and spotted the outline of a shooter on the far roof, maybe thirty meters away.

Who was readjusting his rifle's aim.

At her.

Seventeen

ANTRIM APPROACHED THE TOWER OF LONDON. The ancient taupe-colored citadel nestled near the Thames, the picturesque Tower Bridge nearby. What was once an enormous moat encircling the fortress was now a sea of emerald grass, lit by a sodium vapor glow, that spanned a void between the imposing wall curtain and the street. A cool night breeze, which had blown away the storm, eased off the river.

He knew the area from his childhood, recalling the array of nearby textile sweatshops, clothing stores, and Bengali restaurants. The East End was once the city's dumping ground, a place where immigrants first settled. Tomorrow, Saturday, market day, meant the alleys would be filled with vendors hawking fresh fruit and secondhand clothes. He remembered as a kid roaming these streets, getting to know the peddlers, learning about life.

His target was strolling ahead of him at a brisk pace, but lingered a few moments before a music hall advertising a cabaret show.

Then the man crossed the street.

A multistory car park rose to the right, but the dark-haired gentleman kept strolling, the Union Jack, lit by floodlights, fluttering high above the Tower. The site was closed for the day, the admission booths dark and empty. Beyond, on the banks of the Thames, people milled back and forth, the illuminated Tower Bridge in the distance heavy with stop-and-go traffic. The dark-haired man ventured to the riverbank, then sat on one of the benches.

Antrim approached and sat beside him.

Winter's prelude clawed its way from the cold stone through the seat of his pants. Thank goodness he'd worn gloves and a lined coat.

"I hope this is important," the other man said to him. "I had plans tonight."

"One of my men was just killed."

The man kept his gaze out to the river.

He explained what had happened inside St. Paul's. The man, a senior deputy to America's ambassador to the United Kingdom, faced him. "Do the Brits know what we're doing?"

The meeting had been arranged by Langley, after he'd reported some but not all of what happened. He'd specifically omitted who'd killed his man in St. Paul's and what happened in the Temple Church.

"I don't know," he said. "But it's under control."

"Is it, Antrim? Really? Under control?"

They were in public, so decorum was required.

"Do you understand what's at stake here?" the man asked.

Sure he did, but thought it best to cast a smoke screen of goodwill. "Why don't you enlighten me?"

"The Scottish government is about to release al-Megrahi. That insanity is happening. Forty-three United Kingdom citizens died on that plane. Eleven Scots died on the ground. But everyone seems to have forgotten all that."

"The CIA lost a station chief on Pan Am 103. So did the Defense Intelligence Agency and the Diplomatic Security Service. Four agents flying home. I understand what's at stake."

"And we were told that you had a way to stop it. That, of course, was a year ago. Yet here we are, no closer to stopping anything. That prisoner release will show just how weak we are in the world right now. Can you imagine how this is going to play? Kaddafi will laugh in our faces. He'll parade al-Megrahi before every news camera he can find. The message will be crystal clear. We can't even get one of our allies to hold on to a mass murderer—a man who killed some of their own people. I need to know. Can you stop this?"

He was awaiting word that everything had gone right in that mews with Cotton Malone and Ian Dunne, but was a bit disturbed that he hadn't received any further reports.

"The way to stop this," he said, "is to force the

British to intervene. The Scots normally can't take a crap without London's consent. They have little to no home rule. So we both know the Scottish government is acting with the Brits' tacit consent. One word from London and that deal with the Libyans would be off."

"Like I don't know that."

"I'm working on leverage that could force the British to act."

"Which we have not been briefed on."

"And you won't, until we have it. But we're close. Real close."

"Unfortunately, your time is about up. We're told this transfer is going to happen within the next few days."

News to him. Langley had omitted that tidbit, most likely since, per the flash alert earlier, King's Deception was about to be scrapped. The death of an agent just made that decision more imperative. He wondered, were they setting him up to fail? He'd seen it done before. Nobody at the director level was going to take the blame for these mistakes when there was someone lower on the pole available.

You are a worthless little man.

Denise's words from Brussels, which still stung.

"The sorry son of a bitch Libyan," the diplomat said, "should have been hung or shot, but the stupid Scottish have no death penalty. Progressive, they call it. Stupid as hell, if you ask me."

For some reason, on this issue, the British were

willing to snub their closest ally in the world. If not for the CIA learning of the private talks no one would have known until the deal had been done. Luckily, negotiations had dragged on through back channels. But apparently, that time was coming to an end.

"You're it," the man said. "We have no way to force London to do anything. We've tried asking, offering, reciprocating, even pleading. Downing Street says it's not getting involved. Your operation is all we have left. Can. You. Make. It. Happen?"

He'd worked for the Central Intelligence Agency long enough to know that when a frustrated politician, in a position of power, asked if you could make something happen, there was but one correct response.

But he knew that would be a lie.

He was no closer to solving the problem than he had been a month ago, or a year ago. Ian Dunne's reemergence offered hope but, at this point, he had no way of knowing if that hope would be salvation.

So he said the only thing he could, "I don't know."

The diplomat turned his head back toward the river. The last of the day's scenic cruises motored by, headed west, from Greenwich.

"At least you're being honest," the man said, his voice low. "That's more than others can say."

"I want to know something," Antrim said. "Why are the British unwilling to intervene? It seems out of character. What do they have to gain by letting that murderer go?"

The diplomat stood.

"It's complicated and not your concern. Just do your job. Or at least what's left of it."

And the man walked off.

Eighteen

OXFORD

Kathleen dove behind a damp stone bench, just as the shooter aimed her way. Her body was coiled, poised for action. Each exhale of her breath clouded in the brisk night air.

She spotted the gunman, who was using the crenellated roofline high above for cover, the dark slate roof behind him absorbing his shadow. The rifle appeared sound-suppressed—she'd spotted a bulge at the end of its long barrel. She was unarmed. SOCA agents rarely carried guns. If firepower was needed, policy mandated that the local police be involved. The quadrangle was devoid of cover, save for the few concrete benches scattered along the crisscrossing walkways. Six ornamental lights burned with an amber glow. She stole a look at Eva Pazan, who lay facedown, motionless on the steps leading up to the archway.

"Professor Pazan," she called out.

Nothing.

"Professor."

She saw the shooter disappear from his perch.

She used the moment and darted left into a covered porch, the mahogany door that led into the building decorated with a shiny brass knob and knocker.

She tried the latch. Locked.

She banged on the knocker and hoped somebody was inside.

No reply.

She was now flush against the building, below the shooter, out of his firing angle, protected by a stone awning above her. But with the door locked and no one responding to her pleas, she remained trapped. Another doorway opened ten meters away, this one more elaborate and pedimented with palms and cherubs in the tympanum. Lights from inside illuminated tracery windows in a dim glow. Greenery formed a narrow bed between a concrete walk and the exterior façade. A bower of wisteria hugged the stone wall and rose toward the roof. If she hurried and stayed close she could make it. The shooter above would have to lean straight down in order to acquire a shot. With a rifle that would take time.

Maybe just enough.

She kept her back to the locked door and stared out into the quadrangle. Training came to mind, where she'd been taught to flatten against a wall to offer the slimmest target.

Her mind raced.

Who was trying to kill her and the professor?

Who knew she'd be here?

She sucked in a breath and steeled herself. She'd certainly been in tight situations before, but always with backup nearby. Nothing like this.

But she could handle it.

A quick peek beyond the covered doorway and she saw nothing.

One.

Two.

With a burst of adrenaline, she rushed out and ran the ten meters toward the other entrance, quickly finding cover beneath its stone pediment.

No shots came her way.

Was the shooter gone?

Or was he coming down to ground level?

An arched oak door stood closed, but its latch opened. Inside was the college chapel, the nave long and narrow, lined on either side with carved benches beneath tracery windows.

Like St. George's Chapel, only smaller.

Elaborate patterns of marble made up the floor and a muted stained-glass window loomed over the altar at the far end. Three fixtures threw off an orangey glow. Though she was inside, away from the shooter, a quick look around confirmed that the door she'd just entered was the only way in or out. Above her rose an organ nestled against the building's rear wall, its pipes reaching toward a vaulted ceiling. A narrow set of stairs led up to where the instrument was played.

From behind the organ, three meters above her, a man appeared.

His face was hooded, and he wore a dark jacket.

He aimed a weapon and fired.

IAN RODE IN THE CAB WITH COTTON MALONE, holding the plastic bag with its varied contents. Malone had returned it to him.

He unzipped the top and lifted out the books.

Ivanhoe and **Le Morte d'Arthur.**

Malone pointed to the title pages. "My books are owner-stamped like that, too."

"Where'd you get that name? Cotton?"

"It's shorter than my full name, Harold Earl Malone."

"But why Cotton?"

"It's a long story."

"You don't like answering questions, either, do you?"

"I prefer when **you** do that." Malone pointed. "Good taste in books. **Ivanhoe** is one of my favorites, and King Arthur is hard to beat."

"I like Camelot, the Knights of the Round Table, the Holy Grail. Miss Mary gave me a couple of other stories on Merlin and Guinevere."

"I like books, too."

"Never said I liked books."

"You don't have to. The way you hold them gives it away."

He hadn't realized there was a way to hold a book.

"You cradle it in your palm. Even though those books have seen a lot of use, they're still precious to you."

"They're just books." But his denial sounded hollow.

"I've always considered them ideas, forever recorded." Malone motioned to one of the paperbacks. "Malory wrote King Arthur in the late part of the 15th century. So you're reading his thoughts from five hundred years ago. We'll never know Malory, but we know his imagination."

"You don't think Arthur existed?"

"What do you think? Was he real or just a character Malory created?"

"He was real." The force of his declaration bothered him. He was showing too much of himself to this stranger.

Malone flashed a smile. "Spoken like a true Englishman. I would have expected no less from you."

"I'm Scottish, not British."

"Really now? As I recall, Scots and English have been British since the 17th century."

"Maybe so. But those sassanacks' noses are too far up their arses for me."

Malone let out a chuckle. "I haven't heard an

Englishman called a sassanack in a while. Spoken like a true jock."

"How did you know we Scots are jocks?"

"I read, too."

He'd come to realize that Cotton Malone paid attention, unlike most people he encountered. And he did not seem like a man given to having his knickers in a twist. In that mews, when faced with those fake police and a gun, he'd handled himself as a man in charge, strong and confident, like one of the horses at the track bolting from the gate. His wavy hair, cut neat and trim, carried the burnished tint of old stone. He was tall and muscular, but not overly so. His face was handsome, the features suited to him. He didn't smile a lot, but there really wasn't all that much to be happy about. Gary had said his father was a barrister, like the ones Ian had sometimes watched in London courts, parading about in wigs and robes. Yet Malone did not seem cursed with any of that pompousness.

He actually appeared like someone Ian could trust.

And he'd trusted precious few people in his life.

KATHLEEN HAD NO TIME TO REACT. THE MAN pulled the trigger and something propelled toward her. It took an instant for her to realize that the weapon was not a gun, but a Taser.

Electrodes pierced her shoulder.

Electricity stiffened her body, then buckled her legs, dropping her to the floor.

The voltage stopped.

Her head hummed with a high-pitched violence. Every muscle cramped for a few excruciating seconds. Then came the shakes. Uncontrollable.

She'd never felt anything like that.

She lay on the checkerboard marble and tried to regain control. Her eyes were closed and she suddenly felt pressure on her right cheek, her head clamped to the floor. Someone had the sole of their shoe on her face.

"I'm sure you now realize that you were led here."

That she did.

"Next time, Miss Richards," the voice said. "It will be bullets."

Anger surged through her, but there was little she could do. Her muscles were still convulsing.

The foot came off her cheek.

"Lie still," he said, "and listen." The man was behind her and close. "Don't turn your head, unless you want more electricity."

She lay silent, wishing her muscles would respond to her brain.

"We told Antrim. Now we're telling you. Leave this be."

She tried to assess the cool, clipped voice. Young. Male. Not unlike Mathews' tone, but less formal.

"We are the protectors of secrets," the man said.

What in the world was he talking about?

"Pazan is dead," the man said. "She knew too much. At the moment you know little. A word of advice. Keep it that way. Knowing too much will prove fatal."

Her body was relaxing, the pain gone, her wits returning, but she kept her head to the floor, the man still behind her.

"Domine, salvam fac Regnam."

She'd studied Latin in school and understood what he'd said.

O Lord, keep the queen safe.

"That is our duty," he said. **"Et exaudi nos in die qua invocaerimes te."**

And hear us in the day in which we call on thee.

"Our reward for that duty. We live by those words. Don't you forget them. This is your first and final warning. Leave this be."

She had to get a look at him. But she wondered—was he the one who fired the Taser? Or was there someone else here, too?

A gloved hand came across her body and the electrodes were removed.

She heard the chapel door open.

"Lie still, Miss Richards. Wait a few moments before rising."

The door closed.

She immediately tried to stand. Her skin felt itchy all over. She was woozy, but she forced her legs to work and stood, staggering a moment, then regaining her balance. She stepped to the chapel door and turned the latch. Easing it open, she spied out into the lit quadrangle.

Empty.

She stepped out. The cool night air helped clear her head.

How had the man disappeared so fast?

She glanced right, to the doorway ten meters away, where she'd first sought cover. The closest exit.

She walked over and retried the latch.

Still locked.

Her eyes found the steps and the archway that led back into the dining hall.

Eva Pazan's body was gone.

Nineteen

ANTRIM SAT ON THE BENCH AND STARED AT THE dark Thames. The arrogant bastard from the State Department was gone. He was a twenty-year veteran and resented being ordered around like the hired help. But he had a dead operative on his hands and Langley had made clear that there'd be repercussions.

Now this time crunch.

A few days.

Which nobody mentioned.

Was he being set up? That seemed the way of this business. You were only as good as your last act. And his last few had not been memorable. He was hoping King's Deception would be his salvation.

He'd stumbled across the idea in a 1970s CIA briefing memo. An obscure Irish political party had investigated a radical way to end the British presence in Northern Ireland. A legal, nonviolent method that utilized the rule of law. But no evidence to support their theory been found, though the memo detailed a host of clues that had been uncovered. Once he proposed the concept, moles within British intelligence, most likely the same eyes and ears who'd alerted Langley to the Libyan prisoner transfer, had provided information from long-buried MI6 files. Enough for Operation King's Deception to be approved and counter-intelligence assigned. But after a year's worth of work, nothing significant had been discovered.

Except the information that died with Farrow Curry.

And this Daedalus Society.

Both of which seemed to confirm that there was something to find.

His mind ached from months of worrying, scheming, and dreaming.

Five million pounds. That was what Daedalus had offered, just to walk away. Maybe he should take it? Things seemed destined for failure anyway. Why not leave with something for himself?

Especially after the text he'd just received.

Have one boy in custody, but Dunne escaped.

Idiots. How could they allow a fifteen-year-old kid to elude them? Their orders were simple. Take Malone, his son, and Dunne from Heathrow to a house near Little Venice. There, Malone should have been incapacitated and his son and Dunne transported to another locale. Apparently, everything had happened, except the most important part.

Corralling Ian Dunne.

Another text.

Mews video recording interesting. Watch.

The house in Little Venice was wired both for sound and pictures. So he accessed the feed and found the mews' hidden camera. A recorded image sprang onto his smart phone and he saw Cotton Malone, gathering clothes back into a travel bag.

And Ian Dunne.

Watching.

He brought the phone close to his eyes.

What a break.

Malone and Dunne left the mews together.

Yesterday, he'd formulated a plan. One he'd thought smart and workable. But a new idea streaked through his brain. A way to perhaps reap all five million of the rewards.

First, though, he had to know something, so he texted his men.

Did you enable the phone?

He'd told them to make sure the locator feature was working on Malone's cell and to learn the phone number.

The response came quick.

Done.

MALONE, WITH IAN, EXITED THE TAXI. LUCKILY, the driver agreed to accept U.S. dollars and he tipped an extra twenty for the favor.

Ian's special hiding place was located behind a set of Georgian buildings in a part of London known as Holborn. The block faced a park encircled by a narrow one-car lane, multistory brick buildings in varying colors on all sides. From the name plates he noted that most were occupied by lawyers—who, he knew, had long dominated this section of London. A rich confection of cloisters, courtyards, and passageways defined the place. What had Shakespeare allowed Richard III to say? **My lord of Ely, when I was last in Holborn I saw good strawberries in your garden.** The strawberry patches were gone and the old marketplace had become a diamond exchange. Only the lit park across the street seemed a remnant of the Middle Ages—meticulously landscaped and dotted with bare sycamore trees.

The time was approaching 9:00 PM, but the sidewalks remained busy. The sight of a boy being urged by his mother not to dawdle made him think of Pam. She'd always been a calculating woman, careful with her words, stingy with her emotions. He resented her for forcing this situation with Gary on him. Sure, she was tugged by a long-held guilt. But couldn't she see that there were skeletons behind those doors—none of which should have ever been opened? Six months ago, when she informed him about Gary's parentage, her explanation was that she wanted **to be fair.**

Since when?

She'd kept the secret this long. Why not forever? Neither he nor Gary would have ever known.

So what prompted her sudden need for truth?

Long ago, he'd been a foolish navy lieutenant and hurt her. They'd attended counseling, worked through it, and he'd thought his sincere request for forgiveness had been granted. Ten years later, when she walked out, he came to see that their marriage had never had a chance.

Trust broken is trust lost.

He'd read that somewhere and it was true.

But he wondered what it took to watch, day in and day out, while a father and son bonded, knowing that it was, at least partly, an illusion.

He felt for the cell phone in his pocket and wished it to ring. He hadn't told Ian the substance of the earlier conversation. Of course, he had no intention of handing the boy over.

But he needed that flash drive.

His and Gary's travel bags were slung over his shoulders and he followed Ian into a darkened alley that led to an enclosed courtyard, brick walls from the buildings encasing all sides. Lights from a handful of windows cast enough of a glow for him to notice a small stone structure on one side. He knew what it was. One of London's old wells. Many of the city's districts took their names from water sources that once supplied residents. Camberwell. Clerk's. St. Clement's. Sadler's. Then there were the holy wells. Sacred healing springs that dated back to Celtic times, most of which were long gone, but not forgotten.

He stepped over and peered down past the waist-high stone wall.

"There's nothing down there," Ian said. "It's sealed off a meter or so below with concrete."

"Where's your special place?"

"Over here."

Ian approached what appeared to be a grate in one of the brick walls. "It's a vent that leads into the basement. It's always been loose."

He watched as Ian hinged the panel upward and reached inside, feeling around at the top.

Another plastic shopping bag, from Selfridges, appeared in the boy's hand.

"There's a ledge above the grate. I found it one day."

He had to admire the boy's ingenuity.

"Let's go back to the street, where there's more light."

They left the courtyard and found a bench beneath one of the streetlights. He emptied the contents of the bag and inventoried the assortment of items. A couple of pocketknives, some jewelry, three watches, twenty pounds sterling, and a flash drive, 32G. Plenty of room for data.

"Is that it?" he asked.

Ian nodded. "It felt like a lighter or a pocket recorder when I first got my hand on it."

He scooped up the drive.

"What do we do now?" Ian asked.

Some insurance would be good.

"We find a computer and see what's on this thing."

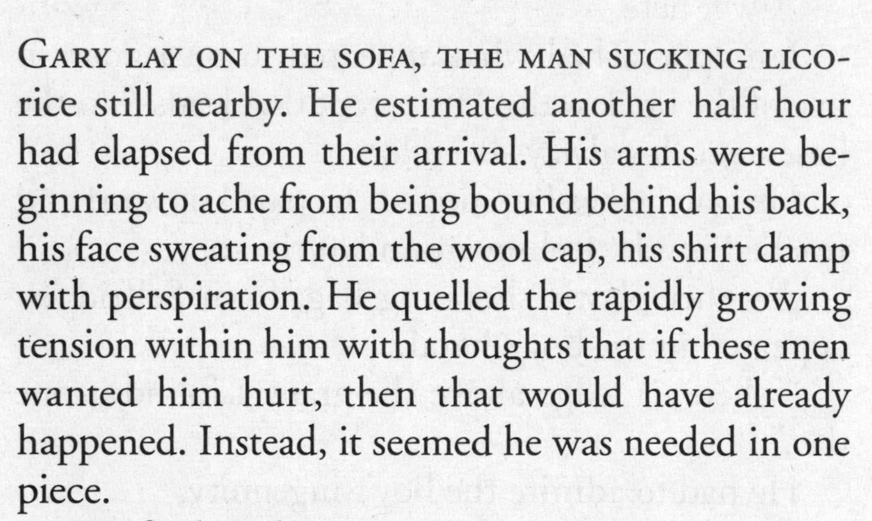

GARY LAY ON THE SOFA, THE MAN SUCKING LICOrice still nearby. He estimated another half hour had elapsed from their arrival. His arms were beginning to ache from being bound behind his back, his face sweating from the wool cap, his shirt damp with perspiration. He quelled the rapidly growing tension within him with thoughts that if these men wanted him hurt, then that would have already happened. Instead, it seemed he was needed in one piece.

But for how long?

He heard a pounding, then a crack.

Wood splintering.

"What the—" the man nearest him said.

"Drop it," a new voice screamed. "Now."

He heard something hard thud to a rug or carpet.

"On the floor. Hands where I can see them."

"We have the other one," a voice said from farther off.

Footsteps, then, "Down, beside your buddy."

No British accents anywhere. These guys were American.

The wool cap was ripped from his face and the bindings on his hands cut. He rubbed his wrists and blinked away the burning lamps that lit the room. When he finally focused he saw worn gold carpet, brown walls, and a pair of matching chairs on either side of the sofa. The exit door had been splintered from its hinges. His two captors, Devene and Norse, lay facedown on the floor. Three men stood in the room, all armed. Two kept weapons trained on his captors.

The third sat beside him on the sofa.

Relief swept over him.

"You okay?" the man asked.

He nodded.

The man was older, near his dad's age, but with less hair and a few more pounds at the waist. He wore a dark overcoat, buttondown collared shirt, and dark pants. Pale gray eyes stared at him with a look of concern.

"I'm okay," Gary said. "Thanks for finding me."

Something about him was familiar.

He'd seen this face before.

"We met in Atlanta."

The man smiled. "That's right. Your mom introduced us. Back in the summertime, when I was there on business."

He recalled the day, at the mall, near the food court. They'd stopped to buy some clothes. The man had called out, walked over, and chatted with his mother while he shopped. Everything had seemed cordial and pleasant. After they left, she'd said he was an old friend she hadn't seen in a long time.

And here he was.

He tried to remember a name.

The man offered his hand to shake.

"Blake Antrim."

Twenty

OXFORD

Kathleen's mind swirled. She'd faced drug traffickers who'd fired fourteen hundred rounds from Uzis and AK-47s at her. A hotel room on Tenerife shot up by a child sex offender who'd not wanted to return to England. Being submerged in a car that had catapulted off a bridge. But she'd never experienced anything like the past few minutes. A woman assassinated by a sniper. Her own body Tasered. And some man who was protecting royal secrets, threatening her life, disappearing into nowhere.

She stood alone in the dark quad.

Her phone buzzed in her coat pocket.

She found the unit and answered.

"Are you finished with Professor Pazan?"

Thomas Mathews.

"The professor is dead."

"Explain yourself."

She did.

"I am here, in Oxford. My plan was to speak to you after your talk. Come to Queen's College now."

She walked the few blocks, following the curve of elegant High Street. She knew it as The High. Many of Oxford's colleges fronted the busy thoroughfare that ran from the center of town to the River Cherwell. Though after 9:00 PM, frenetic activity raged around her. Cars and packed buses, each trailing plumes of exhaust, ferried people to and from town, the busy weekend unfolding. Her nerves were rattled, but she told herself to stay calm. After all, she could be sitting in her flat waiting to be fired.

The foot to her face had rubbed her the wrong way. Had that been the idea? To put her in her place? If so, it was a bad move. If she and that man crossed paths again, he'd pay for the insult.

Queen's College was one of the ancients, founded in the 14th century and named as a counterpart to the already established King's College in the hope that future queens would extend their patronage. The huddle of its original medieval houses was long gone, the fate of time and lack of funding. What remained was a baroque masterpiece, a touch out of place among so much Gothic splendor, centered by a dome-covered statue of Queen Caroline, the wife of George II. Many thought the college was named after her. In reality, it acquired its name from a much earlier benefactor—Philippa, wife of Edward III.

She entered the front quad through the domed gatehouse, the lit walkway ahead framed on either side by winter grass. An illuminated cloister lined with archways stretched left and right, the rusticated stone crusty and brittle, casting the appearance of a mountain monastery.

She spotted Mathews at the far end to her right and marched toward him. He still carried the look of a well-groomed diplomat with his pressed suit and walking stick. In the incandescent light she noticed something not caught earlier. A pale, sullen cast to his skin, along with fleshy jowls.

"I enjoy returning here," the older man said. "Queen's College is impressive, but I always thought Pembroke turned out the best-looking, most talented men."

A tight twist of his thin lips conveyed that he'd made a joke. About himself. Something told her that was a rare event.

"I should have known you were a Pembroke man."

"Forty-two years ago I took my degree. Not much has changed here since then. That's the lovely thing about this town. Always the same."

She wanted to know about Eva Pazan.

"A disturbing thing you reported," he said. "I failed to realize the scope and breadth of what is clearly afoot. The man who accosted you inside the chapel, we have dealt with his group before. They also confronted Blake Antrim earlier in the Temple Church."

"Which you obviously knew, since you brought me there."

"That is right. But we did not know they were aware of your involvement. The idea had been for you and me to observe Antrim, unnoticed. That means I have a security problem."

"What is this group?"

"In years past they have not presented any major problems. The last time they became so brazen was before the Second World War, when Edward VIII abdicated."

Every British citizen knew the tale of the king who fell in love with an American divorcée.

"What is this group?"

"It is called the Daedalus Society. Best we can tell it was formed at the beginning of the 17th century by Robert Cecil."

"Pazan told me about him. He was close to both Elizabeth and James I."

"He was responsible for James becoming king, with Elizabeth's help of course. The Scot owed Robert Cecil his throne."

"Should we not be searching for the professor?"

"No, Miss Richards, **we** should not. There are people who will deal with what happened, and have already been dispatched. Our task is to move forward. In this business, no one person can do it all."

His rebuke came in a voice hard as steel, the tone daring her to challenge him.

"What do you want me to do?"

"The presence of this Daedalus Society complicates matters. I urge you to keep your wits about you."

Your first and final warning.

Leave this be.

"I think I should be issued a firearm."

Mathews fished beneath his coat, removed an automatic pistol, and handed it to her. "Take mine."

She checked the magazine and ensured it was fully loaded.

"Don't trust me?" he asked.

"At the moment, Sir Thomas, I don't know what to think."

"I would have thought the excitement you experienced mild, considering your past history."

He was beginning to rub her the wrong way. "I do what I have to when I have to."

"I have managed other agents with a similar attitude, most of whom are either now dead or no longer in my employ."

"I didn't ask for this assignment."

"Quite right. I chose you, and I knew what I was getting, right?"

"Something like that."

He nodded. "You have a healthy attitude, that I will grant you."

She was waiting for him to tell her what was next.

"If you recall," he said. "At the Inns of Court I told you about the two Henrys and Katherine Parr, and the great secret that passed among them. A sanctuary, perhaps the vault where the majority of the Tudor wealth was hidden."

"This is about buried treasure?"

She caught his annoyance.

"Only partly, Miss Richards. And why do you sound so incredulous? That vault could hold a wealth of information. We know that secret passages connected then, and still do, many of the Whitehall government buildings. Something you surely are aware of."

She was. Accessible today through coded doors. She'd once ventured down into one of the tunnels.

"Henry VIII used similar passages to access his tennis court and bowling alley at Whitehall Palace. We think there were other passages with different uses, ones his father either created or discovered. Ones that have remained hidden for five hundred years."

Which made sense, as London was crisscrossed with tunnels, dug at differing points in history, new ones discovered all the time.

"Katherine Parr was duty-bound to pass that secret on to Henry's minor son, Edward, but there is no evidence that she ever did. Twenty-one months after Henry died, Parr herself passed. We think she may have told the secret—**not** to Edward, but to someone else."

"Who? The Cecils?"

"Not possible. Henry VIII died fifteen years **before** William Cecil rose to power with Elizabeth, and thirty years **before** Robert Cecil succeeded his father. No, Katherine Parr told someone other than the Cecils."

"How do you know that?"

"Just accept that I do. Professor Pazan was asked to instruct you on Robert Cecil's notebook and the various possibilities. The deciphering of that notebook holds the key to all of this. The Tudor wealth was never found, nor accounted for. In today's market it would be worth billions."

"And the Americans want our treasure?"

"Miss Richards, do you continually question everything? Can you not accept that there are matters here of the highest national security. To know what those matters may be is irrelevant to what is expected from you. I have some specific tasks I need you to perform. Can you not simply do as I ask?"

"I am curious of one thing," she said. "SIS is charged with protecting against threats on foreign soil. Why isn't the Security Service, MI5, handling this investigation? Domestic threats are **their** jurisdiction."

"Because the prime minister has ordered otherwise."

"I was unaware the prime minister could violate the law."

"You truly are impertinent."

"Sir Thomas, a woman died a little while ago. I'd like to know why. What's curious is you don't seem to care."

She caught the annoyance on the older man's face. He was clearly unaccustomed to challenges.

"If I did not require your assistance, I would join with your supervisors in terminating your employment."

"Lucky for me I'm so valuable at the moment."

"And lucky for you the situation has changed. Antrim has involved that ex-American-agent I mentioned to you before. Cotton Malone. He has gone out of his way to draw Malone into this fray. I need you to find out why. As I mentioned, the deciphering of Robert Cecil's journal is vital to the resolution of this matter. Within the next few hours Antrim may well possess the means to do just that. Tell me, is he capable of capitalizing on his good fortune?"

"He's not daft, if that's what you're asking. But he's not overly clever, either. More devious and deceitful."

"Exactly my assessment. His operation has not

gone well. He is frustrated. His superiors are pressuring for results. Thankfully, time is short and what he seeks is difficult to find."

Mathews checked his watch, then stared out into the quad. People hustled back and forth from the street toward the college.

"I want you to travel back to London," he said. "Immediately."

"Professor Pazan did not tell me what I need to know. She was on her way back inside to show me more of the coded pages."

"Nothing was found in the dining hall."

Why wasn't she surprised? "Seems everything here is unexplained. I'm not accustomed to working like this."

"And how many intelligence operations have you worked on?"

Another rebuke, but she had to say, "I've handled thousands of investigative cases. Granted, none involved national security, but lives, property, and public safety were at stake. I understand the gravity of situations."

Mathews leaned on his walking stick, and she noticed again the unique handle.

"That cane is quite unusual."

"A gift to myself several years ago." He held up the stick. "A solid piece of ivory carved with the world on its face. I hold it in my hand every day as a reminder of what is at stake with what we do."

She caught the message.

This is important. Work with me.

"All right, Sir Thomas. No more questions. I'll head back to London."

"And I shall arrange for another briefing for you. In the meantime, be alert."

Twenty-one

MALONE FOUND AN INTERNET CAFÉ NOT FAR FROM Holborn and immediately surveyed the crowd. Mostly middle-aged. Unassuming. Probably lawyers, which made sense as they were not far from the Inns of Court. He purchased time on a desktop and logged in. Ian stayed close and seemed interested, not making any attempt to flee. His phone had yet to ring and he was becoming concerned. He was accustomed to pressure, but things were definitely different when one of your own was at risk. What provided him solace was the fact that the men who had Gary knew the boy was their only bargaining chip.

He inserted the drive.

Three files appeared.

He checked the kilobytes and noticed that they varied, one small, the other two quite large.

He clicked on the smallest first.

Which opened.

ELIZABETH I WAS FOURTEEN WHEN HER FATHER, Henry VIII, died and her half brother, Edward VI, became king. Katherine Parr, her father's widow, quickly discovered what it meant to be an ex-queen, having been denied any involvement with her stepson. The regency council provided for in Henry VIII's will assumed complete command. Edward Seymour, the king's uncle, maneuvered himself into the role of Protector. To placate Parr, the young Elizabeth was placed in Parr's household at Chelsea, a redbrick mansion that overlooked the Thames, where Elizabeth lived for a little over a year.

In 1547 an old suitor of Katherine Parr's reemerged—Thomas Seymour, brother to the Protector, and the second uncle to Edward VI. Thomas had lost Katherine to Henry VIII when the king decided she would become his sixth wife. A near-contemporary description of Thomas said he was "fierce in courage, courtly in fashion, in personage stately, in voice magnificent, but somewhat empty of matter." He was also recklessly ambitious, ruthless, and self-absorbed. Today he would be called a confidence man, someone who, through charm and guile, convinces his victims to do what they otherwise might never do.

Befitting the new king's uncle, Thomas was

made Duke of Somerset and bestowed the title Lord High Admiral. This should have placated him, but he was furious that his brother was Protector. So Thomas decided to change his lot. Being a bachelor provided him options, and a smart marriage could shift things dramatically. Henry VIII's will specifically provided that his daughters, Mary and Elizabeth, could not marry without the regency council's approval. Thomas tried to secure permission to marry one or the other, but was rebuked. So he turned his attention to the Queen Dowager.

Katherine Parr was thirty-four in 1547 and still retained a great beauty. She and Seymour had once been lovers so, when he appeared at Chelsea and began to romance her, the result was inevitable. They married secretly sometime in the spring, the young king not providing his blessing until months later.

It was after this that something curious began to occur. Seymour, Parr, and Elizabeth lived together at Chelsea, or in the country at Hanworth, or at Seymour Place, Thomas' London residence. The atmosphere was light and merry. When at Chelsea, Seymour began to visit Elizabeth's chambers, early, and bid her a good day, occasionally striking her upon the bottom. This he also did with other maidens in her household. If Elizabeth was still in bed, he'd open the curtains and attempt to climb into the bed with her. Witnesses reported that Elizabeth would shrink beneath her covers, seeking refuge. One morning he even attempted to kiss her but Kate Ashley, Elizabeth's governess, chased him away. Eventually, Elizabeth began to rise earlier and be dressed, ready for his visits. Lady Ashley eventually confronted Seymour, who was unrepentant about his actions. Parr herself at first thought the matter harmless, but soon changed her opinion. She became angry at her husband's flirtations with the princess, realizing that he'd married her only because his attempts to secure Mary or Elizabeth were refused by the council. She was, in essence, third choice. Now he was trying to directly ingratiate himself with Elizabeth.

But to what end?

By January 1548, Parr was pregnant with her first child by Seymour. She was thirty-five years old and birthing at that age, in that time, was perilous. In February 1548 Parr caught Seymour and Elizabeth together, the princess in the arms of her husband. Parr confronted Lady Ashley about the matter, a conversation that history has never recorded, until now.

The Queen Dowager's anger burst forth to Lady Ashley. She blamed the governess for not properly chaperoning the young princess. But the Lady Ashley made clear that the Lord Admiral Seymour had ordered her away.

"Do you not understand?" the Queen Dowager asked Ashley. "Surely you, of all people, understand."

Silence passed between them, the pause long enough for Parr to know that the Lady Ashley did in fact understand, in the fullest sense. The Queen Dowager had wondered how much this dutiful woman knew. Now that depth was clear.

This passage has been translated exactly as it appeared in Robert Cecil's journal (with some adjustment for modern word usage). I managed to break the code so that the journal can be read. These words have confirmed all that we suspected. Katherine Parr knew not only the secret her husband, Henry VIII, told her on his deathbed. She also knew what had occurred before that. What Henry himself never knew. Her ultimate response to Seymour's amorous overtures was to have Elizabeth, in April 1548, removed from their household. Never again did Elizabeth and the Queen Dowager see one another as, five months later, Parr was dead. Thomas Seymour did not even attend his wife's funeral. Instead, he immediately sought out the princess Elizabeth, renewing his intentions to marry her. But nothing ever came of such.

Malone stopped reading.

Ian stood beside him and had read along with him.

"What does it mean?" Ian asked.

"A good question. Farrow Curry seems to have been conducting some interesting historical research."

"Is that the man who died in Oxford Circus?"

He nodded. "These are his notes, some kind of report he was working on."

He scanned farther down the screen.

WE NOW KNOW FROM ROBERT CECIL'S JOURNAL that Katherine Parr left a letter to Elizabeth, which was delivered at Christmas 1548, four months after Parr died. It appears to have been penned before Parr gave birth to her daughter in September 1548, and is a revealing piece of correspondence that, once placed in proper context, answers many questions. I have translated and adjusted the wording to compensate for modern spelling and usage.

> There was no choice but to send you away. Please forgive me child, and that is what I have always considered you, my child, though no common blood flows between us. We are linked instead by the bond of your father. My current husband is a man of no character, who cares nothing for anyone save himself. Surely you have seen this and recognize the evil and danger he represents. He knows nothing of what he seeks and would be unworthy to be privy to your truth. God has given you great qualities. Cultivate them always

and labor to improve them, for I believe you are destined by heaven to be Queen of England.

This came directly from Cecil's journal. There are other similar references, all equally compelling. Each confirming that the legend is in fact true.

The narrative continued with a series of shorthand references, as if Curry would return later and finish. Malone scanned them, noticing several mentions of Hatfield House, Robert Cecil's country estate north of London, and the Rainbow Portrait of Elizabeth I that hung there. No further mention of the legend, whatever it might be, and its truth appeared. But a notation at the end explained, **only way to know for sure is to go and see.**

A second file, the largest in kilobytes, contained images from a handwritten journal, the green-and-gold pages filled with a cryptic script. The file was labeled CECIL JOURNAL ORIGINAL. Apparently what Curry had managed to translate. No explanations or other entries were in the file.

The final file he could not open.

Password-protected.

Which, obviously, was the most important.

"How do you get the password?" Ian asked.

"Experts can get around it."

His phone rang. He closed the drive.

"Mr. Malone," a new voice said. "We rescued Gary."

Had he heard right?

"We're pulling up at your location now."

His gaze shot out the café's front windows.

A car was wheeling to the curb.

"Stay here," he told Ian, and he darted for the front door.

Outside, the car's rear door opened and Gary bounded out.

Thank God.

"You okay?" he asked his son.

The boy nodded. "I'm fine."

A man exited the car. Tall, broad-shouldered, thinning hair. Maybe fifty years old. He wore a navy, knee-length overcoat that hung open. He rounded the trunk and approached, offering his hand to shake.

"Blake Antrim."

"This is the man who found me," Gary said.

Two more men emerged from the car's front seat, both dressed in overcoats. He knew the look.

"You CIA?" he asked Antrim.

"We can talk later. Do you have Ian Dunne?"

"He's here."

"Get him."

Malone turned back to the café, but did not see Ian through the window. He hustled back inside to the computer.

The drive was gone.

And so was Ian.

His eyes raked the room and he spotted a door that let back into the kitchen. He rushed through and asked the two women busy preparing food about Ian.

"Gone out the back door."

He followed and found himself in a dark, empty alley that right-angled fifty feet away.

No one in sight.

Twenty-two

ANTRIM, WITH GARY IN TOW, ENTERED THE CAFÉ and spotted Malone pushing through a rear door.

"Ian ran," Malone said. "He's gone."

"We really needed him."

"I get that."

"Was he okay?" Gary asked.

But Malone did not answer.

The patrons inside were all focused on what was happening, so Antrim motioned for them to leave. On the sidewalk, near the car, while his men kept watch, he stepped close to Malone and said, "This is an ongoing CIA operation."

"A lot of attention for a covert op."

"Caused by having to rescue your son."

"Is the operation yours?"

He nodded. "For over a year now."

Malone appraised him with a cool gaze. "I was

to drop Ian Dunne off at Heathrow to Metropolitan Police. That's all. The next thing I know, I'm facedown unconscious and my son is taken."

"All I can say is that some problems have surfaced. But I still need to find Ian Dunne."

"Why?"

"That's classified."

"Like I give a crap. How'd you find me?"

"Gary told us about your phone, so we tracked it, hoping you still had it with you."

"And how did you find Gary?"

"Let's just say a little birdie tipped us off and leave it at that."

"More classified information?"

Antrim caught the sarcasm. "Something like that."

Gary stood beside his father, listening.

"What's so important?" Malone asked him. "What are you doing here in London?"

"When you were one of us, did you go around discussing your business with strangers?"

No, he didn't. "We're leaving. Thanks for finding my boy." He faced Gary. "Our bags are inside. We'll get them, then find a hotel for the night."

Antrim took stock of the ex–Magellan Billet agent. Personnel records had noted Malone to be forty-seven years old, but he looked younger, a thick mane of blondish brown hair barely tinted with gray. They were about the same height and build, and even their features were similar. Malone seemed in good shape for a man out of the game for over a year. But the eyes were what really interested him. As noted in the Justice Department personnel jacket, they were a pale shade of green.

He'd played this right so far.

Now for the finish.

"Wait."

MALONE WAS PLEASED THAT HE'D GUESSED RIGHT.

Blake Antrim was in trouble. He'd sensed it almost immediately, especially when Antrim realized Ian was gone. Whatever was happening was not going right.

He stopped and turned back.

Antrim came close and said, "We have a big problem. A national security problem. And Ian Dunne may have something we desperately need to solve it."

"A flash drive?"

"That's right. Did you see it?"

He nodded. "Ian has it. He took it when he ran."

"Did you read it?"

"Some."

"Care to share what was on it?"

"I don't remember."

"Really? Your eidetic memory gone?"

"You been checking up on me?"

"After I learned you were here, with Ian Dunne, and your son was in trouble."

He'd been born with a memory for details. Not photographic. Instead, he could recall the simplest of details, nearly at will. A curse at times, but more often a blessing. So he summarized for Antrim what Farrow Curry had written, noting that one file was password-protected.

"Any idea where Dunne might be?" Antrim asked.

"I just met the boy yesterday. He wasn't the friendliest."

"How about you, Gary?" Antrim asked. "He say anything to you?"

His son shook his head. "Not much. He lives on the streets. But he did say something on the plane about a bookstore he would sleep in sometimes at night. The lady who owns it, Miss Mary, was nice to him."

"He say where that is?"

"Piccadilly Circus."

"Seems like a good place to start," Antrim said.

Malone could not resist. "Particularly considering it's the only place you have."

"That make you feel better?" Antrim asked. "I've told you I'm in trouble. Admitted the problem. What more do you want?"

"Call Langley."

"Like you called Stephanie Nelle every time you got yourself into a tight one?"

He'd never made that call. Ever.

"That's what I thought," Antrim said. "You handled it yourself. How about another favor? Go to that store and see if Dunne shows up. You two seem to have made a connection, more than any of us."

"Who were the guys at the airport? The ones who jumped me and took Gary?"

"They work for a shadow group called the Daedalus Society. They've been interfering with this operation for some time. I thought we had things under control with them, but I was wrong."

"Ian was allowed into the country without a passport."

"I did that. When he was located in the States, I asked British Customs to authorize his entry. I had men at the airport waiting for you. But the other two found you first. Just one more thing that went wrong."

Malone could see that he'd struck a sore point. But he could sympathize. He, too, had experienced operations that simply would not go right.

"All I can tell you," Antrim said, "is that things here are important and time is short. We need that flash drive."

"So did the other two men who jumped me."

"Like I said, the Daedalus Society is after the same thing."

"Dad," Gary said. "Go find him."

The comment surprised Malone. "We don't have a dog in this fight. We need to get home."

"What's a few more hours?" Gary said. "It's late. We have the time. See if you can find him. I'll go with you, if you want."

"No way. Your mother would kill me with what's already happened. And I wouldn't blame her."

"I'll keep an eye on him for you," Antrim said.

"I don't know you."

"Make your calls. Check me out. You'll find everything I've told you is the truth. Gary can stay with us a few hours. I have agents, and I'll personally look after him."

Malone hesitated.

"A few hours to see if Dunne can be found. That's all I'm asking."

"Do it," Gary said.

"I need to make that call," he told Antrim.

The agent nodded. "I understand. I'd do the same thing. But remember, I'm the one who found your boy."

Point made. But he recalled Ian's fears. "If I go after Dunne, I do it alone. None of your guys around."

"Agreed."

"You really cool with this?" he asked Gary.

His son nodded. "You gotta do it."

IAN HAD NOT LIKED THE LOOK OF THE MEN WHO'D emerged from the car. Too official. Too determined.

He was glad to see Gary was okay, back with his dad. But the fake police from Heathrow had definitely spooked him, so he decided it was time to leave.

He'd taken the flash drive for two reasons.

One, he wanted to show it to Miss Mary. She was the smartest person he knew, and he was interested in what she had to say.

The second was maybe Cotton Malone might come looking for it.

If he did, he'd know where to go.

So he headed for Piccadilly Circus.

Twenty-three

OXFORD

KATHLEEN WAS IRRITATED.

She'd resented Mathews ordering her about, treating her like some rookie. He'd ignored her questions, was evasive when he did answer, then summarily dismissed her, telling her to head back to London.

But a woman died at Jesus College and her body had been carted away.

By who? For what?

And she did not believe that **others** were investigating what happened.

Nothing about any of this rang right.

She wondered if Mathews had expected her to be too eager or too grateful to question anything. Or was it that he simply had become accustomed to people obeying? True, she was glad to still have a job. And despite the fact that she could at times be a problem, she'd not forged a career by being either stupid or complacent. So before leaving Oxford she headed back to Jesus College and the quad. There, she found the same quiet scene, the soporific drone of diesel engines drifting in from the nearby streets. She approached the stone bench where she'd sought cover and recalled the shots. On the stone steps leading back to the dining hall, where Pazan's body had laid, she bent down and rubbed the coarse surface, noticing not a speck of blood anywhere. Her gaze drifted to the roof and the parapets, where the shooter had hidden. The down angle was unobstructed. Nothing to prevent a clear shot.

She crossed to the oak door with the brass handle and tried the latch.

Still locked.

Inside the chapel, which remained empty, she climbed the steep stairs to the organ and saw where her attacker had hidden, near the keyboard, behind the pipes, between the instrument and the wall. Which meant he was waiting long before she'd sought refuge inside.

With a Taser?

I'm sure you now realize that you were led here.

That's what he'd said.

So they'd known she'd be in Oxford, at Jesus College, meeting Pazan. Enough in advance to be ready. Then they'd shot Pazan, but not her.

Why?

Because they needed to deliver a message?

An awful lot of trouble when so many simpler options were available.

And what happened to Pazan's body?

She decided as long as she was being insubordinate, she'd be thorough. Though Oxford University was composed of thirty-nine separate collegiate parts, there was a centralized administration that included security patrolling the streets, quads, and buildings. She recalled them from her student days and found the main office near the city police station. Her SOCA credentials earned instant respect, and the personnel on duty were more than happy to answer her questions.

"Do you have a roster of university employees?"

The young woman smiled. "Everyone is badged and credentialed on hiring. They have identity cards that have to be carried."

Which made sense.

"Is there an employee for Lincoln College named Eva Pazan?"

The woman worked a keyboard, then scanned her monitor. "I don't see one."

"Any Evas or Pazans, separately?"

A pause as the screen was searched, then, "Nothing."

"Any employee anywhere, at any of the colleges, with those names?"

More taps on the keyboard.

None.

Why wasn't she surprised?

She left the building.

Pazan could have simply been lying. But why? She'd specifically mentioned teaching history at Lincoln and attending Exeter College.

And that Mathews sent her.

Which the spymaster confirmed.

Then, she was shot.

Had she died? Or was she able to walk away? If so, why no blood anywhere?

Now, apparently, the woman didn't even exist.

She didn't like anything about this.

A few hours ago she'd been dispatched to the Inns of Court precisely at the same time Blake Antrim had been present. Everything had been coordinated, timed with precision.

Which wasn't so shocking.

After all, she was dealing with the Secret Intelligence Service.

In Middle Hall she'd thought herself a knight or a rook on the chessboard. Now she carried the distinct feel of a pawn.

Which made her suspicious.

Of everyone.

MALONE LISTENED TO STEPHANIE NELLE.

He'd found her by phone twenty minutes ago

and told her what he needed to know. Now she'd called back.

"Antrim is CIA, special counterterrorism. Most of it is off the charts, lots of black ops buried deep under national security. He's got twenty years. And he's the one heading the operation there. It's called King's Deception, but Langley would not give me any particulars."

"What happened to all that post-9/11 cooperation?"

"It ended on 9/12."

Which he already knew. "Any problems with Antrim?"

"I couldn't get that much that quick, but I think my source would have told me if he's a loose cannon. Sounds like a typical career man."

Which jibed. Counter-operations required patience, not heroics. If anything, Antrim would lean toward hesitancy instead of being a Lone Ranger.

"Is everything okay there?" she asked.

"It is now. But it was touch and go for a while."

He filled her in on the details. Then said, "I should have flown coach."

"You realize you can go home," she said.

He did. "But before Gary and I go to sleep, I'm going to give Ian Dunne one shot."

Besides, he wanted to know why the boy ran, and why he snatched the flash drive.

"I wouldn't get too deep into this," Stephanie told him.

"I don't plan to. But the stuff on that flash drive got me curious. What the hell are they up to over here?"

"No telling. But I'd leave the kids to play in their sandbox and head on home."

Good advice.

They'd left the café and driven to a house beyond Portman Square. He knew this part of London, near busy Oxford Street, since he always stayed at the Churchill, located at the west edge of the square. Gary, Antrim, and the other two agents were inside the house. He'd stepped out to take the call.

"It's getting late here," he said. "We can't leave until morning anyway. And Antrim did find Gary. So I owe him one."

"Sorry for all this. I thought it was a simple favor."

"It's not your fault. I seem to have a way of finding trouble."

He ended the call.

The front door opened and Gary walked toward him on the sidewalk.

"What are you going to do?" his son asked.

"I'll take a quick look for Ian. Antrim is the real deal. He's CIA. You'll be okay here with him."

"He seems like a good guy. He told me I could see some of the things he's working on."

"I won't be long. Just a few hours. Then we'll find a hotel and get out of here in the morning."

He'd meant what he'd said to Stephanie. Farrow Curry had definitely been into some odd stuff—especially for a government counter-intelligence operation being conducted within the borders of an American ally.

"You know why I wanted to spend Thanksgiving with you."

He nodded.

"Mom told me about my real . . . I mean, my **birth** father."

"It's okay, son. I know this is tough."

"She won't tell me who he is. I want to know. She really never told you?"

He shook his head. "Not until a few months ago and she never mentioned a name. If she had, I'd tell you."

And he wasn't trying to undercut Pam, it was just that you can't choose to tell half a story. Especially one this explosive.

"When we get out of here," Gary said, "I'd like to know what happened before I was born. Everything."

Not his favorite subject. Who enjoyed reliving their mistakes? But thanks to Pam, he had no choice. "I'll tell you whatever you want to know."

"I wish Mom would do the same."

"Don't be too hard on her. She's kicking herself bad on this one."

They stood on the street, the curbs on both sides

lined with parked cars. A busy avenue, a hundred feet away, hummed with traffic.

"You think Ian could be in trouble?" Gary asked.

He heard the concern and shared the anxiety.

"I'm afraid so."

Twenty-four

Antrim was pleased. He'd connected with Malone and convinced him to go after Ian Dunne, feigning enough frustration to telegraph that his entire operation was in trouble. Which had not been all that hard since it was the truth. Ordinarily, though, he would have never shared those problems with a stranger.

But he wanted a little private time.

After all, Gary was the whole reason he'd maneuvered Malone to London.

"You lied to me," he said.

Pam Malone stared back. She stood behind her desk on the twelfth floor in a downtown Atlanta office building. Two days ago he'd run into her at a mall. They hadn't seen or spoken to each other in sixteen years. Back then he'd been a CIA operative, assigned to a duty station in

Wiesbaden, Germany. Pam was a navy wife, her lawyer husband a lieutenant commander, part of the United States' NATO contingent. They'd met, had a brief affair, then she ended it.

"I never lied," she said. "I just never told you anything."

"That boy is mine."

He'd known it the first moment he met Gary Malone. Everything reminded him of himself as a teenager. And—

"He has my gray eyes."

"My ex-husband's are gray."

"There you go. Lying again. I remembered your ex-husband's name. In fact, I've come to hear it many times since you and I were together. He was quite the agent. But I pulled his jacket yesterday. His eyes are green. Yours are blue."

"You're delusional."

"If I am, why are you shaking?"

He'd located her with a quick check of the Georgia State Bar directory. Their talk in the mall had been brief and light. She'd mentioned that she was now a lawyer so it had not taken much to find her. He'd appeared unannounced, wanting to catch her off guard. She'd at first informed the receptionist that she was busy, but when he told the woman to pass on that he'd "just see her at home," he was led to her office.

"You're a sorry, useless bastard who likes roughing up women."

Their breakup was not without consequences. She'd rebuked him with no warning or provocation. Which hurt. He'd actually cared for her. More than most. He'd always been partial to the unhappily married ones. They were so giving, so grateful. All you had to do was pretend you cared. She'd been no different. Convinced that her husband was cheating on her, she'd wanted reciprocity and eagerly gave herself.

"I made a huge mistake with you," she said. "One I prefer to forget."

"But you can't. You have a reminder every day, don't you?"

He saw that his assessment was correct.

"It's the only part of my son I despise. God help me."

"There's no need to feel that way. And, by the way, he's our son."

Her eyes flashed hot. "Don't you say that. Don't you ever say that. He's not our son. He's mine."

"What about your ex-husband? I'm sure he has no idca."

Silence.

"Maybe I'll tell him."

More silence.

He chuckled. "This is obviously a sore spot with you. I can understand that. Seeing me in that mall had to have been a shock."

"I was hoping you were dead."

"Come on, Pam. It wasn't that bad."

"You broke my ribs."

"You broke my heart. Just up and told me to get out and never come back. And after all the sweet times we shared. You surely didn't expect me to just walk away."

"Get out of my office."

"How long was it after that you found out you were pregnant?"

"What does it matter?"

"Did you know when you broke it off?"

She said nothing.

"I . . . should have . . . ended the pregnancy then and there."

"You don't mean that. Aborted your child? That's not you."

"You condescending prick, you have no idea who I am. Don't you get it? To this day I look at that boy, whom I worship, and see you. Every day I have to deal with that. I came so close to ending that pregnancy. So damn close. Instead, I carried the child and lied to my husband, telling him the baby was his. You have any idea what it's like to live with that?"

He shrugged. "You should have told me."

"Get. Out."

"I'm leaving. But if I were you, I'd tell your ex-husband and son the truth. 'Cause now that I know, you haven't seen the last of me."

And he'd meant it.

Immediately, he'd hired private surveillance to keep tabs on both Pam and Gary Malone. It cost a couple thousand dollars a month, but had been worth every penny to learn their comings and goings, their wants and desires. The person he'd hired cared nothing about the law and even managed to tap the landlines on Pam's home phone. Every other day a recording would be forwarded by email of the calls in and out. That's how he learned Cotton Malone knew that Gary was not his biological son. The conversation between the two of them had been heated, Pam telling Malone that Gary was upset, wanting to spend Thanksgiving break with him in Denmark. Even better, neither Gary nor Malone knew Antrim's identity. Both had been kept in the dark by Pam.

Good girl.

He'd never followed through on his threat to contact either Malone or Gary. Neither path seemed the way to go. Instead, he'd remained patient, doing what intelligence officers did, gathering information from which smart decisions could be made. Originally, he'd intended on connecting with Gary in Copenhagen sometime next week.

But the unexpected surfacing of Ian Dunne changed that plan.

Making contact here, in London, worked much better.

So he'd ordered Dunne flown from Florida to Georgia and informed Langley that Malone was in

Atlanta, headed back to Europe. How about a favor among agencies? The Magellan Billet, or at least a former Magellan Billet agent, helping out the CIA. Simple babysitting. **This way we'll know Dunne will be safely delivered.**

Which worked.

Thanks to everyone's anxiety about what the Scottish government intended doing.

During the rescue he'd studied Gary closely, noting the pinched nose, long chin, high brow, and, most important, the gray eyes. Now he had Gary to himself. Pam Malone was nowhere to be seen. Cotton Malone clearly had no idea of the connection, and, based on Malone's comment earlier outside the café, he doubted that he'd be checking with his ex-wife. All he had to do was not allow Gary to call Georgia.

And that would be easy.

The next few hours were critical.

He told himself to handle things carefully.

But it should not be a problem.

After all, he was a pro.

Twenty-five

11:02 PM

MALONE ALWAYS LIKED THE THROB OF PICCADILLY Circus. It was boisterous and brash, and comparisons to Times Square were inevitable. But this tangle of noise had existed centuries before its American interpretation. Five roads met at the circular junction and surrounded the plinth of Eros, the statue a London landmark. St. James Palace sat a few blocks away, one of the last remaining Tudor residences. Reading about Katherine Parr and Elizabeth I earlier had set his mind on the Tudors, who ruled from 1485 to 1603. He'd read many books about them and even maintained a Tudor section at his bookstore in Copenhagen, as he'd learned others shared his interest. Now he was privy to something he'd never read in any of those books.

Some secret.

Important enough to have attracted the attention of the CIA.

Cars slithered to a standstill at the busy intersection and he crossed among them, heading deeper into London's entertainment district that stretched out beyond Piccadilly. Cinemas, theaters, restaurants, and pubs filled the olden buildings, all of them alive with a late-Friday-night business. Wood fronts and plate glass cast him back to another era. He zigzagged a path through the menagerie of people, heading for the address he'd located on his iPhone.

Any Old Books occupied a space not unlike his own shop, a turn-of-the-century structure squeezed between a pub on one side and a haberdashery on the other. Its front door was stained oak and half glass with a worn brass knob. Inside was also similar to his shop. Rows of wooden shelves from floor to ceiling packed with used books. Even the smell, that combination of dust, old paper, and aged wood, reminded him of Copenhagen. He immediately noted an order to the madness, placards jutting from the shelves announcing the various subjects. Organization seemed an affliction common to all successful bookstore owners.

The woman who stood behind the counter was small and thin with short, silver hair. Only a few noticeable lines had settled over her dainty features, like a faint net of age. She spoke in a gentle voice that he noticed was never raised, a smile accompanying every word.

And not a phony one.

She seemed to genuinely care, ringing up a purchase, dispensing change, thanking customers for their business.

"Are you Miss Mary?" he asked her when she finished with a purchase.

"That's what they call me."

"Is this your store?"

She nodded. "I've owned it a long time."

He noticed the stacks of books dominating the counter, surely ones she'd just acquired. He did the same, every day, "buying for pennies, selling for euros." He hoped his two employees were taking care of things back in Denmark. He was supposed to work there tomorrow.

"You're open late."

"Friday and Saturday nights are busy for me. The stage shows are just ending, everyone off for a late dinner or a drink. I learned long ago that they also enjoy buying books."

"I own a bookshop. In Copenhagen."

"Then you must be Cotton Malone."

GARY WATCHED BLAKE ANTRIM AS HE DIRECTED his two agents and made things happen. He'd never met anybody who actually worked for the CIA. Sure, you saw them on television and in movies, or read about them in books. But to deal with one in person? That had to be rare. His father had been an agent for the Justice Department, but never, until recently, had he understood what that meant.

"We appreciate your dad helping us out," Antrim said to him. "We can use the assist."

He was curious. "What's happening here?"

"We're after some extremely special things, and have been for the past year."

They'd driven to a warehouse located near the Thames River, which Antrim described as their command station. They were inside a small, sparsely furnished office near the warehouse entrance, a tight rectangle with a window that opened into the cavernous space.

"What's out there?" he asked.

Antrim stepped close. "Things we've collected. Pieces of a large puzzle."

"Sounds cool."

"Would you like to take a look?"

MALONE SMILED. "I SEE IAN HAS ALREADY arrived."

"He told me you might be coming, and he described you perfectly."

"I need to find him, and fast."

"There are a lot of people looking for Ian, and have been ever since that man died in the Underground."

"He told you about that?"

She nodded. "He and I have always been close, ever since he wandered in here one day."

"And could read."

She smiled. "Exactly. He was fascinated by all of the books, so I indulged his interest."

But he wasn't fooled. "As a way to get him to sleep here at night, instead of on the streets?"

"If Ian ever knew my real motives he never said a word. I told him he was my night guard, here to keep an eye on things."

He immediately liked Miss Mary, an entirely practical woman with a seemingly good heart.

"I never was blessed with children," she said, "and I am way past the time where I could have one. Ian seemed a gift. So he and I spend a lot of time together."

"He's in trouble."

"That much I know. But he's lucky."

He was curious what she meant. "How so?"

"For the second time"—she tossed him a hard gaze—"he's taken to someone he can trust."

"I didn't know that we were buddies. In fact, our relationship has been a bit rocky."

"Surely you realize that he took that flash drive hoping you would come after it. His way of asking for your friendship. I can see that he made a good choice. You look like a man to be trusted."

"I'm just a guy who can't quit doing favors."

"He told me you were once a secret agent."

He grinned. "Just a humble servant of the U.S. government. Now I'm a bookseller, like you."

Which he liked the sound of.

"He told me that, too. Like I say, you **are** a man to be trusted."

"Have others really been looking for Ian?"

"A month ago men came around to the shops. Some of the owners know Ian and they pointed them my way. But I lied and told them I had not seen him. Unfortunately, Ian disappeared a week after that and did not return. Until today. I prayed he'd be okay."

"Like I said, he's in trouble. He has something those other men want."

"The flash drive."

He caught the meaning in her words. "You've read it?"

"I read the same two files you viewed."

Then he saw something in her eyes. "What is it?"

ANTRIM LED GARY FROM THE OFFICE OUT INTO the warehouse, the space brightly lit by an array of overhead fluorescent fixtures. Two tables held stacks of old books, some tucked safely inside plastic bags. Another table supported three iMacs connected to an Internet router and a printer. This was where Farrow Curry had worked, trying to make sense of Robert Cecil's journal, deciphering what seemed impossible to understand.

But the past twenty-four hours had changed his mind.

Not only was it possible, somebody was willing the pay him five million pounds just to walk away from whatever was there.

Gary noticed the stone slab lying on the floor. "What is that?"

"We found that in an interesting place. Not far from here, near a palace called Nonsuch."

"Is it a big castle?"

"The palace no longer exists. Only the ground where it stood. Henry VIII built it as the grandest of all his residences. A magical site. He called it Nonsuch because there was nothing else its equal. None. Such. All we know of what it looked like now comes from three watercolors that survived."

"So what happened to it?"

"Centuries later, Charles II gave it to his mistress and she sold it off, piece by piece, to pay her gambling debts. Eventually, there was nothing left but the dirt on the ground. We recovered this slab from a nearby farm where it had been used for centuries to support a bridge."

Gary bent down and examined the stone. The CIA memo from the 1970s had made mention of the slab's existence.

A series of symbols were carved on its face.

He stepped close and said, "They're mainly

abstract markings, but some are Greek and Roman alphabet letters. They turned out to be the key, though, to a four-hundred-year-old mystery."

He could see that the boy was intrigued. Good. He wanted him to be impressed.

"Like a lost treasure?" Gary asked.

"Something like that. Though we're hoping there's even more to it."

"What do these symbols mean?"

"They're the way to solve a code that was created long ago by a man named Robert Cecil."

Back in the 1970s, when those Irish lawyers first delved into the mystery, there were few sophisticated computers and the decryption programs were little more than elementary. So the slab's secrets had remained concealed. Thankfully, modern technology changed all that.

He watched as the boy traced the symbols with his fingers.

"Would you like to see the most important thing we found?"

Gary nodded.

"It's over here."

MALONE WALKED WITH MISS MARY BETWEEN THE shelves. Her store was a tad smaller than his, but she possessed his same penchant for hardcovers.

Not too many repeats, either, which evidenced how careful she was with her buying. No danger of running out of inventory ever existed, since people loved to trade books. That was the great thing about the business. A steady supply of inexpensive inventory always came and went.

She turned into the history section and scanned the spines.

"I'm afraid I'm going to need your help," she said, pointing to one of the top shelves.

He was six feet tall. She stood a good foot shorter.

"At your service."

"It's there. The fourth book from the left."

He spotted the red-bound volume and reached for it, maybe ten inches tall, four inches wide, and not quite an inch thick. In good condition, too. Late 19th century, he estimated from its bindings and cover.

He read the title.

Famous Impostors.

Then noted its author.

Bram Stoker.

Twenty-six

KATHLEEN PARKED HER CAR. DURING THE DRIVE back from Oxford she'd become convinced that she was being played. There was no Eva Pazan, or at least not one who worked at Lincoln College. Maybe Pazan was told to lie. But why? Weren't they all on the same side? And Mathews had sent her specifically to meet with the professor. If Pazan was a sham, what had been the point? She'd rechecked Jesus College and found a deceit. Now she'd returned to the Temple Church. Things about what happened here earlier bothered her, too.

She parked again outside the walls and entered the Inns of Court through the unmanned vehicle gate. King's Bench Walk was wet and, thanks to the late hour, empty of cars.

Sometimes she regretted never actually practicing law. Neither her father nor her grandfathers had been alive when she chose SOCA. She hardly knew her father—he died when she was young—but her mother kept his memory alive. So much that she decided that the law would be her career path, too. Being back among the Inns, recalling her days here and at Oxford, had definitely reawakened something inside her. At thirty-six she could easily re-hone her skills and perhaps earn entry into the practicing bar. A tough path, for sure. But soon that might be her only option. Her SOCA career seemed over, and her short foray into intelligence work would probably end before it ever started.

Quite a mess she'd made of her life.

But she had no time for regrets.

Never had, really.

She knew that tomorrow, Saturday, visitors would be everywhere among the Inns, enjoying the grounds and touring the famous Temple Church. But little about the ancient building was original. Centuries ago Protestant barristers, wanting to efface all emblems of Catholicism, whitewashed the interior and plastered the columns—a puritanical cleansing that destroyed all of the olden beauty. Most of what the visitors now saw was a 20th-century reconstruction, the aftermath of German bombs during World War II.

At this hour the church was dark and locked for the night. Midnight was fast approaching. Lights burned, though, in the nearby master's residence, the custodian charged with the church's upkeep, a servant of both the Middle and Inner Temples.

She approached the front door and knocked.

The man who answered was in his forties, dark-haired, and identified himself as the master. He seemed perplexed she was there, so she displayed her SOCA identification and asked, "What time does the church close each day?"

"You came here, at this hour, to ask me that?"

She tried a bluff. "Considering what happened earlier, you should not be surprised."

And she saw that her words registered.

"It varies," he said. "Most days it's 4:00 PM. Sometimes it's as early as 1:00 PM, depending on if we have services or a special event planned."

"Like earlier?"

He nodded. "We closed the church, at four, as requested."

"No one was there after that?"

He tossed her a curious look. "I locked the doors myself."

"And were the doors reopened?"

"Are you referring to the special event?" he asked.

"That's exactly what I'm referring to. Did everything perform brilliantly?"

He nodded. "The doors were reopened at six, locked back at ten. No personnel were on site, as requested."

Improvise. Think. Don't waste this opportunity.

"We are having some . . . internal issues. There were problems. Not on your end. On ours. We're trying to backtrack and trace the source."

"Oh, my. I was told that everything must be precise."

"By your supervisor?"

"By the treasurer himself."

The Inns were run by benchers, senior members of the bar, usually judges. The senior bencher was the treasurer.

"Of the Middle or Inner Temple?" she asked.

The church sat on the dividing line between the two Inns' respective land, each contributing to its upkeep. Southern pews were for the Inner Temple, northern pews accommodated the Middle.

"Inner Temple. The treasurer was quite emphatic, as was the other man."

"That's what I came to find out. Who was the other man?"

"Quite distinguished. Older gentleman, with a cane. Sir Thomas Mathews."

MALONE LAID THE BOOK ON THE COUNTER. MORE customers wandered in through the front door and browsed the shelves.

"They do come after the final curtain in the theaters, don't they?" he said.

"The only reason I stay open this late on weekends. I've found it to be quite worthwhile. Luckily, I am a bit of a night person."

He wasn't sure what he was. Night. Morning. All day. It seemed he simply forced his mind to work whenever it had to. Right now, his body was still operating on Georgia time, five hours earlier, so he was okay.

Miss Mary pointed to the book he held. "That was published in 1910. Bram Stoker worked for Sir Henry Irving, one of the great Victorian actors. Stoker managed the Lyceum Theatre, near the Strand, for Irving. He was also Irving's personal assistant. Stoker penned most of his great works while in Irving's employ, **Dracula** included. Stoker idolized Henry Irving. Many say the inspiration for the title character in **Dracula** came from Irving."

"I hadn't heard that one."

She nodded. "It's true. But in 1903, while searching for some land Irving might be interested in purchasing, Stoker came across an interesting legend. In the Cotswolds. Near Gloucestershire and the village of Bisley."

She opened the red volume to the table of contents.

"Stoker became fascinated with hoaxes and pretenders. He said that **'imposters, in one shape or another, are likely to flourish as long as human**

nature remains what it is and society shows itself ready to be gulled.' So he wrote this account and detailed some of the more famous, and not so famous."

He studied the table of contents, which listed thirty-plus subjects scattered over nearly 300 pages. The Wandering Jew. Witches. Women as Men. The False Dauphin. Doctor Dee.

"Stoker wrote four nonfiction books to go with his novels and short stories," Miss Mary said. "He never quit his day job and worked for Irving right up to the great actor's death in 1905. Stoker died in 1912. This book was published two years before that. When I read what was on that flash drive, I instantly thought of it."

She pointed to the last section noted in the table of contents, starting on page 283.

The Bisley Boy.

He carefully turned to the page and started reading. After only a few lines he glanced up and said, "This can't be real."

"And why not, Mr. Malone?"

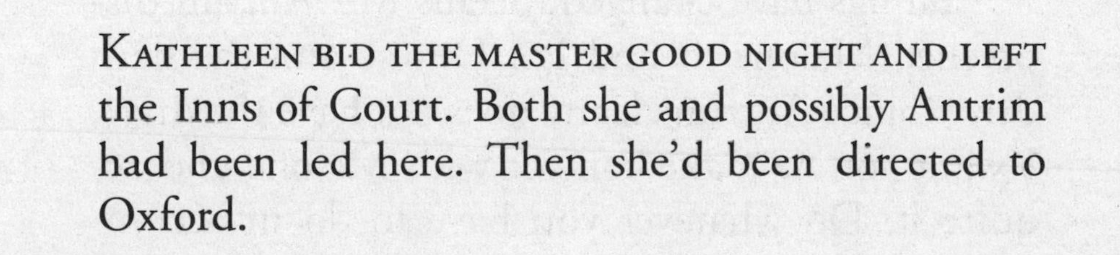

KATHLEEN BID THE MASTER GOOD NIGHT AND LEFT the Inns of Court. Both she and possibly Antrim had been led here. Then she'd been directed to Oxford.

I am of the Inner Temple. A member fifty years.

That was what Mathews had told her earlier.

Then, at Oxford, about the Daedalus Society.

The man who accosted you inside the chapel, we have dealt with his group before. They also confronted Blake Antrim earlier in the Temple Church.

Yet it had been Mathews, through the treasurer of the Inner Temple, who'd arranged for the church's use.

Not some Daedalus Society.

What was happening here?

Her suspicions had turned to outright distrust.

Her phone vibrated.

She found the unit and noted the number.

Mathews.

"Are you back in London?" he asked.

"As you ordered."

"Then proceed to a shop, on Regent Street and Piccadilly Square. Any Old Books. The American agent, Cotton Malone, is there, as may be the young man we are seeking, Ian Dunne. The flash drive could also be there."

"What about Antrim?"

"Things have changed. Seems Mr. Antrim dispatched Malone to find Ian Dunne and the flash drive. Since Antrim clearly does not have the drive, I want you to make contact with Malone and acquire it. Do whatever you have to do in accomplishing that task. Make haste, though."

She wondered why.

"Mr. Malone is about to find a spot of bother."

GARY WALKED WITH ANTRIM TO ANOTHER TABLE, where a book rested beneath a glass lid, similar to one his mother used for cakes and pies.

Antrim lifted off the cover. "We keep this one protected. It's the whole ball of wax."

"Mr. Antrim, why—"

"Call me Blake."

"My parents always tell me to address adults properly."

"Good advice, until the adult says otherwise."

He smiled. "I guess that's okay."

"It'll be fine."

He wasn't real comfortable with the switch to first names, but kept that to himself as he stared down at the old book.

"This is a journal created by Robert Cecil, the most important man in England from 1598 to 1612. He served Queen Elizabeth I and James I as their chief minister. Go ahÔead. You can open it."

The gold-and-green pages, their edges dried and frayed, each one as brittle as a potato chip, contained line after line of handwritten symbols and letters.

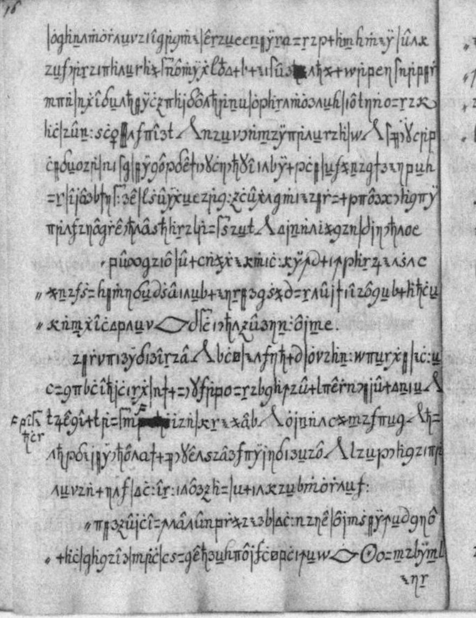

"There are 75,000 characters on 105 pages," Antrim told him. "All in code. Indecipherable since 1612. But we were able to break it."

"What does it say?"

"Things that may change history."

Antrim seemed proud of the accomplishment.

"Was it tough to break?"

"Modern computers helped, along with that stone on the floor over there you just saw. The symbols on it match the ones here and act as a translator. Thankfully, Cecil left it behind as a way to decipher the code."

"Seems like a waste of time then even writing it in code."

Antrim smiled. "That's what we thought, too. Until we studied the personality of Robert Cecil. Your father mentioned some of that earlier. What he read on the flash drive. Knowing Cecil, though, it all makes sense." Antrim pointed to the computers. "Lucky for us those are capable of breaking down ciphers far tougher than Cecil's."

He studied the pages. "This book is four hundred years old?"

"Every bit."

He wanted to know something else and mustered the courage to ask, "I remember that day in the mall back in the summertime. How do you know my mom?"

"We were friends a long time ago. I knew her when she lived in Germany. When your dad was stationed there in the navy."

He knew little about his father's navy days. Just the big picture—a fighter pilot, stationed around the world, who became a JAG lawyer. There was a plastic bin in the basement at home with uniforms, caps, and photographs. He'd rummaged through it once. Maybe he should do that again?

"When we saw you at the mall, that was the first time you'd seen her since then?"

Antrim nodded. "In sixteen years. I moved on to other duty stations and they moved on, too. Never saw her again, until that day with you."

He glanced down at the journal and its coded pages.

"Your mother ever talk about her time in Germany?" Antrim asked.

He'd already done the math. Sixteen years was

before he was born. He wanted to ask more questions. Maybe Blake Antrim knew the man his mother had been involved with?

"All she said was that she and my dad had a rough time then. Both of them were seeing other people. You don't know who my mom might have been seeing?"

Antrim studied him with an intense gaze.

"As a matter of fact, I do."

Twenty-seven

QUEEN ELIZABETH, THE LAST OF THE HOUSE OF Tudor, died unmarried. Since her death in 1603, there have been revolutions in England due to varying causes, but all more or less disruptive of family memories. The son of James I had his head cut off, and after the Commonwealth which followed, Charles II's son James II, had to quit on the coming of William III, by invitation. After William's death without issue, Anne, daughter of James II, reigned for a dozen years, and was succeeded by George I, descended through the female line from James I. His descendants still sit on the throne of England.

There are quite sufficient indications throughout the early life of Queen Elizabeth that there was some secret which she kept religiously guarded. Various historians of the time have

referred to it, and now and again in a way which is enlightening. In a letter to the Protector Somerset in 1549, when the Princess Elizabeth was 15, Sir Robert Tyrwhitt says:

> I do verily believe that there hath been some secret promise between my Lady, Mistress Ashley, and the Cofferer [Sir Thomas Parry] never to confess to death, and if it be so, it will never be gotten of her, unless by the King's Majesty or else by your Grace.

The place known to the great public as Bisley is quite other than that under present consideration. Bisley, the ground for rifle competitions, is in Surrey, thoughtfully placed in juxtaposition to an eminent cemetery. It bears every indication of newness, so far as any locality of old earth can be new. The most interesting spot in the whole district is the house Overcourt, which was once the manor-house of Bisley. It stands close to Bisley church from the grave-yard of which it is only separated by a wicket-gate. The title-deeds of this house, which is now in possession of the Gordon family show that it was a part of the dower of Queen Elizabeth. But the world went by it, and little by little the estate of which it was a portion changed hands; so that now the house remains almost as an entity. Naturally enough, the young Princess Elizabeth lived there for a time; and one can still see the room she occupied.

One other thing must be distinctly borne in mind regarding Bisley in the first half of the sixteenth century; it was comparatively easy of access from London for those who wished to go there. A line drawn on the map will show that on the way as points d'appui, were Oxford and Cirencester, both of which were surrounded with good roads as became their importance as centres. The tradition is that the little Princess Elizabeth, during her childhood, was sent away with her governess for change of air to Bisley where the strong sweet air of the Cotswold Hills would brace her up. The healthy qualities of the place were known to her father and many others of those around her. Whilst she was at Overcourt, word was sent to her governess, Kate Ashley, that the king was coming to see his little daughter; but shortly before the time fixed, and whilst his arrival was expected at any hour, a frightful catastrophe happened. The child, who had been ailing in a new way, developed acute fever, and before steps could be taken even to arrange for her proper attendance and nursing, she died. Lady Ashley, the governess, feared to tell her father. Henry VIII had the sort of temper which did not make for the happiness of those around him. In her despair she, having hidden the body, rushed off to the village to try to find some other child whose person could be substituted for that of the dead princess so that the evil moment of disclosure of the sad fact might be delayed till after his Majesty's departure. But the population was small and no girl child of any kind was available. The distracted woman then tried to find a living girl child who could be passed off for the princess, whose body could be hidden away for the time.

Throughout the little village and its surroundings was to be found no girl child of an age reasonably suitable for the purpose required. More than ever distracted, for time was flying by, Lady Ashley determined to take the greater risk of a boy substitute, if a boy could be found. Happily for the poor woman's safety, for her very life now hung in the balance, this venture was easy enough to begin. There was a boy available, and just such a boy as would suit the special purpose for which he was required, a boy well known to the governess. Moreover, he was a pretty boy as might have been expected from the circumstance. He was close at hand and available. So he was clothed in the dress of the dead child, they being of about equal stature; and when the King's fore-rider appeared the poor overwrought governess was able to breathe freely.

The visit passed off successfully. Henry suspected nothing; as the whole thing had happened so swiftly, there had been no antecedent anxiety. Elizabeth had been brought up in such dread of her father that he had not, at the rare

intervals of his seeing her, been accustomed to any affectionate effusiveness on her part; and in his hurried visit he had no time for baseless conjecture.

Then came the natural nemesis of such a deception. As the dead could not be brought back to life, and as the imperious monarch, who bore no thwarting of his wishes, was under the impression that he could count on his younger daughter as a pawn in the great game of political chess which he had entered on so deeply, those who by now must have been in the secret did not and could not dare to make disclosure. Fortunately those who must have been in such a secret, if there was one, were but few. If such a thing occurred in reality, three persons were necessarily involved in addition to the imposter himself: (1) Kate Ashley, (2) Thomas Parry, (3) the parent of the living child who replaced the dead one. For several valid reasons I have come to the conclusion that the crucial period by which the Bisley story must be tested is the year ending with July 1546. No other time either earlier or later would, so far as we know, have fulfilled the necessary conditions.

Malone looked up at Miss Mary. "I've never heard this story before."

"It's a tale that stayed close to the village of Bisley, until Bram Stoker discovered it. Maybe it is just a tale. But for centuries after Elizabeth I died, the annual May Day celebration in Bisley always included a young boy dressed in Elizabethan costume. Odd, wouldn't you say, unless there was some truth there?"

He really did not know what to say.

"Don't seem so shocked," she said to him. "Imagine if it were true."

He was doing just that, trying to see how that fact would be meaningful enough—four hundred years later—that the CIA had mounted an operation directed specifically toward it.

"When you think about it," she said, "in the context of what is known about the first Elizabeth, it begins to make sense."

He was already recalling everything he knew about the last Tudor monarch.

"She lived to be an old woman," Miss Mary said, "yet never gave herself to a man. She knew her duty. To produce a male heir. She knew what her father went through to have a son. In her case, even a daughter would have sufficed. Yet she consciously chose not to have a child, and expressed that intent many times in public."

One particularly noteworthy statement came to mind, where the queen said she would not marry, **even were they to give her the King of Spain's son or find any other great prince.**

"We should talk about this more."

She reached into one of her pockets and handed

him a folded scrap of paper. "My sister is the expert on all things Elizabethan. She could be far more help to you. I spoke with her earlier and she was fascinated by what I told her. She said she would welcome your call in the morning."

He accepted the offering.

"She lives in East Molesey."

He'd pass the information on to Antrim. "Right now, I need Ian and that flash drive."

"He's upstairs. He told me you would most likely be along before the day was through." She motioned. "Around the shelves, to the right."

Some patrons left through the front door and a few more entered.

He grabbed Stoker's book. "May I?" He noted the price on a slip of paper inserted within the pages. "Two hundred pounds. Pricey."

"A bargain, actually. I've seen it for more."

"You take American Express?"

She shook her head. "My gift from one bookseller to another. I'll hold it for you behind the counter."

He thanked her and headed upstairs.

His building in Copenhagen was also multistory. The ground floor housed the shop, the first and second were for storage of his overflow books, the top floor an apartment that, for the past year he'd called home. This place was similar except there were only three floors. He climbed to the top and found Ian inside a roomy flat.

"Why'd you run?" he asked.

The boy stood at a window, glancing out. "You have to see this."

He stepped over and glanced down.

Two men stood across the street.

"They came a minute ago, dropped off by car."

People hustled back and forth on the sidewalk, yet the duo never moved.

"They don't look right," Ian said.

He agreed.

The two men crossed the street, heading straight below.

Twenty-eight

Antrim had been waiting for an opening. Sure, this should be handled slowly and carefully, but he had to maximize the short amount of time he'd managed to snare. His only hope was that Gary Malone would demand more time. Thanks to the Georgia surveillance and wiretaps he had some idea what had happened between mother and son. But apparently, more significant face-to-face conversations had occurred for Gary to specifically ask about his mother's sordid past.

"Who was my mother seeing?" Gary asked him. "She won't tell me much."

"Why is it so important?" He was hoping the boy would realize that he had to give in order to receive.

"It involves my dad." Gary paused. "Actually it involves another dad. Or birth father. Whatever you call him. My mother had an affair and I was born."

"How do you feel about that?"

"I don't know what to think. But she lied to me and my dad for a long time."

He'd imagined this moment since that day in the mall when he first saw Gary. He'd been involved with a lot of women. But none had ever, to his knowledge, become pregnant. He'd actually thought the time for him to be a father had passed, but Pam Malone's admission had changed his thinking. Now here he was with an opportunity—one Pam never would have provided him. Her bitter denials alone had been enough to spur him forward. Who the hell did she think she was? He almost smiled. No failure had occurred in **this** operation. Everything had played out perfectly.

"Come with me," he said to Gary.

He led the boy back toward the office. The warehouse landlord thought this was a start-up operation for a manufacturing concern, Antrim part of the advance team. So far no one had questioned anything, nor interfered, the rent paid far in advance. A restroom jutted from one side of the office, its door opening into the warehouse. He stepped inside, switched on the light, and motioned for Gary to come close.

He pointed at the mirror. "Look at your eyes. What color are they?"

"Gray. They've always been that."

"Your mother's are blue and your dad's are green. Look at mine."

He watched as Gary focused on his irises.

"They're gray," the boy said.

He said nothing and allowed the moment to sink in.

And it did.

"You're the man my mother was seeing?"

He nodded.

Shocked filled Gary's face. "And you didn't know, either?"

He shook his head. "Not until that day in the mall, when I saw you. I then went to your mother's office and confronted her and she admitted it was true."

"She never told me that."

"I'm afraid she didn't want either of us to know the truth."

"How did you manage to find me and my dad?" Gary asked. "How did we get here?"

He couldn't tell him the truth. That he'd been watching both Gary and his mother. That he'd arranged for Malone to escort Ian Dunne to London. So he simply said, "One of those lucky breaks in life."

Of course, he also could not say that Norse and Devene worked for him and that Gary's "capture" had been a ruse, a way not only for father and son to connect but for Gary and Cotton Malone to both feel grateful. Of course, his men were supposed to corral Ian Dunne, too. But when Dunne ultimately fled, he'd modified the plan as a way to occupy Malone.

"I'm your birth father," he said to Gary.

GARY DID NOT KNOW WHAT TO SAY. HE'D WRESTLED with the fact that there was another man responsible for his creation, wanting to know who that was, demanding from his mother that she tell him the truth.

Now here he was.

But was it real?

His doubts must have been evident because Antrim laid a hand on his shoulder and said, "There's a simple way to be sure. We can do a DNA test."

"Maybe we ought to."

"I thought you might want to do that. I have some swabs in the office. Just a swish around your cheek and we can have it done. I know a lab here in town that can do the test fast."

"It's only going to say what we both know, right?"

Antrim nodded. "Your face. Your eyes. Your build. They're all mine. And your mother admitted that it was true. But I don't want there to be any doubt."

He was ill prepared for this. He'd come to the conclusion that he would never know the identity of his birth father.

"What do we do now?" he asked Antrim.

"Get to know each other. Neither one of us had that opportunity before."

"But what about my dad?"

"We tell him when he gets back."

For some reason, the prospect of that conversation bothered him. He felt awkward. Uncomfortable. Two men. Both his father.

Only in different ways.

Again, Antrim sensed his anxiety. "Don't worry. Cotton seems like a good guy. Maybe he'll be relieved to know, too?"

Maybe so.

ANTRIM DID HIS BEST TO CALM THE BOY'S FEARS, but he had no intention of telling Cotton Malone anything. Prior to this moment he hadn't made any final decisions as to what would be done **after** he told Gary the truth.

He'd wanted to see the boy's reaction.

Which had been good.

He doubted there'd be room for two dads in Gary's life. That could become awkward. But why should there be? This boy was **his.** Not a drop of Malone blood flowed in his veins.

One dad was plenty enough.

His **real** dad.

So he made a decision.

Operation King's Deception would end.

He'd be paid his five million pounds from the Daedalus Society.

But he'd also demand one other thing.

The death of Cotton Malone.

Twenty-nine

MALONE BOLTED FOR THE DOOR, BUT STOPPED AT the top of the stairs. Just like back in Copenhagen, the flights here right-angled downward, the only difference being that instead of three there were two landings. Ian was right behind him, but Malone turned and whispered, "Stay here."

"I can take care of myself."

"I'm sure you can. But Miss Mary may be in trouble and I can't worry about you, too."

The boy seemed to understand. "Help her."

He pointed. "Stay put."

A wooden rail lined both sides of the stairway. He planted a hand on each and pivoted his weight upward, easing down to the landing. He repeated the process to the next and stared down the final flight of stairs at the ground floor, into the bookstore. Fifteen wooden steps were between him and there, any one of which would announce his presence. But before he could decide on what to do, a shadow appeared below.

Then a man.

Headed onto the stairs.

He retreated into the second-floor doorway and peered past the jamb, spotting one of the men from the street coming his way. He waited until the man was halfway up, then burst from his hiding place and, using the two handrails again as pivots, hoisted his body up and slammed the soles of his shoes into the man's face. He released his grip and fell forward, feet pounding the oak steps, legs leaping to the ground as his target hit the floor and tumbled between a row of shelves. Groggy, the man tried to stand, but a fist to the jaw sent him back down. Malone quickly searched and found a 9mm automatic.

Gun ready, he crept to the end of the shelves.

Three more rows lay between him and the counter.

"Here," a man's voice said. "I'm waiting for you."

His gaze darted to the front door, which was closed. Through its glass people could be seen milling back and forth on the dark sidewalk. Someone stopped and tried the locked knob, then walked off.

He leveled the weapon and allowed it to lead the way.

At the third row of shelves he stopped and peered past.

The second man held Miss Mary from behind, a gun to her right temple.

"Nice and easy," the man said.

He kept his weapon aimed and ready. "The point of this?"

"The flash drive."

Who was this guy? And how did he know to be here?

"I don't have the flash drive," he made clear.

He kept his gun aimed.

Just one opening, that's all he'd need to take the bastard down.

"The kid has the drive," the man said. "Where's the kid?"

"How do you know that?"

"I want the drive."

"Give it to him," Miss Mary said.

No fear laced her words.

"Do you have it?" Malone asked her.

"In the metal box. Beneath the counter."

News to him. But what he saw in the woman's eyes gave him comfort. She wanted him to do it.

He crept toward the counter.

The man and his captive stood at the far end, on the outside. He stepped inside and reached below, finding a metal container. With his left hand, the right one still aiming the gun, he snapped open the lid to see pounds, pennies, and pence scattered inside, along with a flash drive, the same size and shape as the one he'd read earlier.

He retrieved it.

"Toss it."

He did.

IAN HAD MADE HIS WAY DOWN FROM THE TOP floor, using the handrails just as Malone had done. He found the bottom of the stairs and, to his right, saw a man holding a gun to Miss Mary.

The sight of her in danger frightened him.

She was the only person in the world who'd ever showed him real kindness. Never asking or expecting anything, she simply cared. Her suggestion that he sleep in her store and keep an eye on things was just her way of making sure he was out of the cold. Neither one of them ever voiced the truth, but they were both aware. Earlier, he'd returned to the mews for the plastic bag because the two books were a link to her. Seeing them reminded him of this store, her soft voice, her gentle ways. If he was to ever have a mother, he hoped she would be like Miss Mary.

He heard Malone's voice, then Miss Mary's, both discussing the drive in a metal box.

He smiled.

She was good.

He watched as the man with the gun told Malone to **toss it,** then used the moment when the man caught the drive to slip a book from the nearest shelf.

If he could catch the man off guard, Malone could act.

He gripped the book, cocked his arm, and said, "Hey, you bugger."

MALONE HEARD IAN'S VOICE AND SAW A BOOK FLY through the air. The man with the gun raised an arm to deflect it. Malone seized the moment to re-level his weapon, but before he could fire, his target lunged left.

"Get down," he yelled.

Miss Mary dropped to the floor.

Malone fired into the books, toward where the man had fled, careful with his aim.

Where was Ian?

He found the end of the first row of shelves and tried to spot any movement through the books toward the store's far side. He spotted a shadow two rows over. He darted down the aisle, between the rows and the front windows, using the solid wooden ends for cover.

"Stay down," he yelled again to Miss Mary and Ian.

At least he had the front door covered.

Then he remembered.

The stairs.

He heard footfalls pounding upward and dashed down an aisle toward the doorway that led to the upper floors. He approached with caution, keeping to one side. A quick glance past the jamb and he saw the man on the landing.

Two rounds pinged off the concrete floor a foot away.

Behind him, Miss Mary had retreated to the counter, seeking cover with Ian. Knowing they were okay, he made his move, firing a shot to clear the way, then rushing up the stairs.

He found the landing and hugged the wall beside the doorway leading into the second floor. The room beyond was empty, but a window at the far side was open. He spotted a fire escape, rushed over and glanced down, spotting the man fleeing down an dark alley behind the building.

He heard shots.

From below.

In the bookstore.

And glass shattering.

Then more gunfire.

KATHLEEN STARED INTO ANY OLD BOOKS through one of its plate-glass windows, spotting an older woman and a young boy near the counter. To their right, amid the shelves, she saw a man coming to his feet. He bent down and lifted one pant leg to reveal a gun strapped to his leg. She reached beneath her coat for the weapon Mathews had given her and, at the same time, tried the knob to the front door.

Locked.

She kicked its wooden half, but the door held.

The man was now standing, gun in hand, advancing forward to the end of the shelves.

The woman and the boy were unaware.

She stepped back and braced her weapon.

The man saw her.

He hit the floor and she fired through the door's glass half.

Shards crashed down.

People on the sidewalk scattered.

A woman screamed.

She searched for the man with the gun.

Gone.

Then he appeared, to her right, in another row of shelves, farther from the woman and the boy, but with a clear shot of her. She shifted left and fired again, through the opening her first round had made in the glass. The man was using the end of the shelving for cover, which seemed solid wood. His gun appeared and, as he fired, she dove to the sidewalk yelling, "Everyone get down."

Most people had fled, some out into the street.

A few lay on the chilly pavement.

Three rounds came their way.

Others were approaching the store from behind her, seeing the commotion but unaware of what was happening.

A new surge of people crowded the sidewalk.

Somebody was going to get hurt.

Her attention returned to the store and she saw the man rushing out the door, into the crowd ahead of her.

She came to her feet and aimed.

But too many people were in the way.

MALONE DASHED BACK TO THE STAIRS AND rushed down, stopping at the bottom. "Ian. Miss Mary."

He heard people outside and realized that the glass in the door was gone.

"We're here," Miss Mary called out.

He darted toward the counter and saw that both were okay.

A new face stood ten feet away. A woman. She was maybe mid-thirties, short auburn hair, thin, attractive, wearing a beige overcoat. Her right hand held a gun, its barrel pointed to the floor.

"Who the hell are you?" he asked.

"Kathleen Richards. SOCA agent. Here on official business."

He'd worked with the Serious Organized Crime Agency while with Justice.

"Why are you here?"

"Actually, Mr. Malone, I was hoping you could answer that question."

Part
Three

Thirty

Gary was still stunned by Blake Antrim's revelations. All of the doubt that had filled him ever since his mother told him the truth had been replaced with a strange anxiety. He hadn't had a chance to prepare himself. Instead, reality just found him.

He and Antrim were back inside the office.

"Do you want to take the DNA test?" Antrim asked him.

"I think so."

"It'll tell us with certainty."

Antrim produced a sealed plastic bag that contained two vials, a swab in each. He opened the bag and swirled one of the swabs inside his cheek, then sealed it into one of the vials.

"Open up."

Gary stood while Antrim did the same to his mouth.

"We'll have the results by tomorrow."

"We may not be here then."

Which brought to mind the next uncomfortable step. Telling his dad. Or Cotton Malone. Or whatever he should call him. He suddenly realized that finding his birth father called into question the man who'd raised him all of his life.

A man entered the office.

Antrim handed over the bag with the samples and provided an address where they were to be taken.

The man nodded and left.

"We haven't heard from your dad yet," Antrim said. "Hopefully, he'll find Ian Dunne."

"What is it Ian stole?"

"The guy who died in the Underground station, Farrow Curry, worked for me. He deciphered the coded book I showed you out there. Unfortunately, he took his work with him on a flash drive that we think Ian stole. We just want it back, that's all."

"What does the coded book say?"

Antrim shrugged. "I don't know. On the day Curry died he called and said he made a breakthrough. He asked that one of my men meet him at Oxford Circus. My man arrived just as Curry fell onto the tracks. He spotted Ian Dunne, with the flash drive, but lost him in the crowd."

"How did you meet my mom?"

He truly wanted to know.

"Like I said, she and your dad were living in

Germany. So was I. She was unhappy. Your father had cheated on her. She was hurt. Angry. One day, there she was, in Wiesbaden, at the produce market. We started to talk. That led to more talking and then to other things."

"Were you married?"

Antrim shook his head. "I've never been married."

"But she was."

"I know. It was wrong. But I was much younger then. So was she. We all do things when we're young that we regret later. I'm sure she feels the same."

"She said something close to that, too."

"Gary, your mother was lonely and felt betrayed. I have no idea what happened between her and . . . your dad. All I did was make her feel better for a little while."

"Doesn't seem right."

"I can see how you'd think that. But put yourself in your mother's shoes. Our relationship was a way for her to deal with the hurt she was feeling. Was it right? Of course not. But it happened and you're the result. So how can it be all bad?"

"Why do you think she wouldn't tell me about you?"

Antrim shrugged. "Probably because everything she'd say would only raise more questions. She surely doesn't want you to think bad of her. Unfortunately, she didn't take into account your—or my—feelings."

No, she hadn't.

"I don't think she'd like it that you and I met."

"Probably not. She made that clear to me when we spoke at her office. She never wanted us to meet. Told me to get out and not come back."

"I don't agree with that."

"Neither do I."

ANTRIM TOLD HIMSELF TO CHOOSE EVERY WORD with caution. This was the moment when he would either win the boy over or scare him away. There was no doubt that Gary believed him to be his birth father. Having their DNA matched was a good thing for them both, but Pam had already made clear the results of that test. What he needed was for this fifteen-year-old to start questioning who **was** his father. The man who raised him? Or the man who provided his genes? It wasn't Antrim's fault that he hadn't been a part of the boy's life, and it seemed that Gary realized that, too.

His mother was to blame.

But he didn't want him questioning her just yet.

That would come later.

Pam would be furious once she discovered what had happened here and, if he knew her at all, there was no telling what she'd say to Gary about him. But if this were played right, it wouldn't matter. By then the boy would be far more suspect of her than of him. After all, she was the one who'd lied all of his life. Why should Gary believe her now?

But there was still the matter of Cotton Malone, who was nearby and could reassert himself before Gary had time to digest everything.

He could not allow that to happen.

Hopefully, the chat they'd just had would begin to raise questions in Gary's mind. He needed him to recognize that his dad bore some responsibility for this, too. Worked right, the boy might just begin to blame Cotton Malone. Which would make what he'd decided to do that much easier for Gary to accept.

"I need to make a call," he said. "Wait here. I'll be back in a few minutes."

GARY WATCHED AS ANTRIM LEFT THE OFFICE, LEAVING him alone inside. Through the window he saw the tables with the books and computers. He had no idea what all of this was about, only that it seemed important. He wondered what his dad was doing.

And he hoped Ian wasn't in too much trouble.

His mother had made clear that she never wanted his birth father to be part of their life. No reasons had been offered and he'd not understood why.

Now he was even more confused.

Blake Antrim seemed like an okay guy. And just

like everyone else, he hadn't known the truth until recently.

And when he did find out, he'd immediately acted.

That said something.

What was he to do?

He'd been presented with an unexpected opportunity. He had a ton of questions for both Antrim and his dad. Tops on the list? Would his mother have ever been with another man if not for what his dad had done with other women? Antrim had been there. He saw things firsthand. And he'd made clear that his mother was really hurt.

He needed to talk about this with someone.

But who?

He couldn't call his mother. Big mistake.

And his dad was seeing about Ian.

There was no one who'd even possibly understand his anger and confusion.

Other than Blake Antrim.

Thirty-one

MALONE WATCHED AS KATHLEEN RICHARDS KEPT her gun lowered but her gaze locked on him. He, too, still held his weapon. He turned to Miss Mary and asked, "What happened?"

"The man who fell from the steps tried to leave, but this officer was outside and shot through the glass."

"He had a gun strapped to his leg," Richards added. "I decided not to wait around and see what happened."

"The bloke started firing," Ian said. "People were scattering everywhere. She"—Ian pointed at Richards—"hit the pavement. Then he darted away."

"I couldn't get a clean shot at him," Richards said, "because of the crowd."

"And no one was hit?"

Richards shook her head. "Everyone is okay."

Sirens could be heard, growing louder.

"The Met," Richards said to him. "Let me handle them."

"Gladly. We're leaving."

"I wish you wouldn't do that, Mr. Malone. I must speak with you. Can you hang around a bit, just until I've dealt with the police? A few minutes is all I need."

He considered her request. Why not?

Besides, he had a few questions of his own.

"Upstairs," Miss Mary said. "In the apartment. Wait there until they're gone. I'll help this young lady. I can say it was a robbery attempt gone wrong. She interrupted the thieves and scared them off."

Worked for him.

"Okay. Ian and I will be upstairs."

Kathleen had made a fast summation of Cotton Malone. Intense. Focused. And gutsy. He'd challenged her without a hint of concern.

She'd had no choice but to fire at the man in the store. He'd returned fire and she'd been concerned about people on the sidewalk. But either the man was the worst shot she'd ever seen, or he'd aimed high, intentionally not placing anyone in danger. Because of what she'd learned during the past few hours she gravitated to the latter conclusion, which only added to her mounting confusion.

The sirens grew loud and two Metropolitan Police cars stopped on the street, their lights flashing. Four uniformed officers emerged and rushed to the store. She already held her SOCA identification, which the lead officer seemed not to care about.

"Hand over your weapon."

Had she heard him right? "Why do I have to do that?"

"Someone tried to rob my store," the older lady said. "He had a gun. This woman stopped that."

Two officers guarded the front door. The other two seemed unconcerned about the possibility that any crime had occurred.

"The weapon," the officer said again.

She handed him the gun.

"Take her."

The other officer grabbed her arms and twisted both behind her back.

She whirled, reversed his grip, and slammed her knee into his stomach. He doubled forward and she kicked him hard, turning to deal with the other policeman.

"Down on the floor," the officer ordered, the gun now aimed at her.

She held her ground. "Why are you doing this?"

"Now."

The two other officers fled their position at the front door and appeared to her right. She debated challenging them, then decided three-to-one odds were not good.

"Hands in the air," the first officer said. "And down to the floor."

She complied and they secured her wrists behind her back with a plastic binding that dug into her flesh.

Then they wrestled her up and led her from the store.

MALONE FACED IAN AND ASKED, "WHERE'S THE flash drive?"

The boy smiled. "I didn't think you were fooled by what Miss Mary did."

She'd been far too eager to direct him to that metal box—and the color of the drive was not the same from earlier.

Ian stuffed a hand into his pant pocket and removed a drive, which he tossed over.

"Miss Mary is pretty smart, isn't she?" Ian asked.

That she was. And bold, too. With a gun to her head she'd managed to play out the bluff. "I imagine those men might be a little agitated when they realize they were fooled."

"That could be a bother. Can you look after Miss Mary?"

"You can count on it."

He studied the drive, recalling all that he'd read.

And the password-protected file—that had to be the prize.

"Why did you run at the café?" he asked Ian, not having received an answer when he inquired earlier.

"I don't like strangers. Especially those who look like police."

"I'm a stranger."

"You're different."

"What spooked you in the car that night, after you stole this drive?"

Ian's face froze as he considered the question. "Who said I was scared?"

"You were."

"Those two men would have killed me. I could see it on the old guy's face before I pepper-sprayed him. He wanted the drive, then he was going to kill me. I never faced that before." The boy paused. "You're right. It scared me."

He realized how hard that admission must have been, especially for someone who trusted no one and nothing.

"It's why I ran from you at the café. I saw men in coats with a look in their eye. I don't like that look. I never had anyone wanting me dead before."

"Is that why you left for the United States?"

Ian nodded. "I stumbled onto the bloke one day. He offered me a trip to the States and I thought it the best place to go. I could see he was trouble. But it was better than here. I just wanted to get away."

Downstairs was silent.

Malone found his phone and punched in the number provided to him earlier.

"I have Ian and the drive," he told Antrim. "But there's a problem." And he reported what had happened, including the appearance of a SOCA agent, name unknown.

"I don't like that the authorities are there," Antrim said. "Can you get out?"

"That's the plan. How's Gary?"

"Doing great. All quiet here."

"And where's here?"

"Not on this open phone. When you're ready to leave, call me back and I'll provide a meet point. And, Malone, the sooner the better."

"You got that right."

He clicked off the phone and wondered what was happening below.

So he stepped over to the window for a look.

KATHLEEN WAS LED OUTSIDE, HER WRISTS BOUND behind her back. People on the sidewalk were stopped by the officers so she could pass and she hated the looks on their faces, wondering who she was and what she may have done. What was the purpose of taking her into custody? Of humiliating her? She was a veteran SOCA officer who'd done nothing wrong.

They crossed the street and the rear door to one of the police cars was opened. She was helped inside, the door slammed closed. She sat in muted silence, people hustling back and forth outside. Through the tinted window she could see inside the bookstore and the older woman. None of the four officers had made any effort to speak to the proprietor, which only made her more suspicious.

What was this about?

MALONE WATCHED AS RICHARDS, HANDS BEHIND her back, was led across the street and stuffed into the back of a police car.

"Why did they take her?" Ian asked.

"Maybe she wasn't SOCA at all."

"She was real," Ian said.

He agreed. Everything about her had rung true.

Traffic on the narrow street had returned, cars edging along in both directions, the two police cars parked against the far curb, their lights still flashing. What should he do now? Obviously, there'd be no talk between them. Should he just hand over the flash drive to Antrim and go home?

Something was wrong.

How had the two men known to come here to this bookstore? How had a SOCA agent known to be here, one who knew his name?

And Ian's safety.

That was still in question.

A black sedan stopped in the street and a man stepped out. Older. Silver haired, dressed in a three-piece suit. He walked with the aid of a cane, crossing the opposite lane of traffic, rounding the police car that held the bound agent, then opening its rear door and easing inside.

IAN COULD NOT BELIEVE HIS EYES AS HE WATCHED the older man with the cane.

A face he would never forget.

"In the car that night, outside Oxford Circus," he said. "The man who wanted the flash drive. The man who told the other bloke to kill me. That's him."

Thirty-two

Kathleen should have known.

Sir Thomas Mathews.

Who sat beside her in the car.

"Will you never learn?" he asked. "Shooting up that store. People could have been killed."

"But they weren't. Odd, wouldn't you say?"

"Is there some implication in that observation?"

"Why don't you tell me?"

"I can see now why your supervisors warned me against involving you in this matter. **Not worth the bother,** I believe, was the phrase they used."

"The man had a gun. There was a woman and child inside. I did what was necessary."

"And where are Mr. Malone and Ian Dunne?"

"The Metropolitan Police didn't find them?"

Mathews smiled, a wiry grin that signaled more agitation than amusement. "You would think that, at some point, you might actually learn from your mistakes."

Actually, she had. "Where's Eva Pazan?"

"Dead, I presume. As you reported."

"You and I both know that is not the case. She doesn't exist. At least not at Oxford."

Mathews sat with both hands resting atop the ivory globe at the end of the walking stick. He kept his gaze out the car's windscreen.

"I underestimated you," he finally said.

"Does that mean I'm not as daft as you thought I would be?"

He turned his head and faced her. "It means I underestimated you."

"What are you doing?"

"I am protecting this nation. At the moment it faces a serious threat, one with potentially dire consequences. It's all quite remarkable, actually. Something that occurred five hundred years ago, and yet could still cause so much trouble today."

"I don't suppose you would share what that is?"

"Hardly. But let me make something clear. It is a real threat, one that cannot be ignored, one that your Blake Antrim has forced us, after many centuries, to finally face."

MALONE STARED AT IAN. "ARE YOU SURE THAT'S the man?"

"He had that same cane. A white ball on the end with markings on it, like a globe. Wore a suit just like that one he has on now. It's him."

The boy's revelation was even more incredible considering the man.

Thomas Mathews.

Longtime head of the Secret Intelligence Service.

While with the Justice Department he'd several times worked with MI6, twice dealing with Mathews. The man was shrewd, clever, and careful. Always careful. So his presence outside Oxford Circus a month ago, when Farrow Curry was killed, raised a ton of questions.

But one rose to the top.

"You told me that the man who forced you into the car was the same guy who pushed Curry into the train. That still true?"

Ian nodded. "Same bloke."

He realized that killing was part of the intelligence business. But outright murder? Here, on British soil, by British agents? The victim an employee of a close ally? And the head man himself personally involved? That raised the stakes to unimaginable levels.

Antrim was into something massive.

"He's been in that car with her awhile," Ian said.

He caught the concern and agreed.

"You think she's in trouble?" Ian asked.

Oh, yeah.

KATHLEEN REALIZED HER SITUATION WAS STRAINED. She was at Mathews' mercy.

"Miss Richards, this is a vital matter the prime minister himself is aware of. As you noted at Queen's College, laws have been bent, if not outright broken. National interests are at stake."

She caught what had not been uttered. **So why are you so much trouble?**

"You came to me," she said.

"That I did. A mistake, as I now realize."

"You never gave me a chance to do anything."

"That's where you are wrong. I gave you every chance. Instead, you ventured out on your own." He hesitated. "I am aware of your questions at Oxford to the security personnel and your visit to the master at the Inns of Court. You should have listened to me at Queen's College and did as told."

"You should have been honest with me."

He chuckled. "Unfortunately, that luxury is not available here."

She did not agree. "What now?"

"Rogues, such as yourself, eventually reach the end of the road."

"So I'm unemployed?"

"I wish it were that easy. Those national interests I mentioned, the ones we are protecting, require extraordinary measures to safeguard. Not ones I normally resort to within our borders, but here, I have no choice."

She did not like the sound of that.

"The last thing we can allow is for an uncontrollable soul, like you, to speak of this."

He reached for the door latch.

"You're going to have me killed?" she asked.

He opened the door and slipped out, quickly slamming it behind him.

A panic gripped her.

Two men immediately climbed into the front.

She wiggled her body across the backseat and kicked one of the doors. Then she realized the better play was the window and slammed her foot into it. One of the men curled over the front seat and a gun barrel was pressed into her stomach.

Her eyes found his.

"Stay still," he said, "or I'll shoot you right here."

MALONE WATCHED AS THOMAS MATHEWS EXITED the car and two men immediately entered. He saw Richards' head disappear then the soles of her shoes pound the rear window.

"She's in trouble," Ian said.

The street had again congealed with traffic.

The car wasn't going anywhere fast.

"Let's help her," Ian said.

"You have an idea?"

"I think so. At least it's always worked for me before."

KATHLEEN HAD NEVER EXPERIENCED THIS LEVEL of fear. She'd found herself in tight situations, her life endangered, but she'd always managed to dodge the worst consequences. Sure, there'd been repercussions with her bosses for the risks she took, but those came later, after the fact, when the danger had long passed.

This was different.

These men intended to kill her.

Inside a police car? She doubted it. But if she continued to resist, they just might shoot her here. So she gave the gun jammed into her gut the respect it deserved and stopped kicking.

"Sit up," the man ordered.

He dropped back into the front passenger seat but kept a watchful eye and the gun aimed at her. The car eased from the curb and merged with the two-laned traffic, vehicles in both directions stopping and starting on the narrow lane.

Be patient, she told herself.
Stay calm.
Wait for an opportunity.
But when? Where? How?
The prospects did not seem promising.

Thirty-three

ANTRIM STEPPED FROM THE WAREHOUSE INTO THE late night and walked another fifty yards, where he could talk in private and watch the door, making sure Gary Malone stayed inside. He called the phone number from the book in the Temple Church. Three rings and the same gravelly voice from the Round answered.

"I'm ready to deal," he told the man on the other end.

"And at so late an hour. Something must be even further wrong."

He resented the condescending tone. "Actually, no. Things are going good for me. Not so good for you."

"Care to enlighten me? Before I agree to pay five million pounds."

"I have an ex-agent, Cotton Malone, who's freelancing for me. He was one of the best we had, and he found what I've been searching for."

"Ian Dunne?"

It shocked him that the voice knew. This was the first time the name had been mentioned.

"That's right. Along with the flash drive. Since you know about Dunne, I assume you know about that, too."

"A correct conclusion. We thought we might acquire both the boy and the drive before you, but that was not the case. Our men failed in that bookstore."

"Now you know how I feel."

The older man chuckled. "I suppose I deserve that. After all, we have made a point to remind you of your lack of success. But since the drive is now secure, it seems fortune has smiled on us both."

Yes, it had.

"Now that you have decided to make a deal," the older man said, "there are two other matters that must be addressed."

He waited.

"The materials stored in the warehouse. We want them."

"You know about those?"

"As I told you in the church, we have been watching closely. We even allowed you to violate Windsor Castle and Henry's tomb."

"Probably because you were curious what might be there, too."

"We were only curious as to how far you might actually take all this."

"All the way." He wanted this man to believe that he was not afraid.

A chuckle came from the other end of the line. "All right, Mr. Antrim. We'll work under the assumption that you would have taken this **all the way**." The voice paused. "We have a precise inventory of what you have accumulated in the warehouse. So please make sure nothing disappears."

"And the other matter?"

"The hard drives."

Damn. These people knew all of his business.

"We know that you replaced the hard drives from the three computers Farrow Curry utilized, hoping to retrieve his encrypted data from them. We want those, too."

"This is that important?"

"You seek a truth that has remained hidden a long time. We want to ensure that it stays buried. In fact, we plan to destroy everything you uncovered so that this worry will never arise again."

He could not care less. He just wanted out. "I have one other matter, too," he said.

"Five million pounds is not enough?"

"That buys you the end of the operation, with no residual effects, no loose ends from Washington. It goes away, never to be restarted. That's what you wanted. I'll make sure it happens, taking the blame and the heat for the failure."

"Five million pounds buys a comfortable retirement."

"That's the way I look at it. Now, you want the physical evidence we accumulated and the hard drives. Okay. I get that. But there's a matter regarding the flash drive. Cotton Malone needs to be eliminated."

"We're not assassins."

"No, just murderers." He'd not forgotten about his man in St. Paul's or Farrow Curry. "Malone read what's on the flash drive."

"You know this?"

"He told me. So if you want this operation closed permanently, Malone has to go away. He has an eidetic memory, so he's not going to forget any detail."

Silence on the other end of the phone confirmed that the Daedalus Society had no good argument in rebuttal.

"Your point is made," the older man said. "Does Malone also have the flash drive?"

"He does."

"How do we find him?"

"I'll let you know where and when."

And he ended the call.

MALONE LEAPED FROM THE FIRE ESCAPE. IAN WAS already on the ground. They'd descended to the first floor and fled the building through the same open window the shooter had utilized earlier. No police were in the dark alley.

They rushed away from the bookstore.

Ian had told him what he had in mind. With his options limited he'd decided to trust the kid.

Besides, the idea could actually work.

At the end of the alley they merged onto a lit sidewalk thick with night revelers and approached an intersection. Two hundred feet to their right was the bookstore, where one police car still sat parked at the curb on the opposite side of the street. The second, the one with the SOCA agent inside, was stuck in traffic fifty feet away, waiting for the signal to turn green. He hoped no one in the car, besides Kathleen Richards, knew him or Ian.

Thomas Mathews was nowhere to be seen.

He signaled and, as Ian trotted off, he dissolved into the weekend crowd bustling before the pubs and shops, easing his way closer to where the police car waited in traffic. Ian was now across the street, on the far sidewalk, keeping pace.

The traffic signal changed to green and cars began to creep forward.

IAN LIKED THAT MALONE HAD LISTENED TO HIM.

He wanted to help.

The old man with the cane was dangerous. He knew that firsthand. The lady SOCA agent had flushed the other man from the bookstore, protecting both himself and Miss Mary.

So she was all right with him.

What they were about to do he'd done several times before. A two-person operation, sometimes even three, where the rewards could be great.

But so were the risks.

He'd seen it go wrong twice.

And hoped tonight would not be the third time.

MALONE WATCHED AS IAN DARTED IN FRONT OF the police car.

Brakes locked and tires grabbed pavement.

The vehicle jerked to a stop.

Ian collapsed, grabbing his legs, howling in pain.

Malone smiled. This kid was good.

The uniformed driver emerged, leaving the door open.

Malone crossed between two stopped cars, whirled his target around, and caught him under the rib cage with a right jab.

The man staggered against the car.

He found the man's shoulder harness and quickly freed the weapon. The officer seemed to recover but Malone gave him no chance, swiping the gun butt across the right temple, the body going limp to the street.

He aimed the gun at the windshield.

The passenger-side door flung open, but Ian was already on his feet and kicked the panel back, preventing any escape. Malone slid into the driver's seat and aimed the gun straight at the second officer, relieving him of his weapon.

"You ready to go?" he asked Richards, not taking his eyes off the policeman.

The rear door opened.

She climbed out, helped by Ian.

"Stay here," Malone told the officer.

He exited the car and recrossed the street. Ian and Richards, her hands still bound behind her back, joined him.

"I suggest we leave," he said.

Thirty-four

Ordinarily, Antrim would be concerned at the level of knowledge the Daedalus Society possessed and the extent of his security leak. Two agents and two analysts had been assigned to King's Deception. Two more freelancers had been hired separately for his dog-and-pony show with Malone. Two of the six were now dead. Had his man at St. Paul's been the problem? What were his last words? **Not supposed to happen.** He'd not understood then what that meant, but he did now. And he wondered. What **was** supposed to happen in St. Paul's?

It made sense that the dead man from St. Paul's could be the leak. But the other four were not beyond suspicion, especially the freelancers. He knew little about any of them except they were sanctioned for this level of operation.

But he didn't care.

Not anymore.

He was retiring. Played right, thanks to Farrow Curry's death, Operation King's Deception would simply end. Langley would definitely blame him and he'd fall on his sword, offering his resignation, which they'd accept.

Nice clean break for all involved.

There'd still be the matter of the dead man in St. Paul's, but how far could any investigation be pursued? The last thing Washington would want was more attention, especially from the British. Better to allow the shooting to go unexplained, the body unaccounted for. Only he knew the culprit, and he doubted anything could be linked to the Daedalus Society. The only connection was his cell phone, which was a throwaway, bought in Brussels under another name, which would soon be hammered to pieces, then burned.

Only the three hard drives remained.

So he left Gary at the warehouse with one of his men and drove to an apartment building on London's East End. The man who lived there was Dutch, a computer specialist used on other assignments. An independent contractor who understood that the obscene amounts of money he was paid not only compensated for services rendered, but also kept his mouth shut. He hadn't involved the CIA's own decryption specialists because they were too far away. And counter-operations did not routinely employ in-house people anyway. Its whole purpose was to operate outside the system.

"I need all three hard drives back," he told the man once inside the apartment with the door closed. He'd roused the man from a sound sleep with a phone call.

"This over?"

He nodded. "Plug's been pulled. The operation is ending."

The analyst found the three drives on a work-table and handed them over with no questions.

Antrim was curious, though. "Did you find anything?"

"I retrieved about sixty files and was working on the password-protected stuff."

"You read anything?"

The analyst shook his head. "I knew better. I don't want to know."

"I'll make sure the rest of your fee is deposited tomorrow," he said.

"You know, I could have retrieved the protected stuff."

That information grabbed his attention.

"You broke through?"

The man yawned. "Not yet. But I think I could have. I broke one of Curry's passwords and an encryption. I could get the others. Of course, all of us being on the same side made it easier than normal."

In order to satisfy the Daedalus Society he would have to turn over everything accumulated in the warehouse, along with the hard drives. But a little backup might be welcomed. Especially when dealing with a total unknown like Daedalus. Besides, after a year's worth of work he wanted to know what, if anything, had been found.

Curry was so excited on the phone that day.

He seemed to have made a significant breakthrough.

"Did you copy the three hard drives?"

The analyst nodded. "Of course. Just in case. You're going to want those, too, right?"

The man started to retrieve them.

"No. Keep working with the copies. I want to know what those password-protected files say. Call me the second you have them."

KATHLEEN HAD NEVER BEEN SO GLAD TO SEE A FACE as the one that had darted before the car, which she'd instantly recognized. She'd hoped Ian Dunne had not come alone and was relieved when Cotton Malone appeared. Now they were blocks over, just outside a closed souvenir shop. Ian carried a pocketknife, which was used to cut her plastic restraints.

"Why did you do that?" she asked Malone.

"You looked like you needed help. What did Thomas Mathews want with you?"

"So you know the good knight."

"He and I have met. In a past life."

"He told me you were an ex-agent. CIA?"

Malone shook his head. "Justice Department. An international investigative unit, for twelve years."

"Now retired."

"That's what I keep telling myself. Unfortunately, I don't seem to be listening. What's Mathews' interest here?"

"He wants me dead."

"Me too," Ian said.

She faced the boy. "That so?"

"He killed a man in Oxford Circus, then he wanted to kill me."

She glanced at Malone, who nodded and said, "He's telling the truth."

Then she faced the boy. "You took a chance walking in front of that car. I owe you."

Ian shrugged. "I've done it before."

"Really? Is it a habit of yours?"

"He's a street pro," Malone said, adding a smile. "One of them would stop the car and pretend he was hurt, another would steal whatever he could from inside. You were saying? Mathews wants you dead?"

She nodded. "I have apparently outlived my usefulness."

"Could it have been a bluff?"

"Maybe. But I didn't want to stay there and find out."

"How about we trade what we know. Maybe, among the three of us, we'll actually begin to make some sense out of all this."

Which they did.

She told Malone everything that happened, since yesterday, at Windsor and Oxford, adding her suspicions about Eva Pazan and what Mathews had told her in the car. Malone recounted his past twenty-four hours, which seemed about as chaotic as hers. Ian Dunne filled in what occurred a month ago at Oxford Circus.

She omitted only three things.

Her current state of SOCA suspension, her past connection to Blake Antrim, and the fact that she'd been led to the Inns of Court specifically to see Antrim.. None of that seemed necessary to reveal.

At least not yet.

"How did you find us at the bookstore?" Malone asked.

"Mathews sent me. He knew you'd be there."

"He say how he knew that?"

She shook her head. "He's not the most forthcoming individual."

Malone smiled "What's a SOCA agent doing working with MI6?"

"I was specially assigned."

Which was true.

To a point.

MALONE WASN'T ENTIRELY SATISFIED WITH KATHleen Richards' explanations. But they were strangers, so he couldn't expect her to provide everything at once. Still, she'd said enough for him to make a few decisions. The first involved Ian. He needed him out of the line of fire, back with Antrim and Gary, but he realized that maneuvering the boy to leave would be tough.

"I'm concerned about Miss Mary."

He explained to Richards that she was the older woman in the bookstore, then said, "Those men could come back, and we left her there."

"The Met are no help," Richards said. "They're working with Mathews."

He stared at Ian. "I need you to look after her."

"You said **you** would do that."

"I will, by getting both you and her to where Gary is."

"I want to go with you."

"Who says I'm going somewhere?"

"You are."

This kid was bright, but that didn't mean he would get his way. "Miss Mary looks after you when you need it. Now it's your turn for her."

Ian nodded. "I can do that."

"I'm going to contact Antrim and have him come get both you and her."

"And where are you going?" Richards asked.

"To get some answers."

The slip of paper Miss Mary had given him with the phone number was still in his pocket. **My sister. I spoke to her a little while ago. She'll take your call in the morning.**

"You going to let me tag along?" Richards asked.

"I'm assuming that you wouldn't take no for an answer."

"Hardly. But my SOCA badge could prove helpful."

That it could. Especially for toting weapons.

He handed her one of the guns he'd snatched.

"I have to make a call to Antrim and check on my son," he said. "Then I'm going to get a few hours' sleep."

"I'd offer my flat," Richards said. "But I'm afraid that's the first place they're going to look for me."

He agreed. "A hotel is better."

Thirty-five

SATURDAY, NOVEMBER 22
8:00 AM

MALONE FINISHED OFF SOME CEREAL AND FRUIT FOR breakfast. He and Kathleen Richards had spent a few hours at the Churchill, he on the pullout sofa bed, she in the bedroom. They'd arrived after midnight and a suite was all the hotel had to offer. Jet lag from the flight over had finally caught up to him and he'd fallen asleep almost immediately after lying down. But not before calling Antrim and making sure Ian and Miss Mary had arrived and that Gary was okay. Richards had told him that they still needed to have a chat, and asked him to keep her identity between themselves until after they talked. So he'd honored that request and not mentioned her to Antrim.

"I was sent by Mathews because of Blake Antrim," Richards said to him from across the table.

The Churchill's restaurant opened off the main

lobby with a wall of windows that overlooked busy Portman Square.

"He and I were once involved. Ten years ago," she said. "Mathews wanted me to use that relationship and make contact."

"Is Antrim a problem?"

He needed to know, since Gary was in his custody.

She shook her head. "Not that way. Not at all. Your son is fine with him. Now, if he were a girlfriend breaking up with Antrim." She paused. "Different story."

He thought he understood. "Doesn't let go gracefully?"

"Something like that. Let's just say our parting was memorable."

"And you agreed to reconnect with him?"

"Antrim is apparently into something that threatens our national security."

That grabbed his attention.

"Unfortunately, Mathews did not say how."

"So he sent you to the bookstore last night to connect with me and Ian. Let me guess. He wants the flash drive?"

She nodded. "Exactly. I don't suppose you would share what's on it?"

Why not? What did he care? This wasn't his fight. Besides, it wasn't all that much. "As amazing as it sounds, Antrim is trying to prove that Elizabeth I was actually a man."

He caught the surprise on her face.

"You must be daft. Mathews was willing to kill me over that?"

He shrugged. "It gets worse. Mathews was there when Farrow Curry was pushed into an Underground train. One of his men did the pushing. Ian saw that, firsthand."

"Which explains why he wants Ian Dunne."

"He's a witness to a murder, on British soil, which runs straight to MI6. Good thing Ian is in the safest place he can be, at the moment, with Antrim, whose interests are clearly opposed to Mathews'."

"Does Antrim know all of this?"

He nodded. "I told him last night on the phone. He said he'd keep a close eye on Ian."

Which also explained why Malone was still here. If not for the fact that Ian was clearly in trouble, he and Gary would leave today. But he could not simply walk away. He wanted to play this out a little longer and see if he could help the boy into the clear.

"Mathews provided me information," she said, "that points to some sanctuary the Tudors concealed that held their personal wealth."

"A point you omitted last night."

She nodded. "I'm sure you held back a few things, too."

He listened as she told him about what happened when Henry VII and Henry VIII died.

"I got the impression," she said, "that the flash drive might lead to this location."

But he could recall nothing from what he'd read that pointed the way.

"Go ahead and finish your breakfast," he said. "I have to print out some stuff."

"From the flash drive?"

He nodded. "A hard copy would be a good thing to have."

"We going somewhere?"

"To Hampton Court. There's somebody there we have to talk with."

KATHLEEN SURVEYED THE RESTAURANT. NOTHING and no one seemed out of the ordinary. Both she and Malone had switched off their cell phones, since Malone had said Antrim had tracked him through his. She was familiar with the technology and knew that a dead phone was a safe phone.

She wondered why they were going to Hampton Court. Who were they seeing? And what did it matter to her anymore? She'd lost two jobs in the past twelve hours. Not much left for her in this fight. Perhaps she should simply cut her losses and leave. But would that stop Thomas Mathews? Hardly. She still had to make things right with him. Had he seriously intended on killing her? Still difficult to say, but that Met officer would have shot her if she'd not quit resisting.

She finished her breakfast and waited for Malone, half listening to the murmur of other conversations. The waiter came and cleared the dishes, refilling her coffee cup. She didn't smoke, drink much, gamble, or do drugs. Coffee was her vice. She liked it hot, cold, sweet, straight—didn't matter, as long as it was full of caffeine.

"This is for you."

She glanced up.

The waiter had returned and held an envelope, which she accepted.

"The front desk brought it over. A woman left it for you."

Her mouth dried. Her senses came alive. Who would know she was here? She opened the envelope and removed a single sheet of paper, upon which was written in black ink.

CONGRATULATIONS, MISS RICHARDS. YOU ARE IN A UNIQUE POSITION. NO ONE IS CLOSER TO COTTON MALONE AT THE MOMENT THAN YOU. MAKE THE MOST OF THAT. SECURE THE FLASH DRIVE AND DETERMINE EXACTLY WHAT MALONE KNOWS. I GIVE YOU MY WORD, AS A KNIGHT OF THE REALM, THAT YOU SHALL BE REWARDED WITH A POSITION IN MY ORGANIZATION IF YOU ACHIEVE THIS RESULT.

OUR COUNTRY IS IN PERIL AND IT IS OUR DUTY TO PROTECT IT. YES, I REALIZE YOU ARE SUSPICIOUS OF ME. BUT CONSIDER THIS. I HAVE KNOWN YOUR LOCATION ALL NIGHT, YET DID NOT ACT. THE FACT THAT YOU ARE READING THIS MESSAGE IS PROOF OF MY CAPABILITIES. ALSO, KNOW THIS. DAEDALUS IS STILL OUT THERE AND THEY TOO ARE CAPABLE OF A GREAT MANY FEATS. THIS IS YOUR FINAL CHANCE AT REDEMPTION. MAKE YOURSELF USEFUL. IF YOU CONCUR IN THIS COURSE, NOD YOUR HEAD. ONCE YOU HAVE THE FLASH DRIVE, CONTACT ME AT THE NUMBER PREVIOUSLY USED.

TM

She could not believe what she'd read.

Thomas Mathews was watching.

She told herself to stay calm.

Doing what Mathews wanted entailed betraying Cotton Malone. But he was a stranger. Of no consequence. Sure, she'd shared a room with him last night and he seemed like a decent man. But national interests were involved. Her career was at stake. And not as a SOCA agent, but perhaps as a member of Secret Intelligence. People did not apply for jobs there. You were recruited, then proved yourself.

Like now.

Provided, of course, that Thomas Mathews' word—**as a knight of the realm**—meant anything.

She sucked in a breath.

Steeled herself.

And nodded her head.

Thirty-six

8:30 AM

ANTRIM PAID HIS ADMISSION FEE FOR WESTMINster Abbey and made his way into the massive church. He passed the black marble slab that marked the grave of the Unknown Warrior, then the choir with its famous wooden benches. Beyond the altar rails, in the sanctuary, was where British kings and queens were crowned. He caught site of a placard that identified the tomb of Anne of Cleves, Henry VIII's fourth wife, the only one smart enough to walk away. Over the past year he'd read a lot about Henry, his wives and children, especially Elizabeth. He once thought his own family dysfunctional, but the Tudors proved that there was always something worse.

Crowds were heavy—no surprise as it was the weekend and this one of those must-sees for any visitor to London with its Poets' Corner, the elaborate chapels, and the dust of so many monarchs. America had nothing to equal it. This church was a thousand years old and had borne witness to nearly everything associated with England since the Norman invasion.

He followed the ambulatory around the sanctuary to polished marble stairs that led up to the chapel of Henry VII. Built by the first Tudor king as his family's tomb, it eventually acquired the name **orbis miraculum,** wonder of the world, and rightly so. The massive entrance gates were of bronze, mounted to oak, embellished with roses, fleurs-de-lis, and Tudor badges. Inside was a three-aisled nave with four bays and five chapels. Wooden stalls lined both sides, above which were hung the banner, sword, helmet, and scarf of a Knight of the Bath.

Another one of those ancient groups.

Created by George I, revived by George V, now part of English lore as the fourth most senior order of chivalry.

Unlike the Daedalus Society.

Which seemed to exist only in the shadows.

Richly carved niches, each displaying a statue, encircled the chapel beneath fragile-looking, clerestory windows. But it was the ceiling that captivated. Fan-vaulted with tracery and pendants, suspended as if by magic, the fretted roof more like a fragile cobweb than carved stone.

At the far end stood Henry VII's tomb. A focal point and a contradiction. More Roman than

Gothic. Understandable, considering an Italian created it. Maybe seventy-five people were admiring the chapel. He'd made the call last night, after leaving the analyst's apartment, and was told to come at opening time, with the hard drives, which he carried in a plastic shopping bag. This place, with its many visitors, offered him some comfort regarding security, but not much. The people he was bargaining with were connected, determined, and bold.

So he told himself to stay on guard.

"Mr. Antrim."

He turned to see a woman, late fifties, short, petite, gray-blond hair drawn into a bun. She wore a navy pantsuit with a short jacket.

"I was sent to meet with you," she said.

"You have a name?"

"Call me Eva."

GARY HAD BEEN GLAD, LAST NIGHT, TO SEE IAN. And he instantly liked the older woman who introduced herself as Miss Mary. She was a lot like his dad's mother, who lived a few hours south of Atlanta in middle Georgia. He always spent a week with her in the summer, as his mother maintained a good relationship with her ex-mother-in-law. But it was hard not to like Grandma Jean. Soft-spoken, easygoing, never a bad word uttered.

They'd spent the night at the house where he and his dad had been taken yesterday. Ian had told him what happened at the bookstore, then after when they rescued the SOCA agent. Gary was concerned but pleased that his dad had handled things. Antrim had not stayed with them, but called to say that all was well with his dad.

"He's going to follow up on a few things in the morning," Antrim said. "I told him you were fine here."

"Did you mention anything about you and me?"

"We'll do that together, face-to-face. He's got a lot to deal with at the moment. We can tell him tomorrow."

He'd agreed.

Now they were back in the warehouse office, alone, the other two agents outside. Antrim nowhere around.

"Do you know where my dad was headed?" he asked Ian and Miss Mary.

Ian shook his head. "He didn't say."

Yesterday he'd wanted to talk more with Antrim, but that had not been possible. He had to talk about it. So he told them what he'd learned last night.

"Are you sure this is true?" Miss Mary asked him when he finished.

He nodded. "We took a DNA test that will prove it."

"What a shock this must be to you," she said. "Finding your birth father. Here."

"But at least you found out," Ian said. "Your mom should have told you."

"Perhaps she had a good reason for keeping that name to herself," Miss Mary said.

Gary, though, was sure. "I'm glad I know."

"And what will you do with this information?" Miss Mary asked him.

"I don't know yet."

"And where is Mr. Antrim?"

"He'll be here. He's a CIA agent, on assignment. My dad's helping him out."

But he was still concerned.

He recalled his parents' divorce, when his mother had explained how years of worrying had taken a toll. He'd not understood what she meant then, but he did now. The uncertainty of not knowing if someone you loved was in trouble worked on you. He'd only experienced it for a few hours. His mother had endured it for years. He'd been angry when his parents divorced, unsure exactly why they were **better off apart,** as they'd both made clear. Afterward, he'd witnessed firsthand the bitterness between them. Peace had only been made between his parents a month ago with all that happened in Austria and the Sinai, but he hadn't noticed much of a change in his mother. Still anxious. Still agitated. Still short-tempered.

Then he'd learned why, when she told him the truth.

And he hadn't made things easy for her.

Demanding to know his birth father's identity. She refusing. He threatening to live in Denmark.

Lots of conflict.

More than either of them was accustomed to.

He needed to speak with his mother.

And when Antrim or his dad returned, he'd do that.

ANTRIM DECIDED TO ALLOW EVA HER MOMENT and asked, "Why are we here?"

"Walk with me."

She led him toward the tomb of Henry VII.

"This is, perhaps, the greatest single chapel in all of England," she said, her voice low. "Henry is there, with his queen, Elizabeth of York. Below is the Tudor vault, where James I and the boy Edward VI lie. Around us are the tombs of Mary, Queen of Scots, Charles II, William III, Mary II, George II, and Queen Anne. Even the two princes of the Tower, Edward IV's sons, murdered by their uncle Richard III, are here." She turned left and stopped before one of the pointed arches, opening into a side bay. "And, then, there is this."

He stared at the black-and-white marble monument with its columns and gilded capitals. The woman lying atop, carved in stone, wore regal robes.

"The final resting place of Elizabeth I," Eva said.

"She died March 24, 1603, and was first buried over there, with her grandfather, in the vault beneath. But her named successor, James I, erected this monument, so she was moved in 1606, and has stayed here ever since."

They approached the tomb, along with a small crowd.

"Notice her face," Eva whispered.

He stepped close and saw that it was that of an old woman.

"The Mask of Youth had been imposed by law during the final years of her reign. No artist could depict Elizabeth except as a young woman. But here, on her grave, for all eternity, that mandate was not followed."

The effigy wore a crown and collar and held an orb and scepter in either hand.

"There are two bodies in this tomb," Eva said. "Elizabeth and her half sister, Mary, who reigned before her. By now, their bones have merged. Look here."

She pointed to a Latin inscription at the base of the monument.

"Can you read it?" she asked.

He shook his head.

"Partners in throne and grave, here we sleep, Elizabeth and Mary, sisters, in hope of the Resurrection."

"Odd, wouldn't you say? Burying them together."

He agreed.

"Both were monarchs, each entitled to her own tomb," she said. "But instead they rest together. Another clever move on Robert Cecil's part, allowing the remains to mingle. No one would ever know who was who. Of course, Cecil knew nothing of comparative anatomy and DNA testing. For his day, burying them together would have concealed everything."

"Has anyone ever looked inside?"

She shook her head. "This tomb has never been opened. Not even during the Cromwell years and civil war."

He still wanted to know, "Why am I here?"

The tourists moved on to another site.

"The Lords thought you might like to see how the secret you seek hides in so public a place."

"The Lords?"

"You met them, in the Round. They govern our society. Each acquires his post hereditarily, and have since 1610 when Daedalus was first started by Robert Cecil. You, of course, understand Cecil's connection to Elizabeth."

Yes, he did. He served as her secretary of state at the time of her death. "But Cecil died in 1612."

She nodded. "He was always a sickly man. The Daedalus Society was part of his legacy. He knew of the great secret, one nobody has really cared about until the last few decades. To your credit, you managed to delve deeper than anyone thought possible."

But he'd had help from that old CIA briefing memo, detailing what a few intrepid Irish lawyers had tried to do forty years ago.

Eva pointed at the tomb. "This monument to Elizabeth is the last one ever erected in Westminster over the spot where a sovereign was buried. Isn't it interesting that, though two are buried here, only Elizabeth is displayed on top? And as an old woman, directly contrary to her wishes?"

He was listening.

"Robert Cecil oversaw Elizabeth's funeral and her entombment. He then served her successor, James I, as secretary of state and personally oversaw the building of this monument. Again, only you would understand the significance of that fact."

He did. Farrow Curry had taught him about both Cecils, and especially Robert. He was a short man with a crooked back, who walked awkwardly on splayed feet. He had a penetrating gaze from black eyes, but was consistently noted as courteous and modest, with a **gentle sweetness.** Aware of his lack of physical attraction he became a man of two personalities. One as a public servant—prudent, rational, and reliable. The other as a private gentleman—extravagant, a reckless gambler, a lover of women, subject to prolonged bouts of deep depression. His popularity with the people waned the longer he served. Enemies amassed. His influence eventually slipped and his ability to produce results dimmed. By the time he died he was hated, called the Fox for unflattering reasons. He recalled a rhyme Curry had said was popular at the time.

Owning a mind of dismal ends
As trap for foes and tricks for friends.
But now in Hatfield lies the Fox
Who stank while he lived and died of the pox.

The fact that Cecil created a coded journal was puzzling, and seemed contradictory to his secretive nature. But, as Curry had explained, what better way for posterity to credit him than by leaving the only way to discover the secret's existence? Everyone who mattered would be dead. Control the information and you control the result. And the only one who would benefit from that would be Robert Cecil.

Eva led him to one side of the monument and pointed at another Latin inscription, which she translated.

"To the eternal memory of Elizabeth, queen of England, France, and Ireland, daughter of King Henry VIII, granddaughter of King Henry VII, great-granddaughter to King Edward IV. Mother of her country, a nursing mother to religion and all liberal sciences, skilled in many languages, adorned with excellent endowments both of body and mind, and excellent for princely virtues beyond her sex. James, king of Great

Britain, France, and Ireland, hath devoutly and justly erected this monument to her whose virtues and kingdoms he inherits."

He caught the key words.

Excellent for princely virtues beyond her sex.

More meaningless and unimportant phrases, unless you knew that Elizabeth I was not what she had seemed.

"Clever, wouldn't you say?"

He nodded.

"There is a lot about Robert Cecil that fits into that category. For a Renaissance man it was a sign of a superior spirit to wish to be remembered after death. If Cecil was nothing else, he was that."

Exactly what Curry had told him.

"By 1606, when this monument was placed here, Robert Cecil was the only person left alive who knew the truth. So he was the only one who could leave these markers."

She pointed to the shopping bag and he handed over the drives.

"Two and a half million pounds will be deposited within the hour into the account you provided earlier. Once your operation is officially over and the remaining evidence destroyed, the balance will be paid. We need that to happen within the next forty-eight hours."

"What about **my** other matter?"

"Where is Cotton Malone?"

He knew the answer, thanks to the call from

Malone last night asking him to take custody of Ian Dunne and the bookstore owner. He hadn't wanted to do either, but to keep Malone in the field he'd dispatched an agent to retrieve them.

"He's headed for Hampton Court."

Thirty-seven

9:10 AM

MALONE LOVED HAMPTON COURT. THE GARGANtuan redbrick palace, perched on the Thames' north bank, had stood for five hundred years. Once Templar land, then a possession of the Knights Hospitallers, the locale was eventually acquired by Thomas Wolsey, in 1514, at the peak of his power, just before he became archbishop of York, a cardinal, then lord high chancellor. But six years later Wolsey was falling from favor, unable to secure the divorce Henry VIII wanted from Katherine of Aragon. To placate the king, Wolsey gave Hampton Court to Henry.

Malone loved that story. Especially how the move failed and Wolsey fell victim to the same cruelty he'd meted out onto others, eventually having the good sense to die before he could be beheaded. Henry, though, loved his gift and promptly expanded the palace to suit royal needs. Centuries later, Oliver

Cromwell intended to sell it off for scrap but came to regard it as a welcome escape from the smoke and mists of London, so he lived there. The great architect Christopher Wren intended to raze it and build a new palace, but a lack of funds and the death of Mary II stymied his plan. Instead, Wren added a massive baroque annex that still sat in stark contrast to the original Tudor surroundings.

Here, at a crook beside the slow-moving Thames, in a thousand-room palace reminiscent of a small village, the presence of Henry VIII could still be felt. The stone pinnacles, the walls of red brick embellished with blue patterns, the parapets, myriad chimneys—all were Tudor trademarks. Here Henry built his Great Hall and added an astronomical clock, elaborate gateways, and a tennis court, one of the first in England. He refashioned the kitchens and apartments and entertained foreign dignitaries with unmatched extravagance. His wives were deeply connected here, too. At Hampton Court, Katherine of Aragon was cloistered away, Anne Boleyn fell from grace, Jane Seymour gave birth to the heir then died, Anne of Cleves was divorced, Katherine Howard was arrested, and Katherine Parr was married.

If any place was **of the Tudors** it was Hampton Court.

He and Kathleen Richards had traveled by train the twenty miles from central London. Richards had wisely suggested that her car, parked not far from Miss Mary's bookstore, could be either under surveillance or electronically tagged. The train offered anonymity and brought them to a station only a short walk from the palace, hundreds of others joining them on the trip. He'd made the call to Miss Mary's sister, who worked at Hampton Court, and she suggested a meeting, on site, just after opening time.

He was both perplexed and intrigued.

Elizabeth I, queen of England 45 years, regarded as one of its greatest monarchs . . . a man?

The thought was at first preposterous, but he reminded himself that both the CIA and British intelligence were keenly interested in the revelation.

Why?

Kathleen Richards was also more questions than answers. That Thomas Mathews wanted her dead was troubling on a number of levels. He agreed with her assessment that something was wrong with the "dead" professor at Jesus College, and how the shooter at the bookstore had not injured anyone with stray bullets. Theater? Maybe. He'd seen quite a bit of that during his time with Justice.

But to what end?

They followed a talkative crowd down a wide stone walk, through the main gate, and into a courtyard that led to another gate. Royalty had not lived here in two hundred years, and he knew the tale associated with the second gate. After Henry married Anne Boleyn he had her falcon crest and their initials entwined in a lover's knot carved into its ceiling panels. Soon after Anne's head was chopped off the king gave orders to remove all of the falcon crests and replace each **A** with a **J** for Jane Seymour, his new bride. In their rush to accomplish that task an **A** was missed, and still could be seen in the ceiling of the archway now above him.

Entering the paved courtyard beyond, he glanced up at the astronomical clock. An ingenious device, with the earth at its center and the sun revolving around it. In addition to the time of day, its outer dials reflected the phases of the moon and the number of days since the New Year. Even more clever was its ability to tell the high water at London Bridge, vital information in Henry VIII's time when the tides governed royal travel to and from the palace.

"You described yourself perfectly, Mr. Malone."

He turned to see a woman strolling toward them. Miss Mary? The same slim figure, silver hair, and congenial smile. An identical face, too, with little makeup, only a touch of lipstick.

"I see my sister did not mention we were twins."

"She left that detail out."

The resemblance between the sisters was uncanny, even down to the same mannerisms. She introduced herself as Tanya Carlton and told them both to call her by her first name.

"I live just across the Thames. But I operate the gift shop inside the Clock Court."

Even their voices were identical.

"I bet you two had some fun when you were young," he said.

She seemed to understand what he meant. "We still do, Mr. Malone. People have a difficult time telling us apart."

"You know why we're here?" Richards asked.

"Mary explained. She knows my interest with all things Tudor, especially Elizabeth."

"Is this real?" he asked.

The older woman nodded. "It just might be."

KATHLEEN WAS CAREFUL NOT TO ALLOW HER INterest to show. She assumed Mathews was somewhere nearby, watching. She'd acknowledged her consent back at the hotel, then sat quietly until Malone returned with three sheets that he'd printed in the Churchill's business center.

From the flash drive, he told her.

But he'd not mentioned where the drive was located. She had to assume he was carrying it, but to ask would be foolish.

Just be patient.

And wait for an opportunity.

ANTRIM WAS NOT HAPPY WITH HAVING IAN DUNNE and the bookstore owner around. They interfered with his time with Gary. He had only a few precious hours to make an impact and the fewer interruptions the better. But he could not have refused Malone's request. He needed the ex-agent dead, and for that to happen he needed him in the field. If the price for that was two more joining the party, then so be it. He'd keep them all together a little while longer. Once he returned to the warehouse, he'd have the woman and Dunne taken back to the safe house.

He'd left Westminster and stopped at a pub to grab a bite to eat. He'd also verified by phone that the one-half payment had in fact been deposited in a Luxembourg account. He was three and a half million dollars richer.

And it felt great.

Though it wasn't yet 10:00 AM, he decided some lunch would be good. He placed an order for a burger and chips and sat in one of the empty booths. A television played behind the bar, set to the BBC. Its volume was down, but something on the screen caught his eye.

A man.

And a tag scrolled across the bottom.

ABDELBASET AL-MEGRAHI SET TO BE RELEASED BY SCOTTISH AUTHORITIES.

He spotted a TV remote on the bar, quickly stepped over and increased the volume. The attendant gave him a glance but he told him he wanted to hear what the reporter had to say.

". . . Scottish officials have confirmed that Libyan terrorist Abdelbaset al-Megrahi, convicted of the 1988 Pan Am 103 bombing over Lockerbie, will be sent back to Libya. Al-Megrahi has been diagnosed with terminal cancer and, for humanitarian reasons, will be returned to Libya to live out his final days. Forty-three United Kingdom citizens died that day, December 21, 1988, including eleven on the ground in Scotland. On hearing the news, relatives were shocked. No word, as yet, on Downing Street's reaction. Sources close to the negotiations, ongoing with Libya, say that the release may come within the next few days. Reports of the release first came from Libya, confirmed by Edinburgh within hours. No one has, as yet, spoken publicly about the possibility, but no one has denied the reports, either. We will be following this closely and will provide additional reports, as they are obtained."

He muted the volume and returned to his booth.

He knew the drill. A leak designed to gauge public reaction. The news would be allowed to simmer a few days, then more would be leaked. Done correctly, in just the right amounts, the story's shock value would fade. Unless some groundswell of opposition rose, supported by a relentless media barrage, the story would eventually be forgotten as the world moved on to something else.

Allowing the leak also announced one more thing.

No turning back. Everyone was committed. The idea now was to get it done before anything could stop it. But what were the Brits receiving for their silence? Why allow it to happen? He still wanted to know the answer to that question, along with one other thing.

What was happening at Hampton Court?

Thirty-eight

KATHLEEN WALKED WITH COTTON MALONE AND Tanya Carlton. They'd paid their admission and entered Hampton Court, along with a swarm of other visitors. Two days ago she was home in her flat wondering what to do with the rest of her life. Now she was a clandestine operative working against a retired American intelligence agent, trying to retrieve a flash drive.

And all for a man who might have tried to kill her.

It didn't feel right, but she had little choice. Mathews' invocation of country had worked. Though her mother was an American she'd always felt deeply English, and her entire career had been devoted to upholding the law. If her country needed her, then her path was clear.

They were inside the Great Hall, another Tudor

hammerbeam ceiling overhead. Magnificent tapestries draped the towering walls, a nearby guide explaining to a group that they were commissioned by Henry VIII and hung here then.

"Henry built this room and entertained here," Tanya said. "In his time the bare wood of the ceiling above would have been painted blue, red, and gold. What a sight that would have been."

They passed through what was identified as the Great Watching Chamber, where the Yeomen of the Guard were once stationed to control access to the king's apartments. A narrow hall led to a gallery with cream- and olive-colored walls, broken by a chair rail, a threadbare carpet protecting the plank floor. One wall was lined with windows, the other with three paintings spaced between sets of closed doors. Tanya stopped before the center canvas, rectangular in shape, which depicted Henry and four other persons.

"This is quite famous. It's called **The Family of Henry VIII.** Henry is seated and, from his stout frame and face, it's clear that this was painted late in his life. His third wife, Jane Seymour, stands to his left. His heir and son, Edward, to the right. To his far right is his legitimate firstborn, Mary. To his far left, his legitimate secondborn, Elizabeth."

"It's all imaginary," Malone said. "Jane Seymour died at childbirth. She never lived to see Edward that old. He looks around seven or eight."

"Quite right. On both counts. This was painted,

we think, around 1545. Maybe two years before Henry died. It's a perfect example, though, of how the Tudors thought. This is a dynastic statement about Henry's legacy. His son, standing next to him, embraced by one arm, is his legitimate heir. His third wife, long dead, still a part of his memory. His other two heirs far off to the side. Present, part of the legacy, but distant. Notice the clothing on Elizabeth and Mary. The jewelry they wear. Their hair, even their faces. Nearly identical. As if it were unimportant to distinguish them. What was important was his son, who takes center stage with the king."

"This is the Haunted Gallery," Malone said, looking around.

"You know this place?"

"The chapel entrance is there, into the royal pew. Supposedly, when Katherine Howard was arrested for adultery she fled the guards and ran through here, into the chapel, where Henry was praying. She pleaded for mercy, but he ignored her and she was taken away and beheaded. Her ghost, dressed in white, is said to walk this hall."

Tanya smiled. "In far more practical terms, this was the place where courtiers would lie in wait to be seen by the king on his way to the chapel. But the tour guides love the ghost tale. I especially like the addition of the white gown. Of course, Queen Katherine was anything but pure."

"We need to know about what Miss Mary discussed with you," Malone said.

"I must say, I was fascinated by what she told me. Elizabeth was so different from Henry's other children. None of them lived long, you know. His first wife, Katherine of Aragon, miscarried several times before giving birth to Mary. Anne Boleyn the same, before producing Elizabeth. Edward, the son by Jane Seymour, died at fifteen. Henry also birthed several illegitimate children, none of whom ever reached age twenty."

"Mary, his firstborn, lived to be what—forty?" Malone asked.

"Forty-two. But sickly all of her life. Elizabeth, though, died at seventy. Strong until the end. She even contracted smallpox here, at Hampton Court, nine months into her reign and recovered."

More people entered the Haunted Gallery. Tanya motioned for them to hug the windows and allow the visitors to pass.

"It's exciting to have people so interested in these matters. They are not often discussed."

"I can see why," Malone said. "The subject matter is . . . bizarre."

"Blooming nuts," Kathleen said. "That describes it better."

Tanya smiled.

"Tell us what you know," Malone said. "Please."

"Mary said you might be an impatient one. I can see that now."

"You spoke to your sister again last night?" Malone asked.

"Oh, yes. She called to tell me what happened

and that you had seen to her safety. That I appreciate, by the way."

More people passed them by.

"Mary is the timid one. She runs her bookshop and keeps to herself. Neither one of us has ever been married, though mind you, there were opportunities for us both."

"Are books your passion, too?" Malone asked.

She smiled. "I am half owner of Mary's store."

"And Elizabeth I is a subject you've studied?"

Tanya nodded. "In minute detail. I feel as if she is a close friend. It's a shame that every written account that has survived describes her as not a womanly queen, but masculine in many ways. Did you know that she often spoke of herself as a man, dressing more in the style of her father or the lords of the time than the women? Once, at the baptism of a French princess, she chose a man as her proxy, which would have been unheard of then. When she died, no autopsy was allowed on her body. In fact, no one but a select few were permitted to touch her. During her life she refused to allow doctors to physically examine her. She was a thin, unbeautiful, lonely person with a nearly constant energy. Totally opposite of her siblings."

Kathleen pointed back to the painting on the wall. "She looks like a lovely young woman there."

"A fiction," Tanya said. "No one sat for that painting. Henry's likeness comes from a famous Holbein portrait that, at the time, hung in Whitehall Palace. As Mr. Malone correctly noted, Jane Seymour was long dead. The three children were almost never in the same locale. The painter drew from memory, or from sketches, or from other portraits. Elizabeth was rarely painted prior to assuming the throne. We have little to no idea what she looked like before age twenty-five."

She recalled what Eva Pazan had told her yesterday about the Mask of Youth. "And what she looked like later in life is in question, too."

"Goodness, yes. In 1590 she decreed that she would be forever young. All other images of her were destroyed. Only a few have survived."

"So it's possible that she may have died early in life," Malone asked, "as Bram Stoker wrote?"

"It would make sense. All of her siblings, save one, did. Elizabeth dying at age twelve or thirteen would be entirely consistent."

Kathleen wanted to ask about what it was that Bram Stoker wrote—Malone had failed to mention that nugget before—but knew better. The name was familiar. The author of **Dracula.** So she made a mental note to pass that information on to Mathews.

Tanya motioned for them to leave the Haunted Gallery, which they did through a doorway that led into the baroque sections of the palace—commissioned, she noted, by William and Mary. The tenor and feel of everything changed. Tudor richness was replaced with 17th-century Georgian plainness. They entered a room identified as the Cumberland Suite, decorated with chairs of richly patterned velvet, gilt-wood mirrors, candlesticks, and ornate tables.

"With George II, this was where his second son, William, the Duke of Cumberland, stayed. I've always loved these rooms. Colorful, with a playful feel."

Two windows opened from the outer wall and a pedimented alcove held a small bed covered in red silk. Baroque paintings in heavy frames hung from the walls.

"Mary said that you read Bram Stoker's chapter on the Bisley Boy," Tanya said. "Stoker was the first, you know, to actually write about the legend. Interestingly, his observations were largely ignored."

Kathleen made a further note. That book was obviously important, too.

"I brought something for you to see," Tanya said. "From my own library."

The older woman produced a smartphone and handed it to Malone.

"That's an image from a page I made this morning. It's an account from the day Elizabeth I died."

"I see you've gone high-tech," Malone said, adding a slight smile.

"Oh, these devices are marvelous. Mary and I both use them."

Malone increased the image size and they were able to read.

> To Lord Charles Howard Elizabeth confided that she was in desperate extremities.
>
> "My Lord," she whispered hoarsely. "I am tied with a chain of iron about my neck. I am tied. I am tied, and the case is altered with me."
>
> The Queen lay prone, speechless, cadaverous. All the life that was left in her was centered in one long, still beautiful hand which hung down at the side of her bed and which still made signs to express her wishes. The Archbishop of Canterbury had been summoned to pray for the dying woman, which he did with unction and enthusiasm. It was presumably the last sound that entered the queen's consciousness. A few hours later the breath left her body. At three o'clock in the morning of March 24, 1603 her body was pronounced lifeless. It was prepared for burial by her ladies and was not dissected and embalmed as was the rigorous custom in those days for sovereigns. The leaden mask and the waxen effigy were prepared, but no man's hand touched the body of Elizabeth after it was dead.
>
> She went to her grave with her secret inviolate.

She and Malone glanced up from the screen, both amazed.

"Quite right," Tanya said. "That last sentence is meaningless, except if you know, or suspect."

"When was this written?" Malone asked.

"1929. In a biography of Elizabeth that I have always admired."

What had the writer meant?

Her secret inviolate.

"Mary asked me specifically to show you that. She and I have spoken on this subject before. She always told me I was foolish to consider such a thing. But now I hear that the two of you may have new information on this great mystery."

Malone found the sheets he'd printed out at the Churchill, from the flash drive, and handed them to Tanya.

"Take a look at these."

Malone faced Kathleen. "Keep an eye out here. I have to make a quick call to Antrim."

She nodded her assent and Malone left the Cumberland Suite, heading back out to the busy gallery beyond. When he was gone Kathleen asked Tanya, "Are you saying that there is a real possibility that Elizabeth I was an imposter?"

"I have no idea. But I do know that the Bisley Boy legend is one of long standing. I think others, like the author of the passage you just read, suspected and wondered, but were too timid to say it. Bram Stoker, to his credit, did say it. Of course, he was ridiculed for his assertion. The press was not kind. **Tommyrot,** I believe, is how **The New York Times** described the theory in its review of his book."

"But is this real?"

"From these notes Mr. Malone has just given me it seems others now believe it to be."

She'd learned all she could.

Time to act.

She relieved Tanya of the pages. "I need these. I want you to wait here until Malone comes back."

"And where are you going?"

She'd already noticed that there was but one way in and out of these rooms—the same way Malone had gone. But there were fair numbers of people milling about. Enough for cover.

"This is official SOCA business."

"Mary said you were the impetuous type, as well."

"I can also be the arresting type. So stay here and be quiet."

Thirty-nine

ANTRIM MADE THE CALL FROM THE BOOTH IN THE pub. He'd eaten his burger and chips and decided on the direct approach. His watch read 10:40 AM, which made it 5:40 AM in Virginia. Of course the CIA operations center never slept and his call was routed to the director of counter-operations, his immediate supervisor and the only person besides the director of Central Intelligence who could give him an order.

"It's done, Blake," his boss said. "We tried to stop the Scots from going public, but they were hell-bent. The deal is made. They're just fine-tuning details while they warm up public opinion."

"That killer should die in jail."

"We all agree. Unfortunately, he's not our prisoner."

"I'll shut down things here."

"Do that. And fast."

"What about our fatality?"

"I don't see any way to investigate that without alerting the wrong people. It could have been the Brits. Probably was. But it could have been somebody else. Doesn't matter anymore. The death will have to stand as unaccountable."

That meant the family would be told only that the agent died in the line of duty, serving his country—not where, or when, or how, just that it happened—and a star would be added to the wall at Langley. Last he could recall there were over a hundred stars. Doubtful any name would be noted in the Book of Honor that sat just beneath. Only those agents who'd been compromised in death were recorded there. Not that he really cared. In fact, letting all of this fade away suited his needs perfectly.

"I'll have it ended by tonight," he said.

"This was crazy from the start," his boss said. "But hey, sometimes long shots play out."

"I did my best."

"No one is blaming you. Though I'm sure there will be some here who'll try. It was imaginative and, if it'd worked, a stroke of genius."

"It may be time for me to go," he said, laying the groundwork for what he had in mind.

"Don't be so hasty. Think about that. Don't beat yourself up so bad."

Not the reaction he'd expected.

"I hated losing this one," he said.

"We all do. We're going to look like idiots when that transfer happens. But it's one we're going to have to live with."

He ended the call.

Operation King's Deception was over. He'd first dismiss the two other agents, then shut down the warehouse himself, handing over everything to Daedalus. Then he'd receive the remainder of his money. By then, with any luck, Cotton Malone would have tragically died. Not a thing would point his way, so Gary would naturally gravitate to him.

They'd bond.

Become close.

Father and son.

Finally.

He thought of Pam Malone.

Screw you.

MALONE WAITED FOR HIS PHONE TO BOOT UP. HE'D intentionally left it off to avoid being tracked and realized that for the next few minutes he'd be vulnerable. But he had to talk to Stephanie Nelle. When he'd left the breakfast table earlier at the Churchill he'd not only visited the hotel's business center but also called Atlanta, waking her from sleep. Though he was no longer one of her twelve Magellan Billet agents he was doing the U.S. government a favor, and she'd told him last night, during their call about Antrim, that she was there if needed.

The phone activated and he saw that Stephanie had already called back, twenty minutes ago. So he answered her message with a return call.

"Where are you?" she asked.

"Waiting to see if I'm a fool or a genius."

"I hate to ask what that means."

"What did you find out on Kathleen Richards?"

"She is SOCA. Ten years. Good investigator, but a loose cannon. Does things her way. Lots of damage and destruction in her wake. Actually, the two of you seem perfect for each other."

"I'm more concerned with what she's doing here with me."

"Actually, that is a good question considering she's currently on suspension for an incident a month ago. I was told she was in the process of being fired."

"Learn anything relative to MI6's involvement?"

He'd retreated to a corner in the gallery among the people and the noise. He turned and faced the wall, speaking low, keeping a watch out behind him.

"Not a thing. But I had to be careful with those questions."

More people spilled in, heading from the Tudor to the Georgian portion of the palace.

"And you never said. Are you a fool or a genius?" she asked.

"That hasn't been determined yet."

"There's a complication here."

He hated that word. **Complication.** Stephanie's code for a total, outright, get-your-ass-kicked mess.

"The CIA called back a little while ago."

He listened as she described something called Operation King's Deception, presently ongoing in London, headed by Blake Antrim. She then told him about Abdelbaset al-Megrahi, convicted of the 1988 Pan Am 103 bombing over Lockerbie, and that the Scottish government had decided to send him back to Libya to die of terminal cancer.

"That decision was made public a few hours ago," Stephanie said. "Seems this transfer has been in the works for nearly a year. King's Deception was authorized to stop it."

"Which apparently failed."

"And they just pulled the plug on the operation. But they asked if you could take one last stab."

"At what?"

"That flash drive you have contains information that died with the man in the Underground station. He was a CIA analyst assigned to King's Deception. Langley knows you have the drive. Antrim reported that. They want you to see if it leads anywhere."

He could not believe what he was hearing. "I don't even know what **they** were looking for. How in the hell would I know if I found anything?"

"I asked the same question. Their answer was that the drive should tell you. If it doesn't, then there's nothing there."

"Is there a problem with Antrim? He has Gary **and** Ian Dunne."

"Not that I've been told. It's just that he wasn't successful with his operation and they'd like you to give it one last try. That prisoner transfer is going to be a PR disaster for us."

Which he knew, and the thought of it even happening made him angry. The son of a bitch **should** die in jail.

A tour group drifted in and moved toward his corner of the room. He used them as cover and kept watch on the doorway that led into the Cumberland Suite.

Kathleen Richards appeared.

She hesitated a moment, glanced around, seemed satisfied that all was clear, then darted right.

"I'm a genius," he quietly said into the phone.

"Which means?"

"That I was right about our SOCA agent."

"What are you going to do? The CIA wants to know."

He hadn't seen Stephanie in five months, not since France, back in June, when he'd helped her out. So much so that she told him, before leaving, that she owed him a favor. But he also recalled her warning.

Use it wisely.

"If I look into this, does this mean you owe me two favors?"

She chuckled. "This one's not mine. I'm just the

messenger. But if you can do anything to stop that murderer from being released, you'd be doing us all a favor."

"I'll get back to you."

"One last thing, Cotton. Antrim knows nothing of this request, and they want to keep it that way."

He ended the call and shut down the phone.

GARY SHOWED IAN AND MISS MARY THE ARTIFACTS in the warehouse. The older woman seemed fascinated with the books, some of which she noted were valuable 17th-century originals. He watched as she examined the special one beneath the glass lid with the green-and-gold pages.

"Your Mr. Antrim is a thief," she said. "This volume belongs to Hatfield House. I am familiar with it."

"Blake is CIA," he made clear again. "He's here on official business."

"Blake?"

"He told me to call him that."

He did not like the appraising look she gave him.

"I wonder what gives **Blake** the right to pilfer our national treasures? I have visited the library at Hatfield House. The attendants there would have gladly allowed him to photograph or copy whatever he may have needed. But to steal it? That is unforgivable."

Since his dad retired from the Justice Department, they'd spoken some about fieldwork. Its pressures. Demands. The unpredictability. A month ago he'd even experienced some of that firsthand, so he was not about to judge Blake Antrim. And what did this woman know, anyway? She owned a bookstore and could not possibly understand what intelligence agents did.

She lifted the glass lid. "Did Mr. Antrim explain what this is?"

"It's a codebook," he told her. "From a guy named Robert Cecil."

"Did he explain its significance?"

"Not really."

"Would you like to know?"

KATHLEEN HAD NOT SPOTTED COTTON MALONE, so she used the moment and embraced the crowd. Hopefully, the information on the sheets she'd obtained would satisfy Mathews. She felt bad about deceiving Malone, but she intended to do her job. Without questions.

She headed away from where they'd entered, deeper into the baroque portions of the palace, and came to what was identified as the Communications Gallery. One wall was lined with windows that overlooked a fountain court, the other was wood-paneled and dotted with doors and oil portraits. Decorative iron posts supported a red velvet rope that prevented visitors from approaching too close to the paintings. Surely there was an exit from the palace if she just kept moving forward.

A quick glance back and she saw a face she recognized.

Eva Pazan.

Back from the dead.

Ten meters away.

A man at her side.

A chill swept through her. Even though she was sure Pazan had not been killed at Jesus College, seeing the woman alive unnerved her.

Was she really part of Daedalus?

Or something else?

Pazan hung back, fifty people in between them admiring the gallery. No effort was made to approach.

Apparently, they were flushing her ahead.

With no choice she kept moving.

At the end of the gallery she decided to buy some time. So she grabbed the last two iron rails, swinging them both around and blocking the path crosswise. The people behind her stopped at the velvet rope, which caused traffic to congeal, her two pursuers trapped at the rear. She caught the quizzical looks, visitors thinking she was someone official and that they could not proceed any farther.

But she didn't hang around to explain, darting into a doorway and turning left, hustling down what was labeled the Cartoon Gallery. Fifty more people filled the gallery admiring the ambience. She caught sight of a video camera high in the corner at the far end, right of the exit doorway, and realized she was going to have to avoid those.

She heard a shout from behind and saw Pazan and her pal appear twenty meters away. She turned another corner and passed through one elegant room after another, identified as the Queen's bedchamber, dining room, dressing room, and drawing room.

In the last one she hooked right.

A man blocked her way.

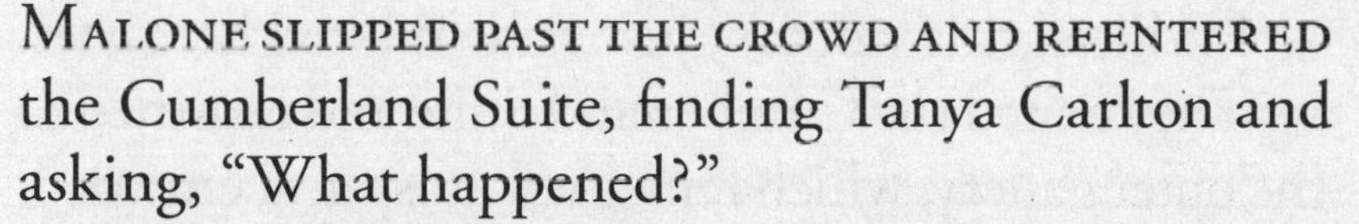

MALONE SLIPPED PAST THE CROWD AND REENTERED the Cumberland Suite, finding Tanya Carlton and asking, "What happened?"

"She snatched the papers you gave me and left. Threatened to arrest me."

He'd wondered what Richards would do, so he'd provided her an opportunity. True, she had the information from the unprotected files but, to his way of thinking, there wasn't much there.

Nothing at all, in fact.

"You don't seemed surprised," Tanya said.

"I'm not."

"I must say, Mr. Malone, I think you are a bit of a conjurer."

"Comes from getting burned by dishonest people."

"What will she do now?"

He shrugged. "Go back where she came from. Or at least we can only hope."

He had a new problem.

Helping the CIA.

"Mary told me that you and young Ian might have saved that woman's life," Tanya said. "Strange way for her to repay the debt."

"But not unusual in my former line of work."

"I managed to read the papers before she took them. Nothing there shocking. Not to me, anyway. But I have long been familiar with this legend."

"Let's get out of here. I'd like to talk with you some more, but with fewer people around."

"Then we must see the gardens. They are magnificent. We can have a lovely walk in the sunshine."

He liked this woman, just as he'd liked her sister.

They exited the Cumberland Suite and returned to the outer gallery, which remained noisy and crowded.

Two men appeared to their right.

Both faces he recognized.

The officers from the bookstore, out of uniform, dressed casually, both of whom appeared not to have forgotten what happened earlier. One had a nasty knot to his left forehead.

"We have a bit of a problem," he whispered. "Seems there are some people here who would like to detain us."

"That sounds dangerous."

"Can you get us out of the building?"

"I worked here for many years as a guide, before being assigned to the gift shop. I know Hampton Court intimately."

He pointed out the two problems. A small camera hung from the ceiling in one corner of the gallery. He'd seen others throughout. That meant people were watching, and dodging those electronic eyes would be tough.

"Angry-looking chaps," she said. "Who are these men?"

Excellent question. Probably MI6. "Some type of police."

"I've never been arrested before," Tanya said.

"It's not fun, and usually leads to a lot of other bad things."

"Then it is no bother, Mr. Malone. No bother at all. I can make our escape."

Forty

HENRY VIII FATHERED AT LEAST TWELVE CHILdren. Eight of those were either stillborn or miscarried, six by his first wife, Katherine of Aragon, and two by his second wife, Anne Boleyn. Three were legitimate. Mary, Elizabeth, and Edward, all mothered by different women. One was illegitimate, Henry FitzRoy, born in 1519 to Henry's mistress Elizabeth Blount. FitzRoy itself is a surname that meant "son of the king" and was commonly used by the illegitimate sons of royalty. Henry openly acknowledged FitzRoy, his firstborn child by any woman, calling him his worldly jewel, making him at age six the Earl of Nottingham, Duke of Somerset, and Duke of Richmond, the title Henry himself held before becoming king. He was raised like a prince in Yorkshire and Henry held a special place for the boy, especially considering, at the time, his wife, Katherine of Aragon, had failed to give birth to a son. FitzRoy was proof, in Henry VIII's mind, that the problem did not lie with him. Which was why he pressed so hard to have his marriage to Katherine annulled—so that he could find a wife who could actually provide him a legitimate heir.

Henry took a personal interest in FitzRoy's upbringing. He was made lord high admiral of England, lord president of the Council to the North, warden of the marches towards Scotland, and lord-lieutenant of Ireland. Many believe that if Henry had died without a legitimate son there would have been a Henry IX in the form of FitzRoy, his illegitimacy be damned. An act made its way through Parliament that specifically disinherited Henry's first legitimate born, Mary, and permitted the king to designate his successor, whether legitimate or not.

But fate altered that course.

FitzRoy died in 1536, eleven years before his father. The same tuberculosis that would eventually claim Henry's second son, Edward, at fifteen stole the life from FitzRoy at seventeen. But not before FitzRoy married Mary Howard. She was the daughter of the second most senior noble in England, her grandfather the most senior. They were joined in 1533 when Mary was fourteen and FitzRoy fifteen.

Henry VIII's older brother, Arthur, had died at age sixteen, never ascending to the throne. Henry always believed that too much sexual activity hastened his brother's death, so he forbade FitzRoy and Mary from consummating their marriage until they were older. That command was ignored and Mary became pregnant, giving birth to a son in 1534. The child was raised in secret by the Howard family, far from London, his existence concealed from the king, who never knew he'd become a grandfather.

Gary listened as Miss Mary told them about the wayward grandchild.

"He resembled his father, FitzRoy, in many ways. Thin. Frail. Fair-skinned. Red-haired. But he acquired his constitution from the Howard side of the family. Unlike Tudor offspring, he was healthy. Unfortunately, that wasn't the fate of Henry's second daughter, Elizabeth. Her mother, Anne Boleyn, was also a Howard, through her mother. But Elizabeth inherited her father's curse of early death and died when she was barely thirteen."

"I thought Elizabeth was queen?" Gary asked.

Miss Mary shook her head. "Her illegitimate nephew, Henry FitzRoy's son, assumed that honor in her place, after she died young."

The door to the warehouse squeaked open and Antrim stepped inside, walking across to the tables and introducing himself to Ian and Miss Mary. They hadn't met last night, Antrim's men handling everything.

"You, young man," Antrim said to Ian, "caused us a lot of problems."

"In what way?" Miss Mary asked.

"He stole a flash drive that held some important information."

"What could possibly be so important as to endanger a child's life?"

"I didn't realize his life was in danger."

"He has been fleeing for the past month."

"Which was his own fault, for stealing. But that isn't a concern any longer. In fact, none of it is. This operation is over. We're out of here."

"It's over?" Gary asked.

Antrim nodded. "The order I received is to close this down."

"What happens to these treasures?" Miss Mary said. "That **you** stole."

Antrim threw her a hard gaze before saying, "That's not your concern, either."

"And what about Mr. Malone and the other lady?" Miss Mary asked.

"What other lady?"

"The SOCA agent," Ian said. "The one who shot up the bookstore when those men came to get the drive."

"Malone didn't mention the agent was a woman," Antrim said. "And I've spoken to him twice."

"Maybe he thought that information none of **your** concern," Miss Mary said.

"Where is my dad?" Gary asked.

"Hampton Court."

"Then she's with him," Ian said.

"Did **she** have a name?"

Miss Mary nodded. "She showed me her badge. Kathleen Richards."

KATHLEEN GAVE THE MAN BLOCKING HER WAY NO time to react, tackling him to the floor, then planting her knee in his groin.

He cried out in pain.

She sprang to her feet.

The gun was still nestled against her spine, beneath her coat. People around her looked on in surprise, some retreating, giving her space. She withdrew her SOCA badge and displayed it.

"Official matter. Leave him be."

The man was still on the floor, writhing in pain.

A camera caught her eye.

Which was a problem.

She hustled through more baroque rooms, then turned and realized she was in a rear corner of the palace. A closed door to her right was marked EXIT, to be used only in an emergency.

This certainly qualified, so she yanked it open.

A stairway led down.

ANTRIM WAS STUNNED. HE HADN'T HEARD THAT name in ten years. Kathleen Richards was in the middle of this?

That could not be a coincidence.

"Describe this woman."

From the sound of it, she hadn't changed much.

"Malone and I saved the SOCA lady from the same men who tried to kill me," Ian said. "They were going to kill her, too."

"Tell me what you know."

He listened as Ian Dunne recounted what had happened in Oxford Circus and since. At one point he interrupted and asked, "Do you know who those men were in the Bentley the night my man died?"

"The old guy was named Thomas Mathews. That's what Malone called him when we saw him outside the bookstore last night."

Another stunner.

Head of the Secret Intelligence Service.

What in the world?

He listened to the rest of the story, and now he was panicked. What had seemed like a smooth ride out had just turned treacherous. Bad enough last night when Malone reported about a SOCA agent, but if his superiors learned that MI6 was directly involved there's no telling what they would do. He'd definitely be abandoned. Left on his own. Subject to arrest.

Or worse.

He had to speak with Daedalus.

They wouldn't want this to escalate.

Not at all.

MALONE AND TANYA REENTERED THE HAUNTED Gallery, following the same threadbare runner, except they were now moving against the flow of traffic back toward the Great Hall.

They fled the gallery and passed back through the Watching Chamber, entering a connecting space that led left, into the Great Hall, and right down to ground level by way of a staircase. Antlers adorned the plain white walls. Tanya avoided the Great Hall and headed straight for the staircase.

"This way, Mr. Malone. It leads to the kitchens."

He sidestepped more visitors.

A metal chain blocked the stairs with a sign that warned NO ENTRY, but they hopped over and started down.

One of the uniformed attendants stepped to the railing above and called out, "You cannot go there."

"It's quite all right," Tanya said. "It's just me."

The attendant seemed to recognize her and waved them on.

"They are quite diligent," Tanya said, as they continued to descend. "So many visitors every day.

People like to take a wander. But it helps to have worked here for twenty years."

He was grateful for both her presence and that he still carried the gun from earlier beneath his jacket.

They came to the ground floor and he heard footfalls behind them, on the risers, descending.

Surely the two fake cops.

"We must not dawdle," Tanya said.

They exited through a door with no latch. Too bad. A simple dead bolt would have been wonderful. But this was surely a modern fire escape from the first floor, once the path where prepared food in the kitchens was transported up to the Great Hall.

A long, narrow corridor stretched in both directions.

Visitors milled about.

Tanya turned left, then right, and entered the Great Kitchen. He recalled what he could about this part of the palace. Over fifty rooms, three thousand square feet, once staffed by two hundred people. Two meals a day were provided from here to the 800 members of Henry VIII's court. They were inside a spacious room with two hearths, a fire raging in each, the high ceilings and walls more whitewash. People were everywhere, snapping pictures, chattering, probably imagining themselves 500 years in the past.

"Come, Mr. Malone. This way."

She led them through the kitchen, stopping at a doorway that opened into a covered courtyard.

"Have a quick look and see if our minders are there."

He peered around the doorway's edge, allowing more tourists to pass, and caught sight of one of the men in the same corridor they'd originally entered after the stairway. Tanya had led them on a U-shaped path back around to it.

"One of them is behind us," she told him.

He turned and spotted the problem in the kitchen, who had not, as yet, seen them.

"Come on," he said.

They crossed the courtyard and he saw the man farther down the long corridor, moving away, but the one behind them would soon be here.

"We need to enter that doorway," Tanya said, pointing to the right side of the corridor, twenty feet away. If they hurried they could be inside before either man noticed.

"Why didn't we just go there first?" he asked her.

"And be seen? They were right behind us. This provided a little confusion."

He could not argue with that.

She scampered off with determined steps, disappearing inside the doorway.

He followed and quickly stepped down a short set of stone stairs to a brick floor into what once served as the palace's wine cellar, the vaulted ceiling supported by three columns. Windows allowed sunlight to pour through. Huge wine casks, lying on their sides, lined the outer walls and filled the center space between the columns.

Tanya headed for the chamber's rear and he spotted another set of steps that led down to a closed door. She descended and he saw an electronic lock, but she knew the code, punching it in, then beckoning him to follow.

The two men appeared behind them, at the entrance.

One reached beneath his jacket.

He knew what that meant.

So he reached faster and found his gun, firing one round to the right of the entranceway. The closed space and the stone walls amplified the shot to an explosion. People admiring the wine barrels winced, then realized he held a gun and panicked. He used the moment to hop down the steps and into the open doorway. Once inside, Tanya slammed the door.

"The electronic lock engaged," she said. "Unless they know the combination, they won't be following."

His best guess was the men were MI6, working for Thomas Mathews, maybe with the help of the Metropolitan Police. But who knew. So involving local security was not an impossibility.

He studied where they were, a pitch-black space, the air dank and moldy.

He heard Tanya moving and suddenly a flashlight switched on.

"The staff keep them here," she said.

"Where are we?"

"Why, in the sewers. Where else?"

KATHLEEN REACHED THE BOTTOM OF THE STAIRway, back on ground level. She exited into a long corridor, then immediately entered a narrow room identified as the Upper Orangery. The outer walls were one closely spaced window after another. Sunlight filled the chamber. People were here, too. Not as many as on the first floor, though.

If Thomas Mathews was on site, why wasn't he helping?

Instead, Eva Pazan was after her undaunted. It would not take long for her pursuer to realize that her target had fled downward. She was unsure which side Pazan was on, but after her experience at the bookstore she decided to trust no one.

Just leave.

But not by one of the exits, as those were certainly being watched.

Past the windows she spotted the magnificent Privy Garden, which stretched from the palace to the river.

That seemed the way to go.

She stepped to one of the windows and noticed no alarms. And why would there be? There were hundreds of windows in the palace, the cost and logistics of wiring every one incalculable. Instead, motion sensors were the way, and she spotted them inside the orangery, positioned high to catch anyone who might enter through one of the windows.

But those would be deactivated during the day.

She surveyed the room and saw none of the uniformed staff. So she unlatched the pane and hoisted the bottom panel upward.

The drop down was maybe two meters.

A few of the people nearby gave her a stare.

She ignored them and climbed out.

Forty-one

IAN WANTED TO KNOW MORE ABOUT HENRY FITZ-Roy. He'd been fascinated by what Miss Mary had said.

"This bloke, FitzRoy, married at fifteen to a fourteen-year-old girl?"

"That was quite common at the time. Marriages among the privileged were not for love. They were for alliances and the acquisition of wealth. Henry VIII saw the marriage to a Howard as a way to cement his relationship with that rich, powerful family. At the time his son's illegitimacy was not considered a problem, since Henry was so open in his affections."

"What did Henry's wife think about that?" Gary asked.

"She was not pleased. It created tension, and probably accounted for some of the miscarriages.

Katherine of Aragon was, in many ways, a fragile woman."

The American named Antrim had retreated into the office with the two other men. Though he'd just met the man, Ian sensed something not right about him. And he'd learned to trust his instincts. He'd immediately liked Miss Mary and Cotton Malone. Gary was okay, too, though the younger Malone had little idea how tough life could be. Ian had not known either his mother or his father, and probably never would. His aunt had tried to tell him about his family, but he'd been too young to understand and, after he left, too angry to care.

Gary had two fathers.

What was the problem?

He'd caught the caution in Miss Mary's eyes as she challenged Antrim. She had a bad feeling, too. That was clear. Gary, though, was too absorbed in his own problem to think straight.

That was okay.

He could think for him.

After all, Malone had told him to look after Gary.

"Eventually," Miss Mary said, "Henry VIII married a Howard, too. Her name was Katherine, and she became his fifth wife. Unfortunately, this Howard was promiscuous and the king had her head chopped off. The Howards never forgave Henry for that, nor did the king forgive them. The Howards began to fall from grace, no longer in favor. Mary Howard's brother, Henry, the Earl of Surrey, was executed for treason, the last person Henry sent to the block before he died in January 1547."

"How do you know all this?" Gary asked.

"She reads books," Ian said.

Miss Mary smiled. "That I do. But this particular subject has always interested me. My sister, especially, is knowledgeable about the Tudors. It seems Mr. Antrim shares our interest."

"He's doing his job," Gary said.

"Really? And what is his great interest in British history? The last I was aware, Great Britain and the United States were close allies. Why is it necessary to be spying here? Holed up in this warehouse? Why not just ask for what you want?"

"Spying is not always that easy. I know. My dad was one for a long time."

"Your father seems like a decent man," Miss Mary said. "And, I assure you, he is as perplexed by all of this as I am."

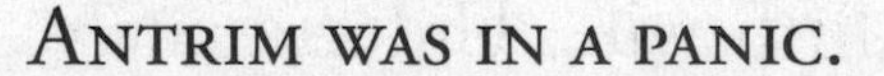

ANTRIM WAS IN A PANIC.

MI6 had been involved with Farrow Curry's murder? Which meant they were aware of Operation King's Deception. Daedalus said they killed Curry. Which meant either they or Ian Dunne lied.

But which one?

And now Cotton Malone was at Hampton Court with Kathleen Richards?

What in the hell was she doing there?

He had to know, so he dispatched both of his agents to immediately find out what was happening.

He stared out into the warehouse to where the woman and the two boys sat among the items that would shortly be destroyed. He was waiting for the call that confirmed Cotton Malone was dead. He'd tell the sad news to Gary himself. Pam would certainly then become involved, but he should be okay. Gary would not allow her to block him out a second time, and there'd be no other father to interfere. The thought of victory made him smile. He'd already alerted his investigator in Atlanta to step up surveillance. Taps on Pam's phone lines could prove useful in the months ahead. Information was the intelligence operative's greatest ally. The more the better. And with seven million dollars in the bank, there'd be no worries about financing.

But first things first.

Operation King's Deception had to end.

As agreed.

Gary was bothered by Miss Mary's criticism of Antrim. She had no right to say anything negative about him. And though her words seemed carefully chosen, he'd caught her meaning loud and clear.

Are you sure about this man?

As sure as he could be. At least Blake Antrim had not lied to him. Unlike his mother. And Antrim had not hurt his mother. Unlike his father. He still needed to speak with his mother. She wouldn't like what was happening, but she'd have to accept it. If not, he would follow through on his threat and move to Denmark. Maybe his dad would be more understanding.

"Henry FitzRoy," Miss Mary said, "and Mary Howard had a child. A boy. He was thirteen when his grandfather, Henry VIII, died in 1547. This boy was thin and pale, with red hair, like the Tudors. But strong and determined, like the Howards."

"Is this what my dad is looking into?" Gary asked.

"I don't know. I truly don't."

Gary had seen that Antrim was bothered by something. He'd quickly excused himself and hustled back to the office. A few minutes ago the two other agents left the building. Antrim was still inside the office. He needed to talk to him. Movement across the interior caught his attention.

Antrim called out, "I'll be outside. I have to make a call."

"Where's the toilet in this place?" Ian asked.

"Over here. The door right of the window into the office."

IAN DECIDED TO ACT.

He did not need the toilet. What he needed was to know what Antrim was doing. The American had seemed surprised to learn about the old codger, Mathews, being involved. And even more interested in the SOCA lady. Malone was at Hampton Court? He wondered why. He'd visited there several times, the free-admission courtyards and gardens attracting a horde of tourists with pockets to pick. He also liked the maze. One of its gate handlers had taken a liking to him and allowed him to roam among the tall bushes for free.

He walked toward where Antrim had pointed out the toilet. Then, after a quick glance back to make sure Gary and Miss Mary were talking, their attention not on him, he detoured to the warehouse exit door. Carefully, he turned the knob and eased open the metal slab, just enough to peek out. AnÔtrim was twenty meters away, near another building, a phone to his ear. Too far away to hear anything and too out-in-the-open to approach closer. But it was clear Antrim was agitated. His body stiff, head shaking while he talked.

He closed the door.

And thought about how he might get his hands on that phone.

Forty-two

MALONE GRABBED ONE OF THE FLASHLIGHTS HANGING from an aluminum rack, a modern addition to something that was clearly from long ago. He followed Tanya down a brick incline that ended at another tunnel, this one stretching left and right.

"Mr. Malone, you must count your blessings. Few get to see this. Two miles of culverts crisscross beneath the palace. State-of-the-art for its day. They brought water from sources miles away and removed the stinking waste from the toilets and kitchen rubbish." She pointed her light to the right, then swung it left. "To the River Thames. That way."

The stooped, narrow passage was tight and U-shaped, fashioned of bricks coated with white paint stained with mold.

"There's a tale that Henry's mistresses came in and out through here."

"You seem to enjoy those tales."

She chuckled. "That I do. But now we must hurry."

She turned left. The floor angled downward slightly, surely to allow gravity to assist with the flow toward the river. A trough filled the center, pooled with standing water, alive in places with movement.

"Eels," she said. "They are harmless. Just keep your steps to either side of the water."

Which he was already doing. He thought himself capable of enduring a lot. He'd flown fighter jets for the navy. He'd jumped from planes and dove deep beneath the ocean. With the Magellan Billet he'd faced guns and men who'd wanted to kill him. But one thing he truly detested was being underground. He'd found himself there more than he liked, and always forced his brain through it, but that did not mean he was comfortable being surrounded by solid earth. And with eels, for godsakes. Tanya Carlton, though, seemed utterly at home.

"You've been here before?" he asked, trying to take his mind off the situation.

"Many times. We were once allowed to explore these. They're quite remarkable."

He noticed protrusions from the walls, beyond dark holes, about two-thirds of the way up. He examined a few with his light.

"Drainpipes from above. They bring the rainwater down and out to the river."

He noticed that nothing around him was

screwed, nailed, bolted, or mortared. The bricks fit to one another without the benefit of any binding. If not for the fact that they'd existed here for five centuries he'd be a little worried.

"We'll pass the palace soon," Tanya said. "It's quite wide above us. Then we traverse the garden for a little while until there is an exit."

The kitchens were located on the palace's north side, the river to its south, maybe three football fields in between. A lot of being underground, as far as he was concerned.

"For a sewer, this doesn't smell that bad."

"Oh, my, this hasn't been used for waste in centuries. Can't go dumping in the river anymore. It's mainly for rainwater. There are staff that keep it cleaned out. The entrance we used was the way servants would come here in Henry's time to keep the flow from clogging."

She seemed at ease with all this intrigue, as if it happened every day. But he had to say, "I'm sorry for involving you in this."

"Goodness, no. Most excitement I've had in a long while. Mary said there might be an adventure, and she was so right. I once worked for SIS. Did Mary tell you that?"

"She left that detail out."

"I was an analyst in my younger days. Quite good, too, if I do say so." She kept plowing ahead. "Not as exciting as things you once did, but I learned to keep a cool head on things."

"I wasn't aware you knew what I did."

"Mary said you were an American agent."

He was forced to stoop as they walked. Tanya had no such problem. Their lights revealed only about twenty feet ahead of them.

More eels splashed beside his feet.

He heard a sound from behind.

Voices.

"Oh, dear," Tanya said, stopping. "I'm afraid the palace staff must be involved. They are the only ones who could open that door."

KATHLEEN DROPPED TO A GRAVELED PATH. THE Privy Garden stretched out before her, the space full of pyramid yews, round-headed holly trees, fall bulbs, statues, and annuals edged with box hedges. Graveled paths and wide avenues routed traffic through the natural décor.

She decided to head away from the river, to the rear side of the palace. From there she could double back to the train station and catch a ride somewhere. Anywhere but here. She needed to think. Make some decisions. Smart ones this time. The problem was she had only one place to turn. She was through at SOCA. Her employer would do nothing to protect her. The police were likewise useless. Only Thomas Mathews could help.

Or could he?

And if so, **would** he?

She followed the path to the palace rear and turned left.

Fifty meters away stood Eva Pazan and the same man from inside.

Both spotted her.

She turned and raced away, shielded by the corner of the building.

Ahead was nothing but more buildings with more cameras.

So she decided to go left, toward the river, into the riot of color and order that was the Privy Garden.

MALONE REALIZED THEY HAD A HEAD START BUT wondered where Tanya was taking them. The concern for what lay behind them was helping with his unease at being underground. He thought about just stopping and confronting their pursuers. If it was MI6, why would there be a problem? If the police, same thing? What was the worst that could happen? Arrest? Stephanie Nelle could get him out of that.

"It's just ahead," Tanya said.

He assumed the men behind them carried flashlights, but he could not spot their beams. In absolute darkness weak pencils of light carried only so far. But that meant their flashlights were not visible, either. Ahead he saw a ladder that led into an opening in the ceiling.

"Mr. Malone," a voice said from the blackness behind them, with an echo, which signaled distance. "One chance. Stop and wait for us."

Tanya grabbed the ladder.

He motioned for her to climb and fast.

"This is not your fight," the voice called out. "No need to die for it."

Die?

He grabbed hold of the metal ladder. Aluminum. Sturdy.

"Who are you?" he called out.

"That's not your concern."

He stared back into the darkness to his left. A pale glow, far off, to his right, revealed the emerging end at the Thames. Light appeared above him as Tanya opened a hatch in the short tunnel that led through the brick ceiling.

He climbed up, free of the tunnel below.

A bang.

Which startled him.

Then another.

More.

Gunfire raged through the passage beneath him.

Bullets ricocheted off the brick. He was above it, near the exit, but was concerned about a stray. He quickly emerged at ground level, slamming down a metal hatch.

"Thank goodness this portal is never locked,"

Tanya said. "It was added years ago as a safety measure."

He grabbed his bearings.

They were south of the palace, west of the great Privy Garden, a brick wall and tall hedges in between. The compact Banqueting House, which fronted the river, nearby. No people here, but he could hear voices beyond the hedges in what he knew were the Pond Gardens. He'd strolled through them before, where the fish served in the palace were once kept alive before heading to the kitchens.

"Was that gunfire I heard below?" Tanya asked.

"Afraid so. We need to disappear. Fast."

Things had just changed.

Those men came to kill him.

He studied the hatch and saw a lever that allowed it to be opened from the top side, which moved in conjunction with the one below. He looked around for something, anything, and found what he needed near a pond in the center of the garden. A walk leading to and from, bisecting the grass and the flowers, was paved with flat stones. He darted over and managed to dislodge one, about a foot square, from the moist earth. He carried it back and rested it beside the lever on the hatch.

A workable lock.

When anyone tried to turn it from below the stone would block its path.

"Where to?" he asked Tanya, since she'd obviously brought them here for a reason.

She pointed beyond the Banqueting House to the river.

"That way."

Kathleen kept moving through the Privy Garden toward the Thames. The manicured hedges were all low, offering no place to hide and no cover. A wide graveled path lined with knee-high box hedges led to a center fountain. Not many people here, but enough. Behind her Eva and her companion found the garden and headed her way.

She still carried her gun and was deciding how best to use it. She'd shoot her way out, if need be, but the lack of effective cover cautioned, for the moment, against that route. Statues dotted the grass to her left and right, large enough to offer some protection, but getting to and from them required crossing open territory.

So she kept hustling ahead.

Malone and Tanya passed around the Banqueting House. Tanya seemed to know exactly where she was going. They crossed a small lawn beneath bare trees and found an eight-foot-high brick wall that separated the palace grounds from a concrete walk bordering the Thames.

"I live just there, on the other side of the river, up a tributary," she said. "I motor to work every day in my boat."

He nearly smiled. This was a smart woman. He'd wondered how they were going to make their way off the hundreds of acres that surrounded Hampton Court. The simplest route? On the water. Which Tanya Carlton had known all along.

An iron-barred gate opened in the wall, it too with an electronic lock. Tanya punched in the code and they passed through.

"I come through here every day, so the grounds-keeper has provided me access. Years ago, I was given a key. I daresay things have progressed since then."

They turned and hurried down the pavement, a white, wooden rail guarding the riverside, heading away from the gardens. He spotted the railway station where he'd arrived across the river. He kept a watch out toward the brick wall, ready to find his gun. A handful of others were also strolling the path.

His mind was in full alert.

Somebody had wanted him dead.

And that underground passage, with its privacy, had offered them a perfect opportunity.

He needed to speak with Antrim.

As soon as they were away from here.

KATHLEEN SPOTTED A DECORATIVE IRON FENCE, the work of some talented blacksmiths, which allowed glimpses of the Thames through its gilded foliage. The fence on either side was over two meters high and spiked on top. Eva and her pal were closing fast. She spied left, then right, and noticed where the fence ended and a high brick wall that further guarded the perimeter began. What caught her attention was a set of steps that led up to another level of the garden, higher, nearly even with the top of the brick wall. It would be easy from there to hop onto the wall and jump down to the other side, where pavement bordered the Thames. She could either run like hell or make a swim for it.

She darted right and ran down the graveled path, then up the steps.

Behind her, she spotted Pazan now running her way.

She came to the top of the stairs and onto more gravel. She'd been right. The iron fence with its spikes ended and the brick wall began, lower here thanks to the new height. A simple matter to hop up and jump down the two meters to the other side. But before she could pivot onto the wall, two men appeared from ahead, guns in hand. Eva was now at the base of the stairs behind her, armed too.

"You will not make it," Pazan said. "Even if you

do, look down. There's nothing but open ground. We will shoot you dead before you get anywhere."

She glanced left. Where were all of the people? The gardens should be crowded on a beautiful Saturday morning. The few who'd been there before were now gone. And where was Mathews? Two large boats were tied to a concrete dock below her, but no one was in sight there, either.

Pazan climbed the stairs and approached. "I need your gun. Slow and careful. Toss it down."

She found the weapon and did as told. "Who are you?"

"Not who you think I am."

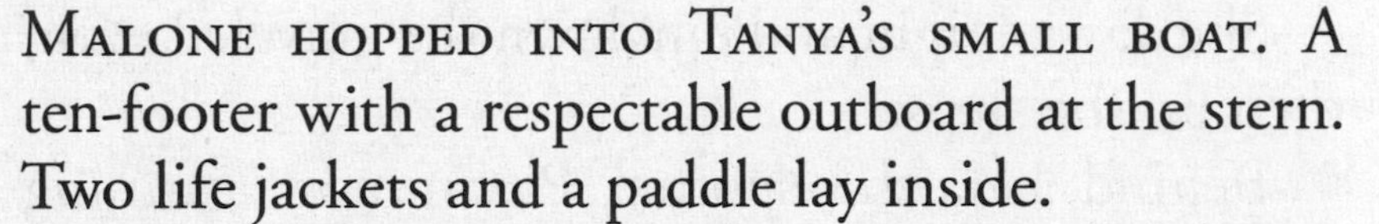

MALONE HOPPED INTO TANYA'S SMALL BOAT. A ten-footer with a respectable outboard at the stern. Two life jackets and a paddle lay inside.

"Never had to use any of those," she said. "Thank heaven."

"You want me to start the engine?" he asked.

"Goodness, Mr. Malone, I've been yanking the cord of that old bully for years. I'm quite capable."

He watched as she pulled the starter twice and the engine groaned to life. He untied the mooring line and she motored them away, turning back toward the palace grounds, heading downstream on the Thames.

"Stick to the far side," he said. "Just in case."

She maneuvered across the brown water, away from the palace. They were approaching another concrete dock, where two large boats were tied. He spotted a woman, standing atop the same brick wall that wound its way around to the Banqueting House. She stood where the iron fence that separated the gardens from the water ended and the high wall began.

Kathleen Richards.

Another woman, along with two men, stood to her right.

All held guns.

Richards was yanked down.

Tanya saw it, too.

"It seems Miss Richards has found some bother."

No question.

And, considering what just happened in that tunnel, he may have been totally wrong about her.

Part
Four

Forty-three

ANTRIM WAS BECOMING MORE AGITATED THE LONGER the conversation progressed. The same gravelly voice from Daedalus had answered his call and seemed to be enjoying the situation.

"Did you hear me?" he said into the phone. "The friggin' head of MI6 is involved in this. **He** killed Farrow Curry, not you."

"I heard you, Mr. Antrim. I simply choose not to believe what a street brat has told you. I know what occurred. We ordered it done."

"Kathleen Richards is SOCA. I know her. What the hell is she doing involved? Did you know about that, too?"

"That is new information. But I hardly see a

problem. Everything is about to end. You will have your money and be gone before dawn."

You got that right. Sooner the better.

"If Thomas Mathews **is** involved here," the voice said, "he could have been deceiving his listener with misinformation."

True. But there was still the matter of Cotton Malone.

"What happened at Hampton Court?"

"I am awaiting word on that right now. The last I was told, Mr. Malone was being herded to a favorable spot where he would be eliminated. All was progressing without a problem."

"I need to know when that happens."

"What's your interest in Malone?"

"I don't have one. You do. He read the drive. He knows things. He's your problem, not mine."

"I truly doubt that. You are not an honest man."

"Like I care about your opinion of me. You murder people. You can believe it or not, but MI6 is in this. That means containment is going to be a big problem. **Your** problem."

"Yours, too. Once known, I imagine your superiors will be wondering what you are truly up to."

"Which means this whole thing will blow up and you can kiss your little secret goodbye."

Silence on the other end signaled that he was right.

"Do you have Ian Dunne in your custody?" the voice asked.

"Safe and sound."

"Keep him there. In the meantime we need to speak, in person."

Like he was going to do that. He wasn't an idiot. He'd already realized that the safest course for Daedalus now would be to simply kill him, too.

"Not going to happen."

The voice on the end chuckled. "I thought that request would concern you."

He remained silent.

"All right, Mr. Antrim, to soothe your fears we'll meet in a public place. One with security, so you might feel more at ease."

"Why do we need to meet?"

"Because there is something you must see. And, look at it this way, you have Ian Dunne. He's your security. I'm sure you're about to hide him away in a spot only you know. He will be your insurance."

"Why do you want the boy? It's the flash drive you want."

"He's a witness to a death, and we detest loose ends."

Made sense.

Unfortunately, he was out of men at the moment, so he'd take Gary with him and leave Dunne and the woman in the warehouse.

A location Daedalus knew.

So what? Who cared?

Both of them dead and gone would be preferable.

A harsh reality hit home.

Daedalus **was** the only friend he had left.

"Name the place."

GARY STOOD WITH MISS MARY.

"You look troubled," she said to him.

"I need to speak with my mom or dad."

He knew this woman carried a cell phone. She'd taken a call last night.

She laid a gentle hand on his shoulder. "I was told not to use my phone again. We have to respect their wishes." She paused. "How difficult is this?"

"More than I thought it would be."

She pointed at the artifacts. "Mr. Antrim's stealing of all this makes me wonder about him."

"He's a spy. Sometimes you just have to do things. I had to do things a month ago."

"Bad things?"

He nodded. "I saved a friend's life."

"That was quite brave."

He shrugged. "I just reacted. He was in danger."

"You know little to nothing of this man who says he is your birth father. And you seem so like the man who raised you as a father."

"How do you know my dad?"

"I don't. I only know what I saw last night. He is a brave soul."

Yes, he was.

"Take this slow," she said. "Don't be rushed. A

lot of truth is coming toward you. Our brains can only absorb so much, so fast. Be careful."

She seemed sincere, which reminded him even more of his grandmother, whom he also wished was near.

"My mother could set it all straight," he said.

Miss Mary nodded. "And it's her job to do that."

"She made this mess."

"You have no idea what happened all those years ago."

"Have you ever been married?"

She shook her head.

"Then how would **you** know?"

"Because I have been in love. And I have broken a heart and had my own broken. Never, ever, is it only one person's fault."

He considered what she said and realized he may have hurt her feelings. "I'm sorry."

She smiled. "For what?"

"You're just trying to help."

"And not doing a good job at it."

He heard the metal door open at the other end of the warehouse and saw Antrim reentering.

"I still need to talk to my mom," he said again, his voice low.

"What will you say to her?"

He thought about that question, along with all of the conflict from the past couple of weeks, especially his mother's unbending position that she would never reveal a thing.

"I don't know."

IAN HAD WATCHED AS ANTRIM FINISHED HIS CALL and replaced the phone in his jacket pocket. Right side. Loose fitting. Perfect opportunity. He retreated to the toilet and waited until he heard the outer metal door open. He then exited, turned, and trotted back toward where Miss Mary and Gary stood.

Following Antrim.

He closed fast.

Five meters.

Two.

Antrim stopped and turned.

He bumped into the American, his right hand slipping into the jacket pocket and finding the phone.

He withdrew his hand.

All in a split second.

"Sorry about that," he said, adding his usual sheepish look. "I didn't see you."

Antrim smiled. "It's okay."

He dropped the hand with the phone to his side and used his leg to shield it until Antrim turned back around. He then slipped the phone into his back pocket and hoped it didn't ring. He'd have a tough time explaining why he stole it.

He kept pace with the American back across the warehouse.

"I have to go out," Antrim said. "Gary, would you like to come with me?"

"Sure."

Ian caught the look on Miss Mary's face. One that said she did not agree with Gary's decision, and that she knew what Ian had just done.

Yet she said nothing.

Which told him plenty.

"You two stay inside and you'll be fine," Antrim said. "We'll be back in a couple of hours."

He watched as Gary and Antrim headed for the exit door.

He stepped close to Miss Mary.

"I daresay," she whispered, "he could not care less what happens to us."

He agreed.

"What did you steal?"

He withdrew the phone.

She smiled. "Brilliant."

Forty-four

Malone stared as Kathleen Richards disappeared off the brick wall. Tanya was speeding the boat away, turning at a crook in the river, a long stretch of trees and grass now between them and Hampton Court Palace. If those men in the tunnel had come to kill him, had they also come to kill Richards? He'd set her up to see where she stood and she'd made her choice. But he wondered. Was that really **her** choice?

"I need to go back," he told Tanya, who sat at the stern, gripping the outboard's throttle.

"You think she might be in danger?"

"I don't know. But I have to find out."

He spied a golf course on the palace-side bank. The only course in England set within a royal park. He'd played it once long ago. He motioned and Tanya motored to shore and idled the outboard.

He faced her. "They'll identify you quickly. You can't go home."

"I wasn't planning to. I thought I would visit Mary."

"She's hidden away. What's your favorite London hotel?"

"Oh, my. There are so many I am partial toward. But my favorite is The Goring, in Belgravia, near Buckingham Palace. Such elegance."

"Go there and book a room. Whatever you want."

Her eyes came alive. "What a wonderful notion. What am I to do with this room?"

"Stay in it, until I come for you. If the hotel is booked out, stay in the lounge until I get there."

"They might not appreciate that."

He smiled. "Order food. They won't care then. If I have a problem, I'll call the front desk and leave a message." He reached into his pocket and found the flash drive. "Take this with you."

"Is this what Mary read?"

He nodded. "I'm counting on you to keep it safe."

"And I shall, Mr. Malone."

"Get off this river quick."

"Just ahead. I'll leave my boat and find a taxi."

"You have money?"

"I am quite well off, thank you," she said. "Fully capable."

He had no doubt this woman could handle

herself. She'd proven that. He hopped onto shore. The gun was still wedged in the crook of his back, beneath his jacket, its presence reassuring.

"Use cash," he said. "And stay put. Don't leave until I get there."

"I can follow directions. Just you don't go and get yourself hurt."

He wasn't planning on it. But he also wasn't betting against it.

Tanya engaged the throttle and glided the boat back out into the Thames. He watched as the motor's growl faded downstream.

A wide graveled path fronted the river. On its far side he spotted a tuft-grass fairway and headed toward it. Copses of oak framed the edges. He recalled the links feel to the course, with its undulating terrain and contoured greens framed by deep bunkers. He spotted a few players and some deer roaming, but kept moving toward the palace, about six hundred yards away.

He left the fairways and found a grassy avenue, lined on both sides with lime trees. A long canal stretched to his right. He recalled that there was a tree around here somewhere, Methuselah's Oak, that was said to be 750 years old. He headed toward an open iron gate at the avenue's far end, where the grass ended and another graveled path began. Tall, toadstool-shaped yews lined the path. Past the trees a fountain spewed water.

He slowed and told himself to be careful. He was

back in the vicinity of cameras. Visitors crowded the paths around him, admiring the lovely trees and flowers. The palace's baroque east façade rose ahead, many of the older Tudor buildings to his right, nestled tightly together. Beneath more ornamental yews trimmed bare eight feet up he caught sight of Kathleen Richards, flanked by two men, a woman leading the way. He stopped his advance and used the trees for cover, retreating behind one of the thick trunks.

Richards was led past the baroque section to the end of the Tudor buildings and a far corner, where the rear palace right angled back toward its main entrance. He crossed the graveled avenue to another tree for a better view and saw the entourage enter the last building. A pitched roof topped the long rectangle, a line of tall windows, side by side, stretching the length of the second floor.

Which he knew was not a floor at all.

He'd been inside that part of Hampton Court before.

Kathleen was powerless to do anything. Make a break? Nowhere to run. The gardens were like an open field, purposefully designed to offer clear lines of sight in every direction, which only worked to her detriment. She'd been led back from the riverbank, through the Privy Garden to the palace, then around to where a placard announced THE ROYAL TENNIS COURT.

They stepped through an opening in a brick wall and entered another portal, a louvered metal door closing behind them. She was led down a narrow corridor with plate-glass windows on one side that offered views into what was once Henry VIII's tennis court, one of the first ever in England. No one was around. No visitors or staff anywhere.

They turned at the end and proceeded down the court's short side to another door that led to what appeared to be storage and workrooms. She was motioned inside one that had a table and chairs along with a coffee machine, cups, and condiments. Some sort of break room.

Eva Pazan came inside with her.

The three men waited outside.

Pazan closed the door and said, "Sit down. We have things to discuss."

MALONE LEFT THE FOUNTAIN GARDEN AND headed for the entrance to the royal tennis court. There, beyond a brick wall that encircled the Tudor portions of the palace, he saw that the entrance to the court was shut, a sign announcing that the exhibit was closed.

He tried the latch.

Locked.

The door was metal with a set of thin and pliable louvers at the top and bottom, no glass or screen inside. He bent one of the slats in the top set up and the one beneath it down enough for him to reach inside and find a lock.

A twist and the door was opcn.

He readied the gun and slipped inside, closing and relocking the door.

A narrow passage stretched to his right, which paralleled the indoor court, windows above, lining both long sides, bathing the court with sunlight. Through glass, past what appeared to be seats within compact viewing booths, he saw a man in a three-piece suit standing at the net.

Thomas Mathews.

"Please, Mr. Malone," the older man called out. "Come in. I've been waiting for you."

Forty-five

Ian stared at Antrim's cell phone. He and Miss Mary had examined the most recent calls from the log, three to a number noted as UNKNOWN.

"The call he just made was also to an unrecorded number," he said.

"I wonder if it can be called back."

"You think we should?"

"I don't like or trust Mr. Antrim. He seems . . . preoccupied."

He agreed. "That last call got his knickers all in a twist. He didn't like what he was hearing."

"He will soon know that the phone is missing."

He shrugged. "I'll say it fell out of his pocket and I found it outside."

Miss Mary smiled. "That he will never believe, especially considering your background."

"Gary should not have gone with him."

"That's true. But neither you nor I could have stopped him. He wants to know his birth father. You can understand that."

They'd rarely discussed his past. That was what he liked best about Miss Mary. She didn't dwell on things that could not be changed. She was always positive, looking forward, seeing the best.

"I told him I never knew my dad. Or my mum. And it really doesn't matter."

"But it does."

She always could see through him.

"I'll never know them, so why get upset over it?"

"There are ways to find people," she said. "You know that whenever you are ready we'll try and find your parents."

"I don't want to know them."

"Maybe not now, but you will."

The phone vibrated in his hand.

Miss Mary took it from his grasp. "Perhaps we should answer." She studied the screen. "It's only an email alert, not a call."

"You're good with that thing."

She smiled. "I do a respectable business in book sales from the Internet."

He watched as she punched the screen a few times.

"It's from a gentleman who says he was successful in opening the files on the drive. Attached is the password-protected file, as requested."

Ian knew exactly what that meant. "There were

three files on the drive I lifted. One could not be opened without a password. Malone said experts could get around that."

"That they can," Miss Mary said. "I think I will forward this email to my own account."

He smiled. "That way we can read it?"

"I certainly hope so."

She punched the screen and waited a few moments. "There. It's gone. Now to delete the fact that I sent something from this phone. That should give us a little cover from Mr. Antrim noticing."

She handed the phone back to him.

"Place it in the office. On the desk. He can wonder how it found its way there."

"He'll never believe that."

"Maybe not. But we won't be anywhere around."

ANTRIM FOLLOWED A CORTEGE INTO THE ROYAL Jewel House, located within the walls of the Tower of London. The voice on the phone from Daedalus had proposed a safe location, and no better one could have been chosen. Security was everywhere, from armed guards, metal detectors, and cameras, to motion sensors. The hall was packed with tourists, all eager to view the British royal regalia of crowns, scepters, orbs, and swords proudly displayed behind wafers of bulletproof glass. No way to bring a weapon in here and little chance existed of anything bad happening since the entrance and exit were both heavily protected.

He felt a little better, but not much.

He wondered why this meeting was necessary.

He listened to one of the tour guides explaining how the Crown Jewels were, during World War II, moved from the nearby Wakefield Tower to an underground chamber beneath the Waterloo Barracks for secure keeping. There, a magnificent star-shaped case had been constructed and elaborately lit to showcase one of the last set of crown jewels left in the world. But the swarm of visitors that flocked each year to view them had proven too much for the cramped chamber and this larger location, back at ground level, was built.

Bright sunshine from outside was replaced by a cool semi-darkness. A wide corridor led forward, equipped with a conveyor-belt walkway designed to keep viewers moving. The cases themselves were illuminated with a combination of halogen floods and miniature lasers. The effect was magical. Another impressive British display.

Gary was outside, wandering the tower grounds. He'd told him not to leave the walled enclosure and that he would not be long inside.

"This is quite a spectacle," a female voice said from behind.

He turned.

And was shocked by who he saw.

Denise Gérard.

Gary roamed the grounds outside the Jewel House. He stopped at a sign that identified the magnificent White Tower, which dominated the enclosure. He'd already examined the Tower Green, near the spot where, one of the uniformed Beefeaters had explained, executions once took place. Two of Henry VIII's wives lost their heads there, as had Lady Jane Grey, a seventeen-year-old who ruled for nine days as queen until Mary, Henry VIII's first daughter, chopped her head off, too.

His gaze focused on the White Tower and he read the sign. Its hundred-foot walls of stone formed an uneven quadrilateral, defended on the corners by three square towers and one round one. Once the exterior had been whitewashed, giving the building its name, but now its stone glistened a golden brown. High above, the Union Jack fluttered in a light breeze. He knew that this ancient citadel was one of the symbols of England, like the Statue of Liberty was to America.

He wondered what they were doing here. They hadn't spoken much on the taxi ride over. Antrim had simply said that there were a few loose ends he had to deal with, which shouldn't take long, then they'd return to the warehouse and wait for his dad to call. He'd asked about speaking to his mother and Antrim had assured him that they would do that, too.

She needs to hear from you, Antrim had said. **Then I need to speak with her again, too. But we should talk to your dad first.**

He agreed.

That should be first.

The day was bright and sunny, the sky a deep blue. Lots of people were visiting the site. Antrim had bought them both tickets to the grounds, which he noticed also included access to the Jewel House, where Antrim had gone.

What was happening inside?

Why were they here?

He decided to find out.

ANTRIM WAS IN SHOCK. "WHAT ARE YOU DOING here?"

Denise looked gorgeous, wearing a pale blue bouclé skirt with a stylish jacket.

"I'm what they wanted you to see."

He was confused and cautious.

"Don't be so lame," she said. "I was there, in Brussels, watching you all along."

Could that be? "You're with Daedalus?"

A slight nod of her head. "I was sent to monitor your whereabouts. That I did, for nearly a year."

Shock filled him. He'd been the leak?

For a moment his gaze drifted through the polished glass a few feet away where he saw the four-hundred-year-old St. Edward's Crown, the same crown the Archbishop of Canterbury reverently placed upon a monarch's head, as echoes of **God save the king** or **queen** bounced from the walls of Westminster Abbey. What was happening here?

He gathered his thoughts.

"The whole thing with the man I saw you with in Brussels. Not real?"

"It was time that we parted ways. So we manufactured a reason that you would not question. We know how you become violent with women. There's quite a trail behind you, Blake. We needed you to move on, in your own way, where you would be comfortable."

"What would have happened? Another woman would have taken your place?"

She shrugged. "If need be. We decided to motivate you through other means."

"By killing my agent in St. Paul's?"

"The Lords wanted you to know then, and now, what they are capable of accomplishing. It's important you fully grasp the extent of their resolve."

She motioned for them to step off the conveyor belt, where they could linger for a few moments. He did, exhaling a short breath.

"These are symbols of what once was," she said.

"Reminders of a time when kings and queens held true positions of power."

"Everything between us was an act?"

She chuckled. "What else would it have been?"

Her dig hurt.

She motioned at the jewels. "I've always believed that the English monarchy did itself a great disservice when it gave up real power in return for survival. They allowed Parliament to rule in exchange for being allowed to stay kings and queens. That downfall started in 1603, with James I."

He recalled Farrow Curry's lessons. James, the first from the house of Stuart to sit on the throne, was a weak ineffectual man who cared more about pomp, circumstance, and pleasure than ruling. His first nine years were bearable, thanks to Robert Cecil's strong hand. But with Cecil's death in 1612 the remaining thirteen years of his reign were characterized by a calculated indifference, one that weakened the monarchy and ultimately led to his son Charles I's beheading twenty-three years later.

"Elizabeth I was the last monarch who enjoyed true power on the throne," she said. "A queen, in every way."

"Except one."

Denise pointed a slender finger at him, the nail manicured and polished, like always. "Now that's the wisdom and wit that you can, at times, express. Such a shame that, otherwise, you are a worthless excuse for a man."

She was taunting him. In total control.

And he was powerless to respond.

"What does Daedalus want?" he asked.

"Unfortunately, that seems to be changing by the moment. Your Cotton Malone escaped Hampton Court. He's still alive. Your two agents, though, were not as fortunate."

Now he realized.

He was alone.

"I work for the CIA. There are plenty more agents."

She seemed not in the mood for bravado. "But, sadly for you, none is here. We want Ian Dunne."

"You can have him. He's at the warehouse, which you obviously know about since your head Lord told me what's in it."

"That we do. But I wonder, Blake. I know that deceitful part of you. I've seen it. I told the Lords that you are not a truthful man. So, one chance, one opportunity. What else is there we don't know about?"

And he suddenly realized that he may have a trump card, after all.

The copies of the hard drives.

No one had mentioned those.

"You know all I know."

She stepped back toward the conveyor belt. Before leaving she stopped and brushed her lips across his cheek. A gentle gesture. More for the benefit of the people around them.

"Dear Blake," she whispered. "We already have the copies of those hard drives you left with the man you hired. I told the Lords you would lie."

She stepped onto the conveyor.

"Take care, darling," she said, blowing him a kiss.

Forty-six

MALONE APPROACHED THOMAS MATHEWS. THEY stood at center court, the spacious rectangle that enclosed them lit from a bright sun pouring through the upper windows.

"Haven't seen you since London," he said. "What? Seven years ago?"

"I recall."

"So do I," Malone said, and he meant it. Mathews had nearly cost him his life.

"Tell me, Cotton. Did you come back solely for Kathleen Richards?"

"So you've been watching?"

"Of course."

"You make it sound like that was a mistake."

The older man shrugged. "All depends on your point of view."

He could tell Mathews was treading lightly, unsure of what, where, and when, at least insofar as things related to a retired American agent right in the middle of an active CIA operation.

"You attacked my men outside the bookstore," Mathews said.

"Your men? I don't recall anyone saying that. But it seemed like Richards needed help." He paused. "And she did."

"The question is why you felt the need to render assistance."

But he had no intention of volunteering an answer to that inquiry.

"Henry VIII himself played tennis here," Mathews said. "It is said he learned of the execution of Anne Boleyn while engaged in a match. A different game from what we call tennis, but nonetheless exciting."

Everything around him, though encased within an ancient shell, was more modern, the refurbished court still in use today. Real Tennis the game was called, which utilized not only the floor but also the walls and ceiling to maneuver the ball over the net.

"It's impressive how things so old can still be relevant today," Mathews said, tossing out more bait—which, this time, Malone decided to snag.

"Like that Elizabeth I may have been male?"

The older man appraised him with cool eyes. This was one of the world's premier spymasters. Even Stephanie Nelle spoke of him with awe and respect. He vividly recalled their encounter from seven years ago. Mathews had proven formidable. Now Malone was, once again, within the Englishman's sights.

"I was saddened by your retirement," Mathews said. "You were an excellent operative. Stephanie must miss your talents."

"She has plenty of other agents."

"And modest. Always modest. That I recall about you, too."

"Get to the point," he said.

"You may not think the fact that Elizabeth I was an imposter would matter four hundred years later but, I assure you, Cotton, it does a great deal."

"Enough to kill Farrow Curry?"

"Is that what the boy said?"

He nodded. "That's why you want him. Not the flash drive. You want the boy. He's a witness. You want to shut him up."

"Unfortunately, these circumstances demand extraordinary actions. Ones, normally, I would never sanction. Especially here, on British soil."

"You won't harm a hair on that kid's head. That much I guarantee."

"From anyone else I would take that as unsubstantiated bravado. But I believe **you**. What about your own son? Is his life equally valuable?"

"That's a stupid question."

"It may not be, considering who has him, right now, as we speak."

He stepped close to Mathews. "Enough bullshit. What the hell is going on here?"

KATHLEEN SAT AT THE TABLE INSIDE THE SMALL room, Eva Pazan positioned near the door.

"That show at Jesus College was for your benefit," Pazan said. "A way to invest you in the situation."

"Seems like a waste of time. You could have just told me. Who pressed my face to the floor with their shoe?"

Pazan chuckled. "I knew you wouldn't like that. That was my colleague outside the door. We thought a demonstration of violence, coupled with an attack on me, might keep you focused. Unfortunately, we were wrong."

"Are you part of the Daedalus Society?"

"It doesn't exist."

That did not surprise her. "Thomas Mathews created it. Right?"

Pazan nodded. "If you realized that, why run inside the palace?"

"It's hard to be sure of anything around here. And, the last I checked, Mathews wanted me dead."

Her captor smiled. "The intelligence business is not like yours. You hunt down facts and work for convictions. We have no courts. No prisons. This is life or death, and success is the only thing that matters."

"Mathews created Daedalus for Antrim, didn't he? He wanted to manipulate him, but could not reveal SIS was involved."

"Smart girl. We've been watching Antrim and his operation since the beginning. We needed a way to get close, without any fingerprints. A fictional, ancient society seemed the best way and, lucky for us, Antrim bought it. But you didn't."

"Is that a compliment?"

"Hardly. You've proven quite a chore. We thought you might be helpful with Antrim, but things have changed."

And she knew why.

"Because of Cotton Malone."

MALONE WAITED FOR AN ANSWER TO HIS QUESTION, but decided to add, "I know about the release of Abdelbaset al-Megrahi."

"Then you also know that your government doesn't want that to happen. They want us to stop Edinburgh."

"Which you can."

He'd been thinking about why that wasn't possible. And only one explanation made sense.

Oil.

"What is it you want from the Libyans? What's the deal they offered for al-Megrahi's release?"

"Let's just say that we could not ignore their humanitarian request."

"So you sold out for oil price concessions?"

Mathews shrugged. "This nation has to survive. We are stretched, as is everyone, to the limit. We have something they want. They have something we want. It's a simple trade."

"He murdered British, Scottish, and American citizens."

"That he did. And he will soon meet his maker and atone for those sins. He has terminal cancer. It isn't like we are releasing him to live a long life. If letting him go gains us more over the long run, then why not do it?"

He now understood why the British government had stayed silent. If any hint of a trade leaked out, the repercussions would be enormous. The headlines devastating. GREAT BRITAIN DEALS WITH TERRORISTS. The American position was, and always had been, no negotiations with terrorists, period. That didn't mean no talking with them, just use the talk to buy enough time to act.

"Cotton, look at this another way. After World War II, both the United States and Britain utilized former Nazis. Your space program was born from them. Your aviation and electronics industries excelled. Intelligence services expanded. All thanks to ex-enemies. Postwar Germany was governed with their open assistance. We **both** used them to keep the Soviets off base. Was that any different than here?"

"If it's such a great idea, why not tell the world what you're doing?"

"I wish things were so black and white."

"That's another reason I got out. I can actually do what's right now."

Mathews smiled. "I always liked you, Cotton. A man with courage and honor. Unlike Blake Antrim."

He said nothing.

"Antrim has been running a CIA-sanctioned operation called King's Deception, here, on British soil, for over a year now. He's been systematically stealing our national treasures. Delving into our secrets. Over the past forty-eight hours he sanctioned the violation of Henry VIII's tomb in St. George's Chapel. He used percussion explosives to crack away the marble slab, then rummaged through the royal remains. He also accepted five million pounds to end Operation King's Deception. Half has been paid, another half will soon be owed."

That grabbed his attention. "How do you know that?"

"Because I engineered the payment. I created a mythical opponent. The Daedalus Society. And convinced Antrim of its sincerity."

"By killing Farrow Curry?"

"You know that course is necessary, at times. Curry became far too knowledgeable. He learned our secret. I thought his death would solve the problem. Unfortunately, we had to kill another."

That he knew nothing about.

"One of Antrim's operatives who provided us information in return for compensation. But he became greedy and wanted more than he was worth. So we used his death as a way to ingratiate ourselves directly to Antrim. Which, I must say, worked. All was fine, and would have been, but for your appearance."

"So you sent men to kill me in the tunnel?"

Mathews glared at him.

"That I did."

KATHLEEN WAS BECOMING ANGRIER BY THE SECOND.

"Malone was an unknown," Eva said. "His presence has accelerated everything. But this is going to end here, now, today."

"What is going to end?"

"The Americans want us to do something. We don't want to do it. So they decided to find some leverage. A way to force us to do what they want. Thankfully, we've prevented that. All that remains is to tidy up the mess."

"Meaning me?"

"And Antrim."

She thought fast and knew what to do.

"I don't want to die."

She stared straight at Pazan.

"I'll do whatever you want. But I don't want to die."

She stood from the chair.

Her eyes watered as she kept her gaze locked on the other woman.

"Please. I'm begging you. I don't want to die."

Pazan stared at her.

"I'm tired of running. I get it. You people have the upper hand. I'm in your custody. Can't you contact Mathews and tell him I did what he wanted?" She found the sheets in her pocket. "I stole these from Malone. It's what was on the flash drive. I was bringing them to Sir Thomas when you cornered me. I didn't know you were working with him. How could I?"

She crept closer, the pages leading the way in her trembling left hand.

Pazan reached out to take them.

She handed them over. "I just don't want any more problems."

Her right hand balled to a fist and swung up to meet Pazan's left jaw in a perfect uppercut that propelled the woman backward off her feet. She grabbed one of the chairs and pounded Pazan's midsection. The SIS agent crumpled forward. A rage consumed Kathleen. She swung the chair upward, then down on Pazan's head, sending her captor to the floor, not moving.

The door burst open.

The other man who'd been with Pazan inside the palace rushed ahead, the one who'd planted his foot on her face, a gun leading the way.

She whirled the chair into the hand with the gun, jarring the weapon away.

Another swing into his chest stopped him cold.

Raising the chair and slamming it down, she surely cracked the man's skull, dropping him beside Pazan. She tossed her weapon aside, then found the gun and the pages.

"That makes us even," she whispered to the man on the floor.

Forty-seven

IAN STOOD BESIDE MISS MARY AS THEY BOTH READ the file emailed to Miss Mary's phone.

A translation of Robert Cecil's journal.

I WAS TOLD OF THE DECEPTION BY MY FATHER. He called me to his deathbed and revealed something extraordinary. When but a child of thirteen, the young princess Elizabeth had died of fever. She was buried in the garden at Overcourt House, inside a stone coffin, with no ceremony, the Lady Kate Ashley and Thomas Parry the only two privy. Both feared for their lives, as King Henry VIII had charged them with his daughter's safety. Henry was then unhealthy, enormous in girth, his temperament violent and irritable. Though Elizabeth's death came from no person's fault, both Ashley and Parry would

have paid for the girl's death with their lives. But circumstances worked in their favor. First was that the father rarely saw the daughter, his mind consumed with other matters. Thankfully, there were two wars ongoing, one with Scotland, the other with France. Henry's fifth wife, Katherine Howard, had been unfaithful and was executed for infidelity. Then the wooing of Katherine Parr and his marriage for a sixth time became overriding. The perpetual worry for his legitimate son and heir, Edward, along with his own mortality, further dominated the final years of his reign. So his second daughter was relatively unimportant.

It helped that Elizabeth lived an isolated life away from court, the Lady Ashley, her governess, her only constant companion. With the child dead something had to be done and it was Thomas Parry who proposed a solution. Parry was aware of the illegitimate grandchild of Henry VIII, the son born to Henry FitzRoy and Mary Howard. Until his death in 1536 FitzRoy had stood in great favor with the king. Henry had known of FitzRoy's marriage to Mary Howard, and approved, but he had forbidden the consummation of the marriage until the young lovers were older. This decree was ignored and a son was born to them in 1533. Of this, Henry was never told.

Parry proposed a substitution. The unknown

grandson for the deceased princess. Lady Ashley thought the idea absurd and said they would all lose their heads. But Parry lay forth five principles in making his case. First, the imposter must have the likeness of the princess, as to create no suspicion. This was satisfied since the grandson had inherited the Tudor fairness of skin, the red hair, and the features of his grandfather. Second, there must be a familiarity with the circumstances of the princess's life. The grandson had been raised in isolation by the Howards, but had been taught of his noble heritage. Third, there must be both education and knowledge similar to what the princess received. This, too, had been provided, the boy schooled in geography, mathematics, history, mechanics, and architecture. Fourth, a skill in the classics and foreign tongues was important. The grandson could speak and write French, Italian, Spanish, and Flemish. Finally, there must be an ease of body and the courtliness of a highborn. This the grandson possessed in abundance, as the Howards were the wealthiest in the realm.

Thomas Parry traveled to where the grandson lived and proposed his plan to Mary Howard, the boy's mother, who readily agreed. Thirteen years had passed since her husband died. She'd lived a quiet life, though her brother, the Earl of Surrey, was one of Henry VIII's favorites. But unbeknownst to Parry controversy was brewing within the Howard family. Mary's father had petitioned the king for permission to marry his daughter to Thomas Seymour. That permission was granted, but Mary, aided by her brother, refused. Her brother then suggested that she seduce the king and become his mistress. But she refused, considering the thought repulsive. She and her brother became estranged after that, and she eventually testified against him when Henry tried and executed him for treason.

Mary agreed with all that Parry proposed, breaking off relations with her family. She never remarried and died in 1557, a year before her son was proclaimed queen of England. I inquired of my father how the deception was maintained since, surely, some Howard relations would have wondered what happened to the boy. But after the Earl of Surrey's execution in 1547, the Howards harbored a great hate for Henry. If any of them were privy to the deception, none ever revealed a thought. Mary Howard, herself, knew of her family's quest for royal power and, while resenting her father and brother, surely took amusement in how she, the lowly daughter, obtained what no male Howard had managed.

My father was told of the deception shortly after Elizabeth was proclaimed monarch. He was called to the new queen and found her alone in her chambers. She was twenty-five years old and had, for many years, worn the robe of a nun's habit. She had, in every way, been overlooked in favor of her brother Edward, her sister Mary, and her father's many wives. She had become accustomed to being forgotten. Now she was queen. She stood that day full of height and with a steady gaze, providing a commanding presence. Rings, fans, jewelry, embroidery, pearls, and lace garnished her attire. Her hair was yellowish red, the skin a dead white. Her eyes were set deep in their sockets and their stare was aggressive.

"My Lord Cecil, you are a man whom we have long trusted, both for your wisdom and your discretion."

My father bowed at the compliment.

"We desire for you to serve as principal secretary. We have no doubt that you shall be faithful to us all. But there is something we must discuss."

It was then that the imposter revealed himself, explaining all that I have detailed so far. My father listened with a patience that would characterize his life, realizing that he had been offered a unique opportunity. This man, of Tudor blood, but not born to reign, was now queen. No one, save for Lady Ashley and Thomas Parry, knew the truth. To expose the imposter would be to plunge the kingdom into civil war, as many would lay claim to the empty throne. Nothing would be gained by that. For the past twelve years this man had existed as a woman and no one was the wiser. He had become, in every way, Elizabeth Tudor. For my father to now know this would bind them together until one or both left this world. What was being proposed was not a position at court, but a partnership bound by a great deception.

My father stared up from his deathbed, watching as I absorbed all that he had said.

"I told the imposter that I was his servant and will forever remain such."

I said nothing.

"The queen is aware that I am passing on this great secret. She desires for you, my son, to serve her as I have done. I too want that."

"My only wish is I can be merely half the faithful servant that you have been."

My father died a day later, August 4, 1598, and I was summoned to the queen. She was sixty-five years old that day, her cheeks hollow, the high forehead, long chin, and aquiline nose exaggerating the gauntness of a dry and wrinkled face. Most of her teeth were gone. A curled red wig covered her head and an enormous lace ruff wrapped her neck. She stared at me with the same gaze that had kept England safe the past forty years.

"What say you?"

I dropped to one knee and bowed my head. "I shall serve, as my father served, faithful and forever loyal."

"Then it shall be, Lord Secretary. Together, we will keep England strong."

"He knew the truth," Miss Mary said.

They were inside an Underground station, blocks from the warehouse. Miss Mary had wanted to see what the file contained, so they'd lingered and allowed two trains to pass through while they read.

"This confirms everything I've ever heard of the Bisley Boy," Miss Mary said. "Most of the legend's tale seems true."

Ian watched as she sat silent for a moment.

Few people were inside the station.

"This could change everything," she muttered.

"How?"

"Mr. Malone needs to know."

Her phone vibrated. Both their gazes locked on the screen.

"I don't recognize that number."

"Answer it," he told her.

She did.

"Goodness, Tanya. I was just thinking of you," Miss Mary said into the phone. "I need to speak with Mr. Malone. Is he still with you?"

Silence came as Miss Mary listened, then said, "We will be right there."

The call ended.

Her face was solemn. Concerned. He waited for her to explain.

"There was trouble at Hampton Court. People tried to kill my sister and Mr. Malone. We have to go."

Forty-eight

Antrim exited the Jewel House into the midday sun. He'd felt safe inside, with its crowds, cameras, guards, and metal detectors. Back out in the open he was less secure. The enormous White Tower dominated the center of the walled enclosure, surrounded by more walks, grass, and trees.

Terror engulfed him.

Denise an agent for Daedalus? Playing him the whole time? Apparently Operation King's Deception had been known from the start. But what sparked all of the recent attention from British intelligence? Thomas Mathews supposedly killed Farrow Curry. Not Daedalus. Or had he?

His gaze searched for Gary. He'd told the boy to wait outside. Thousands of people filled the walks, here to see one of England's signature sites. A hundred feet away, through the crowd, stood Denise Gérard and another man.

Both headed his way.

Now he realized.

This was where they wanted him.

He decided to head back inside the Jewel House, but the line of people waiting to enter was too great, and forcing his way through would only draw the attention of guards. He could seek their help, but that might not be wise in the long run. The better play was to get the hell out of there.

But what about Gary?

No time.

The boy was on his own.

There was nothing he could do. He'd told Gary to stay close. Searching for him was not possible. So he kept walking around the White Tower, working his way back toward the exit gate in the outer brick wall. He reached for his phone, deciding to see if Denise's claim about his two agents at Hampton Court was true. Was he actually alone now? But the unit was not in his pocket. He felt around, but it was gone. He shook his head and kept walking, zigzagging a path through the congestion. A quick glance back confirmed that Denise and her companion were still there.

He'd never faced one of his lovers, after the fact, like this. The partings were always on his terms, clean and permanent, which was the way he liked it. He didn't enjoy smacking women, and usually harbored deep regrets afterward. But sometimes it was just necessary. It was all his father's fault—but he doubted Denise would care about that.

This operation, which was once business, had turned personal.

More so than he'd ever experienced.

GARY FLED THE JEWEL HOUSE.

He'd had trouble leaving, hanging back in the crowd, trying not to be seen by Antrim or the woman. They'd stood off the moving conveyor, near one of the display cases, talking. He'd merged with the mass of people, keeping watch, staying hidden, Antrim clearly agitated with her.

What was going on?

And where was Antrim now?

He stepped left, passing the length of the Jewel House, then turned right, following the pavement between the White Tower and what signs identified as the hospital and Armory. A tower and part of the outer wall loomed fifty yards ahead, signaling the outer perimeter. The path he was following angled back to the right, passing before the White Tower's impressive forward façade. A stretch of emerald grass formed a front lawn, upon which roamed a few black birds, which the visitors were photographing. Beyond, on the pavement that paralleled the far side of the White Tower, he spotted Antrim.

Heading for the exit gate.

Why?

Then he saw the woman from inside the Jewel House, a man at her side, following. His gaze drifted left, to the exit gate, where he spotted two more men. Standing. Waiting. Their heads pointed straight at Antrim, who seemed more concerned with the two following him than what lay ahead.

Now he knew.

Antrim was clearly in trouble.

He had to help.

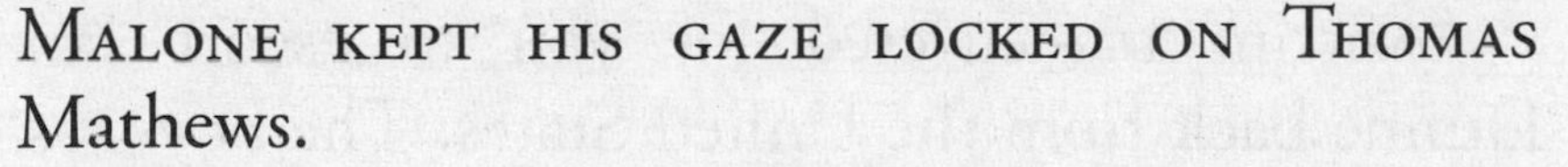

MALONE KEPT HIS GAZE LOCKED ON THOMAS Mathews.

"I had no choice," Mathews said. "Ordering those men to shoot you was not done with any joy."

He kept his cool. "Yet you still did it."

"Your presence has altered everything," Mathews said. "And not in a positive way."

"You killed two Americans."

"One was greedy. The other smart. But as you know, in this business such moves are quite common. I have a task to perform, and there is little room to maneuver."

"You want to kill Ian Dunne, too. No. That's not right. You actually have to kill him."

"Another unfortunate circumstance."

He needed to leave. Every second he lingered only increased the risk that he was already taking.

"Do you have any idea why Antrim involved you?" Mathews asked.

The older man stood tall and straight, his signature cane held by the right hand. Malone recalled something about a bad hip, that had progressively worsened with age, necessitating the walking stick.

"He asked me to find Ian Dunne. That's all."

A curious look came to Mathews' face. "That's not what I mean. Why are you here, in London?"

"I was doing a favor."

A curious look came to Mathews face. "You truly don't know."

He waited.

"Antrim maneuvered for you to escort Ian Dunne back from the United States. The boy was caught in Florida, then transported to Atlanta to meet up with you. Why was that necessary? Are there not agents in Florida who could have escorted him home? Instead, he specifically asked for you to do it, having his supervisor call Stephanie Nelle."

"How in the hell do you know that?"

"Cotton, I've been in this job a long time. I have many friends. Many sources. You do realize that Gary was taken by men hired by Antrim?"

No, he did not.

"The entire thing was a show for your benefit."

He had a horrible feeling, like he was three steps behind everyone else.

And that usually meant trouble.

He found his phone, switched it on, and called

Antrim's number. No answer. No voice mail. Just ringing. Over and over.

Which signaled more trouble.

He clicked the phone off and said, "I have to leave."

"I can't allow that."

He still held his gun. "I'm not Antrim."

He heard a noise and saw two men enter the court from one of the doors leading to the viewing booths that lined the walls.

Both were armed.

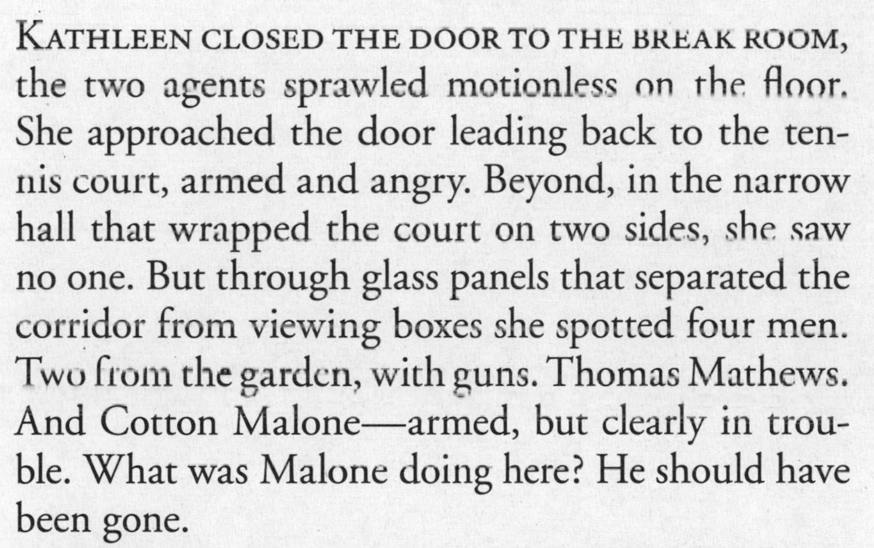

KATHLEEN CLOSED THE DOOR TO THE BREAK ROOM, the two agents sprawled motionless on the floor. She approached the door leading back to the tennis court, armed and angry. Beyond, in the narrow hall that wrapped the court on two sides, she saw no one. But through glass panels that separated the corridor from viewing boxes she spotted four men. Two from the garden, with guns. Thomas Mathews. And Cotton Malone—armed, but clearly in trouble. What was Malone doing here? He should have been gone.

"Please lay down your weapon," Mathews said to Malone.

Her vantage point was at the court's far end, short side, where none of the others could see her.

A door stood open a few meters away.

She crouched below the glass and crept toward it, slipping inside one of the viewing booths. Three rows of seats ran parallel. She stayed low and approached another door that opened into the court.

Time to repay a debt.

Forty-nine

Ian followed Miss Mary onto the train.

He knew the London Underground, having many times explored parts that were off limits to the public. Several of the tunnels offered a respite from either winter's cold or summer's heat, places where he could linger in safety, so long as the police or a worker didn't find him. He hadn't utilized them in a while, ever since Miss Mary allowed him to guard her shop. He was grateful to her, more than he could ever express, glad she was here with him now.

They sat in two empty seats.

"I don't know about you," she whispered. "But I am anxious to read more of what Robert Cecil wrote."

He agreed.

She found her phone and again accessed the

email she'd sent herself, locating in the attachment where they'd left off.

I BEGAN MY SERVICE TO THE QUEEN AUGUST 4, 1598. Though I knew not at the time, barely five years remained in her reign. The queen and I discussed the deception on a mere six occasions. Four of those were in the final months of her life. The first time was the most memorable.

"Ask us what you want," the queen said to me.

I stood inside the bedchamber at Nonsuch. Henry VIII had built the palace as a place of fantasy. Unlike Henry's first daughter, Mary, this queen had enjoyed it.

"Your father was of great service to us," the queen said. "Our success and longevity is thanks to him. It is our hope that you will also bring us good fortune."

"That would be my only desire."

"Then ask what you will and let us be done with this subject."

We spoke for nearly two hours. The tale was one of amazing doing and dare. He was the grandson of Henry VIII, his father the bastard child of Elizabeth Blount, his mother a Howard, the daughter of a great lord. He had lived in obscurity, raised by the Howards, his existence unknown to any Tudor. He was but thirteen, innocent, highly educated, and taught from birth that he was special. But no chance existed of him

ever being anything more than the son of a bastard. All titles and privileges which his father had enjoyed ended with his father's death. Barely a year after that Jane Seymour gave the king a legitimate son and, thereafter, no Tudor cared a moment for Henry FitzRoy or any child he may have sired. But with the unexpected death of princess Elizabeth, and the appearance of Thomas Parry with a plan to substitute the grandson for the daughter, Mary Howard saw an opportunity.

At the time he'd worn his red hair long, his muscles and bones slim, trim, and feminine. In fact, he'd always thought himself trapped. His body that of a man, his mind a woman. The conflict had raged in him since he was old enough to remember. The opportunity his mother offered would end that debate. He would become a woman, taking the princess Elizabeth's identity in every way.

That happened in 1546. No one at the time considered that he might one day be queen. The idea had simply been to placate Henry and save the lives of Kate Ashley and Thomas Parry. Many obstacles remained in the path to the throne. Edward still lived, as did Mary. Elizabeth, at best, was third in line but only if a half brother and sister died without heirs. The subterfuge, though, worked and, as years passed, the grandson blossomed behind the heavy makeup,

wigs, and billowing dresses that became his trademark. Lady Ashley tended to his every need, as did Thomas Parry, and no one ever suspected any deceit. Twelve years passed and both Edward and Mary died with no heirs. His mother, Mary Howard, also died. He was alone, no identity save for the one created by him as the princess Elizabeth. Then, at age 25, he became queen. When I inquired how the deception was maintained after he was crowned, he became whimsical. He assured me that so long as one was careful and diligent, there was no fear of any revelation. Lady Ashley served the queen until 1565, when she died.

"One of the saddest days of our life," he told me, eyes reddening, though 33 years had passed.

Thomas Parry died in 1560, barely two years into the reign. He was never a popular man at court, and many said he left this world of mere ill humor. Of course, he conceived the deception so he always remained close to the queen. Knighted, he served as controller of the royal household. My father told me that the queen paid for his funeral in Westminster, which was never understood by me until that day at Nonsuch.

Blanche Parry became the queen's Chief Gentlewoman of the Privy Chamber after Lady Ashley's death and served until 1590. Though never acknowledged, Lady Parry was surely aware of the deception. The queen treated her

as a baroness, granting her two wardships in Yorkshire and Wales, and burying her in St. Margaret's Chapel, Westminster, with all the pomp of royalty.

"So long as we do certain things in private," the queen explained, "no one could ever know."

Which explained many of the habits. He dressed in private and bathed only with either Lady Ashley or Parry in attendance. He owned an array of eighty wigs and insisted on clothing that concealed his chest and lacked contour from the waist down. He wore heavy white makeup on his face, a sign of purity many observers noted, but it also allowed a masking of features. Always more feminine than masculine, he had sparse hair on his body, including the head, as he'd inherited the Tudor tendency toward baldness. Doctors were allowed to treat him, but never to examine anything more than his eyes, mouth, and throat. At no time could anyone touch his person, and few ever did.

I left the encounter that day feeling both scared and satisfied. This man, who had by then ably ruled England for thirty-nine years, perhaps better than any monarch before, was an imposter. He possessed no right to the throne, yet he occupied it, as completely and thoroughly as if Elizabeth herself had survived. The people loved him, the queen's popularity never in question. My father had made me pledge to serve

him and that I did, until the day he died in 1603. Ever vigilant, he left specific instructions that no autopsy would be performed and none was. I was told by the queen exactly what to do with the body, which I followed only somewhat precisely.

"It seems Robert Cecil lived up to his nickname," Miss Mary said. "The Fox."

Ian was curious. "What does that mean, **somewhat precisely**?"

"That he chose what he wanted to respect and ignored the rest. Which explains why his journal even exists. He seems to have wanted people to know the truth."

The train stopped at a station.

He and Miss Mary exited, then wound their way around to a connector line that would take them to The Goring Hotel.

Once inside the new train he asked, "Can we read some more?"

Miss Mary smiled in her warm way. "Of course. I'm as curious as you seem to be."

WHEN MY FATHER SERVED THE QUEEN I, ALONG with a great many, wondered why she never married. King Henry was obsessive in his desire to secure a male heir. Queen Mary likewise tried and failed to birth a child. There were many offers of marriage toward Elizabeth, both domes-

tic and foreign. Lord Robert Dudley seemed the favorite, but my father openly despised him and the queen publicly bowed to his will and did not marry Dudley. The queen also rejected Philip II of Spain, Archduke Charles of Austria, and two French princes. When Parliament urged a marriage or the nomination of an heir, the queen refused to do either. Since my father knew the truth, he understood why that could not be. But every offer, every insistence, every Parliamentary urging was maximized for political advantage. She told the House of Commons that, "in the end, this shall be sufficient, that a marble stone shall declare that a queen, having reigned such a time, lived and died a virgin."

For the poets she became the virgin queen, married to her kingdom, under the divine protection of heaven. "All my husbands, my good people," were the words used on more than one occasion. But the queen was not unmindful of the duty to ensure that the kingdom survive. The fear of civil war was great. So it came to be that he urged me to correspond with James, king of Scotland, son of Mary, Queen of Scots, whom he'd executed for treason. In conciliation of that unavoidable act I was to offer that James assume the throne of England upon the queen's death. In return, James would cease all opposition and threats toward the English crown. The Scotsman harbored deep resentment for what happened to his mother, but the prospect of the throne eased his anger. He was a shallow man, with few principles, easily swayed. So, when the queen died, the succession occurred without one drop of spilled blood.

I came to admire and respect the imposter. He governed with care and wisdom. My father likewise held him in high esteem. I often wonder if the true Elizabeth would have faired better or worse. What England received was a monarch who ruled forty-five years, providing much needed stability. The imposter was blessed with a countenance unlike his Tudor ancestors, one that provided him long life and reasonable health. In the only other time we spoke of his substitution he told me of his mother and father.

"Our dear mother died before we became queen. We regret she never lived to know. We never saw each other again, once Thomas Parry returned us to Overcourt and we became the princess."

"But twelve years passed before you rose to the throne."

"That it did. My mother lived for eleven of those. Lady Ashley and Parry kept me informed as to her life and health. I was told that she was pleased with all that happened. She loved my father dearly, but hated my grandfather, King Henry. On the day Parry took me to Overcourt she told me that it was right and just that this be happening. I would finally become a Tudor, in every way. Her wish was that I would one day become queen. That thought frightened me. But I have since become accustomed to my duty and comfortable with my charge."

I noticed that when he spoke, for the first time, the label for himself became not "us" or "we" but "me" and "I." Here was a man, a son, who'd never asked for what befell him but who likewise had not failed in his duty.

"You are the ruler of this nation. Your word is our command," I told him.

"Except for one fact, dear Robert. One fact that might one day become overriding."

I knew of what he spoke since I too had considered that since he was not the princess Elizabeth, he was not the rightful and lawful ruler of England. Every act done in his name would be void *ab initio*, from the beginning, as more of the fraud.

As if he never existed.

Fifty

GARY USED THE CROWD, MAKING HIS WAY TOWARD the exit gate, still a hundred feet away from Antrim. Though clearly aware of the woman and man behind him, Antrim had not, as yet, noticed the two men at the gate. If he did, why keep heading straight toward them?

While Antrim had been inside the Jewel House, Gary had roamed the walks, admiring the White Tower rising to his right. He'd listened to the colorfully dressed Beefeaters as they entertained groups gathered around one spot after another. Everything here seemed attached not to the present, but the past. History was not a subject he enjoyed in school, but here it was all around him. What a difference from words on a page, or images on a video screen. Surrounding him was one of the oldest fortresses in England, where men had died defending the walls, and something was happening.

Right now.

Right here.

He focused again on Antrim, who continued to hustle toward the exit. The two men still stood at the gate, and Gary watched as one of them reached beneath his jacket. He caught a glimpse of a shoulder holster, similar to one his dad owned, and knew what was there. No weapon was displayed, but the hand stayed beneath the jacket, tucked away, out of view.

Ready.

Antrim kept coming.

Gary was now fifty feet away, still among the crowds.

No one had noticed him.

Antrim stopped, his gaze now focused ahead at the two men.

Surprise and concern filled his face.

The woman and the other man were closing from behind.

Time to act.

ANTRIM SAW THERE WAS NOWHERE TO GO. THE only exit from the Tower grounds was blocked by two men. Any retreat would take him straight to Denise. He'd made a deal with the devil and now the Daedalus Society had decided he, too, was a liability. True, he had several million of their dollars in the bank, but none of that would do him any good dead. He was mad at himself for all of the mistakes he'd apparently made. This operation, which he'd hoped might be his salvation, had turned into a nightmare.

Even worse, it apparently had been one from the start.

The idea had been to find something that could be used to coax the British government into stopping the Scots from releasing a convicted terrorist. An internal CIA assessment on the potential for Operation King's Deception had shown that, if successful, the information might be sufficient. The British prided themselves on an adherence to law. Common law was born here, then exported around the world. Their loyalty to legality had been used more than once to squelch a king, expand Parliament, or subdue a colony. King's Deception had been designed to turn that loyalty against them. Had all gone to plan, Downing Street would have had no choice but to intervene with the Scots. All Washington wanted was a murderer kept in jail. In return, no one would ever know what happened 400 years ago.

But the Daedalus Society had interfered with all of that.

He wished he knew more about them, but there'd been no time to investigate, and any effort to do so would have drawn Langley's attention.

His only thought now was how to get the hell

out of here in one piece. Would they shoot him here? With all of these people around? Who knew. These people were fanatics, and fanatics were unpredictable.

The idea had been to kill Cotton Malone.

But things had changed.

Now he was the one in the crosshairs.

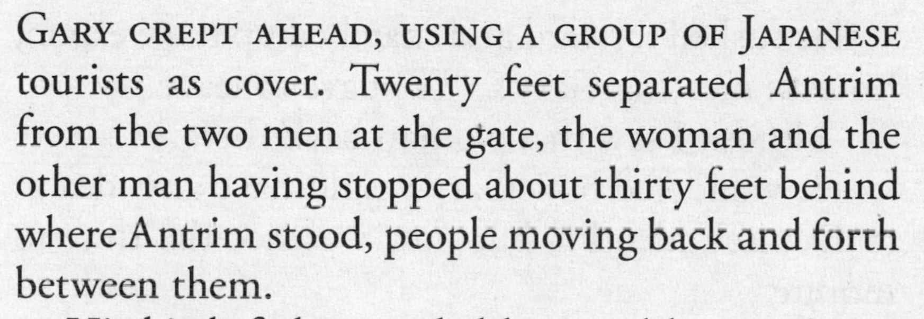

GARY CREPT AHEAD, USING A GROUP OF JAPANESE tourists as cover. Twenty feet separated Antrim from the two men at the gate, the woman and the other man having stopped about thirty feet behind where Antrim stood, people moving back and forth between them.

His birth father needed him and he wasn't going to turn away.

The two men at the gate still had no idea he was there, their attention totally on Antrim.

He was approaching from their right and unless they had eyes in the sides of their heads

He burst from the crowd and leaped forward, propelling his body into the air, rolling sideways so his full length crashed into both men.

Down they all went to the pavement, their bodies cushioning his fall.

He heard a grunt, then a thump as heads slapped hard stone.

Both men were stunned and groggy.

Gary sprang to his feet.

ANTRIM REALIZED WHAT HAD HAPPENED.

As one of the men crumpled down, a hand slipped from beneath his jacket, holding a gun. The grip was released when the man's head pounded the cobbles.

He rushed forward and snatched up the weapon, his eyes meeting Gary's. "We have to leave."

"I know. I saw that woman back there."

He wondered how Gary would have any idea as to Denise's identity, but now was not the time to inquire.

His finger curled onto the trigger.

He turned and aimed the weapon straight at Denise. Someone yelled, "Gun." It took an instant for the scene to register with the people pouring in and out of the gate. Two Beefeaters flanked either side and both fled their posts, racing toward him.

Denise dove toward a patch of grass to her left, beyond the walk.

He followed her leap with the gun and ticked off one round.

The retort sent the people engulfing him into a frenzy, which blocked the Beefeaters from reaching him. He turned, saw Gary, and motioned for them to leave, slipping the gun into his pant pocket. Everything happened in a matter of seconds, the next few critical, so he told himself to calm down, blend in, use the chaos to his advantage.

He gently grabbed Gary's arm. "Nice and slow. Draw no attention."

Gary nodded and they turned right at the Thames and followed the concrete walk away from the Tower. Loud voices and congestion loomed behind them. A sea of excited people acted like a moat, guarding their flank.

His heart raced.

They kept moving back toward the busy street, where Antrim flagged a taxi.

They climbed in and sped away.

He caught the driver's attention. "Take us to any tube station a few blocks from here."

The Underground was the fastest and safest way back to the warehouse. A station was located less than half a mile away from it. Though Daedalus knew its location, there were things he needed.

Like Cecil's journal.

If he was quick, he could stay ahead of them.

"That was brave, what you did," he said.

"You needed help. That woman was behind you."

"How did you know about her?"

"I went into the Jewel House and saw you talking to her."

How much else had he seen or heard? Could not

have been much. No one had been nearby when he spoke to Denise. And he hadn't seen Gary inside.

Let it go.

He gently grabbed Gary by the shoulders. "You saved my hide."

The boy smiled. "You would have done the same for me."

Fifty-one

Kathleen stayed low and made her way to a door that opened from the viewing booth into the tennis court. Her gaze alternated between the scene before her and what might be behind her. She doubted the two from the break room would be awake anytime soon. Both were going to need a doctor. A familiar surge of adrenaline charged her nerves. One she liked. Or at least that's what the therapist had told her and she'd not disagreed. Right now the rush helped her think, making decisions that her life may depend on.

But she liked it that way.

Relying on herself.

Cotton Malone was in a tight spot. Thomas Mathews had him corralled. And though Malone held a weapon, it would do him little good.

"What now?" Malone asked, his eyes locked on the two armed men standing ten meters away.

Mathews stood to Malone's left, between him and where Kathleen was hiding.

"It would seem," Mathews said, "that two of you will be shot and a third will walk away."

The old man was right. The best Malone could hope for was to take down one.

"What's the point of this?" Malone asked, still staring at his problem.

"This is not personal, Cotton. Strictly business. That, you surely understand."

"All I care about is making sure my boy is okay. The rest of this is your mess, not mine."

"Are you aware that Blake Antrim performed a DNA test on himself and your son?"

MALONE WAS SHOCKED BY WHAT HE'D HEARD. "What the hell are you talking about?"

"I actually know the results of that test."

Was he hearing right?

"I told you that Antrim maneuvered your initial stateside involvement with Ian Dunne. He wanted you **and** your son in London. Once here, he managed to divert you off in search of Dunne while he kept watch over your son."

"He found Gary, after he'd been taken."

"It was all staged."

"For what?"

"The DNA test showed that Antrim is Gary's birth father."

"I don't have time for your bullshit."

"I assure you, Cotton, I speak the truth."

And something told him that was the case.

"I was unaware of your personal situation," Mathews said, "until recently. Your son is not biologically yours. A fact you did not know until a few months ago."

"How could you possibly know that?"

"Antrim has been watching your ex-wife for several months. We monitored calls made to a person in Georgia he employed for surveillance."

"Why would he do that?"

"It seems your ex-wife despises him. She refused him any contact with the boy. So, apparently, he decided to create his own opportunity for them to meet."

Reality slammed him hard.

Gary's birth father was here?

"Does Gary know this?" he asked.

Mathews nodded. "I'm afraid so."

"I have to leave."

"I can't allow that," Mathews said.

KATHLEEN LISTENED TO THE CONVERSATION. Apparently, there was a direct connection between Blake Antrim and Malone's son.

One that Malone had clearly been unaware existed.

Knowing Antrim, she was not surprised. He'd fathered a child? And the mother hated him? Probably because he'd pounded her at some point, too.

The two men with guns continued to aim their weapons at Malone.

She decided to even the odds and burst from the darkened viewing box, firing, taking down one of the armed men with a bullet to the thigh.

The other man instantly reacted to her attack and readjusted his aim.

Toward her.

MALONE HEARD THE SHOT AND SAW ITS RESULT, his gaze darting left where Kathleen Richards appeared. She'd shot one of the men, the other now swinging his weapon around. He followed her lead, shooting the second man in the thigh, collapsing him. Richards ran forward and gathered both weapons, the two men writhed in pain, blood gushing from the wounds, staining the court surface.

"We're leaving," he told Mathews.

"A mistake."

He stepped close to the spymaster. "I'm going to see about my boy." What he'd just learned, coupled with the fact that he could not contact Antrim, spelled big trouble. "Stay out of my way."

"You might not like what you find."

"I can handle it."

But he wondered.

"You've got four agents who are going to need medical care," Kathleen said, her gun trained on Mathews.

Mathews shook his head. "You are quite the personality."

"I did your man over there a favor with only a leg injury. Next time I won't be as generous."

"Neither will I," Malone added.

"Are you willing to risk your life for this?" Mathews asked him.

"The question is, are you?"

He motioned to Richards and they fled the building, back out into the afternoon sun. No more agents were in sight and they ran left, past the famous garden maze, to a street that they followed back to the palace front. Taxis were lined near the main walk. They hailed one, climbed inside, and left.

"I appreciate that," he said to her.

"Least I could do."

His mind reeled.

He found his phone and tried Antrim's number again. No answer.

"You can't find him?" Richards asked.

He shook his head.

"Where to?" the driver asked from the other side of the Plexiglas shield.

"The Goring Hotel."

"I heard what Mathews said about your boy."

He faced Richards.

"I need you to tell me everything you know about Blake Antrim."

Fifty-two

THE QUEEN DIED PEACEFULLY IN HER BEDCHAMBER, having fallen into a long sleep from which she never awoke. Sadness filled me. I never once thought of the imposter as anything other than my sovereign. He strengthened both the monarchy and the nation while dodging the royal duty of marriage and procreation. King Henry would always be remembered for follies. Elizabeth would be recalled by accomplishments.

The queen left precise instructions on what was to be done after death. On the day before he died, the imposter dismissed all and called me close.

"Listen," he said, the hoarse voice only breath.

He spoke uninterrupted for several minutes, the act taxing what little strength remained. He told me of Queen Katherine Parr, at a time soon after the deception began, when King Henry was dead and he was sent to live in the queen dowager's household.

"She discovered the ruse," he said to me. "She knew I was not the princess."

Which made sense, as the queen dowager, when King Henry was alive, had spent much time with both the princesses Mary and Elizabeth.

"But she did not reveal me. Instead, she saw a certain irony, a justice, that befit her departed husband. She was not Henry's champion. She had not wanted to marry him, but was forced into that decision. She cared little for him, regarding his surly attitude as that of a tyrant. She discharged her duty as queen with no joy and longed only to be free, which the king's death finally granted her."

But the queen dowager chose poorly for her fourth husband. Thomas Seymour was a scheming manipulator. His desire had been to marry the princess Elizabeth and he tried to ingratiate himself at every opportunity. The queen dowager watched his amorous advances toward the young princess with great amusement, knowing nothing would ever come from them. When it became clear that her husband would not cease his folly, to avoid a scandal and the possibility of discovery, she removed the imposter from their home.

"Seymour's advances toward me were unexpected. They remain the only time in my life when the secret was in jeopardy. But the queen dowager protected me and was sad to see me go. We spoke on the day I left, privately, and she told me to take care and always be careful. She wanted me know that the great deception was safe with her. She died a few months later, but not before writing me a letter, which arrived after her death, in which she told me that I would one day be queen."

He handed me the letter.

"Bury this with me."

I nodded my acceptance of the charge.

"During that final talk Queen Katherine also told me something my grandfather had told her. A secret. One only for royal Tudors. But there are no more of us. So listen to me, good Robert, and follow my instructions without fail."

I nodded again.

"King Henry called the queen dowager to his deathbed, as I have called you. Before that, my grandfather had been summoned to his father's side. Each time the secret was passed. King Henry wanted the queen dowager to tell his son, Edward. But she did not. Instead, she told me, and trusted that I would do what was best with the information."

I listened with an intensity that surprised me.

"There is a place, known only to four souls. Three of those are now dead, as I soon will be. You will be the fifth to know. In this place I have stored much wealth, as my grandfather and great grandfather had done. There also I placed the body of the princess Elizabeth. Thomas Parry long ago dug her from her grave at Overlook and brought her there. You cannot bury me in a royal tomb. There is no assurance that the grave might not one day be opened. Unless that occurred at a time when my remains are but dust, my secret, that which I have guarded so zealously during my life, would then be revealed. Place the princess Elizabeth in my grave and me in hers. That completes the circle and all will be safe then. I want your pledge, upon God's hand, that you shall do this."

I offered the pledge, which seemed to please him.

He laid a trembling hand onto mine. "The wealth there should be for James. Tell him to use it wisely and rule this nation with wisdom and justice."

Those were the last words we spoke.

The queen's death spurred an occasion of universal mourning. It fell to me to provide for the final resting place. I personally supervised the body's preparation. Then the imposter lay beside his great grandfather, Henry VII, in the Tudor vault, while a fitting tomb was constructed. This required three years. During that time the body of the young princess, Elizabeth, found

in the locale detailed to me, was substituted for that of the imposter. That task I personally accomplished without any assistance. I chose to join Queen Mary and the princess Elizabeth, sisters in life, together in death, their bones in one tomb, intermingling. It seemed a proper way to further mask the truth. When the bodies were finally entombed inside the marble, I composed the epitaph that would define the imposter's life.

> Sacred to memory: Religion to its primitive purity restored, peace settled, money restored to its just value, domestic rebellion quelled, France relieved when involved with intestine divisions; the Netherlands supported; the Spanish Armada vanquished; Ireland almost lost by rebels, eased by routing the Spaniard; the revenues of both universities much enlarged by a Law of Provisions; and lastly, all England enriched. Elizabeth, a most prudent governor 45 years, a victorious and triumphant Queen, most strictly religious, most happy, by a calm and resigned death at her 70th year left her mortal remains, till by Christ's Word they shall rise to immortality, to be deposited in the Church, by her established and lastly founded. She died the 24th of March, Anno 1603, of her reign the 45th year, of her age the 70th.

I varied on my pledge to the queen in two respects. First, I kept the letter that Katherine Parr had sent to him. It seemed the last remnant of physical proof that existed. But I burned it on completion of this journal. Second, the wealth that lay within the secret chamber I never revealed to anyone. King James was not an honorable man. I harbored little respect and no admiration for this first of the Stuart family. If he be a prelude of what is to come, I daresay the monarchy could be doomed.

The time of my own death now draws near. If this journal is being read that means someone with intellect and perseverance found the stone I commissioned for Nonsuch Palace. The odd assortment of letters seemed to fit the whimsical world of that royal residence. What be a secret if it cannot be revealed? Fitting that the means of its revelation rested in plain sight. This journal will stay among my papers, guarded by my heirs. If one day someone discovers the connection between it and the stone, then let the truth be told. For that intrepid soul, if you dare, seek out that place which the Tudors created for themselves. But be warned. More challenges shall await you there. If you further doubt this account, I left one other marker. A painting of the queen, commissioned by myself, and designated in my will to hang in Hatfield House for as long as my heirs own the property. Study it

with care. To be remembered is a good thing. My father's memory is one of honor and respect. Perhaps mine will be the same.

Ian glanced up from the computer screen.

He and Miss Mary had found The Goring Hotel in Belgravia, a posh, expensive neighborhood just beyond Buckingham Palace in the heart of the city. He was surprised at Miss Mary's sister, Tanya. Identical twins in not only looks, but also manner and voice, though Tanya seemed more excitable and a bit less patient. Tanya had let a room on the hotel's third floor, a spacious suite that came with deep sofas and soft chairs and a wall of windows that faced a quiet street. The hotel had provided her a laptop computer, which they'd used to access Miss Mary's email account, so they could read more of what Robert Cecil wrote four hundred years ago.

"This is quite amazing," Tanya said. "What a life that imposter led."

"How could no one know?" he asked.

"Because Elizabethan England wasn't like today. There was no television or newspapers to invade one's privacy. If you breached royal etiquette you could lose your life, and many did. The journal makes clear that those closest to the queen—Lady Ashley, Thomas Parry, and the two Cecils—were aware. Which certainly helped."

He wanted to know, "Why would they do that?"

Tanya smiled. "For the most basic of reasons.

They would all, forever, be closest to power, and to be close to the Crown was the goal of all courtiers. The imposter clearly knew he required assistance and he chose wisely in his accomplices. Quite remarkable. The Bisley Boy legend is true."

"I still can't see how it was possible to fool people all those years," Ian said.

Tanya smiled. "We truly have little idea what Elizabeth actually looked like. All of the surviving portraits are suspect. And she was definitely a person of strange habits. As Robert Cecil noted, she wore wigs, heavy makeup, and unflattering clothing. By all accounts she was not a pretty woman, her language coarse, her manner brusque. She controlled her life, and her world, totally. No one could, or would, question her decisions. So it is entirely possible that the ruse could have worked."

He noticed that Miss Mary had stayed quiet.

"What's wrong?" he asked.

"I worry about Gary. Perhaps we should not have left the warehouse."

Fifty-three

ANTRIM, WITH GARY, APPROACHED THE WAREhouse. Outside seemed quiet, the district crammed with storage facilities, which was one reason he'd chosen the locale. Even so, he approached the main door with caution and eased it open. Inside was still lit, the tables with artifacts unaffected, but the bookstore owner and Ian Dunne were nowhere to be seen.

"Where are they?" Gary asked.

He heard the concern. "I told them to stay here. Check the bathroom."

Gary ran around the walls that formed the interior office, and Antrim heard the metal door open.

The boy reappeared and shook his head. "Not there."

The other exit door, on the far side, remained closed, secured by a digital lock. Where **had** they gone? Had someone taken them? No matter. Their being gone saved him the trouble of ditching them. He entered the office and spotted his cell phone on the metal desk.

How did it get there?

Then he realized.

When Ian Dunne bumped into him. The little delinquent picked his pocket.

It was the only explanation that made sense.

He snatched up the unit and saw only one email. From the man who was hacking into Farrow Curry's hard drive. He read the short message, which offered success and the password-protected file, deciphered, attached.

He quickly opened it and scanned the text.

"What is it?" Gary asked.

He kept reading, then said, "Something I was waiting for."

He made another decision. What had, at first, seemed a good idea was now becoming a problem. There were things he needed to do himself. Screw the Daedalus Society. He already possessed half of what they owed him and that would be enough. From the little he'd just read from Robert Cecil's journal, there may be more to this than he'd ever believed. Those Irish lawyers from forty years ago were onto something that could be worth a hundred times more than five million pounds. He recalled how excited Farrow Curry was that day, and the source of that anticipation might lie within Cecil's journal, which he needed to carefully read.

None of which could be done with Gary Malone underfoot.

He'd been childless all of his adult life. Maybe he should keep it that way. He was going to have to disappear, escape both Daedalus and the CIA. That could prove next to impossible with a young boy around. Especially one whose mother hated him and whose father was an ex-agent with an attitude.

Malone had escaped Daedalus.

It was unlikely that there would be other opportunities to take him out.

Time to get the hell out of here.

But what was he to do with Gary?

First, secure the email. It had been sent to the account he'd provided the analyst. His more secure locations he kept to himself. So he forwarded the message and attachment to an address where it would be safe behind multiple firewalls, then deleted it from the phone.

"We need to find Miss Mary and Ian," Gary said.

He ignored the boy and kept thinking.

"Can I use that phone to call my dad?" Gary asked.

He was about to say no, but a rumbling from outside caught his attention. Car engines. Switching off. Then doors opening and closing. He whirled toward the lone window in the outer wall and spotted two vehicles.

Two men exited the lead car.

The same faces from the Tower.

Denise emerged from the other.

All carried pistols.

He darted to the desk and yanked open the drawer. No weapon. Then he remembered. He'd taken it last night and left it in his hotel room. Why would he have needed it today? This morning he'd thought this a day of cleanup, nothing more. Then off to enjoy his money and kindle a relationship with his son, rubbing it all in the face of Pam Malone.

But none of that mattered anymore.

Except the money part.

To enjoy that, though, he had to escape the warehouse in one piece.

Then it hit him.

"Come on," he said to Gary.

They ran from the office and across the interior, toward the tables and artifacts. He assumed that before Denise and her entourage plunged ahead, they'd scope out the landscape.

Which should buy him a few moments.

He spotted the plastic container resting on the concrete and lifted it onto a table. He snapped off the lid to expose eight clumps of pale gray clay, the remainder of the percussion explosives, the same substance used to violate Henry VII's grave inside Windsor.

Nasty stuff.

Tricky, too.

Eight detonators lay inside. He pressed one each into four of the clumps and activated them. He snatched up a small remote, his thumb resting atop its single button. He stuffed the remaining four packets and detonators into a knapsack from one of the tables. Before popping the lid back on, he tossed the cell phone inside. No need for it any longer.

He pointed behind them. "That door across there is bolted from the inside with a digital lock. Go open it. 35. 7. 46."

Gary nodded and ran off.

He retrieved Cecil's journal from beneath its glass dome and slipped it into the knapsack.

The main door to the warehouse burst open.

Denise led the way in with the two men, guns drawn. Antrim shouldered the knapsack and ran toward where Gary stood, at the other door, nearly a hundred feet away.

"Stop," he heard Denise yell.

He kept moving.

A bang.

One round zinged off the concrete near his right foot.

He froze.

Denise and the two men stood across the warehouse, each with their pistols aimed. He was careful, palming the detonator in his right hand, hidden by his cuffed fingers, thumb still on the button.

Get the door open, he mouthed to Gary, before turning around.

"Hands up," one of the men said. "Keep them where we can see them."

He slowly raised his arms, but kept his right hand facing away, four fingers open, thumb holding the controller in place.

"Your computer analyst told us he sent you what Farrow Curry deciphered," Denise called out.

"He did. But I didn't get a chance to read it before you showed up."

She approached the tables and admired the stolen books and papers.

"A five-hundred-year-old secret," she said. "And these are the keys to its unraveling."

He hated the smug look on her face. She thought herself so clever. So in charge. Her rebukes of him, both in Brussels and at the Tower, still stung. He hated everything about cocky women, especially that arrogance bred from good looks, wealth, confidence, and power. Denise possessed at least three of those, and knew it.

She approached the empty glass lid. "Where is Robert Cecil's journal?"

"It's gone."

She'd yet to pay any attention to the plastic container.

"Not good, Blake."

"Do you know what it says?" he asked her.

"Oh, yes. Your man talked freely. He was almost

too easy to persuade. We have the copies of the hard drives and the entire translation."

The two other men stood behind her, now closer to the tables, their guns still aimed. He kept his arms raised, hands still. Percussion explosives were state of the art. Lots of heat, a manageable concussion, and minimum noise. Their effect came from high temperatures directed at a targeted focal point, which could do far more damage to certain surfaces.

Like stone.

Where intense heat weakened its structure.

Here was a no-brainer.

Lots of paper, plastic, glass, and flesh.

"We need that journal, Blake."

He was a good fifty feet away.

Which should be enough.

"Rot in hell, Denise."

His thumb pressed the button.

He dove back, toward Gary, pounding the concrete and covering his head.

GARY HAD EASILY SPOTTED ANTRIM HOLDING THE controller with his right hand, concealed from the three people across the warehouse. He'd wondered what the clumps of clay could do.

Now he saw.

Antrim dove to the floor just as a bright flash erupted from the tables and a swoosh of intense heat surged his way. He'd managed to release the lock before the three had corralled Antrim, the door slightly ajar. Now he fell outside, the door banging against the warehouse's exterior wall, his body slapping the pavement. Heat rushed past him and sought the sky. He stared back through the open doorway. The flash was gone. But the tables were charred and everything on them annihilated. The woman and two men lay on the warehouse floor, their smoking bodies black.

He'd never seen anything like it before.

ANTRIM ROSE.

He'd been just far enough away to escape the carnage, the heat intense but lasting only a few seconds.

Denise and her cohorts lay dead.

Good riddance.

Everything was reduced to ash. Only the stone tablet remained, lying on the floor, charred and of no use.

Screw the Daedalus Society.

Three dead operatives just about made them even.

He shouldered the bag and hustled out the door to find Gary lying on the concrete.

"You okay?" he asked.

The boy nodded.

"Sorry you had to see that. But it had to be done."

Gary stood.

There could be more trouble nearby, so he said, "We have to get out of here."

Fifty-four

Malone listened to what Kathleen Richards had to say about Blake Antrim and didn't like any of it. She and Antrim had been involved a decade ago, their split violent. She painted a picture of a narcissistic individual who could not accept failure, especially when it came to personal relationships. He doted on women, but his ways eventually wore thin and he despised rejection. Malone recalled what Mathews had said in the tennis court. Pam hated Antrim. Refused him all contact with Gary. Richards told him about her final encounter and surmised that a similar incident most likely occurred with Pam. Which explained why she'd refused to tell Gary the man's identity.

But Gary now knew.

Or at least that's what Mathews had said.

They were headed back into London inside the cab, toward The Goring Hotel, where Tanya Carlton should be waiting. He'd trusted the older woman with the flash drive, as it seemed the only play at the time. Now he needed its information.

"That's twice you've come to my aid," Richards said to him.

She was confident and certainly capable, both attractive qualities. Since the divorce he'd been involved with a couple of women like her. He seemed to gravitate toward the smart and the bold. But he wanted to know, "Why'd you take those sheets in Hampton Court and leave?"

"I thought I was doing my job. Sir Thomas wanted that flash drive. He said national security was involved. I thought I was doing the right thing for once, without questioning."

Which made sense.

One part of his brain was worried about Gary, the other was dissecting the situation. Why would it matter that Elizabeth I may have been a fraud? Why would the CIA want to know, and the British government want that truth suppressed? Vanity? A matter of history? National pride? No. More than that.

He rolled over several scenarios and one kept recurring. So he found his phone and called Stephanie Nelle in Washington.

"This is a mess," Stephanie said to him. "I learned a little while ago that a CIA agent was killed in St. Paul's Cathedral yesterday, just as you were arriving. He was on Antrim's team, part of King's Deception."

"And I know who killed him."

So he told her.

Thomas Mathews.

"This just got worse," she said. "I only learned that information through a back-channel source. The people at Langley, who called me about you, failed to mention it."

No surprise. Honesty was not prevalent in the intelligence business, and the higher up the liar the more lies told. That was the thing about Stephanie Nelle he'd always admired. A straight shooter. True, her frankness sometimes tossed her into political trouble, but she'd survived more than one White House administration, including the current one under President Danny Daniels.

He told her what Gary was facing.

"I'm sorry about this," Stephanie said. "I really am. I got you into this one."

"Not really. We were all conned. Right now, I have to find Antrim."

"I'll see what I can do with his bosses at Langley."

"Do that. But tell them they have one pissed-off ex-agent over here with absolutely nothing to lose."

He knew that would open their ears.

"What about Mathews," she asked. "He's seriously breached protocol. I doubt anyone here is going to roll over and allow two dead agents to go unavenged."

"Keep that to yourself. For now. I need Gary safe first."

"You got it."

He ended the call.

"I don't think Blake would hurt the boy," Richards said to him.

But her words did not help. He'd left Gary with Antrim. Made that choice. **He** placed him in the situation. Of course, if Pam had been honest and told him the name of the man she'd had the affair with, he would have known. If she'd been open with Gary, then they both would know. If Malone had not been an ass sixteen years ago and cheated on his wife, none of it might ever have happened.

And if . . . and if . . . and if.

He told his brain to stop.

He'd been in tight spots before.

But never like this.

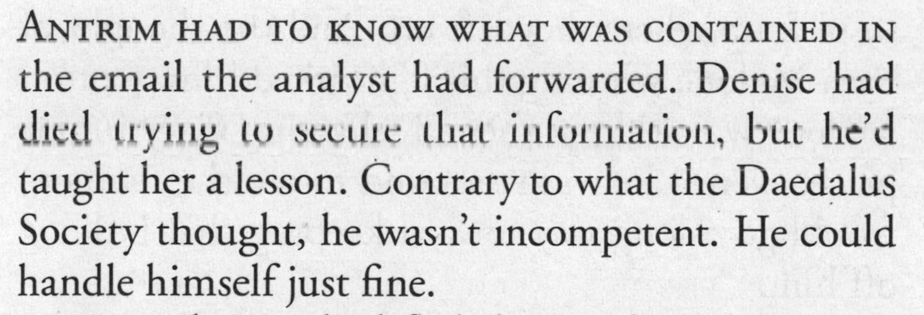

ANTRIM HAD TO KNOW WHAT WAS CONTAINED IN the email the analyst had forwarded. Denise had died trying to secure that information, but he'd taught her a lesson. Contrary to what the Daedalus Society thought, he wasn't incompetent. He could handle himself just fine.

He and Gary had fled the warehouse, running several blocks to the nearest Underground station and boarding the first train that appeared. He decided to take a page from Malone's playbook and find an Internet café. From there he could access his secured account and find out what was so important.

"Why'd you have to kill those people?" Gary asked him as they exited the train in a station near the Marble Arch.

He was in survival mode, and the presence of an inquisitive fifteen-year-old seriously complicated things. But this was a question he wanted to answer.

"In every operation there are good guys and bad guys. Those were the bad guys."

"You blew them up. They had no chance."

"And what would have happened if I hadn't? We'd both be either dead or in custody. I didn't want either of those to happen."

His words came sharp, his voice tight.

They headed for the WAY OUT signs and the street above. Gary stayed silent. He decided that he shouldn't alienate the boy too much. Once this was over and things calmed down he might want to pick up where they left off. And the thought of Pam Malone winning this fight irked him. Cotton Malone was still out there. Delivering Gary in one piece, even if he wasn't around to see the reunion, would go a long way toward keeping that bulldog off him.

He stopped.

"Look. I didn't mean to jump all over you. A lot is happening and I'm a little tense."

Gary nodded. "It's okay. I get it."

Kathleen followed Malone into The Goring Hotel. She knew this place. A hundred years ago a man named Goring persuaded the Duke of Westminister to sell him a plot of land at the rear of Buckingham Palace. There he built the last grand hotel of the Edwardian era, each room a suite, equipped with central heating—which, for its time, was quite remarkable. She'd once enjoyed afternoon tea on its terrace, the biscuits and clotted cream heavenly.

No time for such niceties today, though.

Malone was clearly troubled. He'd tried twice more to call Blake Antrim, but with no answer. She sympathized, though she could only imagine his torment. Her SOCA badge made it easy for the front desk to provide Tanya Carlton's room number. They found the door on the third floor, which was answered by Ian Dunne, who seemed glad to see them both.

"Why aren't you two with Gary?" Malone immediately asked.

She caught the heightened level of concern in Malone's voice.

"You were all supposed to be together."

Tanya Carlton sat at a small desk, her twin sister standing behind her. A laptop computer was open before them.

"Gary left with Antrim," Ian said. "We didn't want him to go, but he went anyway."

"So I decided we should leave," Miss Mary said. "It was clear Antrim was through with us. I had a bad feeling about that place."

"What place?" Malone asked.

Miss Mary told them about a warehouse near the river.

"Any idea where Antrim and Gary went?" Malone asked.

Miss Mary shook her head. "He didn't say. Only that they would be back soon. But something told me that wasn't going to happen, so we left. Prior to that, though, Ian managed to steal Mr. Antrim's cell phone. Which turned out to be a good thing."

"How is that?" Malone asked. "I've been trying to contact Antrim on that phone."

"We left it in the warehouse," Ian said.

Which meant either Antrim and Gary had not returned to find it, or something else had happened.

Tanya pointed to the laptop. "We have discovered what this is all about."

Malone nodded.

"So have I."

Fifty-five

WITHIN THESE PAGES I HAVE REVEALED A MOMENTOUS secret, one that would have deep repercussions if ever revealed. My hope is that by the time these words are deciphered the fact that her majesty, Elizabeth I, was not as she appeared would be nothing more than a historical curiosity. My father taught me that truth is fleeting, its meaning fluid, depending on time and circumstances. No greater example of that wisdom exists than what has transpired here. I am sure that the reader has not forgotten what the two King Henrys passed down and what Katherine Parr told the imposter. Your reward for deciphering this journal is the opportunity to see that which only royalty has been privy to visit. There I have left the wealth of the Tudors. Also, there rests the imposter, safe from all prying

eyes, peaceful in his eternal sleep. England was lucky to have him, no matter the fact that he was illegitimate in every legal way. But no more remorse. The time for that is over. I go to my grave with no regrets, glad that I will not be here to witness the downfall of all that my family holds dear. I fear a grave mistake was made in empowering the Stuarts. Kingship is more than a crown. Once I thought of telling James what I know. That was before I realized he was wholly unfit to be king. He knows nothing, nor does any other living soul. I am the last. You, reader, are now the first. Do what you may with your knowledge. My only hope is that you show the wisdom that the good Queen Elizabeth demonstrated during his forty-five years on the throne.

What you seek can be found beneath the former Blackfriars Abbey. It was placed there long before the abbey existed and found by one of the friars during the reign of Richard III. Access is through what was once the wine cellar, an opening in its floor concealed by one of the casks. Upon the cask is carved an old monk's prayer. "He who drinks wine sleeps well. He who sleeps well cannot sin. He who does not sin goes to heaven."

Antrim finished Robert Cecil's narrative.

He was inside an Internet café before one of the desktops, Gary standing beside him.

"Where is Blackfriars Abbey?" the boy asked.

A good question.

He knew the name. A locale near the Inns of Court, within the City, on the banks of the Thames, but there was no abbey there. Only an Underground station that bore the name. He typed BLACKFRIARS into Google search and read what he found on one of the sites.

IN 1276 DOMINICAN FRIARS MOVED THEIR ABBEY FROM HOLBORN TO A SPOT ON THE RIVER THAMES AND LUDGATE HILL. THERE THEY BUILT AN ABBEY, WHICH ACQUIRED THE NAME BLACKFRIARS, THANKS TO THE DARK ROBES WORN BY THE MONKS. THE ABBEY BECAME QUITE FAMOUS, REGULARLY HOSTING PARLIAMENT AND THE PRIVY COUNCIL. IN 1529 THE DIVORCE HEARING OF HENRY VIII AND KATHERINE OF ARAGON WAS HEARD THERE. HENRY VIII CLOSED THE PRIORY IN 1538, PART OF HIS DISSOLUTION OF MONASTARIES. SHAKESPEARE'S GLOBE THEATER SAT JUST ACROSS THE RIVER, SO A GROUP OF ACTORS ACQUIRED A LEASE TO SOME OF THE BUILDINGS AND STARTED A COMPETING THEATER. THE SOCIETY OF APOTHECARIES EVENTUALLY OCCUPIED ANOTHER OF THE BUILDINGS IN 1632. THAT STRUCTURE BURNED IN THE GREAT FIRE OF 1666, BUT THE APOTHECARIES HALL REMAINS TODAY. BLACKFRIARS RAILWAY

STATION NOW STANDS AT THE LOCALE, ALONG WITH A STOP ON THE CIRCLE AND DISTRICT LINES FOR THE LONDON UNDERGROUND.

"It doesn't exist anymore," he said. "The abbey is gone."

A sense of defeat filled him.

What to do now?

"Look," Gary said. "On the screen."

His gaze locked on the monitor. An email had appeared in his secured account. He read the FROM line. THOMAS MATHEWS. Then the subject. YOUR LIFE.

"Wait over there," he said to Gary.

The boy's gaze signaled defiance.

"This is CIA business. Wait over there."

Gary retreated across to the other side of the room.

He opened the email and read the message.

Clever, your escape from the Daedalus Society. Three of their operatives are dead. They will not be pleased. I am aware of Operation King's Deception, as I am sure you now realize. I am also aware that you have learned the location of the Tudor sanctuary from Farrow Curry's translation. We must speak in person. Why would you do such a thing? Because, Mr. Antrim, if you do not, my next communication will be to the United States and you surely know what the substance of that conversation will be. I know about the money the Daedalus Society paid. Actually, you and I now desire the same thing. So our intentions are similar. If you would like to see that which you have sought, then follow the directions below. I want you there within the next half hour. If not, then I will leave you to your superiors, who will not be pleased to learn what you have done.

He glanced up from the screen.

MI6 knew all of his business, too.

What choice did he have?

He read the directions. Not far away. He could be there within the half hour. The knapsack he'd taken from the warehouse sat at his feet. Inside was Cecil's original journal and the remaining PEs. He should have retrieved one of the guns from the bodies in the warehouse, but his main concern had been to get the hell out of there.

He glanced across the room at Gary, who was staring out of one of the café's street-front windows.

Mathews had not mentioned a thing about him.

Maybe Gary could be used.

To his advantage.

GARY WAS CONFUSED.

This man who was his birth father was so different from his father. Moody. Emotional. Sharp-tongued. But he was a big boy and could handle it, though all of this was a new experience.

He'd also just watched as this man incinerated three people, then showed no remorse. The woman had obviously known Antrim since she'd twice called him by his first name and, just before Antrim ignited the explosives, he'd taunted her. **Rot in hell, Denise.**

His dad had only once spoken about killing. That happened a month ago, when he, his father, and his mother were all in Copenhagen. **Not something you like to do, but something you sometimes have to do.** He could appreciate that.

Blake Antrim seemed to take another approach. But that did not make him wrong. Or bad. Just different.

Antrim now seemed agitated. Upset. Concerned.

Not the same confidence from yesterday, when he first revealed that he was the man who'd been with Gary's mother.

Things had changed.

He watched as Antrim hoisted the knapsack from the floor and walked over.

"We have to go."

"Where to?"

"To the place the journal mentions. I know where that is now."

"What about my dad?"

"I have no way of contacting him. Let's check this out, then we'll figure out how to find him."

That sounded logical.

"But I'm going to need you to do something for me."

Fifty-six

MALONE WAS READY TO DO SOMETHING. ANYthing. Yet he was stymied as to the proper course. He had no way of contacting Blake Antrim and no way of finding Gary. He was furious at himself for making a multitude of poor decisions, his son's welfare now in jeopardy thanks to his carelessness. Miss Mary and Tanya had shown him the translation of Robert Cecil's journal, which he and Kathleen Richards had now read in its entirety.

"Blackfriars Abbey is gone," Tanya told him. "It has been for a long time."

Another piece of bad news, which he added to the growing heap.

"There's an Underground station there now," Tanya said. "It's presently closed, being totally rebuilt."

He listened as the sisters told him about the

station, which had existed on the site since the 19th century. Both rail and Underground lines converged there. Last year, the station was demolished and a sleek new glass-fronted building was erected, which was slowly taking shape. No rail trains stopped there now, and hadn't for over a year. But the Underground still passed beneath.

"The place is a mess," Miss Mary said to him. "Construction everywhere. The pavements are closed all around it. That station sits on the riverbank beside a busy street."

"What you're saying is that this four-hundred-year-old puzzle is at a dead end."

"Then why is SIS so interested?" Richards asked. "If there's nothing to find, why does Thomas Mathews care?"

He knew the answer. "Because there is something to find."

He quickly ran through his options and determined that the choices were down to a precious few. Doing nothing? Never. Calling Stephanie Nelle back? Possible, but the time lag before anything happened could be a problem. Trying to find Antrim on his own? Impossible. London was a big place.

There seemed only one path.

He faced Richards. "Can you contact Mathews?"

She nodded. "I have a number."

He pointed to the room phone. "Dial it."

KATHLEEN FORGAVE MALONE FOR HIS ATTITUDE. Who could blame him? He was in a quandary, the only way out possibly coming from a man who'd just tried to kill them both. This spy business was so different from her everyday experience. Things seemed to change by the minute, with no warning and little time to react. That part she actually liked. Still, it was frustrating not knowing who was on what side, and where she fit in.

But at least she was still standing.

In the game.

And that meant something.

She dialed the number from the note Mathews had provided earlier.

Two rings.

Then it was answered.

"I assumed you would be making contact sooner rather than later," Mathews said in her ear.

She handed over the phone.

MALONE GRIPPED THE HEADSET AND SAID, "Listen to me. My son is God knows where. He didn't ask to be put into this—"

"No. He was maneuvered into this."

"Which you allowed to happen. I didn't know. **You** did. You used me, and you used Richards."

"I just communicated with Blake Antrim."

That's what he wanted to hear.

"Does he have Gary?"

"He does. They're on the run. Antrim killed three of my agents."

"How?"

"He blew them up, thinking they were his enemy."

"And Gary?"

"He was there. But he's fine."

Not good. Time to play his trump card. "I have the flash drive, which contains a complete translation of Robert Cecil's journal. I read it. Which means I'm not forgetting it."

"I have that translation now myself."

"I also know what this is all about."

He paused.

"Ireland."

Silence on the other end of the phone confirmed his suspicion.

"What do you want?" Mathews finally asked.

"My son, and to be gone from here."

"And what of all that you know?"

"That's my insurance to make sure you behave. I can email that drive to Stephanie Nelle with one click. In fact, I have it loaded up right now. Would you like me to send it along to her? The CIA would probably love to know that what they were after is real. They'd also love to know that you killed two of their men. Maybe they'll pay you back by releasing it all to the world, just to spite Downing Street."

Mathews chuckled. "We both know that once you do any of that I have nothing left to gain. You, on the other hand, still have something to lose. Your son."

"That's right, you son of a bitch. So cut the crap and let's make a deal."

"I know where Antrim is headed. He, too, has Cecil's translation."

"Blackfriars Abbey is gone."

"I see you do know. And you're right, it is gone. But the Tudor sanctuary is not. If I give you Antrim, will you give me the drive?"

"I can still tell Washington."

"You could, but you won't. This is personal, not business. Your son is at stake. For me, it's the other way around."

He knew better, but said what was expected. "Deal."

"Then here is where you must go."

IAN COULD HEAR THE ENTIRE CONVERSATION through the phone, the hotel room dead quiet. The other three women were likewise listening. Malone was playing the old man, controlling his anger, keeping himself calm, using his brain. He could relate to that. He'd survived on the streets doing the exact same thing. But he was bothered by the fact that most of this seemed his fault. **He** stole the flash drive. Then pepper-sprayed the old man. **He** fled to America. And ran from that mews.

But he came back.

And stole Antrim's phone. Which gave them the translation.

Without that, Malone would have nothing to bargain with.

So he'd also helped.

But he still felt responsible for Malone's anguish.

And he wanted to help.

MALONE HUNG UP THE PHONE.

He turned to see Kathleen Richards staring at him, realizing they'd all heard what Mathews had said.

"He cannot be trusted," Richards said.

"Like I don't know that."

His mind raced.

One more phone call.

He lifted the receiver and dialed overseas for Stephanie Nelle.

"I'm about to engage Thomas Mathews," he said.

Then he told her what had happened.

"I need a straight answer," he said to her. "No bullshit. Did the CIA explain to you Operation King's Deception?"

"Your asking that question means you already know the answer."

That he did. "It's Ireland. Right?"

And she explained.

THE MODERN TROUBLES BEGAN IN 1966 AND LASTED until 2003, the violence claiming 3,703 lives. Nearly 40,000 people were injured. A shocking amount of mayhem considering only about 900,000 Protestants and 600,000 Catholics lived in Northern Ireland during that time. For three long decades violence, distrust, fear, and hatred marred that country, eventually exported to England and Europe.

The seeds of that conflict, though, stretched way back.

Some experts point to the Anglo-Norman invasion of Ireland by Henry II in 1169 as the beginning. More realistically, it all began with the Tudors. Henry VIII was the first to take an interest in Ireland, invading and controlling the area in and around Dublin, slowly extending his hold outward, conciliation and innovation the weapons he used to subdue the local

lords. Henry was so successful that an act of the Irish Parliament in 1541 proclaimed him king of Ireland. But rebellion was a constant threat. Troops were occasionally dispatched and skirmishes fought. Complicating matters was the fact that Ireland was overwhelmingly loyal to Rome and the pope, while Henry required allegiance to his new Protestant religion.

So a spiritual divide emerged. Local Irish Catholics versus the newly arrived English Protestants.

Ireland remained relatively unimportant during the short reigns of the next two Tudors, Edward VI and Mary.

Under Elizabeth I everything changed.

Personally, Elizabeth viewed the island as a wilderness and preferred to ignore it. But a series of rebellions, which called into question her entire foreign policy, forced her into action. A great army was sent, the rebellions crushed, and, as a consequence for defiance, Irish land was seized. The influence of Gaelic clans and Anglo-Norman dynasties, which had existed there for centuries, ended. Title to all land shifted to the Crown. Elizabeth then granted ownership, leases, and licenses to English colonists who formed plantations. This confiscation had first started during the time of Henry VIII, and continued in small doses through Edward and Mary, but it accelerated during Elizabeth's reign, then reached its peak with her successor, James I. To work the newly acquired land, large numbers of Englishmen, Scots, and Welsh immigrated to Ireland. The idea of encouraging both colonists and plantations was to conquer Ireland from within, settling the country with loyal Englishmen beholden to the Crown. The English language would also be imported, as would English customs and beliefs. Irish culture would be eradicated.

This sowed the seeds of a bitter cultural and religious conflict, one that would endure for centuries. Catholic Irish Nationalists versus Protestant English Unionists.

Cromwell came in the 1640s and massacred thousands. The United Irish Rebellion, during the 1790s, was also brutally suppressed. The famine years of the 1840s nearly crushed everyone. Home rule was tried in the late 19th and early 20th centuries, where the Dublin Parliament governed Ireland, but remaining answerable to London. A farce, which only widened the division. Irish society progressively grew more militant and radical. A war of independence, fought in 1919 between the Irish Republican Army and the British, ended with a solution neither side wanted. Ireland was partitioned, reduced from 32 to 26 counties, all in the south, where Catholic Nationalists dominated. The remaining six counties, all in the north, where

Protestant Unionists were a majority, became the separate country of Northern Ireland.

Violence started immediately.

One factional group after another arose with its own radical agenda. Riots became commonplace. Minority Catholics in Northern Ireland began to feel threatened and lashed out, then Unionists retaliated, establishing a vicious cycle of strike and counterstrike. Coalition governments were tried. All failed. The Irish to the south and the Nationalists in the north wanted the English Protestants gone. The Protestant Unionists wanted their rights and lands protected by London, since it was the British Crown that had granted them in the first place. The six counties of Northern Ireland were initially chartered by Elizabeth I from seized Irish land, and every incoming owner there traced their title to a royal grant. At a minimum, the Unionists argued, London must protect their legal rights.

And London did.

Sending troops to suppress Nationalists.

Eventually, at the height of the Troubles, Nationalists brought the conflict to London and Europe and bombings became commonplace across the continent. An uneasy peace came in 1998, which has held ever since. But both sides remain deeply suspicious of the other, only tentatively willing to work together to avoid further bloodshed.

None of the root causes of the conflict has ever been resolved.

The same debate that started long ago continues.

Bitter feelings remain.

Nationalists want a united Ireland ruled by Irish.

Unionists want Northern Ireland to continue as part of Great Britain.

IAN LISTENED AS THE FOUR ADULTS TALKED. Malone had finished his call and told them that his former boss, a woman named Stephanie Nelle, had confirmed that Antrim was focused on Northern Ireland—he'd listened to the history—and on some Arab terrorist who was about to be released from a Scottish jail. The Americans wanted the British to stop the release, and to get them to do that they intended on finding evidence that Elizabeth I was not what she appeared, calling into question her entire reign, throwing into doubt the legitimacy of Northern Ireland itself.

"What a reckless scheme," Malone said.

"And a dangerous one," Richards said. "I can see why Mathews is concerned. It would not take much to reignite massive amounts of violence within Northern Ireland. Periodically, there are attacks here and there from both sides. The fight is definitely not over. It's just simmering, each waiting for a good reason to start killing the other."

"The peace was made," Tanya said, "because at the time it was the only course. The British are there, in Northern Ireland. They aren't leaving. And killing people wasn't accomplishing anything."

"Think what would happen if the truth were known," Miss Mary quietly said. "If Elizabeth I was indeed a fraud. That means everything done during that reign was fraudulent. Void. Illegal."

"Including every acre of land seized and every land grant made in Northern Ireland," Malone said. "Not one would have any legal effect. The six counties that form the country were all seized by Elizabeth."

"Would it matter?" Tanya asked. "After five hundred years?"

"Definitely," Malone said. "It's like if I sold you my house and you live there for decades. Then one day someone shows up with proof that the deed I gave you is a fraud. I didn't have the power to actually convey title to you in the first place. It's elementary real property law that the deed would be void. Of no legal effect. Any court here, or in America, would have to respect the true title to that land, not the fraudulent act of my transfer."

"A battle that would be fought in court," Richards said.

"But one the Irish would win," Malone added.

"Worse, though," Richards said. "The truth alone would be more than enough for Unionists and Nationalists to restart the Troubles. Only this time they'd actually have a legal reason to fight. You can almost hear the Irish Nationalists. They've been trying to get the British to leave for 500 years. Now they'd scream, **Your fake queen invaded our country and stole our land. The least you can do is give it back and leave.** But that wouldn't happen. London would resist. It would have to. They've never abandoned the Unionists in Northern Ireland, and they won't start now. There are billions of pounds invested there. London would have to stand and fight. Whether that's in court or in the streets. It would be an all-out war. Neither side would bend."

"Of course," Malone said to her, "if your government would simply stop Edinburgh from handing a murderer back to Libya, there wouldn't be a problem."

"I don't like that any more than you do. But that doesn't excuse this foolhardy tactic. Do you know how many thousands of people could die from this?"

"Which is why I'm going to give the flash drive to Mathews," Malone said.

"And what about Ian?" Richards asked.

"Good question. What about me?"

Malone faced him. "You know that Mathews wants you dead."

He nodded.

"The question is," Malone said, "how far is he willing to go to clean up this mess? Especially now that a lot more people know about it. He has more than one loose end. So I'll take care of that, too."

Malone looked at Richards.

"We have to go."

"Sir Thomas never mentioned me coming."

"I need your help."

"I'm going, too," Ian said.

"Like hell. Mathews never mentioned you on the phone. That means one of two things. He doesn't know where you are, or he's waiting for us to leave to make a move. I'd say the former. Too much happened too fast for him to know anything. If he did, he'd have acted already. Also, I need you out of the way so I can bargain for your safety. If he has you I have no bargaining power."

Malone faced the twin sisters.

"Stay put here, with Ian, until you hear from me."

"And what happens if we never hear from you?" Miss Mary asked.

"You will."

Fifty-seven

Antrim approached the construction site, Gary walking with him. The old Blackfriars tube station had been demolished, replaced by a shiny, glass-fronted building that seemed about half complete. A plywood wall separated the work site from the sidewalk, the Thames within sight less than a hundred yards away. A newly reconstructed Victorian rail bridge now spanned the river, upon which was being built a modern railway station. He'd read somewhere that this was London's first transportation center ever built over water.

Through a break in the plywood barrier he spotted no workers. Though it was Saturday, some should be here. Mathews had told him to head for this particular corner of the site. To his right, traffic raced by on a busy avenue that headed south across the Thames. He still carried the knapsack with explosives inside, the only weapon he possessed, and he had no intention of entering this trap unarmed.

A maze of heavy equipment littered the scarred earth. Deep gouges in the ground, yards wide and extra deep, stretched toward the riverbank. Train tracks lay at the bottom, straight lines disappearing inside the new bridge station, heading toward the far south bank. He recalled this place from his youth. A busy station. Lots of people in and out every day. But not today. The site was deserted.

Which was exactly what Thomas Mathews would want.

So far he'd followed directions.

Time for some improvising.

MALONE RODE IN THE UNDERGROUND, TAKING A train from Belgravia east to a station near the Inns of Court, close to Blackfriars. Kathleen Richards sat beside him. He could still hear what Stephanie Nelle had told him on the phone half an hour ago.

"It's the CIA attempting to save the day," she said. "Forty years ago a group of Irish lawyers actually tried to prove that Elizabeth I was a fraud. It's called the Bisley Boy legend—"

"Just like Bram Stoker said in his book."

"To their credit, they were trying to find a legal, nonviolent way to force the British to

leave Northern Ireland. At that time the Troubles were in full swing. People were dying every day. No end seemed in sight. If they could prove in court that all British claims to their lands were false, legal precedent could be used to reunite Ireland."

"Clever. And it might have been a good idea then, but not now."

"I agree. The slightest provocation could restart the violence. But the CIA was desperate. They worked hard to find al-Megrahi, then bring him to trial. To see him just walk away galled them to no end. The White House wanted something. Anything to stop it. So Langley thought a little blackmail might work. Unfortunately, they forgot that this president isn't the type to do that, especially to an ally."

On that he agreed.

"The CIA director and myself just had a spirited discussion," she said. "Currently, the White House is unaware of what they've been doing, and they'd like to keep it that way. Especially since the whole operation failed. But with SIS now involved, this could become a source of extreme embarrassment for everyone."

"And they want me to clean up the mess."

"Something like that. Unfortunately, that prisoner transfer is going to happen. The goal now is not to allow an international PR disaster to amplify the situation. It seems the British

know everything about King's Deception. The only thing going for us is they don't want the world to know."

"I don't give a damn."

"I realize that Gary is your only concern. But, as you say, he's with Antrim. And Langley has no idea where that might be."

Which was why he'd called Mathews.

And was walking into a trap.

"What do you want me to do?" Richards asked him.

He faced her. "Why are you on suspension?"

He saw that she was surprised he knew that.

"I caused a lot of bother trying to arrest some people. But that's nothing new for me."

"Good. 'Cause I need some bother. Lots of it, in fact."

IAN HAD NOT LIKED MALONE'S REFUSAL TO ALLOW him to go along. He was not accustomed to people telling him what to do. He made his own decisions. Not even Miss Mary gave him orders.

"This is all so unbelievable," Tanya said. "So incredible. Imagine the historical implications."

But he didn't care about that.

He wanted to be where things were happening.

And that was Blackfriars station.

He sat on one of the chairs inside the hotel room.

"Are you hungry?" Miss Mary asked him.

He nodded.

"I can order you something."

She stepped across the room to the phone. Her sister sat at the desk with the laptop. He bolted for the door and fled into the hall. The stairs seemed the best route down, so he headed for the lighted sign.

He heard the room door open and turned back.

Miss Mary stared at him with a look of concern.

He stopped and faced her.

She didn't have to say a word. The watery gloss in her eyes told him what she was thinking.

That he should not go.

But her eyes also made clear that she was powerless to stop him.

"Be careful," she said. "Be ever so careful."

GARY FOLLOWED ANTRIM ONTO THE CONSTRUCTION site. They wove a path through heavy equipment across the damp soil, dodging puddles from yesterday's rain. A massive concrete shell lay inside one of the open trenches, twenty feet down, its damp walls being dried by the afternoon sun. Eventually, the entire structure would be covered with dirt. For now, though, its sides, roof, pipes, and cables were exposed, the rectangle stretching fifty yards toward the river, where it disappeared into the ground, beneath a section of closed-off street.

They climbed down into the wet trench, using one of the wooden ladders, and made their way toward a yawn in the earth that opened into a darkened chasm. He blinked the sun from his eyes and adjusted to the dim light. Concrete wall rose to his left, bare earth to his right, the path well traveled, the dirt here dry and compact beneath his sneakers.

Antrim stopped and signaled for quiet.

He heard nothing save for the rumble of the nearby traffic.

An opening in the wall could be seen ahead.

Antrim approached, glanced inside, then motioned for him to follow. They entered and saw that the exposed structure housed a rail line, the tracks in disrepair, rebar everywhere awaiting wet cement. Incandescent floodlights burned bright, illuminating the windowless space. He wondered how Antrim knew where to go, but assumed the email earlier in the café had provided the necessary information.

Antrim hopped up to another level from the dirt around the tracks and they crept deeper inside. The cool air smelled of wet mud and dry cement. More tripods with flood lamps lit the way. He estimated they were at least twenty feet underground, beneath the glass-fronted building overhead. They came to a wide-open space that funneled to shafts angling farther down into the ground.

"This foyer is where passengers will come down

from above, then make their way to the tracks," Antrim whispered.

Gary glanced into one of the down shafts. The next level was fifty feet beneath him. No steps or escalator were present. More lights burned below. Another wooden ladder, one of several propped in the shaft, allowed a way down.

"That's where we have to go," Antrim said.

KATHLEEN FOLLOWED MALONE AS THEY EXITED the Underground station and found the Embankment. The dome of St. Paul's rose not far in the distance, the Thames less than fifty meters to their right, Blackfriars station straight ahead. Both of them still carried their weapons. Malone had stayed silent after he explained what he wanted her to do. She hadn't argued. This was a trap, no other way to view it. To walk in unprepared would be foolhardy.

And even though Thomas Mathews held the superior position—since he seemed to know exactly where Blake Antrim would be—Malone had wisely demanded proof of Gary's presence.

So they'd been waiting.

Malone's phone vibrated, signaling an incoming email. He opened the message, which came with a video attachment.

They watched on the screen as Blake Antrim

and Gary walked through what appeared to be a construction site. They were inside a windowless space, Antrim easing himself onto a ladder, disappearing downward.

Then Gary climbed onto the rungs and vanished.

The message contained in the email was concise.

PROOF ENOUGH?

She saw the concern in Malone's face. But she also saw the frustration, as there was no way to know where the video had originated.

Best guess?

Blackfriar's station. About a kilometer away.

They stood just outside the Inns of Court.

Back where it all started yesterday.

"Do what I asked," Malone said.

And he walked off.

Fifty-eight

ANTRIM HOPPED FROM THE LADDER AND SAW HE was standing on what would eventually be a train platform, the tracks there, five feet below the concrete, exiting one tunnel then entering another. He noticed how lights indicated that the rails were active, signs warning to be wary of high voltage. The Circle and District lines ran straight through Blackfriars, two of London's main east–west Underground routes. Millions traveled those lines every week. They could not be blocked. So the trains kept coming, back and forth, though none stopped here.

Gary finished his descent and stood beside him.

More lights on tripods illuminated the work area.

Tile was being applied to the walls, a cheery color in a mosaic pattern. The entire platform was being refurbished, construction materials everywhere.

"Mr. Antrim."

The gravelly voice startled him.

He turned to see Sir Thomas Mathews standing fifty feet away, without his signature cane.

The older man motioned.

"This way."

MALONE ENTERED THE INNS OF COURT AND REplayed Thomas Mathews' instructions in his mind. Beneath the ground on which he walked flowed the Fleet River. Its origin lay four miles to the north, once a major London water source. But by the Middle Ages a burgeoning populace had totally polluted the flow, its odor so horrendous that Victorian engineers finally enclosed it, making the Fleet the largest of the city's subterranean rivers. He'd read about the maze of chambers and tunnels that crisscrossed Holborn, channeling the water to the Thames.

"Go to the Inns," Mathews said. "North of the Temple Church, adjacent to the master's house, is the Goldsmith building. In its basement is access. It will be open and waiting for you."

"Then where?"

"Follow the electrical cables."

He turned right and negotiated King's Bench Walk. He entered the church court, filled with weekend visitors, and passed the Temple Round. He spotted the brick house labeled GOLDSMITH and entered through the main door, locking the latch behind him. A staircase was visible at the end of a short hall. He descended to a basement with walls of hewn stone. Two bare bulbs hung from the low ceiling. In the floor, across from the base of the stairs, an iron door was hinged open.

He stepped over and glanced inside.

A metal ladder led down ten feet to a dirt floor.

The way to Gary.

Or, at any rate, the only one he had.

GARY HOPPED OFF THE CONCRETE PLATFORM AND followed the smartly dressed older man into a train tunnel. Lights attached to its concrete walls burned every fifty feet. He heard a rumble and felt a rush of air. The older man stopped and turned, motioning behind them.

"These tracks are still active. Stay to the wall, but be careful. The electricity in the rails can kill."

He spotted a light out the tunnel's exit, past the new station platform, into another tunnel entrance on the far side. Its brightness grew, as did the vibrations. A train suddenly appeared on the tracks, speeding toward them, passing in a roar, the cars full of people. They hugged the wall. In a few seconds it was gone, the rumble receding, the air still again. The older man resumed walking. Ahead, Gary spotted another man, waiting beside a metal door.

They approached and stopped.

"The boy goes no farther," the older man said.

"He's with me," Antrim said.

"Then you go no farther."

Antrim said nothing.

"Your father is waiting for you at St. Paul's Cathedral," the older man said to Gary. "This gentleman will take you there."

"How do you know my dad?"

"I've known him for many years. I told him I would deliver you to him."

"Go," Antrim said.

"But—"

"Just do it," Antrim said.

He saw nothing in Antrim's eyes that offered any comfort.

"I'll catch up with you in Copenhagen," Antrim said. "We'll have that talk with your dad then."

But something told him that was said only for the moment, and Antrim had no intention of ever coming.

The other man approached and slid the backpack from Antrim's shoulders, unzipping and displaying its contents to the older man, who said, "Percussion explosives. I would have expected no less from you. Were these used to breach the tomb of Henry VIII?"

"And to kill three Daedalus operatives."

The older man cut a long stare at Antrim. "Then,

by all means, bring them along. You may have need of them."

Antrim faced Gary. "Give me the remote."

The idea had been for Antrim to tote the explosives, with their detonators active and in place, while Gary kept the remote, the hope being that no one would search a boy for a weapon.

But that had apparently changed.

"I want to stay," he said.

"Not possible," the older man said, motioning to the second man, who led Gary away.

He yanked free of the man's grasp.

"I don't need your help walking."

Antrim and the older man entered the metal door.

"Where does that go?" Gary asked.

But no answer was offered.

IAN WAS PROUD OF HIMSELF. HE'D MANAGED TO quickly steal a travel card and used the Underground to head across London to a station just east of Blackfriars. He'd avoided Temple station since that was where Malone and Richards would have exited, directly adjacent to the Inns of Court. Instead, he would approach Blackfriars from the opposite direction. On the trip over he'd thought about what to do once there, unsure, but at least he was not waiting around in some hotel room.

He hated that he'd hurt Miss Mary. He'd seen

the look on her face, knew that she did not want him to go. Maybe it was time he listened to her and trusted her judgment.

He spotted the construction site, traffic hectic in both directions on a boulevard that fronted it on two sides. The dome of St. Paul's rose off to his right. A plywood wall formed a makeshift barrier around the work site, but he managed to slip through an opening, past crabbed branches of bushes choked with trash. He saw no one, but kept among the equipment and debris, careful not to stay too long in the open.

He stepped into the main building and crept deeper inside, grit crunching beneath his shoes.

He heard voices.

Scaffolding rose to his right, a stack of crates and boxes nearby.

He dashed over and sought cover behind them.

KATHLEEN ENTERED THE BLACKFRIARS CONSTRUCtion site from the west, making her way toward the new station building. She carried her gun, out and ready. Malone had not wanted her with him. Mathews had made clear that he was to come alone. Instead, he'd told her to check out the site and be prepared. Mathews had said that Antrim was headed below Blackfriars station, and the video they'd watched confirmed that Antrim and Gary Malone were at a construction locale. It stood to reason that this was the place, so Malone wanted it reconnoitered. After that, he'd told her, **improvise**.

She proceeded with caution and entered, finding her way through a series of platforms and corridors. Tripod lights were on, and she doubted they'd been left burning all weekend. From everything she'd read about this project it was a seven-day-a-week venture, time being of the essence. So where were the workers? SIS had surely taken care of them for the day.

Inside the new station building she spotted something familiar.

From the video.

She stared down an opening in the floor to another level, where Underground tracks ran. Ladders allowed access, just like the one she and Malone had seen.

Then a noise.

To her right.

On her level.

She headed toward it.

IAN SPIED GARY MALONE BEING LED BY ANOTHER man. Tall. Young. A copper, no doubt.

"I don't want to leave," Gary said.

"This is not up to you. Keep moving."

"You're lying to me. My dad's not at St. Paul's."

"He is. Let's go."

Gary stopped and faced his minder. "I'm going back."

The man reached beneath his jacket, produced a gun, and pointed the barrel straight at Gary. "Keep. Moving."

"You're going to shoot me?"

Gutsy. He'd give Gary that. But he wasn't as sure of the answer to that question as Gary seemed to be.

His mind raced.

What to do?

Then it came to him. Just like a month ago in that car. With Mathews and the other man who'd wanted to kill him. He'd left the plastic bag with his treasures at Miss Mary's bookstore, but he'd removed the knife and pepper spray.

Both were in his pockets.

He smiled.

Worked once.

Why not again.

GARY STOOD HIS GROUND AND DARED THE GUY TO pull the trigger. The extent of his courage surprised him, but he was more concerned about his dad than himself.

And Antrim, who'd brushed him off.

Which hurt.

He caught movement out of the corner of his eye and turned to see Ian walking toward them.

What in the world was **he** doing here?

The man with the gun saw him, too. "This is a restricted site."

"I take a wander in here all the time," Ian said, still approaching.

The man seemed to realize that he was holding an exposed gun and lowered it. Which only confirmed that there would not be any shooting.

"You a copper?" Ian asked.

"That's right. And you can't be here."

Ian came close and stopped. His right hand whipped upward and Gary heard the hiss of spray. The man with the gun howled, both hands searching for his eyes. Ian swung his foot up and slammed the sole of his shoe into the man's stomach, dropping him to the concrete.

Both boys ran.

"I heard what he told you," Ian said. "Your dad is not at St. Paul's. He's here."

Fifty-nine

ANTRIM CROUCHED LOW AS THEY NEGOTIATED THE narrow passage. Power cables were bolted near the barrel ceiling, lights inside wire cages every seventy-five feet or so, their glow nearly blinding.

"We discovered these tunnels," Mathews said, "when Blackfriars station was first rebuilt in the 1970s. A convenient entrance to them was incorporated into the new station and kept under our control. We ran power into here, and you are about to learn why."

Mathews was shorter and did not need to watch his head. The older man just clipped along, the dirt floor dry as a desert.

"I thought you might like to see what it is you were after," Mathews said. "After all, you did go to much trouble to find it."

"It's real?"

"Oh, my goodness, Mr. Antrim. It is **most** real."

"Who built these tunnels?"

"We think the Normans first dug them as escape routes. Then the Templars refined them, adding the brick walls. We are not far from the Inns of Court, their former headquarters, so I assume these paths served a great many of the knights' purposes."

He heard a rumble, growing in intensity, and wondered if it was another train passing through its own tunnel nearby.

"The River Fleet," Mathews said. "Just ahead."

They came to an open doorway at the end, where the tunnel crossed perpendicularly another man-made expanse, this one tall, wide, and channeling water. They stood on an iron bridge that spanned ten feet above the flow.

"This bridge was added after the discovery of the tunnel we just traversed," Mathews said. "When the Fleet was enclosed centuries ago, the route was unknowingly blocked. It is low tide at the moment, but that will soon be changing. At high tide, the water will rise to nearly where we stand."

"I guess you wouldn't want to be down there when that happens."

"No, Mr. Antrim, you most certainly would not."

MALONE KEPT FOLLOWING THE TUNNEL, THE water now up to his calves and rising at a steady pace.

The entry point from the Goldsmith house had led to this wide passage, maybe twenty feet across and fifteen feet high, the brick walls mortared tightly, their surface smooth as glass. He was surely standing in the Fleet River. Its pollution was long gone, the water cold, but the turgid air carried a rank odor. He'd once read a book about London's many underground rivers—names like Westbourne, Walbrook, Effra, Falcon, Peck, Neckinger—the Fleet and the Tyburn the most prominent. About a hundred miles of subterranean flow, he recalled, the city balanced atop them like a body on a water bed. In the ceiling high above ventilation shafts periodically pierced the brick arch, leading to metal grates that allowed in light and air. He'd seen some of those grates on the streets. Now here he was underground, inside an impressive Victorian creation, the Fleet River washing past him at an impressive pace. His normal discomfort at being enclosed was eased by the wide space and tall ceilings. Also, Gary was here. Somewhere.

And that meant he had to keep going.

Mathews had told him to follow the power cables. The one that had snaked a path from his entry point at the Inns of Court was affixed above him, past any high-water mark, disappearing ahead into the semidarkness. The gun was still nestled to his spine, beneath his jacket. He was being led. No doubt. But not for the first time. His job with the Magellan Billet had been to take these kinds of risks. He knew what he was doing. What he didn't know was what had happened between Antrim and Gary. Had he laid a hand on the boy? Hurt him in any way? At a minimum a stranger had entered their family and come between him and his son. Worse, this stranger was not to be trusted, paid millions of dollars to sell out his country. Were the deaths of the two American agents on Antrim's shoulders? Damn right. And now this traitor had Gary within his clutches.

What a mess.

And all because of mistakes made long ago.

KATHLEEN FOUND THE SOURCE OF THE COMMOTION and watched as Ian Dunne sprayed a man in the face. Pepper spray, most likely, judging from the reaction. Ian had clearly disobeyed Malone's instructions to stay put at the hotel. She was hidden behind a concrete mixing machine, its exterior caked in gray grout. She watched as the boys ran and realized the other was Malone's son, Gary. She heard Ian as he explained that Malone was nearby and Gary saying that he knew where. She decided to stay anonymous, at least for the moment, ducking and allowing them to pass.

She followed, giving them distance.

Plenty of cover was present from the debris and equipment. She saw them find the ladder from the video and climb down. She approached, spotted no one below, and hustled down, too. At the bottom a quick glance to her right revealed Gary Malone disappearing into a tunnel.

Air billowed from another tunnel to her left.

A few seconds later an Underground train roared past, entering the tunnel where the boys had gone. She rushed over and waited for the cars to pass, then peered into the darkness.

The two boys had pressed themselves to the concrete walls and were now hustling ahead, finding a door and entering.

ANTRIM DESCENDED A FLIGHT OF MARBLE STEPS into a lit chamber. The vaulted room was oval-shaped, its ceiling supported by eight evenly spaced pillars. Most of the walls were shelved, the bays divided by chiseled pilasters. Cups, candlesticks, kettles, lamps, bowls, porcelain, chalices, jugs, and tankards were displayed.

"Royal plate," Mathews said. "Part of the Tudor wealth. These objects were of great value five hundred years ago."

He stepped to the oval's center, glancing up at vine and scroll decorations that ornamented the columns. Murals of angels were painted above each support, more colorful paintings in the upper arches.

"This is how it was found," Mathews said. "Luckily, SIS was the first to enter and it has remained sealed since the 1970s."

A stone sarcophagus stood thirty feet away.

Antrim walked close and saw that its lid was gone.

He glanced at Mathews.

"By all means," the older man said. "Have a look."

MALONE CONTINUED TO FOLLOW THE ELECTRICAL cables, which eventually left the river chamber and wound a path through another narrow tunnel back into the earth. Not a long way. Maybe twenty feet. Eventually, he noted, as the river rose, its flow would creep inside. But—thanks to a gradual incline—not all the way to its end.

Which came at an archway with no door.

Beyond he spotted a darkened chamber about thirty feet across and another doorway, bright with light.

He heard familiar voices.

Mathews and Antrim.

He found his gun and entered the first room,

careful with his steps, creeping across the pavement to the second doorway.

Three pillars supported the ceiling of the empty rectangle, offering some cover. He leaned against the wall and drew short breaths through his nostrils.

Then peered inside.

IAN LED THE WAY DOWN THE TUNNEL, GARY CLOSE at his heels. They were following the electrical cables and lights, as that was what Mathews had told Malone to do during the telephone conversation at The Goring. Gary had led him to the metal door, describing the older man who'd been waiting earlier.

Whom he knew.

Thomas Mathews.

He heard a rush of water, growing louder, and found its source just past the place where a metal door hung open. He knew about the Fleet River that ran beneath London, and had even explored the tunnels a couple of times. He recalled a posted warning. High tide came fast and flooded the chambers, so the risk of drowning was great. Now he stood on an iron bridge that spanned the flow, water rushing past its supports, rising rapidly inside a channeled path. The surge vibrated everything beneath his feet.

"We need to stay out of that," Gary said.

He agreed.

They kept moving, entering another open arch, its metal door swung open, following the lights to a small chamber. The electrical cables snaked a path down the wall, then across the floor into another room.

Voices disturbed the silence.

Gary eased to one side of the far doorway.

Ian fell in behind him.

Both listened.

ANTRIM STARED INTO THE SARCOPHAGUS. Nothing elaborate or ornate adorned its exterior. No inscriptions, no artwork. Just plain stone.

And inside only dust and bones.

"The body is that of a man who lived to be in his seventies," Mathews said. "Forensic analysis confirmed that. Thanks to your violation of Henry VIII's tomb, we obtained a sample from the great king himself."

"Glad I could be of service."

Mathews seemed not to like the sarcasm. "DNA analysis between the remains there and here showed that this man shared a paternal genetic link with Henry VIII."

"So this is what's left of Henry FitzRoy's son. The imposter. The man who was Elizabeth I."

"There is no doubt now. The legend is real. What

was once a fanciful tale to the people in and around Bisley is now fact. Of course, the legend had done no real harm—"

"Until I came along."

Mathews nodded. "Something like that."

What Robert Cecil had written was true. The imposter had indeed been buried beneath Blackfriars, and the dead Elizabeth, a mere child of twelve, moved to Westminster and laid to rest with her sister.

Incredible.

"This room, when found," Mathews said, "also contained trunks of gold and silver coin. Billions of pounds' worth. We melted it down and returned it to the state treasury, where it belonged."

"Didn't keep any for yourself?"

"Hardly."

He caught the indignation.

"If you would, please, I'd like Robert Cecil's journal."

Antrim slid off the backpack and handed over the book.

"I saw it earlier," Mathews said.

"I didn't want Daedalus to have it. And what about them? Are they going to be a problem?"

Mathews shook his head. "Nothing I cannot handle."

He was curious. "What are you going to do with this place?"

"Once this notebook is destroyed, this becomes just another innocuous archaeological site. Its meaning will never be known."

"King's Deception would have worked."

"Unfortunately, Mr. Antrim, you are correct. We could have never allowed the truth about Elizabeth to be known."

He was pleased to know that he'd been right.

"I do have a question," Mathews said. "You maneuvered Cotton Malone to London, with his son, for a specific purpose. I managed to learn that purpose. The boy is your natural son. What do you plan to do with that situation?"

"How could you possibly know any of that?"

"Fifty years in the intelligence business."

He decided to be honest. "I've decided having a son is a pain in the ass."

"Children can be difficult. Still, he is your boy."

"But the several million dollars Daedalus paid me is more than enough compensation for the loss of that."

Mathews gestured with the journal. "You realize that what you planned to do with all of this was utter foolishness."

"Really? It seemed to get **your** attention."

"You clearly have no understanding of Northern Ireland. I knew men and women who died there during the Troubles. I lost agents there. Thousands of civilians died, too. There are hundreds of obsessed fringe groups simply waiting for a good reason to start killing one another again. Some want the English gone. Others want us to stay. Both are willing to slaughter thousands to prove their point. To reveal this secret would have cost many people their lives."

"All you had to do was tell the Scots to not release the Libyan."

"Such an interesting way to treat one of your allies."

"We say the same about you."

"This is none of America's concern. The bombing of that plane occurred in Scottish territory. Scottish judges tried and convicted al-Megrahi. The decision as to what to do with their prisoner was the Scots' alone."

"I don't know what you, or they, were promised by Libya, but it had to be substantial."

"Is that moralizing?" Mathews asked. "From a man who sold out his country, his career, and his son for a few million dollars?"

He said nothing. No need to explain himself.

Not anymore.

"You manipulated Cotton Malone," Mathews said. "His son, his ex-wife, the CIA, Daedalus. You tried to manipulate my government, but then decided **you** were more important than any of that. How does it feel, Mr. Antrim, to be a traitor?"

He'd heard enough.

He slid the backpack from his shoulders

and dropped it at the base of one of the center pillars.

The detonators were in place, armed, ready to go.

"What now?" he asked.

Mathews smiled. "A little justice, Mr. Antrim."

Sixty

Malone listened to the conversation between Antrim and Mathews, growing angrier by the second. Antrim cared for nothing save himself. Gary was meaningless. But where was Gary? He was supposed to be with Antrim. He gripped the gun, finger on the trigger, then stepped from the shadows into the harsh wash of light.

Mathews stood facing away. Antrim had a clear view and shock filled the American's face.

"What the hell is he doing here?"

Mathews slowly turned. "I invited him. I assume you have been listening?"

"To every word."

"I thought you two needed a private place to resolve your differences. So I led both of you here." Mathews moved toward the steps and the other doorway out. "I'll leave you two to work through your dispute."

"Where's Gary?" he asked.

Mathews stopped and faced him. "I have him. He's safe. Now deal with Mr. Antrim."

GARY HEARD WHAT MATHEWS HAD SAID.

A lie.

He started forward to reveal himself.

His father needed to know he was there.

Ian grabbed his shoulder and whispered, "You can't. That man's a bloody schemer. He wants to kill me, and probably you, too."

He stared into Ian's eyes and saw truth.

"Sit tight," Ian breathed. "Wait a bit. Let your dad handle it."

MALONE STARED AT BOTH MATHEWS AND ANTRIM, keeping his gun aimed and ready.

Mathews smiled. "Come now, Cotton. You and I both know that you cannot—or, better yet, you will not—shoot me. This entire fiasco was started by Washington. I have done nothing more than defend the security of my country. You understand the gravity of what was at stake. Can you blame me, now? I did exactly what you would have done, if the roles were reversed. The prime minister himself is aware of what is happening here. You can kill me, but that prisoner transfer is going to occur and my death would only make a bad situation for Washington horrendous."

He knew the old man was right.

"Actually, this problem is his creation." Mathews pointed at Antrim. "And, frankly, I hope you make him suffer. He killed three of my agents."

"What the hell are you talking about?" Antrim said. "I didn't kill anybody who works for you."

Mathews shook his head in disgust. "You ass. **I created Daedalus**. The people you encountered with them were my agents. The money paid to you came from me. It was all a show. You are not the only one who can manipulate."

Antrim stood silent, seemingly absorbing reality, then said, "You killed two of my people. And your three agents came to kill me. I only defended myself."

"Which, frankly, shocked me. You are an incompetent fool. How you were able to solve this puzzle is a mystery. It has remained concealed for a long time. But, incredibly, you somehow stumbled into the solution. So I had no choice. You gave me no choice."

"I did my job."

"Really, now? And at the first opportunity offered you sold out your country. For a few million dollars you were willing to forget it all, including those two dead American agents."

Antrim said nothing.

"Your name. I always thought it ironic. There are six counties in Northern Ireland. Armagh, Down, Fermanagh, Londonderry, Tyrone—" Mathews paused. "—and Antrim. It's an ancient place. Perhaps somewhere in your lineage there is Irish blood."

"What does it matter?" Antrim asked.

"That's the point. Nothing really does matter, except you. Now I will leave you two to settle your differences."

And Mathews started up the stone risers.

GARY HAD TAKEN IAN'S ADVICE AND STAYED PUT. Ever since his mother had told him about his birth father, he'd imagined what that man would be like. Now he knew. A liar, traitor, and murderer. Someone vastly different than he'd hoped.

He heard the soles of shoes scrape across gritty stone.

Approaching.

"Someone is coming," Ian whispered.

The area where they stood was small. No exit besides the way they'd come and the doorway into the next chamber. A bright bulb inside a wire cage dissolved the darkness, but not entirely. To their right, near the far wall, shadows remained thick. He and Ian fled there and huddled in a corner, waiting to see who appeared in the doorway.

The older man.

He stepped out and headed for the second exit.

Then stopped.

And turned.

His gaze locked their way.

"It's impressive you both made it here," he said in a low, throaty voice. "Perhaps that's best. You both should see what is about to happen."

Neither he nor Ian moved.

Gary's heart pounded.

"Nothing to say?"

Neither boy spoke.

Finally, Ian said, "You wanted me dead."

"That I did. You know things that you should not."

In one hand the older man held a book, which Gary recognized. "That's Cecil's journal."

"Indeed. Apparently you, too, know things you should not."

Then he left.

Entering the tunnel that led to the bridge and the construction site.

They both hesitated, waiting to be sure he was gone.

Then they stepped back, closer to the doorway.

ANTRIM DID NOT LIKE ANYTHING ABOUT THE situation. Mathews had led him here to confront

Malone, who was staring at him holding a gun. The backpack with the explosives lay against one of the columns. Malone had paid it little attention. The remote detonator was tucked in his pocket. He didn't actually have to remove it. Just a slap to his thigh would do the trick.

But not yet.

He was far too close.

And Mathews had said nothing about the explosives. No warning to Malone. As if he wanted them used. What had the old Brit said. **Bring them along. You may have need of them.**

Malone stood between him and the stairs that led up to the doorway through which Mathews had left. But the second exit, the one from which Malone had entered, beckoned.

That was the way.

Opposite the path Mathews had taken.

He needed to end this, go to ground, and enjoy his money.

"You're a tough man," he said to Malone, "with that gun. I'm unarmed."

Malone tossed the weapon aside.

It clattered across the floor.

Challenge accepted.

KATHLEEN HAD FOLLOWED IAN AND GARY through the metal door and into a lit tunnel, walking slowly, her gun leading the way. She'd stayed back, waiting to see where the path would lead, concerned about the two boys, ready to confront them. A rush of water had grown louder and she came to a metal bridge that spanned a dark, swift current.

The Fleet River.

She'd been into its tunnels twice before, once in pursuit of a fugitive, another time to search for a body. Its subterranean path was one tall tunnel after another, at least ten meters high, the water now up to nearly half that height, just below the bridge.

Movement from the other side caught her eye.

She retreated back into the shadows.

Thomas Mathews emerged onto the bridge, then turned and closed the far door behind him. She watched as he inserted a key into the lock and secured the portal. Before leaving the door Mathews reached beneath his jacket and found a small radio.

She stepped onto the bridge.

Not a hint of surprise spread across the older man's face.

"I was wondering when you would appear," he said.

He approached, stopping two meters away.

She kept her gun aimed at him. "Where are those two boys?"

"Behind that locked door."

Now she knew. "You lured them all here."

"Only Antrim and Malone. But Ian Dunne was

an unexpected bonus. He and Malone's son are now there, too."

What was happening beyond that door?

Then she noticed what else Mathews was holding. An old book, bound in brittle leather, clutched tight.

"What is that?" she asked.

"What I have sought. What, ultimately, you may have discovered for me."

Then she realized. "Robert Cecil's journal."

"You are, indeed, an excellent agent. Quite intuitive. Unfortunate that no discipline accompanies that admirable trait."

"I get what's at stake here," she told him over the water's roar. "I know what Northern Ireland is capable of starting up again. I don't agree with the Americans meddling in our business, but I also understand why they did. That bloody terrorist **should** stay in jail. All of you have handled this wrong."

"Sharp criticism from a disgraced agent."

She absorbed his insult. "A disgraced agent, who gives a damn about two kids in trouble."

"Ian Dunne is a witness to an SIS murder. One, here, on British soil. Which, as you noted at Queen's College, violates the law."

"Quite a scandal for you and the prime minister. Tell me, does he know all that you've done."

His silence was her answer.

"Let us say that I am dealing with it, Miss

Richards. This must end here. It must end now. For the good of the nation."

"And for the good of you."

She'd heard enough.

"Give me the key to that door."

Sixty-one

Malone's nerves jangled with rage, his eyes watching Antrim's every move. "Was all this worth it?"

"Damn right. I have plenty of money. And in a few minutes you'll be dead."

"So sure of yourself."

"I've been around a long time, Malone."

"I'm not one of your exes. You might find beating up on me a bit more difficult."

Antrim shifted to the right, closer to the open sarcophagus. The gun lay ten feet away from them both, but Antrim seemed uninterested, moving in the opposite direction.

"That what this is about?" Antrim asked. "Defending the honor of your ex-wife? You didn't seem to care much about her sixteen years ago."

He refused the bait. "You enjoy beating up women?"

Antrim shrugged. "Yours didn't seem to mind at the time."

The words stung, but he kept his cool.

"If it's any comfort, Malone. The boy means nothing. I just wanted to see if it could be done. Pam pissed me off a few months ago. She thought she could tell **me** what to do. One rule I always live by. Never let a woman be in control."

GARY HEARD MORE OF WHAT ANTRIM SAID.

A wave of revulsion and anger welled inside him.

He moved to rush into the chamber, but Ian again grabbed him and shook his head.

"Let your dad handle it," Ian breathed. "It's his fight right now."

Ian was right. This was not the time. Him suddenly appearing would only complicate things. Let his dad handle it.

"You okay?" Ian breathed.

He nodded.

But he wasn't.

ANTRIM WAS TAUNTING MALONE, PUSHING EVERY button, goading him into a reaction. But he wasn't lying, either. Not about Pam or Gary. Neither mattered anymore. He would have to take Malone down, then flee out the other entrance, detonating the explosives as he left. Fifty feet would be more than enough protection, considering the dirt walls that surrounded him. The resulting heat and concussion would surely crack the stone and collapse the chamber, providing a proper grave for ex–Magellan Billet agent Cotton Malone. All he had to do was get through the doorway ten feet away.

That meant incapacitating Malone for a mere few seconds.

Enough for him to bolt and press the detonator in his pocket.

Careful, though.

He could not engage in too much jostling, as he did not want the button jammed accidentally.

But he could handle this.

MALONE LEAPED, HIS ARMS CATCHING ANTRIM around the waist.

He and Antrim pounded to the stone floor.

But he held tight.

IAN HEARD BODIES THUD AND A GRUNT FROM ONE of the two men. He risked a look and saw that they were fighting, Antrim flipping Malone off him and springing to his feet. Malone, too, was up and swung his fist, the blow blocked, a counterpunch delivered to the stomach.

Gary watched, too.

Ian's gaze raked the chamber and located the gun, to the right of the entrance, at the base of steps that led down into the room.

"We need to get that gun," he said.

But Gary's attention was on the fight.

"Antrim has explosives."

GARY SAW THAT IAN WAS SURPRISED BY WHAT HE'D revealed. "In that pack on the floor. The detonator is in his pocket."

"And you're just now mentioning this?"

He'd seen what those packs of clay could do to bodies.

Special stuff, Antrim had said.

He recalled that Antrim had been around fifty feet away from the carnage in the warehouse and had been unharmed. If he could toss the backpack out the doorway on the other side of the room, that might do it. He doubted Antrim planned to blow anything as long as he was still around.

But the detonator.

In Antrim's pocket.

It could accidentally be pressed in the fight.

His dad was in trouble.

"You get the gun," he said to Ian. "I'll toss that backpack."

* * *

MALONE DODGED A RIGHT JAB AND SWUNG HARD, catching Antrim in the face. His opponent staggered back against the chamber wall, then charged.

More blows rained down.

One caught him in the lip. A salty taste filled his mouth. Blood. He landed more blows to the head and chest but, before he could punch again, Antrim reached for one of the metal pitchers on the shelves and propelled it toward him.

He ducked the projectile.

Then Antrim was on him, slamming something heavy into the nape of his neck, which hurt. He grabbed hold of himself and joined his hands together, sweeping his arms upward, the double fist clipping Antrim below the chin.

A bronze flask clanged to the floor.

His head spun, the throbbing in his temple became a blinding ache.

A kick to his legs twisted him sideways.

He turned, pretended to have lost his breath, and readied himself to attack.

Ian rushed into the room, leaping down the stone stairs, heading straight for the gun.

Then Gary appeared.

What the hell?

Their appearance momentarily stunned him.

Ian reached for the gun, but Antrim was on him, yanking the weapon free, backhanding the boy across the face.

Gary grabbed the backpack from the floor and tossed it into the darkness of the other room.

ANTRIM'S FINGER FOUND THE TRIGGER AND HE aimed the weapon. "Enough."

Malone seemed woozy, the boys staring at him.

Ian rubbed his face from the blow.

Fear surged through him. His sweat cast a sweet, musky scent.

One thought filled his brain.

Leave. Now.

"All of you, over there, by the stairs."

His left eye was swollen from Malone's fist, his chin, temple, and brow aching. He retreated toward the second doorway, his pounding heart rising against his ribs.

Malone moved slow so he aimed the gun straight at Gary and yelled, "Would you rather I shoot him? Get over there."

Malone straightened up and stepped back, Ian and Gary joining him.

"You okay?" Malone asked Ian.

"I'll be fine."

Gary stepped forward. "Would you shoot me? Your own son?"

No time for sentiment. "Look, we haven't known each other in fifteen years. No need to start now. So, yes, I would. Now shut the hell up."

"So this was all about hurting my mom?"

"You were listening outside? Good. So I don't have to repeat myself."

Malone laid his hand on Gary's shoulder and drew him back close, but the boy's gaze never left Antrim.

Antrim found the exit, a quick glance confirming that the chamber beyond was safe. The darkness was thick, but enough light spilled in for him to see the outline of another exit thirty feet away.

He reached into his pocket and found the detonator.

"Stay right there," he told Malone.

He backed from the room, keeping the gun trained.

Sixty-two

Kathleen aimed the gun straight at Thomas Mathews. Never had she imagined that she would be in a face-off with Britain's chief spy. But that's exactly what the past two days had been.

"Give me the key to the door," she said again.

"And what will you do?"

"Help them."

He chuckled. "What if they don't need your help?"

"All of your problems are in there, right? Nice and neat. Tucked away."

"Good planning and preparation made that result possible."

But how could Mathews know that all of his problems would be solved? So she asked, "What makes this a sure thing?"

"Ordinarily, I would not answer that. But I'm

hoping this will be a learning experience for you. Your Blake Antrim brought percussion explosives with him. The same type used in St. George's Chapel."

The dots connected. "Which you want him to detonate."

He shrugged. "It matters not how it ends. Intentional. Accidental. So long as it ends."

"And if Antrim makes it out, after blowing everyone else up?"

"He will be killed."

Now she realized Mathews was stalling, allowing whatever was happening behind the locked door to play out.

That meant time was short.

And those two kids were in there.

"Give me the key."

He displayed it in his right hand, the one that held the radio.

Then he thrust his arm over the side of the bridge.

"Don't do it," she said.

He dropped the key.

Which disappeared into the torrent.

"We do what we have to do," he said to her, his face as animated as a death mask. "My country comes first, as I suspect it does with you."

"Country first means killing children?"

"In this case it does."

She hated herself for not stopping Ian and

Gary sooner. It was her fault they were now behind that locked door. "You're no different from Antrim."

"Oh, but I am. Quite different, in fact. I am no traitor."

"I will shoot you."

He smiled. "I think not. It's over, Miss Richards. Let it be."

She saw his fingers flick a switch on the radio. Surely there were more men nearby, which meant that shortly they would not be alone. She'd heard about moments when a person's entire existence flashed before them. Those instances when life-changing decisions were either made or avoided. Turning points, some called them. She'd come close several times to such an instant, when her life had been on the line.

But never anything like this.

Sir Thomas Mathews was, in essence, saying that she was too weak to do anything.

He'd dropped the key and dared her.

Her professional life was over.

She'd failed.

But that didn't mean that she should fail as a person.

Malone and two kids were in trouble.

And one old man stood in her way.

He brought the radio toward his mouth. "They have to die, Miss Richards. It is the only way for this to end."

No, it wasn't.

May God forgive her.

She shot him in the chest.

He staggered toward the low rail.

The journal dropped to his feet.

A look of shock filled his face.

She stepped close. "You're not always right."

And she shoved him over the side.

He hit the water, surfaced, and gasped for air, arms flailing. Then his strength oozed away and he sank, the current sweeping the corpse into the darkness toward the Thames.

No time existed for her to consider the implications of what she'd done. Instead, she rushed toward the door and studied the lock. Brass. New. The door itself all metal.

She kicked it a few times.

Solid and opening toward her, which meant a metal jam was providing extra strength.

Only one way.

She stepped back, aimed the gun, and emptied the magazine into the lock.

GARY NEVER ALLOWED HIS GAZE TO BREAK.

Everything happened so fast he doubted Antrim realized that the backpack was gone. His attention had been on Ian and the gun. Antrim continued to back into the darkness of the other room, the gun still aimed their way. He was no longer visible but, thanks to the lights, they remained in full view to him.

His dad was watching, too.

"Let him go," Gary said, his lips barely moving.

MALONE HEARD GARY'S WORDS.

"What's he got?" he quietly asked, keeping his eyes on the dark doorway across the room.

"Bad explosives," Gary mumbled. "Superhot. They burn people. He brought them in the backpack."

What had Mathews told him at Hampton Court? About Antrim and Henry VIII's grave? **He used percussion explosives to crack away the marble slab above the remains.** He knew their capabilities. And limitations.

His eyes raked the room, confirming what he'd seen a few moments ago.

The backpack was gone.

"Let him go," Gary breathed again.

ANTRIM GRIPPED THE DETONATOR IN HIS RIGHT hand. He was safe within the second room, Malone and the two boys visible through the doorway in the next chamber. Plenty of protection stood between him and the PEs. He kept his gun aimed, which Malone seemed to respect, as none of the three had moved. A quick glance back and he saw the blackened outline of the other exit only a few feet away. He had no idea where it led, but obviously it was a way out, and far preferable to heading in the direction of Thomas Mathews. His eyes were still accustomed to the lights and he allowed his pupils a moment to dilate, preparing himself for darkness. He carried no flashlight, but neither had Malone, which meant that the way out was easy to follow. He'd just have to keep his eyes shielded during the explosion.

Thomas Mathews wanted him to kill Malone. The boys? Collateral damage. Two fewer witnesses to all that had transpired.

Gary?

It didn't matter.

He was no father.

The past twenty-four hours had proven that.

He was better off alone.

And alone he would be.

He dropped to the floor and prepared to hunker down close.

He aimed the detonator.

And pushed the button.

A flash sparked ten feet away.

Here.

In this room.

The darkness was dissolved by orange, then yellow, and finally blue light.

He screamed.

MALONE SAW A FLASH, HEARD A TERRIFIED WHIMPER, and imagined Antrim's face, a study in horror as he realized what was coming. He dove left and swept Gary and Ian down with him. Together they hit the floor and he shielded both boys from the concussion that poured from the other chamber, intense heat and light surging upward and engulfing the ceiling. The sarcophagus stood between them and the other exit, which blocked much of its effect. Thank goodness those were PEs and not conventional explosives, as the pressure wave would have annihilated both chambers.

But the heat wreaked havoc.

Electrical conduits severed and the lightbulbs burst with a blast of blue sparks. The PEs exhausted themselves in a mere few seconds, like magician's flash paper, the room plunged into total darkness. He glanced up and caught the bitter waft of spent carbon, the once cool air now midday-warm.

"You okay?" he asked the boys.

Both said they were.

They'd all heard the scream.

"You did what you had to," he said to Gary.

"He would have killed us," Ian added.

But Gary remained silent.

A crack broke the silence. Like wood splintering, only louder, more pronounced. Then another. Followed by more. He tensed as a gnawing anticipation grew within him. He knew what was happening. The centuries-old bricks that made up the walls and ceiling of the adjacent chamber had just been subjected to heat intense enough to crack their surface. Couple that with the pressures of holding back tons of earth and it would not take much for all of it to give way.

Something crashed in the other room.

Hard and heavy.

Followed by another thud powerful enough to shake the floor.

Ceiling stone was raining down. Their chamber was okay, for the moment. But they needed to leave.

One problem.

Total darkness surrounded them.

He could not even see his hand in front of his eyes.

No way to know which way to go.

And little time to find out.

KATHLEEN TOSSED THE GUN ONTO THE BRIDGE and lunged for the metal door. She'd planted four rounds into the lock, obliterating it. Risky, considering the ricochets off the metal, but she'd had no choice. The door was equipped with no knob or handle, only the lock that kept it shut, an inserted key the way to ease it open once the tumblers were released.

But she had no key.

Another kick and the panel jarred loose enough from its jamb for her to curl her fingers inside and yank it outward. Two solid tugs and the mutilated lock gave way, the door bursting open.

She immediately noticed the odor. Carbon. Burnt. Just like from Henry VIII's grave at Windsor. Spent percussion explosives.

Something had happened.

A passage stretched before her, everything in solid darkness. The only light was what leaked in from the river tunnel, which was barely illuminated by overhead grates.

She heard a crash.

A heavy mass slamming downward.

No choice on what to do.

"Ian? Gary? Malone?"

MALONE HEARD KATHLEEN RICHARDS.

She'd made it to them.

Elation and panic mingled within him.

More stone cascading downward drowned out Richards' pleas. Then something smashed to pieces only a few feet away. The carnage was spreading and a toxic cloud of dust was enveloping them.

Breathing was difficult.

They had to go.

"We're in here," he called out. "Keep talking."

IAN HEARD RICHARDS, TOO, HER VOICE FAR OFF, probably in the tunnel that led from the bridge.

"She's back from where we came," he said to Malone through the blackness.

More stone cracked to rubble only a few feet away.

"Everyone up," Malone said. "Hold hands."

He felt Gary's grip in his.

"We're in a chamber," Malone called out. "Beyond the tunnel where you are."

"I'll count out," Richards said. "Follow the voice."

GARY HELD HIS FATHER'S AND IAN'S HANDS.

The chamber was collapsing, and the one in

which Antrim had died was probably already gone. The air was stifling and all three of them struggled against fits of coughing, but it was next to impossible not to inhale dust.

His dad led the way and they found the steps.

Stone pounded the floor nearby and his father yanked him up the risers. He held on tight and guided Ian up with him.

He could hear a woman counting from a hundred.

Backward.

MALONE FOCUSED ON RICHARDS' VOICE, CLIMBING the steps. His right hand groped the air ahead, looking for the doorway he recalled seeing, listening to the numbers.

"87. 86. 85."

He moved right.

The voice grew fainter.

Back to the left. More rock crumbled to dust behind them as centuries-old engineering succumbed to gravity.

"83. 82. 81. 80."

His hand found the doorway and he led them out.

The air was better here, breathing easier.

And nothing was falling.

"We're out," he called to the darkness.

"I'm here," Richards said.

Directly ahead.

Not far.

He kept moving, each step cautious.

"There's nothing out here," Gary said. "It's an empty room."

Good to know.

"Keep talking," he said to Richards.

She started counting again. He kept edging the boys toward the voice, picking through the dark, his right hand finding familiarity at a wall.

His fingers, curved into a claw, led the way.

The chamber they'd just fled seemed to be imploding, the crashes escalating to a crescendo.

His hand found air.

And Richards.

She grabbed hold and drew him into another tunnel, leading them away. Around two bends and he spotted a faint glow. Bluish. Like the pale wash of moonlight.

They stepped through an exit.

He noticed the door, its lock shot through. They stood on a bridge above another portion of the river tunnel he'd ventured through earlier. The pull of the tides had thrown up a wall of water, flooding the passage, raising the Fleet another eight to ten feet. Luckily, the bridge spanned above it with three feet to spare.

He checked on Gary and Ian.

Both boys were fine.

He faced Richards. "Thanks. We needed that."

He noticed something lying on the bridge behind her.

Robert Cecil's journal.

Then he saw the gun.

And knew.

He lifted the weapon and snapped out the magazine.

Empty.

"You found Mathews?"

She nodded.

"The older man knew Antrim had those explosives," Gary said. "He told him he might have use for them."

Malone understood. Mathews had clearly wanted Antrim to kill him. He was probably hoping that Antrim would also kill himself in the process. If not, then surely SIS agents would have taken him out. Antrim was either too foolish or too anxious to realize he could not win.

"Mathews also knew Gary and Ian were in there," Richards said.

"He saw us," Ian said. "When he left."

He knew the drill. No witnesses.

The son of a bitch.

He stepped close, still holding the gun, and caught the truth in Kathleen Richards' eyes. She'd killed the head of SIS.

Better not to say a word.

Same rule.
No witnesses.
But he wanted her to know something.
So he stared back and sent her a message.
Good job.

Sixty-three

HATFIELD HOUSE
SUNDAY, NOVEMBER 23
9:45 AM

MALONE ENTERED THE MANSION, LOCATED twenty miles north of London. He'd taken the train with Kathleen Richards, Ian, Gary, Tanya, and Miss Mary, the station located immediately adjacent to the estate. The day had begun typically English in late fall—occasional sunshine, sudden showers. He'd managed a few hours' sleep without any turbulent dreams. They'd all showered, changed clothes, and eaten breakfast. The horror of yesterday was over, everyone relieved but still apprehensive. Calls made long into last night had finally yielded results.

Washington and London had come to an uneasy peace.

And neither side was happy.

Washington was pissed because the Libyan prisoner transfer would occur. London remained angry over what it considered an unwarranted invasion of its historical privacy by an ally. In the end both sides agreed to walk away and leave it alone. The transfer would happen and both sides would drop any notions of retaliation for Operation King's Deception.

The deal would be sealed here, at Hatfield House, the ancestral home of the Cecils, still owned by the 7th Marquess and Marchioness of Salisbury, themselves distant relatives of William and Robert Cecil. In 1607 James I traded the property to Robert Cecil, who then built a massive E-shaped brick residence—two wings joined together by a central block—a mixture of Jacobean style and Tudor distinction. Tanya had told Malone that little had changed about the exterior since Robert Cecil's time.

"This is a place of great history," she said. "Many kings and queens have come here."

Inside was large and lofty, the furnishings simple in a grand style. The air reeked of varnish from the warm paneling, wax off the polished floors, and the smoky remnants of wood fires.

"We've visited here several times since we were little girls," Miss Mary said. "And it always smells the same."

They stood in Marble Hall, a Jacobean marvel that stretched up two floors and spanned the length of the great house. Oriel windows splashed golden blocks of sunshine on the paneled walls. He admired the minstrel's gallery, the wall tapestries, and the namesake checkerboard marble floor. A fire crackled in a hearth before a row of oak tables and benches that were identified as original furnishings.

A few hours ago Thomas Mathews' body had been fished from the Thames, a bullet hole in his chest. A preliminary autopsy had revealed water in his lungs, which meant he actually drowned. Nothing had been told to Stephanie Nelle about Kathleen Richards killing Mathews. The gun had been tossed into the Fleet River where, by now, it was long gone. Only he and Richards knew the truth, the tragedy officially ruled a consequence of a counter-operation gone wrong. Part of the brokered deal had been that Mathews' death, along with those of Antrim and the other five agents, would remain unexplained.

Stephanie reported that SIS had tried to penetrate the subterranean chambers where everything had played out, but both were gone. Tiny cameras, used in earthquake rescue, located charred remains among the moraine of stones and smashed artifacts, confirming Antrim's demise.

Operation King's Deception was finished.

Only one last thing to do.

From the far side of the hall a woman entered. She was tall, thin, and stately, her honey-colored hair neatly shingled in precise waves. She marched toward them at a steady pace, the sharp ring of her heels absorbed by the paneled walls. He'd been told her name. Elizabeth McGuire. Secretary of state for the Home Department. Charged with all matters involving national security, including SIS oversight. Thomas Mathews had worked for her.

She stopped before Malone. "Would the rest of you excuse us? Mr. Malone and I must speak in private."

He nodded to the others that it was okay.

"Enjoy a walk through the house," McGuire said. "There is no one inside but us."

He watched as Richards and the twin sisters led the boys from the hall.

As they departed, McGuire said, "You caused quite a commotion."

"It's a gift," he said.

"Is this amusing to you?"

Obviously, this woman had not come to swap pleasantries or anecdotes. "Actually, the whole thing was stupid as hell. For both sides."

"On that we agree. But let me be clear, the Americans started this."

"Really? It was our idea to trade away a terrorist murderer?"

He wanted her to know on which side of the fence he stood.

Her face softened. "Stephanie Nelle is a close friend. She said you were once her best agent."

"I pay her to tell people that."

"I think she and I were both shocked by all that had happened. Particularly regarding Ian Dunne. And your son. Placing young boys in jeopardy was inexcusable."

"Yet you still get what you wanted," Malone said. "The Libyan goes home and Great Britain derives whatever concessions it is Libya promised."

"As is the way of the world. The United States makes deals like those every day. So there is no need to become sanctimonious. We do what we have to." She paused. "Within limits."

Apparently the out-of-bounds marker on those limits stretched far, but the time for debate was over.

She motioned toward the hall's far end and led him there. "I chose Hatfield House for our meeting because of this portrait."

Malone had already noticed the canvas, hanging in the center of a paneled wall, open archways on either side, flanked by two smaller oil images, one of Richard III, the other Henry VI. A carved oak chest stood beneath, veins of silver and gold streaking the ancient wood.

"The Rainbow Portrait," McGuire said.

He recalled its mention in Farrow Curry's notes and in Robert Cecil's journal. The face was that of a young woman, though the painting, as McGuire explained, was created when Elizabeth was seventy years old.

"Lots of symbolism here," she said.

And he listened as she explained.

The bodice was embroidered with spring flowers—pansies, cowslips, and honeysuckles—to allude to springtime. Her orange mantle, powdered with eyes and ears, showed that Elizabeth saw and heard all. A serpent adorned her left sleeve, from whose mouth hung a heart, representing passion and wisdom.

"It's the rainbow, held in her right hand, that gives the portrait its name."

He noticed its distinct lack of color.

"Elizabeth was always careful in choosing her portraits. This one, though, was finished after her death, so the artist had free rein."

Impressive, he had to admit.

"The last spectacle of Elizabeth I's reign happened in this room," McGuire said. "The queen visited Robert Cecil in December 1602. There was great ceremony and entertainment. A glorious finale to a long reign. Three months later she was dead."

He caught the definitive use of the pronoun **she.**

He'd also already noticed the phrase that appeared prominently on the left side of the portrait.

NON SINE SOLE IRIS.

Latin he understood, along with several other languages, a side effect of his eidetic memory.

NO RAINBOW WITHOUT THE SUN.

He pointed to the words.

"Historians have philosophized about the meaning of that motto," McGuire said. "Supposedly,

Elizabeth was the sun, whose presence alone brings peace to her realm and color to the rainbow."

"Yet the rainbow has no color."

"Precisely. Others have said that the painting is a subversive undercutting. No rainbow shines because there is no sun. Her magnificence is supposedly false." The older woman paused. "Not too far off the mark, would you not say?"

"Then there's another meaning," he said. "Taking the phrase for what it says and changing it. **No rainbow without the son.** S-o-n. Meaning there would have been nothing without him."

"Quite right. I've read the translation of Cecil's journal. He had great respect for the imposter. I imagine he gazed upon this image often."

"What now?" he asked.

"A good question. One I've been thinking about since last night. Unfortunately, Thomas Mathews did not survive to aid in my analysis. Can you tell me what happened to him?"

He wasn't about to fall into that trick bag. "He worked in a risky business, and stuff happens."

"Of course, if we were allowed to debrief all of you we might actually learn something relevant."

Part of the brokered deal was that no one talked to anyone about anything.

He shrugged. "It will simply remain a mystery. As will the deaths of two American agents."

"And three more from our side."

Touché. But this woman was no idiot. She knew

that either he, or Richards, killed Mathews. Nothing she could do about it either way. So he made clear, "My son was placed in grave danger. And, as you said, so was Ian Dunne. They're not players. Never were. Never will be. Go too far in this game and there's a price to be paid."

"I conceded to Stephanie that both sides went too far. Seven deaths is more than enough for us all to learn a lesson."

He agreed.

She motioned to what he carried. Robert Cecil's journal. Stephanie had told him to bring it. The deal included its return.

She accepted the old volume, thumbed through its coded pages, then looked at him. "You asked me, what now?"

She stepped to the hearth and tossed the book into the fire. Flames leaped over the cover. Smoke wreathed the stones, before being sucked up the chimney. In a few seconds the journal was gone.

He said, "I guess history doesn't matter around here."

"On the contrary, it matters a great deal. In fact, it is history that would have caused all of the damage. Elizabeth I was a fraud, so anything and everything done during that reign would be void. At a minimum it would all be suspect. True, four hundred years have passed. But you're a lawyer, Mr. Malone. You know the principles of real property. Chain of title is critical. Elizabeth seized Irish land

and passed title on to a lot of British Protestants. Every one of those chains of title would now be in question, if not void from the start."

"And you British pride yourselves on the rule of law."

"Actually, we do. Which makes this scenario that much more frightening."

"So if Antrim had not been a traitor and deciphered the journal, it just might have stopped that prisoner transfer?"

She threw him a calculating gaze. "We'll never know the answer to that."

But he did.

"There is one other aspect to this, too," she said. "Elizabeth was also solely responsible for the accession of James I, as king. That would have never happened but for the imposter. James' mother was Mary, Queen of Scots, the great-niece of Henry VIII, her grandmother Henry's sister. Henry VIII's will specifically excluded that branch of the family from ever inheriting the throne. It is doubtful that the real Elizabeth would have gone so contrary to her father's wishes. The imposter was a wicked one, that I will say. He could birth no heirs, so he chose the one person to succeed him whom his grandfather expressly rejected. Perhaps he did that in deference to his mother, who hated Henry VIII and all of the Tudors. So you see, Mr. Malone, history does indeed matter. History is the whole reason all of this happened."

He pointed to the hearth. "But it's gone now. No more proof."

"The translations are likewise gone," she said. "As is the email the bookstore owner sent herself."

Miss Mary's cell phone had been confiscated last night.

"I believe you have the last version."

He produced the flash drive from his pocket and handed it to her.

She tossed it into the flames.

Malone found everyone outside, in the garden. Elizabeth McGuire was gone, their business concluded. She'd come to make sure the journal and the flash drive were destroyed. True, Ian, Richards, Tanya, and Miss Mary all knew the secret. And could speak of it. But nothing existed to support any of their allegations. Just a wild tale. Nothing more. Like the Bisley Boy legend and Bram Stoker's account from a hundred years ago.

"Time for us to leave," he said to Gary.

The boys said their goodbyes, then Ian faced him. "Maybe I'll come see you one day in Denmark."

"I'd like that. I really would."

They shook hands.

Miss Mary stood beside Ian, her arm on the boy's shoulder. He saw the pride on her face and realized that maybe now, finally, she had a son.

And Ian a mother.

He said, "Perhaps it's time for your street days to end."

Ian nodded. "I think you're right. Miss Mary wants me to live with her."

"That's an excellent idea."

Tanya stepped close and hugged him. "Good to know you, Mr. Malone. That was quite an adventure you gave us."

"If you ever want a job again in the intelligence business, use me for a reference. You did good."

"I enjoyed the experience. Something I shall not soon forget."

Gary said his goodbyes to the sisters while Malone led Kathleen Richards off to the side.

"What happened in there?" she asked in a low voice.

"The journal is gone, as are all the translations. Officially, this never happened."

He hadn't told her much about his conversations last night with Stephanie, but the confirmation came earlier. "You have your job back with SOCA. That's an order straight from the top. All is forgiven."

She tossed him a thankful smile. "I was wondering how I was going to make a living."

"I appreciate what you did down there. We owe you our lives."

"You would have done the same."

"Do me a favor?"

"Anything."

"Don't stop being you. Go for it. With all you've got, and to hell with the rules."

"I'm afraid it's the only way I can do the job."

"That's what I want to hear."

"But I still killed Mathews. I could have shot him in the leg. Taken him down."

"We both know that wouldn't have worked. The SOB deserved to die and, if given the opportunity, I would have done the same thing."

She appraised him carefully. "I do believe you would have."

"He recalled the last time he'd enountered Thomas Mathews. I told him once, seven years ago, that one day he'd press someone too far. And he finally did."

She thanked him for all he'd done. "Maybe I'll come over to Copenhagen one day and see you, too."

Her eyes held the promise of more.

"Anytime," he said. "Just let me know."

They walked back to the others.

"We made quite a team," he said to them. "Thanks for all your help."

He watched as they left, walking back to the train station for their return trip to London. He and Gary were headed straight to Heathrow, a car waiting for them at the house's main entrance, courtesy of Stephanie Nelle.

"You okay?" he asked Gary.

They hadn't really discussed all that happened

yesterday. And though Gary had not actually killed Antrim, he'd certainly allowed him to die.

"He was a bad man," Gary said.

"In every way."

The world swarmed with hacks, con men, and cardboard cutouts. Parents fought every way they could to shield their kids from each and every one. But here the truth had to be faced. He needed to say something.

"You're my son, Gary. In every way. You always will be. Nothing has changed that, or ever will."

"And you're my dad. Nothing will ever change **that,** either."

A chill swept through him.

"You got an earful yesterday," he said.

"I needed to hear it. That was reality. Mom kept it from me for a long time. But the truth finally found me."

"We now know why your mother kept Antrim to herself."

Gary nodded. "I owe her an apology."

"She'd appreciate that. She and I made a ton of mistakes a long time ago. It's good to know that they're all resolved now. Or at least I hope they are."

"You'll never hear me speak of this again. It's done."

"As it should be. But how about this one thing. Let's keep what happened here to ourselves."

His son smiled. "So Mom won't kill you?"

"Something like that."

Silence grew between them as they admired the gardens. Birds flitted across the grass in quest of tidbits. Thick trunks of mottled yellow and green bark cast a peaceful look. He recalled a story about the crumbling oak he could see in the distance. Where in November 1558 a twenty-five-year-old imposter dressed as the Princess Elizabeth, a role by that day he'd played for twelve years, was told of Queen Mary's death. He'd been reading a book and glanced up from the page at hearing the news that he was now ruler of England.

His words were prophetic.

This is the Lord's doing and it is marvelous in our eyes.

The last two days flowed with a calm finality through his mind. Much had happened. Much was over. But as with the imposter that day in the garden, so much lay ahead.

He wrapped an arm around his son's shoulder.

"Let's go home."

Epilogue

The Present

Epilogue

MALONE FINISHED HIS STORY.

An hour had passed.

Pam had sat at the table, in the quiet kitchen, and listened to every word, her eyes moistened with tears.

"I wondered why I never heard from Antrim again. I lived in fear, every day, that he would show up."

He'd wanted to tell her all of this for some time. She should know the truth. But he and Gary had agreed to keep it to themselves.

"I learned why you suddenly decided to tell me the truth about Gary," he said to her. "Antrim confronted you in that mall. He saw Gary and knew. He surely threatened to tell me himself. You had no choice."

She said nothing for a time.

"It was bad that day in my office. He made it clear he wasn't going away. I knew then you both had to know the truth. So I told you first."

A call he would never forget.

"Gary was so different when he returned from you that Thanksgiving," she said. "He apologized for the way he'd been. Said he was okay with everything. Told me that you and he had worked it all out. I was so relieved I didn't question anything. I was just grateful that he was okay."

"It was just that the 'working out' almost cost us."

The concerned look on her face confirmed that she understood what he meant. Both of their lives had been in jeopardy.

"Blake was a terrible man," she said. "When we were together, back in Germany, I just wanted to hurt you. To lash out. To make you feel the pain I felt from your betrayal. It could have been anybody. But stupid me chose him."

"I might actually understand that, except you never told me that you had the affair. So how was I hurt? Instead, you only hurt yourself, then lived with the consequences inside you."

And they both knew why that happened. She'd never been able to let go of the fact that he'd strayed. Outwardly, she forgave him. Inwardly, the shock of his cheating festered like a cancer. Occasionally it would rear its ugly head during an argument. Eventually, her lack of trust destroyed them both. Her confessing at the time that she had done the same thing might have changed all that. Maybe their marriage would have ended right then.

Or maybe not at all.

"My anger was so strong," she said. "But I was nothing more than a liar and a hypocrite. Looking back, we really never had a chance to stay together."

No, they hadn't.

"Seeing Antrim that day in the mall brought it all back. The past had finally come to reclaim what it had lost." She paused. "Gary."

They sat in silence.

Here was a woman whom he'd once loved—whom in some ways he still loved. Only now they were less than lovers, but more than friends, each knowing the other's strengths and weaknesses. Was that intimacy? Probably. At least partly. On the one hand it bred a measure of comfort. On the other, a level of fear.

"Blake attacked me the day I broke it off," she said. "He'd always been aggressive. Had a temper. But that day he was violent, and what really scared me was the look in his eyes. Like he couldn't help himself."

"That's the same thing Kathleen Richards described."

Richards had called him a couple of months after everything happened and visited Copenhagen for a few memorable days. They emailed a little after that, then lost touch. He'd sometimes wondered what happened to her.

"I never wanted Gary to know that man. Ever. He meant nothing to me, and I wanted him to remain that way."

"Gary saw firsthand what was important to Blake Antrim. He heard what Antrim really thought of him. I know it hurt, but it's good he heard it. We both now understand why you kept him to yourself."

"He's your son all right," she said. "Never once has he ever let on he knew anything about his birth father."

He smiled. "He'd make a great agent one day. Let's just hope that line of work doesn't interest him."

"Part of me hates that Gary saw Blake as he truly was. I don't want him wondering all of his life if that's what he'll become."

"He and I discussed that afterward, back in Copenhagen. I don't think he has that worry. Like you said, he's a Malone. In every way that matters."

"Is Blake still there, in that underground chamber?"

He nodded. "His grave."

Stephanie had told him that no gold star would be added to the wall at Langley. That honor was only for heroes.

"And the truth of Elizabeth I stays secret?"

"As it should. The world is not ready for that piece of history."

He watched as she considered the enormity of all that had happened. He'd learned more of the story from talking to Gary, then to Stephanie a few weeks later. A confidential, cooperative investigation between the Justice Department and the British Home Department had revealed all of the details of Antrim's and Mathews' activities.

Quite an adventure from a simple favor.

"My flight to Denmark leaves in three hours."

He'd come to the States on book-buying business and stopped off in Atlanta for a few days to visit with Gary. He'd never anticipated having the discussion they'd just had, but was glad everything was out in the open.

No more secrets lay between them.

"You can stop beating yourself up," he said to her. "All of this is done, and has been for a long time."

She started to cry.

Which was unusual.

Pam was tough. That was her problem—too tough. Combine that with his own inability to deal with emotions and they'd made for a challenging pair. Their marriage, which included much happiness, in the end failed. Finally now, after so many years, they both seemed to realize that placing blame mattered little. All that mattered was Gary.

They both stood from the table.

She stepped to the counter and tore off a couple of paper towels to deal with her tears. "I'm so sorry, Cotton. So sorry for all of this. I should have been honest with you a long time ago."

True. But that was past, too.

"I almost got you killed. Hell, I almost got Gary killed."

He shouldered his travel bag and stepped to the door. "How about we call it even."

She threw him a perplexed look. "How is that even possible?"

Asked that question three years ago he would have had no answer. But a lot had happened since he left Georgia and moved to Denmark. His life was so different, his priorities changed. Hating an ex-wife was not only meaningless but counterproductive. And, besides, he'd come to realize that he was half to blame for all the hurt anyway.

Better to let it go and move on.

So he threw her a smile and answered with the truth.

"Actually, we're more than even. You gave me Gary."

Writer's Note

FOR THIS NOVEL TWO TRIPS WERE MADE TO England, one of them quite memorable as we were there when the Icelandic volcano grounded all air travel. Good use was made of those three extra days, though, as my wife, Elizabeth, and I scouted more locales that eventually made their way into the novel. For an interesting addition to the novel, check out my short story, "The Tudor Plot," which takes place seven years before **The King's Deception.**

Now it's time to separate fact from fiction.

The death scene of Henry VIII (prologue) happened, and most of the comments made by Henry are taken from historical accounts. The king died without his children present, but whether Katherine Parr visited him during his final days is unknown. Of course, Henry's passing on of a great Tudor secret to his last queen was my invention. The death of Henry VII at Richmond Palace (chapter 10) is likewise faithfully recounted, except I added a visit from the heir. Sir Thomas Wriothesly's description of what happened that day was most helpful.

Many refer to London's Metropolitan Police as Scotland Yard, but I decided to utilize its proper label, "the Met." That was likewise true with the Secret Intelligence Service, which is popularly known as MI6 (responsible for international threats). The Serious Organized Crime Agency (SOCA) (chapter 3) is a domestic law enforcement agency, Great Britain's version of the FBI.

Windsor Castle and St. George's Chapel are both magnificent. Henry VIII is buried there, beneath the marble slab as detailed in chapter 3. The epitaph quoted is accurate, as is the fact that Henry's grave was opened in 1813.

Fleet Street and the City (chapter 9) are correctly described, as are the Inns of Court (chapter 10). Where the Middle and Inner Temples are now headquartered was once a major Templar stronghold. The land grant from Henry VIII and James I to the barristers happened (chapter 13). The Pump Court is also there, as is the Goldsmith house (chapter 58), though I slightly modified the house. The story recounted in chapter 10, of how the War of the Roses may have started in the gardens, is considered true. But nobody knows for sure. The Inns are governed by benchers, led by the treasurer (chapter 26), and act as both a training and governing body for their lawyer-members—similar to the role state bar associations play in the United States. The Middle Hall, featured in chapter 10, is perhaps the Inns' most historic building, but the round Temple Church is its most recognizable (chapters 9 and 10). The Penitential Cell (chapter 12) inside the church can be visited. The Inns of Court are required, by royal decree, to maintain the Temple Church as a place of worship (chapter 13).

The Daedalus Society is not only Thomas Mathews' creation but mine, too. However, the tale of Daedalus (chapter 12) is taken from mythology. Nonsuch palace once existed (chapter 25) and how it disappeared is likewise true. The symbols that were supposedly there (chapter 25) never existed but are based on the Copiale Cipher (an image of which appears in chapter 15). I merely adapted that 75,000-character German manuscript to this British story. Only recently has its array of abstract symbols, mixed with Greek and Roman letters, been fully deciphered.

There are many locales that make appearances. Brussels, with its **Manneken Pis** (chapter 2); Oxford and its many colleges (chapters 16 and 20); Portman Square and the Churchill Hotel (chapter 35); Piccadilly Circus and London's theater district (chapter 25); Little Venice with its longboats and narrow canals (chapter 4); St. Paul's Cathedral and the Whispering Gallery (chapter 5); Westminster Abbey and the chapel of Henry VII (chapter 36); Oxford Circus (chapter 8); and The Goring Hotel (chapter 54). The Tower of London is likewise an amazing site (chapter 17), which includes the Royal Jewel House (chapters 45 and 48). London does indeed sit atop a hundred miles of subterranean rivers, each enclosed within a maze of tunnels, the Fleet being the largest and most famous (chapters 58 and 59). The underground chamber described in chapter 59 is entirely my creation, though similar tunnels and chambers are found beneath London all the time.

The Tudor wealth described in chapter 15 existed. Henry VII amassed huge amounts of gold and silver that Henry VIII (through his closure of the abbeys) increased. The disappearance of all that wealth during the regency of the boy king, Edward VI, remains a mystery.

Jesus College, at Oxford, was founded during the time of Elizabeth I (chapter 16). Its great hall stands as depicted, including the queen's portrait, which still hangs. The chapel and quad (chapter 18) are also faithfully described.

William and Robert Cecil (chapter 16) are historical characters. William's close relationship with Elizabeth I, including his protection of her during the bloody reign of her sister, Mary, is well documented. William served Elizabeth as secretary of state until his death. His son Robert succeeded him. Both men played integral roles in Elizabeth's long reign. Toward the end of his life, though, Robert's popularity and effectiveness waned. The derogatory rhyme quoted in chapter 36, along with his nickname "the Fox," are real. Robert Cecil's journal, first mentioned in chapter 15, sprang from my imagination, but the vast majority of historical information contained within it is true (chapters 47 and 49). Robert Cecil personally supervised the interment of Elizabeth I and the subsequent construction of her tomb in Westminster (chapter 52). Burying Elizabeth with Mary was his idea, and he also composed the odd inscriptions that appear on the tomb's exterior (chapter 36).

At the heart of this story is the all-too-real drama of Abdelbaset al-Megrahi (chapters 37 and 46), a former intelligence officer, convicted of 270 counts of murder for the 1988 bombing of Pan Am Flight 103 over Lockerbie, Scotland. Afflicted with cancer, al-Megrahi was sent back to Libya in 2009 and eventually died in 2012. Both dates have been adjusted to accommodate Malone's fictional world. Much controversy swirled around that so-called humanitarian act, the English playing a pivotal role by not interceding with the Scottish government. The United States strongly opposed the action, and to this day no one really knows the actual motivations behind its occurrence. Operation King's Deception is totally fictitious, but the idea that the United States would seek sensitive information to coerce an ally is not beyond the realm of possibility.

Hampton Court is spectacular, and all of the scenes (chapters 37, 38, and 39) that take place there are faithful to the site. The Haunted Gallery exists, as do the Tudor portraits described in chapter 38. The Cumberland Suite, the gardens, docks, kitchens, golf course, and the tunnels beneath (chapter 42) all are there. Only the door in the wine cellar, leading to the former sewers, was my invention.

Blackfriars Abbey is long gone, but the Underground station described in chapters 56 and 57 remains. At the time this story takes place (two years ago) the station was being rebuilt, but the new facility is now complete. To my knowledge, percussion explosives, as described in chapters 3, 53, and 62, do not exist. I created them, combining the physical characteristics of several different types of reactants.

Elizabeth I was a wonderfully complex person. She never married and openly shirked her duty to provide a royal heir—both of which raise interesting questions. She was thin, unbeautiful, lonely, with nearly constant energy—totally opposite all of her siblings. The idiosyncrasies noted in chapter 49 (and at other points throughout the novel) are taken from historical accounts. Elizabeth refused to allow doctors to examine her, commanded that no autopsy would be performed, always wore heavy face makeup and wigs, donned unflattering clothing that totally concealed her body, and allowed only a select few people close. Those included Kate Ashley, Thomas Parry, both Cecils, and Blanche Parry. If there was any conspiracy, these five individuals would have been at its heart.

The Mask of Youth (chapter 16) existed, so every drawing of Elizabeth must be called into question. Within the novel are five images. On the Part One page is a portrait created in 1546 when Elizabeth was 13 years old. This would have been about the time she supposedly died. This is a famous image, one of the few that exist showing the princess under the age of 25. No one knows, though, if it accurately depicts her. The Part Two page shows the Clopton Portrait from 1560. Elizabeth was 27 at the time, two years into her reign, and never looked less regal and confident. The features are noticeably nonfeminine. On the Part Three page is the Ermine Portrait, painted in 1585. This is an excellent example of the Mask of Youth. Elizabeth was 52 years old at its creation, but her face is that of a much younger woman. The same is true on the title page with the Rainbow Portrait, where Elizabeth was 70 years old but appears far younger. And, finally, on the Part Four page is the Darnley Portrait, painted from life in 1575. Interestingly, the crown and sceptre were placed on a side table, not held, suggesting that they were more props, than symbols of power. Once again, little about the face is feminine. The conclusions are inescapable. We simply have no idea what Elizabeth I looked like.

Elizabeth wanted her Scottish cousin James to succeed her. The Union of Crowns, which Robert Cecil spearheaded (chapter 16), is historical fact. Elizabeth's quote—**I will have no rascal to succeed me, and who should succeed me but a king**—is often cited as authority for her wishes. Its oblique wording is odd. Why not just simply name a successor? But if the possibility that she may have been a fraud is considered, the odd phrasing begins to make more sense. Whether Elizabeth was actually aware of the plan of succession Robert Cecil hatched with James is unknown. But most historians agree that Cecil would have never made the overtures without her blessing. The deathbed scene described in chapter 16, where she supposedly made her succession wishes clear, happened—and in 1603 the English crown passed from the Tudors to the Stuarts with no objections.

The story of what occurred while the young princess Elizabeth lived with Katherine Parr and Thomas Seymour (chapter 21), including Seymour's unseemly advances, was quite the scandal. Parr did eventually send the princess away and wrote a letter, which was delivered to Elizabeth a few months after Parr's untimely death (chapter 21). I modified its wording to fit this story. Parr, though, would have been the only person (outside the conspirators) who could have discovered any switch. Unlike Henry VIII, Parr spent a great deal of time with the young Elizabeth (chapter 52). The former queen also harbored a deep resentment toward anything and everything related to her late husband Henry VIII. So it is unlikely she would have revealed anything she may have known.

Henry FitzRoy was the illegitimate firstborn son of Henry VIII (chapter 40). All of the details recounted about FitzRoy, including his marriage to Mary Howard, are correct. Whether FitzRoy fathered a child before dying at age 16 is unknown.

All agree, though, that FitzRoy physically resembled the Tudors, so it's logical that any child of his would be similar. As detailed in chapter 38, only Henry VIII's secondborn, Mary, lived into her forties. All of Henry's other known offspring died before the age of twenty. Yet Elizabeth lived to age 70, even surviving a bout with smallpox early in her reign (chapter 38)—most uncharacteristic for a child of Henry VIII.

Bram Stoker's book **Famous Impostors,** published in 1910 (chapters 25 and 26), is the first printed account of the Bisley Boy legend. The italicized text in chapter 27 is quoted directly from Stoker's book. The **New York Times'** opinion of the book—**tommyrot**—is also correctly quoted (chapter 38).

I heard the Bisley Boy tale during a visit to the village of Ely, north of London. Stoker was the first in print to link the legend to Henry FitzRoy. Whether the story is truth or fiction we will never know. What is known is that the people of Bisley, for centuries, on May 1 each year, paraded a small boy through the streets dressed in Elizabethan costume (chapter 27).

Why do that?

No one knows.

But the Westminster tomb of Elizabeth and her half sister, Mary, has never been opened. If the remains of the young princess, who may have died at age 13, lie within, the application of modern science could easily solve this riddle.

Research for this novel involved studying around 300 books on Elizabeth I. Many were filled with inexplicable statements, like the one quoted in chapter 38, an excerpt taken verbatim from a 1929 American volume, **Queen Elizabeth,** by Katherine Anthony. The final line certainly resonates. **She went to her grave with her secret inviolate.** The author provided no revelations or explanations for any secret, leaving the reader to only wonder.

Which is the same for the Rainbow Portrait (title page and chapter 63).

Robert Cecil himself commissioned the painting, which was not completed until after Elizabeth I's death in 1603. The portrait still hangs in Hatfield House, replete with all of the symbolism explained in chapter 63. The Latin phrase on its face—NON SINE SOLE IRIS—NO RAINBOW WITHOUT THE SUN—is made all the more interesting in light of the Bisley Boy legend.

If, indeed, Elizabeth I was not who she purported to be, the legal reality is that everything done during that long reign would be void (chapters 49, 56, and 63). That would include all of the massive land seizures that happened in Ireland, much of which eventually formed the country of Northern Ireland (chapter 56). Thousands of Protestant immigrants were granted royal land titles from Elizabeth, every one of which would now be called into question. The Troubles happened (chapters 56, 57, and 59). Thousands died from decades of violence. Prior to 1970 tens of thousands more died in the conflict between Unionists and Nationalists that traces its roots directly back to Elizabeth I. Most observers agree that the hate within Northern Ireland has not disappeared. It merely simmers, both sides waiting for a good reason to start fighting again.

What better one than the entire English presence there being based on a lie?

Elizabeth McGuire in chapter 63 made clear to Cotton Malone that history matters.

And she was right.

About the Author

Steve Berry is the **New York Times** and #1 internationally bestselling author of **The Columbus Affair, The Jefferson Key, The Emperor's Tomb, The Paris Vendetta, The Charlemagne Pursuit, The Venetian Betrayal, The Alexandria Link, The Templar Legacy, The Third Secret, The Romanov Prophecy, The Amber Room**, and the short stories "The Tudor Plot," "The Admiral's Mark," "The Devil's Gold," and "The Balkan Escape." His books have been translated into forty languages and sold in fifty-one countries. He lives in the historic city of St. Augustine, Florida. He and his wife, Elizabeth, have founded History Matters, a nonprofit organization dedicated to preserving our heritage. To learn more about Steve Berry and his foundation, visit www.steveberry.org.

LIKE WHAT YOU'VE READ?

If you enjoyed this large print edition of
THE KING'S DECEPTION,
here are a few of Steve Berry's latest
bestsellers also available in large print.

THE COLUMBUS AFFAIR
(paperback)
978-0-307-99063-1
($27.00/29.95C)

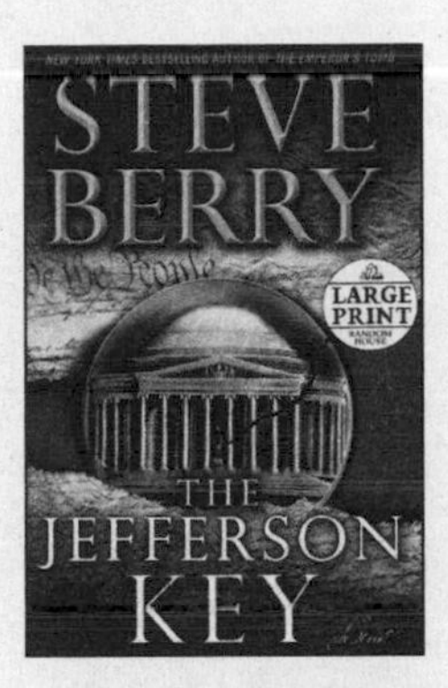

THE JEFFERSON KEY
(paperback)
978-0-7393-7841-0
($26.00/$30.00C)

THE EMPEROR'S TOMB
(paperback)
978-0-7393-7791-8
($26.00/$30.00C)

THE PARIS VENDETTA
(paperback)
978-0-7393-2868-2
($26.00/$32.00C)

Large print books are available wherever books
are sold and at many local libraries.

All prices are subject to change. Check with your
local retailer for current pricing and availability.
For more information on these and other large print titles,
visit www.randomhouse.com/largeprint.